THE MESMERIST

BY THE SAME AUTHOR

The Devil's Memoirs (2 volumes) (*translated by Stuart Gelzer*)

THE MESMERIST

by
Frédéric Soulié

Translated from the French by
Stuart Gelzer
and
Michael Shreve

A Black Coat Press Book

Visit our website at www.blackcoatpress.com

ISBN 978-1-64932-417-7. First Printing: November 2025. Published by Black Coat Press, an imprint of Hollywood Comics.com, 18321 Ventura Blvd. Suite 915, Tarzana, CA 91356. All rights reserved. Except for review purposes, no part of this book may be reproduced or transmitted in any form or by any means, electronic or mechanical, including photocopying, recording, or by any information storage and retrieval system, without permission in writing from the publisher. The stories and characters depicted in this novel are entirely fictional. Printed in the United States of America.

TABLE OF CONTENTS

Introduction

Le Magnétiseur (here translated as *The Mesmerist*) was first published by Gosselin in Paris in 1834. It is a breathtaking tale of dark romanticism, a genre in which Frédéric Soulié was a master.

As the 19th century was about to begin, the English gothic novels hit the French literary scene with a bang. Their extravagant and macabre nature tapped into the emotions released during the French Revolution, and eventually helped the genre to seamlessly evolve into the more modern forms of the *fantastique*.

Horace Walpole's *The Castle of Otranto* had already been published in 1765, but it was Ann Radcliffe, with her *Mysteries of Udolfo* (1794), and Matthew Lewis, with *The Monk* (1796), which both proved enormously successful in their French translations. A subsequent, but no less influential, author was Charles-Robert Maturin, whose *Melmoth the Wanderer* (1820) was praised by many distinguished authors.

Imitation being the sincerest form of flattery, the English gothic writers helped launch a wave of what the French called *romans noirs* (black novels), or *romans frénétiques* (frantic novels), which became the first sub-genre of popular literature.

The first French *roman noir* is usually considered to be *Coelina, ou l'Enfant du Mystère* (Coelina, or The Child of Mystery)(1799), written by François-Guillaume Ducray-Duminil, quickly turned into an equally successful stage play by Guilbert de Pixérécourt -- himself the author of many gothic novela and plays.

From 1800 onward, French enthusiasm for the *roman noir* grew by leaps and bounds. The inventive and talented author Charles Nodier also began his literary career by penning popular gothic novels such as *Les Proscrits* (The Proscribed) (1802), *Le Peintre de Salzbourg* (The Painter of Salzbourg) (1803) and *Les Méditations du Cloître* (The Meditations of the Cloister) (1803

In 1819, a translation of John-William Polidori's *The Vampyre*, falsely attributed to Lord Byron, proved so successful that it was immediately copied by Cyprien Bérard, who authored *Lord Rutwen ou les Vampires* in 1820[1]. That same year, Honoré de Balzac, still an aspiring writer, paid his dues to the *roman noir* by penning *Falthurne*, the tale of a virgin prophetess who knew occult secrets that dating back to Ancient Mesopotamia, and *Le Centenaire, ou Les Deux Beringheld* (The Hundred-Centenarian, or The Two Beringheld) (1822), clearly inspired by *Melmoth*.

In 1821, Vicomte Charles-Victor d'Arlincourt combined Walter Scott's (1771-1832) sense of historical epic with Ann Radcliffe's gothic passions, to write the first historical gothic novel, *Le Solitaire* (The Hermit) about Charles le

---

[1] *The Vampire Lord Ruthwen*, Black Coat Press, ISBN 978-1-61227-004-3.

Téméraire (who in reality died in 1477) continuing to secretly control all the major events of history. Also influenced by Walter Scott was Victor Hugo when he wrote *Han d'Islande* (Han of Iceland) (1823), a bloody tale featuring two monstrous heroes, one a Viking warrior who drank blood from his victims' skulls, and the other a semi-mythical bear, and his classic *Notre-Dame de Paris* (The Hunchback of Notre-Dame) (1831).

In 1829, *L'Âne Mort et la Femme Guillotinée* (The Dead Donkey and the Guillotined Woman) by Jules Janin was hailed as a new masterpiece of the macabre -- often verging on the pastiche -- but was criticized by others for being just too bloody and horrible, anticipating the "Grand-Guignol" by sixty-eight years.

In 1832, *Le Diable* (The Devil) by Étienne-Léon de Lamothe-Langon introduced the incredibly charming yet wholly corrupt character of the Chevalier Draxel, virtually evil incarnate, one more modern literary archetype shaped from the cauldron of gothic literature. Lamothe-Langon, a writer known for his memoirs, had also penned an impressive number of gothic novels such as *L'Hermite de la Tombe Mystérieuse* (The Hermit of the Mysterious Tomb) (1816)[2] as well as the ground-breaking *La Vampire* (1825)[3] which told the story of a young Napoleonic army officer who brought his Hungarian fiancée home to later discover that she was, in reality, a vampire.

The almost sadistic description of the slow, pernicious influence of evil was particularly well handled by Frédéric Soulié who, in 1832, burst onto the literary scene with his first *roman noir*, *Les Deux Cadavres* (The Two Corpses), soon followed by *Le Magnétiseur* (The Mesmerist) in 1834

Melchior-Frédéric Soulié was born in Foix on December 23, 1800. His birth crippled his mother, Jeanne-Marie Baille. His father, François-Melchior Soulié, after having taught philosophy at the University of Toulouse, had enlisted in the army in 1792 and reached the rank of adjutant-general, but was forced to leave the military because of illness. He then joined the public finance administration as an employee in the tax revenue service. Frédéric lived with his mother in Mirepoix, not far from Foix, till the age of four, when his father took him to live with him. Young Frédéric followed his father when he was transferred to Nantes in 1808, then to Poitiers in 1815, where Frédéric completed his secondary education. His sister, Antoinette-Françoise, remained with their mother at Mirepoix. The family had not been reunited by the time of Soulié's death in 1847.

After the fall of Napoleon, Melchior-Frédéric Soulié was fired from the tax service for being a supporter of the exiled Emperor. He went to Paris; Frédéric accompanied him there and attended law school. Expelled for having signed a Republican petition and for taking an active part in a student revolt against the

---

[2] *The Mysterious Hermit of the Tomb*, Black Coat Press, ISBN 978-1-61227-734-9.

[3] *The Virgin Vampire*, Black Coat Press, ISBN 978-1-61227-032-6.

law school dean, he was banished with several of his fellow students to the University of Rennes, where he completed his law studies under the watchful supervision of the police.

Upon getting his degree, Frédéric rejoined Melchior-Frédéric in Laval, where he had been reinstated in his job. He first worked with his father, and then joined the civil service himself. In 1824 Melchior-Frédéric was fired again for supporting the "wrong" candidates in the elections, and Frédéric resigned from the civil service. Father and son resolved to settle once more in Paris.

Frédéric, using the name "F. Soulié de Lavelanet," published some poetry he had written earlier, followed by three elegiac songs, all under the title *Amours françaises* ("French Loves"). That small volume went unnoticed, but it allowed him to make some contacts in the literary world: Casimir Delavigne lavished his encouragement on Soulié, and he became a friend of Alexandre Dumas. To ensure his subsistence, he took a job as the manager of a mechanical sawmill. Driven by his literary vocation, he translated and adapted Shakespeare's *Romeo and Juliet*, which was performed at the Odéon on June 10, 1828. At the same time, Soulié wrote an original play, *Christine à Fontainebleau* ("Christine in Fontainebleau"), which was performed at the Odéon on October 13, 1829, but failed to attract much attention.

Discouraged, Soulié became a journalist and began writing short stories. However, on June 17, 1830, he returned to the theater with a two-act play entitled *Une Nuit du Duc de Montfort* ("A Night with the Duke of Montfort"), which was more successful and generated some income. A little over a month later the 1830 July Revolution broke out, and Soulié fought among the insurgents, rifle in hand, in the streets of Paris. He was decorated with the July Cross.

When order was restored he took up his pen again, contributing stories to many smaller newspapers, including *La Mode* and *Le Voleur*. In the theater, however, he had yet another failure with *Nobles et bourgeois* ("Noblemen and Bourgeois"), a five-act play. But he was not discouraged. His three-act play, *La Famille de Lusigny* ("The Lusigny Family"), performed at the Théâtre-Français on October 15, 1831, was a success.

Encouraged by that, Soulié next simultaneously staged a play, *Clotilde*, first performed at the Théâtre-Français on September 11, 1832, and published his first gothic novel, *Les Deux Cadavres* (q.v.). The play received enthusiastic applause from a large audience; the novel, a tale full of horrors, murders, and bloody scenes, was also a great success. From that moment on, Soulié's reputation as a great playwright and novelist was established.

In 1833 he published a collection of short stories, *Le Port de Créteil* ("Créteil Harbor"), which was also successful. At that time he founded a newspaper, *Le Napoléon*, which he soon sold to Émile Marco de Saint-Hilaire. In the theater, two plays he staged on the Grands Boulevards, *L'Homme à la blouse* ("The Man in the Smock") and *Le Roi de Sicile* ("The King of Sicily"), were his last two failures.

During the two years that followed, Soulié was very prolific. Another play, *Une Aventure sous Charles IX* ("An Adventure under Charles IX"), performed at the Théâtre-Français on May 21, 1834, was highly acclaimed. He also published many novels, including *Le Vicomte de Béziers* ("The Viscount of Beziers"), *Le Magnétiseur* ("The Hypnotist"), and *Le Comte de Toulouse* ("The Count of Toulouse") all in 1834; *Le Conseil d'Etat* ("The High Council") in 1835; and a short story collection, *Un Eté à Meudon* ("A Summer in Meudon") in 1836. On August 6, 1835, his play *Les Deux Reines* ("The Two Queens") was performed at the Opéra-Comique, also to great acclaim. But despite all those successes, Soulié remained in a rather precarious financial position.

His uncle, Marshal Clauzel, on becoming governor-general of Algeria for a second time, made him an offer he had already proposed in 1831: that of a lucrative job in the administration of the colony; but Soulié refused again, preferring to devote himself to his literary career. Nor did he accept the proposal made to him by Count Molé, then President of the Council, to join the High Council of the Republic, on condition that he give up his literary career.

It was around that time that Soulié conceived the idea of *The Devil's Memoirs*,[4] a gigantic, powerful work, probably inspired by Alain-René Lesage's *Le Diable Boîteux* ("The Lame Devil") from 1707. *The Devil's Memoirs* offered a picture of society at its most hideous: crime, incest, adultery, lies, all the evils human souls were capable of, were depicted in characters seemingly good, innocent, and pure. A well-regarded man, enjoying a reputation for probity, was secretly infamous; a woman, lauded for her virtue, was an example of hypocrisy and debauchery. The immense fame that *The Devil's Memoirs* garnered for Soulié placed him at the pinnacle of literary glory.

At the same time, his translation of *Romeo and Juliet*, relaunched at the Odéon, was greeted with unanimous applause. During 1839 three more of his plays were performed at the Théâtre de la Renaissance: *Diane de Chivri*, *Le Fils de la Folle* ("The Madwoman's Son"), adapted from his own 1839 novel *Le Maître d'école* ("The Schoolmaster"), and *Le Proscrit* ("The Banished Man"); all were successful. And that did not stop Soulié from also contributing articles and reviews to *L'Europe littéraire*, *La Mode*, *La Revue de Paris*, and *La Chronique de Paris*, and serialized novels to *Le Journal général de France*, *Le Journal des Débats*, *La Presse*, *La Quotidienne*, *Le Messager*, and *Le Siècle*. He also cooperated with the elite of French literature to publish several collective works.

Between 1840 and 1847 Soulié published more novels, and had several plays performed at the Théâtre de l'Ambigu, all of which were successful, including, on October 14, 1846, the now classic *La Closerie des genêts* ("The House with the Broom Hedge"), which was a triumph. Soon after that, however, Soulié came down with heart disease; after three months of suffering he died in his country house in Bièvres, on September 23, 1847.

---

[4] Black Coat Press, ISBNs 978-1-64932-346-0 & 978-1-64932-347-7.

A large crowd attended his funeral on September 27 at the Church of Sainte-Élisabeth du Temple and his burial at the Père-Lachaise cemetery, where Victor Hugo gave a speech and where Alexandre Dumas, pressed by the crowd to say something, collapsed in sobs.

Of all the *feuilletonistes* of that time, Soulié seems to us the most modern in style. He is casual, chatty, and ironic. He couches his satire in innuendo, allusions, and circumlocutions in order to criticize the falsity of social hierarchy, affectation, marriage, and, most of all, women. Since he was both a dramatist and a novelist, his novels retain some of the theater's techniques. He uses dialogue extensively to delineate character and to move the plot forward when narration would be boring. The poet in him sprinkles verse throughout even the darkest passages. He died dictating a poem he had composed about those gathered at his bedside. His novels and articles became parts of plays, and his plays were turned into novels and short stories, making him one of the best-paid *feuilletonistes*. His allusions, though almost always apt, are sometimes too locked in nineteenth-century life to be completely meaningful to a twenty-first century audience. Many of Soulié's stories never definitively conclude: their open endings resemble modern television series, which always have the next season in mind when one season wraps up. Soulié left his endings vague enough to be followed with a sequence or a spin-off in another *feuilleton*, if it seemed likely to sell. If there was no sequel, readers could continue the story in their imaginations and end it to their own satisfaction.

In most of his output Soulié is a critic of human and society's failings, showing little or no pity or charity. In *Le Lion amoureux* ("The Lion in Love") from 1840, he portrays the rich, vain, useless young men of Parisian society, but does not spare the bourgeois who are awed by them and envy them. In *Physiologie du Bas bleu* ("The Physiology of a Bluestocking") from 1841, he is a misogynist who mocks women writers, including George Sand, sparing only the woman who "scratches" with her pen on paper in order to feed her family. In all his work he castigates pride, vanity, self-interest, self-delusion, the hypocrisy and corruption of government and government officials, and the artificial stratification of society.

The term "Mesmerist" comes from Franz Anton Mesmer (1734-1815), a German physician .In 1774, he theorized the existence of a process of natural energy transference occurring between all animate and inanimate objects; this he called "animal magnetism," later referred to as "Mesmerism."

Mesmer's theory attracted a wide following between between 1780 and 1850. In 1843, the Scottish doctor James Braid proposed the term "hypnotism" for a technique derived from animal magnetism; today the word "Mesmerism" generally functions as a synonym of "hypnosis."

In February 1778, Mesmer moved to Paris and established a medical practice therer. The city was soon divided into those who thought he was a charlatan and those who thought he had made a great discovery.

In his first years in Paris, Mesmer tried and failed to get either the Royal Academy of Sciences or the Royal Society of Medicine to provide official approval for his doctrines. He found only one physician of high professional and social standing, Charles d'Eslon (1738-1786), to become a disciple. In 1779, with d'Eslon's encouragement, Mesmer wrote an 88-page book, *Mémoire sur la découverte du magnétisme animal*, to which he appended 27 "propositions" outlining his theories.

In 1784, without Mesmer having requested it, King Louis XVI appointed four members of the Faculty of Medicine as commissioners to investigate animal magnetism and mMesmerism. At the request of these commissioners, the king appointed Baron de Breteuil, minister of the Department of Paris, to establish investigative commissions. One was composed of individuals from the Royal Academy of Sciences, and the other of individuals from the Academy of Sciences and the Faculty of Medicine. The investigative teams included the chemist Antoine Lavoisier, the doctor Joseph-Ignace Guillotin, the astronomer Jean Sylvain Bailly, and the American ambassador Benjamin Franklin.

The commission conducted a series of experiments aimed not just at determining whether Mesmer's treatment worked, but whether he had discovered a new physical fluid. The commission concluded that there was no evidence for such a fluid. Whatever benefit the treatment produced was attributed to the power of "imagination." One of the commissioners, the botanist Antoine Laurent de Jussieu, took exception to the official reports, authoring a dissenting opinion.

The commission did not examine Mesmer specifically, but instead observed the practice of d'Eslon. They used blind trials, blindfolding the subjects, in their investigation, and found that Mesmerism seemed to work only when the subject was aware of it. Their findings are considered the first observation of the placebo effect. Even d'Eslon himself was convinced by the commission, stating that, "the imagination thus directed to the relief of suffering humanity would be a most valuable means in the hands of the medical profession."

Mesmer was driven into exile soon after the investigation. However, his influential student, Amand-Marie-Jacques de Chastenet, Marquis of Puységur (175-1825), continued to have many followers until his death. Mesmer continued to practice in Frauenfeld, Switzerland, for a number of years. He died in 1815 in Meersburg, Germany.

Jean-Marc Lofficier

THE MESMERIST

I. THE DUCHESS OF AVARENNE
(1787)

"What time is it?"

"Noon, ma'am."

"That's awful!"

The Duchess of Avarenne immediately got up out of her vast arm-chair, took a turn around the enormous room she was in, stopped before a platform bed that filled one end of it, considered the bed for a few seconds, shrugged crossly, and turned quickly away. She continued her tour, as she passed a sofa picked up a muff that had been set on it, turned it inside out, turned it right-side out, smoothed the black fur with her white hand, then tossed it onto another chair. She went to a small table, rearranged three or four cups, opened and closed a book she happened to glimpse, then went and sat at a vanity table covered in white bombazine. There she examined herself in the mirror, her face almost touching the glass. She used the tip of one finger to part her lips so she could study her sparkling white teeth with great care, then drew back a bit, half closed her eyes, turned her head this way and that, tossed a spot of powder on two curls that revealed the jet black of her hair, used the gold blade of a makeup knife to remove the white the powder puff had left on her forehead, blended in with the corner of a handkerchief the rouge that hid her own fresh complexion, and went on, "What are they doing down there?"

"The marquis is receiving the people from the bailiwick who've come to pay him their respects."

"Like who?"

"I believe, ma'am, it's the magistrate and the lawyers from the marquis's jurisdiction, the mayor and the council from the village, and the priest and the canons from the Abbey of Saint Severin."

"What are they like?"

13

"Who, ma'am? The canons?"

"All of them."

"Well, ma'am, they're like… They're like anybody else."

"Ah!"

And the Duchess of Avarenne went back to her business at the mirror, studying her hands, her waist, her bust, simpering at her reflection, bowing to herself, waving a tiny hello to herself. Then she went on, "Ah, they're like anybody else."

"Anyway, the duchess can see them for herself, because I hear the reception ending, and there they are coming out of the great hall now."

"Let's have a look…"

The beautiful duchess went to the window that Honorine had just opened, leaned over the balcony with a long yawn, and began to look around the great courtyard that lay before the Chateau Lagarde. A dozen people were coming down the steps that led to the first floor.

"Who's that man in black velvet, the one my father's talking to?"

"That's Doctor Lussay, ma'am."

"A doctor, him? He can't be thirty!"

"But they say he's a brilliant doctor, ma'am, and also a terrible man."

"Well, he's a shrimp. If he were mine I'd make him into a dwarf. Don't those canons smell bad?"

"They're all very respectable priests, ma'am."

"They're not especially fat. Who are all those other people, over by the stables?"

"Those are the farmers waiting their turn to pay their respects to the marquis."

"Do farmers powder their hair in Auvergne?"

"No, ma'am, never."

"Then who's that peasant talking to those two girls?"

"That's Jean, ma'am."

Hearing the sigh that slipped out of Honorine's mouth when the girl made that answer, the duchess turned and asked, "Is that boy your lover?"

Honorine blushed and looked sad. Shaking her head with a melancholy smile, she replied, "Alas, no, ma'am, he's not my lover."

"Well, why isn't he your lover?"

"Oh, ma'am, Jean pays no attention to a poor girl like me. He's a rich miller, and there's more than one bourgeois from town who'd give him his daughter…"

"In marriage? To a peasant!"

"Certainly, ma'am."

"Those bourgeois would sell themselves for loose change. And yet there's some difference in rank between them and him."

"Oh, ma'am, there are bourgeois women from town, among the poshest and the prettiest, who wouldn't agree with you. And if the mayor and the chief alderman fell out and almost came to blows a few months ago, it's because their wives both wanted him."

"For their daughters?"

"Oh, no, ma'am, for themselves."

"That's quite different. Oh, so that boy has mistresses among your bourgeois women?"

"And among ladies too."

"How so?"

"Damn! They say the Lord of Berbis's wife used to meet him at night in the little woods by the village."

"In the woods! Is the woman out of her mind? Doesn't she have a room?"

"Oh, ma'am, the thing is, you can't make Jean do whatever you want. You have to take him as he comes."

"So the boy is some kind of hero? What's so seductive about him?"

"Damn! You see, ma'am, it's because he's so handsome, with such a gorgeous face, and built like a lord!"

"Oh, he's good-looking? The Apollo of Auvergne!"

"And then, ma'am, there's more: he thinks about nothing but that."

"Nothing but what?"

"They say, ma'am… they say he's mad for women."

That distinctive turn of phrase made the duchess give Honorine a look. But the girl's face was so disingenuous that the duchess could see she attached no particular meaning to an expression she must've heard and that she was repeating quite naively. So the duchess began to laugh, and said two or three times, "Oh, so he's mad for women! Let's have a look at this Adonis. Bring me my opera glass."

Honorine went back into the room; and the duchess, waiting on the balcony, gave a bored look around—which stopped suddenly on the broad avenue that climbed to the chateau from the village of l'Étang. She eagerly took the glass the girl handed her; but instead of aiming it at the handsome miller, as Honorine expected, she carefully looked down the avenue.

After a while she murmured with obvious disappointment, "Yes, it's my uncle's carriage. It's him… Oh, it's too awful!… Exile from the court

15

isn't enough, now I have to endure a sermon. Let the Abbot of Auvergne confine his preaching to his flock! It's true, my father has called in reinforcements. I'll write to the prince; this has to stop—I'm tired of being persecuted."

Angrily, she hurried off the balcony, dropped her glass onto a table, and sat down in her vast armchair, where she remained, lost in thought, till the sound of the wheels warned her that the carriage was entering the courtyard. She rose abruptly. Picking up a parasol, she got ready to go out, saying to Honorine, "I'm sick all day. I can't leave my room and I can't receive anyone, you understand? You'll tell my father that if he asks for me or if he tries to bring my uncle here."

"Yes, ma'am."

"If a messenger arrives, have Dubois ring the bell to come back, without telling him why. I'll know what that means."

"Yes, ma'am…"

The duchess followed a long corridor to a staircase at the far end of one of the wings of the chateau, went down it, slipped outside, and hurried into the nearby woods. For a short while she walked quickly, listening anxiously in case she was being followed. Then, when she was deep enough in the thickets so that no one could spot her, she stopped, sat down, and began to think at her leisure.

She was an unusual character, this Mademoiselle Charlotte Diane de l'Étang, become by marriage Duchess of Avarenne. The most offensive aristocratic arrogance and the most tacit adherence to the Philosophes were entangled in her, and even merged, in such a way as to form a kind of personality that was already rare at the time she made it a scandal, and that for us can only be rooted in the romantic past. The Duchess of Avarenne had two affectations, which she was alone in not finding contradictory: the first was that she belonged to a family that had never been stained by a misalliance; the second was that she had no prejudices. One of those affectations is fairly easy to understand; the other requires some explanation.

The first was the pride in pure blood that comes so easily to people that it threatens to infect every shoemaker whose father and grandfather were honest shoemakers. It was the vanity over a distinguished lineage that fastened integrity like a coat of arms to the names of certain bourgeois families, and which, among the nobility, had no other failing than not requiring virtue. That affectation was an ancient inheritance, received at birth, rooted in the cradle, growing over time, till it became part of the duchess's nature. The second affectation was the rotten fruit of a faulty education, or rather of an education wrongly understood. If we were willing to take command, here we could declare war on the misguided ideas that led astray the eighteenth-century need for emancipation.

At that time society groaned, hobbled by the thousand tethers of patronage that feudalism had bequeathed to the petty nobility, and by the ascendancy over every thought that the clergy had arrogated to itself. Each of those tyrannies had its own open and particular enemies. The enemies of the nobility were first of all the City bourgeois, whose vanity was incensed at there still being any line between them and the aristocracy they brushed up against by wealth and education. Richelieu and Louis XIV, by extending the nobility downward so far that it was defended by nothing more than parchment ramparts, were the true destroyers of feudalism. The day a Montmorency could strip himself of all his privileges by tearing up two sheets of paper before the tribunal of the revolutionary Constituent Assembly, that day the true aristocracy was already no more. The noble baron would no doubt have taken more time in handing over his chateaux in Languedoc and in spiking his canons, if he'd still had them. The other enemies of the nobility were the peasants, the only people who actually suffered from the remnants of rural feudalism, which affected them in the form of fees, taxes, tithes, and what was known as "low justice": sufferings almost always made worse by the interference of the bourgeois stewards and magistrates who profited through extortion and seigneurial tyranny.

The struggle of the nobility against both the bourgeoisie and the common people has had its history so gruesomely written in pages of blood and fire and destruction since 1790 that it's pointless to speak of it. But the struggle that preceded and paved the way for that one was the struggle of free thought against the theocratic power. Aside from the adversaries they had in common, arising from the seigneurial rights that belonged as much to the clergy as to the nobility, in addition the Church had enemies that its particular authority pushed to one side or whose progress it hindered: I mean writers, Philosophes, scholars. Those men—worldly, fashionable, witty, with elegant manners, praised and caressed by the powerful—had no hatred for their patrons and no thought of uniting to fight them.
Voltaire wrote *The Henriad*[5] to honor the great names of France; and if he forgot to mention Sully[6] in his history of Henri IV, it wasn't out of hatred for his rank but because the minister's great-grandson had insulted the

---

[5] *La Henriade* (1723), an epic poem celebrating the life of Henri IV.
[6] Prince Maximilien de Béthune Sully (1560-1641), statesman and minister to Henri IV who built a strong, centralized administrative system.

poet. He followed that poem with *Zaïre* for the sake of the House of Lusignan, *Adélaïde du Guesclin* so he could mention Vendôme,[7] and a thousand little witticisms to flatter Richelieu. Montesquieu supported the Nobility of the Robe;[8] d'Alembert cried at the top of his lungs that he was the bastard child of a great lady;[9] Baron d'Holbach was no more a baron than he was German, and yet Rousseau criticized him for claiming to be one only because he was the son of a jumped-up commoner;[10] Marmontel arranged back-alley trysts, like some lackey, to drive Madame de Château-roux out of Louis XV's bed;[11] Diderot praised Monsieur Malesherbes for hiding the manuscript of the *Encyclopédie* in his mansion, when he'd been ordered to seize it in his capacity as a magistrate,[12] and traveled to Russia to thank Catherine the Great for the pension of a thousand pounds she'd paid him fifty years in advance.

Yet all of them, without exception, attacked the clergy to its very core—the clergy who prosecuted, condemned, and burned their books. Not daring to attack the Church's worldly power, they laid siege to its spiritual power: they denied its origins, contested its principles in order to abolish their consequences, and were willing to kill God to take tithes away from the priests and end censorship at the Sorbonne. From that arose the great moral emotion that gave each person the need and the right to argue against any power that existed to his detriment, and which persuaded the Third Estate and the peasantry to rid themselves of the rural seigneury

---

[7]*Zaïre* (1732), a play set during the Crusades, featuring members of the noble Lusignan family from that time. *Adélaïde du Guesclin* (1734), a play set in medieval France, featuring the Duc de Vendôme of that time.

[8]Montesquieu (1689-1755), political philosopher. The Nobility of the Robe was a class of hereditary nobles who acquired their rank through holding high office (versus the more ancient Nobility of the Sword).

[9] Jean le Rond d'Alembert (1717-1783), mathematician, physicist, and co-editor of the *Encyclopédie*.

[10]Paul-Henri Thiry, Baron d'Holbach (1723-1789), atheist Enlightenment philosopher. Though born in Germany, he lived most of his life in France. His father was a vintner.

[11]Jean-François Marmontel (1723-1799), historian, playwright, and contributor to the *Encyclopédie*. Marie Anne de Mailly, Duchess of Châteauroux (1717-1744), one of four sisters who were all (in succession) mistresses of Louis XV.

[12]Denis Diderot (1713-1784), writer, Philosophe, and founder and chief editor of the *Encyclopédie*. Guillaume-Chrétien de Malesherbes (172117-94), statesman and minister; though a staunch monarchist, he was also a liberal supporter of the *Encyclopédie*.

that oppressed them, following the example of the Philosophe who scorned the Christ in whose name his books were being suppressed: 1789 was the outcome of all those destructive forces, the living aphorism of all those written arguments.

But that said, to demonstrate how every power exercised for the first time goes beyond the intended limit, how the first hot-air balloon was lost in the sky, how the first steam engine exploded, and how liberty pushed theory to the point of decreeing in practice the permanent reign of the guillotine—to reduce our observations to those commonplace propositions would be to restate a trivial truth. On the other hand, to trace and analyze that stupendous movement in its entirety and in detail, right up to the moment when it shattered every facet of society, would be to write a history of the human spirit beyond our powers and beyond the ambitions of this book. Everyone can see lightning when it flashes; it takes a Franklin to discover electricity. We'll therefore leave those great questions to wiser heads, and in that abundant mine out of which philosophy has brought so many systems we'll trace one single vein, as tenuous and imperceptible as the thread secreted by a silkworm, and follow it as a guide to the tangled character of the Duchess of Avarenne.

Diane was a woman born passionate in both mind and body; she had a cold heart and little physical vanity, but she was inordinately proud of her lineage. She was happy to be beautiful because she was a woman, but she didn't take a woman's advantage of it. She'd wanted the marriage she'd agreed to because her husband was a great lord, and the name l'Étang was a good alliance for that of Avarenne; but she expected no gratitude for having delivered her
beautiful fair self into the hands of a dirty, swarthy hunchback. When her bold, subtle mind needed exercise and a challenge, she sought out some spirit to conquer, and was flattered by praise from the lowest rascal with a claim to brains. She'd fought for the love of a prince against a courtesan with a shady past; but she'd only enjoyed winning because the prince told her she was prettier and more entertaining than the courtesan. She'd have been ashamed of herself if her rank had been a factor in her victory. When thoughts of her physical youth disturbed her solitary nights, she dreamt not of emperors and kings but of strength and beauty. She found it right that everything had been settled as between equals: Mademoiselle Diane de l'Étang versus the Duke of Avarenne, name versus name, with the prize of the battle being marriage; the witty, beautiful, flirtatious Diane versus the witty, beautiful, flirtatious courtesan, seduction versus

seduction, with the prize of the battle being the admiration of a prince who was a connoisseur. The beautiful, passionate, inexhaustible, exuberant woman, hot-headed and naked, to the handsomest and most inexhaustible man. She had her trinity, that she apportioned like this: the noble girl to the noble husband, Aspasia to Alcibiades,[13] and Messalina to the luggage porter on the street corner.[14] She opened her salon to the greatest names in France, her boudoir to those most accomplished in gallantry, and her bed to the youngest and best-looking.

Her character, of which the memoirs of that time have left us more than one account, seems incomprehensible to the rationality of our own era; it's hard for us to explain how such genuine aristocratic vanity could coexist with such coarse abandonment of personal dignity. This is a case for applying our observations on philosophical changes during the eighteenth century. The philosophy of that century, as we've said, spoke a great deal about natural liberty, but not at all about political liberty. Never—at no time in our history—was less issue made of the right to control the expenses of the state, a right exercised in the fifteenth and sixteenth centuries. But never was more attention devoted to the right to deny the existence of God and the power of religion and priests.

The nobles—and this was a great failing—who didn't foresee that they'd end up getting engaged in the struggle, not against the Philosophes but against the common people, did nothing, and even went so far as to approve of a moral code that suited their own libertine tastes so neatly and that didn't attack their privileges. A few questions about equality certainly arose in all the debates in which the nobles took part; but they were questions of human and not political equality. The nobles were very willing to grant that a peasant was the equal of a noble, in that the peasant's legs and face were as well-made as the noble's; but that was only in the context of one man compared to another—the question of comparing a bourgeois and a gentleman remained untouched. From that arose the subtle distinction that made so many great lords and ladies into divided beings,

---

[13]Alcibiades (circa 450-404 BCE) was a prominent Athenian statesman and general during the Peloponnesian War, notorious for defecting to the enemy, first to the Spartans, then to the Persians. Aspasia of Miletus (born circa 450 BCE), though both mistress to the Athenian statesman Pericles and sister-in-law to Alcibiades, had a well-known relationship with him. Soulié's comparison here emphasizes the match of two superior minds and personalities.

[14]Messalina (circa 17-48 CE) was the wife of the Roman emperor Claudius. Later Roman historians described her as promiscuous and sexually insatiable.

acknowledging the equality of the state of nature in their physical pleasures, but preserving intact their superior social status.

The result was that the Duchess of Avarenne and many others made natural and philosophical use of their lackeys, drawing from philosophical principles that were true in general but wrongly applied to exceptions the conclusions that justified their passions. It was only later that the common people drew from that same philosophy the principles that supported their own interests. You can look through all the writers from the seventeenth century to the reign of Louis XVI—in which concrete financial difficulties led public thinking to a concrete application of the principles of liberty—and you can seek a writer who dared to draw from the principles of human equality, radically expressed, the consequences of the destruction of privilege and the participation of all in government: you won't find a single one. Someone did write, in badly rhymed verse,

All men are equal; birth is no issue,
The only difference is a matter of virtue...[15]

but no one thought to say that men who were equal should have equal rights.

Whether it was their need for natural equality, or whether it was that the protection that so many nobles had granted to the Philosophes blinded the latter to the contradiction between their principles and the existence of an aristocracy, or whether they just hadn't thought through all of their consequences, the fact is that for a long time the nobles believed themselves safe from the movement that overthrew religion and the clergy, and they let it happen, without perceiving that all the privileges of the ancient monarchy were stacked on top of each other, and when one fell, all the others would come down.

What a lot of rumination over a woman's whim, which another writer would've narrated without explanation, leaving the reader, for good or ill, to make what sense he could of it; especially since that whim hasn't yet been consummated, as Beaumarchais would put it,[16] and we've stopped in the middle of our story to ramble on about a character rather than make her act, which is certainly more the practice in real novels. So let's get back to the story.

---

[15]*Les mortels sont égaux; ce n'est pas la naissance, / C'est la seule vertu qui fait la différence.* The lines are by Voltaire, from his play *Mahomet* (1736), here slightly paraphrased by Soulié.
[16]Pierre Beaumarchais (1732-1799), among many other occupations the playwright of *The Barber of Seville* (1775) and *The Marriage of Figaro* (1784).

The Duchess of Avarenne was in the thickets, seated on a chair formed by the lawn, thinking of her immediate situation. Since she referred at will to her own past history, the better to calculate her odds in the future, we'll trace the path of her reflections and make note of them as we go forward.

"So here I am," she said to herself, "shut up in my father's chateau just when I thought I'd reached the pinnacle of wealth and power. In all of Louis XVI's court there's only one prince worth a woman's trouble to make him her lover, and that prince was my slave. Thanks to his respect for me, my husband, away on a diplomatic mission, raised no obstacles to our pleasures, to my triumphs, to the expense of my establishment, to my parties that were the envy of the elite of the Petit Trianon.[17] I'd just begun to be as happy as I deserved, when along came a woman who put herself athwart my future: aiming to take away the man who belonged to me, she made a crime of my liaison—the one she wanted for herself—and because she would only be tomorrow's mistress, she was clever enough to enlist on her side the idiot wife of that prince in dismissing today's mistress. Mix into all that the queen's prudishness, the king's austere virtue, and the piety of the king's sisters. My father was threatened; there was talk of recalling my husband; I was told that the Étang estate required my father's presence, and that my father required his daughter's presence. And for all that to happen without me being able to stop it, the prince was sent back to his provincial estates on the pretext of an assembly of local notables—an assembly that was summoned only for that purpose. I was forced to leave on twenty-four hours' notice, and here I am, stuck in an awful wasteland in which I'm already dying of boredom after being here a day and half. The fact is, everything happened so fast that I haven't had time to think. Still, I have to do something. Should I go rejoin the Duke of Avarenne? That would be surrendering without a fight. Should I go back to Versailles as soon as the prince is there again? That would expose me to a new order to go into exile from the court, which my disobedience this time would make irrevocable. Should I wait here for things to settle down there? But the prince's heart is filled with vanity at best, and he loved me because there was status in having me, and danger in losing me, and he was in competition for me with the most fashionable men. He'd let me die here, and in two weeks I'd be replaced by another woman; who knows, he might already have forgotten me!

---

[17]The Petit Trianon was a palace within the grounds of Versailles that served as a personal residence for the king and his entourage.

After all, I've done the math carefully: he could've sent me a message to tell me what was going on; we traveled here slowly enough for that. That wretched courier! I couldn't hear the hoof beats of a horse behind my carriage without thinking it must be a man in green livery with gold braid catching up to me to hand me an order to return immediately. But the horse passed me by, and it was just some bourgeois going at a gallop. A plague on bourgeois who gallop! That's what my journey here was like: always waiting in expectation, and always mistaken. I got here the day before yesterday, and I've received nothing… It's unthinkable! It's monstrous! That prince can sometimes be so gullible! They can put the fear of the Devil into him—and him such a libertine, wallowing in debauchery! And he's so thoughtless; he spends his time on foolishness. I've definitely been discarded; I'm defeated, I'm…"[18]

She'd reached that point when she heard someone walking in the woods. Whoever was coming seemed to stop from time to time, as if he were examining the places he was passing through in search of someone or something. The duchess's first thought was that they were out looking for her, and her first impulse was to escape; her second was to wait and confront the intruder, whether it was her father or her uncle, to put off being scolded for a while. She'd already prepared a couple of angry expressions, the kind with which women almost always prevail; because if a man said those things to you, you'd have to reply by slapping him, and—that not being an acceptable way to treat the fair sex above a certain social height—all you could do was be silent and accept the insults. We talk a lot about the tyranny of strength, but the tyranny of weakness is cruel and abusive in quite another way. There's also the tyranny of dishonor—the tyranny so firmly seated in vice, swaggering so proudly there, so thoroughly greased in its mud, that not a single spot remains where you can take revenge…

---

[18]God forbid we should offer as our own opinion of an unhappy man the words we give here as the judgment of his angry mistress. A woman who considers herself discarded can sometimes believe every possible evil of the man who's forgotten her, especially when she's capable of doing something she dreads. The youth of a prince is no more exempt from folly than that of the humblest bourgeois, but it's not our place to blame him for it. And if we've chosen, without naming him or bringing him on stage, a character who's become, through age and exile, at the very least respectable, it's because we needed someone of a rank compatible with the events we wanted to depict. (Soulié's own 1834 footnote.)

We've all known some wretch who's dead, and who took pleasure in putting down in his daily newspaper column some slander against the first honorable man who came to mind when he got up in the morning. The insult he wrote down got published, the honorable man read it, flew into a rage, collected a witness and pistols and a sword, and went to find the slanderer. He demanded satisfaction, and the other man laughed in his face. So he insulted him, and the other man just laughed even louder. He called him a coward, and the coward just shrugged. He slapped him, and the man he slapped cried out that he was being murdered. Satisfied and feeling avenged, the honorable man left, believing the punishment he'd just administered had restored his good name. The next day brought another article and another slander, provoking another rage, another visit, another sneer, another insult. That day the honorable man spat in the slanderer's face and thought the matter was settled. The slanderer waited till the door was shut, and an even more deadly, more infamous slander came with the dawn and the next day's paper. In the face of such stubborn ugliness, I've seen peaceable men roar in fury and ask how they can shut up a wretch like that. Then they calmed down, because they'd just had an idea for getting revenge. That same night they waited for their man on a street corner, grabbed him by the collar, thrashed him hard enough to break their walking stick down to the handle, and sent him away with a broken arm. The villain knew how to write with his left hand, and his daily slander woke the next morning, spread across Paris to a few hundred subscribers, and was rushed through the mail to a thousand readers. What to do now? Be silent, or come to terms with it, or turn murderer. The honorable man was the weaker one, and he remained an honorable man, and the wretch laughed and swaggered in his triumph. That's what we're calling the tyranny of dishonor; it has a thousand other ways of proceeding, but we'll confine ourselves to this one example.

We could also expand on the various methods available to the tyranny of misfortune: from the exile who takes pleasure in defying the laws of the country that took him in, and who treats the least reprimand as an attack against his misfortune;[19] to the foundling welcomed into a family who

---

[19]This is just an instance of a general theory, which we wouldn't want to see applied to any particular case, especially in a political context. Between the magnificent Polish exiles and the petty French officials, the tyranny is all on the part of the latter. (Soulié's own 1834 footnote.) Thousands of educated, liberal, prominent Poles fled to France and other countries in the 1830s after the failure of their

protests at the slightest discipline, "It's only because I'm outcast and alone that you're persecuting me!" Both the one and the other can sometimes act with impunity because of the fear—of lacking the respect due to misfortune—that they inspire in well-meaning people.

The Duchess of Avarenne had all three kinds of tyranny at her disposition. Let's imagine that what she dreaded took place, and some sermonizing relative had come to the woods to give her a well-deserved lecture; let's imagine it was her brother:

"Sister, your affair with the prince has shocked the court and brought dishonor to your name!"

"Brother, you had no objection to that affair when it led to your being appointed colonel and then brigadier in the royal army."

"If I'd known that was the reason…"

"Oh, don't try that. You knew, and if your wife wasn't so stupid and ugly you'd have driven her, at sword point, to the prince's bedroom."

"Sister, you're lucky you're only a woman!" And the brother would've gone away, grinding his teeth.

Now let's imagine it was her uncle:

"Niece, your behavior has shocked respectable people and defied the heavens."

"I care little for either the heavens or respectable people."

"What they say about you surpasses all belief."

"What? They say I have a lover? Two? Three? Ten? Well, it's true! It entertains me; it's none of your business; and if you mention it again I'll have a hundred."

"Oh, niece, this is what your Philosophes have taught you!"

"The Philosophes are intelligent people; the devout are imbeciles. Nobody besides brute peasants still fasts and observes Lent and goes without something."

"But do you have any idea what kind of names your behavior deserves?"

"What? Are they going to call me an atheist? That's in fashion now. A whore? Not everyone can be one who wants to. Besides I've heard all that for ages."

"And you're not ashamed?"

"Ashamed! I haven't got the time."

"Oh, niece, I give up. You've sunk even lower than I expected."

---

pro-independence uprising against the division of Poland between Russia, Prussia, and Austria.

"So long, uncle. Give my best to your flock."

And the saintly abbot, his heart broken, went away shocked and stunned, without having found any joint through which he could pierce her armor of impudence and reach her heart.

Now for her father:

"Well, daughter, here's the fruit of your folly: exile from the court, and the loss of any future and any wealth."

"Many thanks, father. My own misery isn't enough, now you have to burden me with your grievances."

"But you brought that misery on yourself."

"Is that a reason to come blame me for it? What have I asked you for? To leave me alone to suffer in a corner."

"But…"

"Have I complained? I'm strong, I've got courage. But if I also have to put up with your anger, I have to admit I'll succumb… Life at that price would be unbearable…"

"But still…"

"Yes, sir, I'd rather die! My God, my God! I'm so miserable! And you, who claim to love me, you're on the side of my enemies… Well then, so be it! All this will come to an end. Life in this chateau… is it happiness, or wealth, or pleasure that would make me cling to it?"

"Come, come, Diane, you're going mad."

"Mad! Oh, no, sir. I know what I'm saying. Look, sir, I'm in despair. Leave me, leave me, or I can no longer answer for what I might do."

"Listen to me."

"Oh, my God, my God! What tyranny!"

And with that the despairing beauty would've pressed a hand to her brow in anger, she would've disturbed three curls of her lovely hair, she'd have pretended to be about to dig her nails into her beautiful eyes; and her fearful father, would've softened and withdrawn cautiously so as not to aggravate that wounded heart.

That's not what happened, but it's what would inevitably have happened if it had been her brother or her uncle or her father who came out of the woods and appeared before the beautiful Duchess of Avarenne. But it was no one with the right to scold her, because it was simply Jean d'Aspert, the handsome miller, who, as soon as he spotted the duchess, came quickly toward her, hat in hand, looking very respectful and ill at ease. As soon as he was near her he pulled a package out of his pocket and handed it to her.

"What's this?"

"Letters that a man who was hanging around outside the chateau wanted to have delivered secretly to madame."

"What man?"

"A kind of postilion in green, with gold braid."

"Ah, very good! Why didn't you let him in?"

"Because he told me no one should suspect he'd been here. If madame had been in her apartment, I could've escorted the stranger secretly to her. But I'd seen madame go out into the grounds and head into these woods. I thought the man's livery might be noticed, and I thought I'd be of more help to him if I took charge of the letters myself and brought them to you, since everybody knows me here and no one would pay me attention."

"And what's become of that man?"

"He's waiting in the village for the answer I said I'd bring him."

"Very good," said the duchess. "Wait." And with a wave of her hand she dismissed the handsome miller, who withdrew.

Then she opened the package. Inside an envelope that hinted at a long explanatory letter she found only a short note folded in half, containing these few lines:

My beautiful lover, it seems to me you've been awfully reckless. The king is angry. I haven't dared speak to him about you yet. Be patient; I predict in a little while I'll be needed, and then I can negotiate your return. I'm still infatuated with you, and very grateful for the love you brought me. You're in such an awful place that I won't ask you to be faithful as proof of your love; I'll reserve that virtue for myself. For lack of that one, have the virtue of thinking of me a great deal and writing to me often. A thousand kisses on your beautiful eyes. If someone sends you the following quatrain, don't believe it:

On my way back from Courbevoie
I got an upset stomach
From a heavy pastry from Savoie;
I took Duthé to make it pass.[20]

The duchess's stillness after reading that odd note was a sign of an uncommon confusion in her thoughts. She believed she'd calculated and foreseen all the miseries of her situation, and now she saw that in a single stroke and all at once everything she'd foreseen and calculated had been

---

[20]Duthé, a person's name, sounds like *du thé* ("some tea"), as Soulié himself notes here.

surpassed. Nothing could've been colder or more curt than that note: not a word of comfort, or of hope for the future, or of devotion to her, or of efforts on her behalf—just some distant negotiation, with results even more distant, and a pretext for infidelity that took the form of a boast. It was enough to make her go mad. But the duchess must've had in reserve some means of extracting from the prince what she would rather have owed to his consideration for her, because she angrily crumpled the note and said aloud as she got up, "Oh, we'll meet again..."

She left the woods and returned to her apartment to write the answer the courier was waiting for. That reply—filled with anger and ill feeling—was soon ready. The duchess threatened her lover with exposure skillfully designed to compromise him, and informed him haughtily that she'd know how to place him between the necessity of defying the will of the court on her behalf and maintaining her there on his own authority, and the disgrace of dropping her like a coward—in which case she'd have no compunction about making public a secret whose irrefutable proof was in her possession. She'd give the prince enough time to send her an answer; but when that time had passed, if she got no answer or if she got an unsatisfactory answer, she'd leave here and return to Versailles. So it was up to him to decide.

When her note was ready, she needed the intermediate messenger who would pass it on to the courier; so she told Honorine to go fetch Jean d'Aspert, who was probably waiting somewhere in the woods. Honorine replied that the miller had spoken to her, and that, since he had business at the neighboring chateau, he'd told her he'd come back that evening, once it was dark, to receive the duchess's orders and pass them on to the courier, who wouldn't leave till the next morning, since he meant to spend all of this day resting after his long journey of riding at full galop.

That delay irritated the duchess a great deal. There are moments of anger when you have to carry out your resolve completely for fear of changing your mind. That note, written but not yet sent, weighed on her, not because it would arrive a day later but because it wasn't yet on its way. The courier could've stopped for a week thirty leagues from the village of l'Étang and it wouldn't have made her especially impatient, since she'd be sure her message would get to its destination and have its effect, and once it was in the prince's hands pride would force her to do what she'd said she'd do. But, by some vague whimsical instinct she was afraid that between two o'clock, which had just rung, and ten o'clock, the hour she had to wait for, something would happen, some thought would occur to her, she'd have some quarrel with her father, that would make her hold back the letter she'd written. That vexation occupied her thoughts for fifteen minutes, after which she went back to being bored.

If idleness is the mother of all vices, then boredom could certainly adopt as its children most of the excesses committed by an imagination accustomed to wearing itself out on a thousand small cares that count not as work but as a pastime. So when dinnertime arrived at three o'clock, and the duchess was told her father was expecting her, Diane was seized by a whim for not dining, and she asked to be left alone. She made herself ill, she pretended to be ill, she took to her bed and called for herbal tea. Bed was boring, the tea was insipid; she threw the second cup across the room, got up, and began to pace around her apartment in her nightshirt. Then she got cold, and ordered a fire made; and on a gorgeous sunny day in June her servants piled entire tree trunks in her vast bedroom fireplace. She enjoyed watching the flames spread from one log to another till all had caught, and when the whole mound of wood was burning she hoped just a little that the chimney would catch fire. That didn't happen, and she grew tired of being warm.

She summoned Honorine; night had fallen. After lighting a candle the girl approached her mistress, who was wrapped up in a damask dressing gown and had tucked her bare feet into black velvet mules. Honorine asked her if she wanted something.

"Is there anything of interest in these parts?" asked the duchess abruptly.

"Nothing, ma'am."

The greatest marvels hold no interest for those who live among them. Notre Dame isn't interesting to the native of the City who passes its magnificent portals every day. The most rustic landscape, the most sublime ruin, is of no interest to the peasant who breaks the soil on the most picturesque hillside with his hoe, or takes shelter from the rain under the ancient arches of a twelfth-century abbey. And therefore Honorine could think of nothing interesting to suggest to a woman who'd seen Paris and Versailles.

"Isn't there even a ghost around here somewhere?' asked the duchess.

Honorine didn't answer; she'd gone pale and was shaking all over.

"Ah!" said the duchess, "so there are ghosts. Great—tell me about it."

"Oh, no, ma'am, there aren't any ghosts. But there are extraordinary things."

"Like what?"

"Alas, ma'am, there are sorcerers."

"Some old shepherd who casts spells? They have them everywhere! They're dirty and they stink."

"Oh, no, ma'am," replied Honorine with a smile that betrayed, through her fright, a trace of pride in the local sorcerers. "They aren't old shepherds. It's much more terrible: It's Doctor Lussay, who can make demons enter the body of whomever he wants, and make them come out again when he pleases."

"Oh, so that little man is a charlatan? That's good to know. And what does he get out of it?"

"Oh, ma'am, the doctor doesn't get paid anything for that; on the contrary, he pays the people who let him do it."

"So what does he do to them?"

"Well, ma'am, it's hard to explain. I saw it done once, but I was so frightened I didn't dare go back."

"Still, you must remember what you saw. Was it the Devil in person, with horns and cloven hooves?"

"No, ma'am. Picture this: it was night, and the sky had clouded over, just as it's threatening to do right now. There was a terrible storm, and I'd stayed in the main room at our house, trembling all over, when suddenly there was Jean coming in, wet, dirty, covered in mud, asking where my father was. My father was in town and wouldn't be back till the next day."

"It was very clever of Monsieur Jean to come looking for him on exactly that day," said the duchess with a little chuckle.

"Well, no, ma'am, since I wasn't able to give Jean what he wanted."

"Oh, you weren't able to give him what he wanted?" said the duchess, looking at Honorine in surprise that a pretty girl like her hadn't been able to give a handsome fellow like Jean what he wanted. So, affecting astonishment, she added, "What was he asking for that was so extraordinary?"

"Ma'am, he was asking for the key to the great wine cellar that leads to the passageways under the chateau."

"So he's a drunkard?"

Honorine waved that away impatiently, almost indignantly.

Seeing that, the duchess went on, "Well then, what did he want with that key?"

"He wanted to go all the way to the doctor's house, which is an ancient outbuilding of the chateau, whose cellars connect with those of this house—so he could catch the doctor performing his necromancy."

"Why?"

"You see, in those days Jean was courting Louise. Louise was slightly ill, and they'd had Doctor Lussay come. But instead of treating her with medicine he'd cured her by laying his hands on her head and talking to her and tracing big circles on her forehead with a metal wand and using all kinds of hocus pocus—to the point that Louise was like the doctor's slave, obeying his every gesture and shaking like a leaf before him. There were others in the area who'd been healed like Louise, and they were all the same way—big strong laborers and carters. Once the doctor treated them, it seemed like they lost all courage, all strength. It's true, ma'am. People around here noticed, and they began to get suspicious. But since the doctor helped everybody, people didn't talk about it much. And yet in the end people noticed that almost every night those who'd been healed by Doctor Lussay left home at the same time and went to the doctor's house and didn't come out till two or three hours later, often looking completely bowled over. Some people hid out to hear what was going on; but since Doctor Lussay's house is surrounded by a garden, they couldn't hear anything that was happening inside.

"And yet all those poor people, after they'd been cured, were visibly wasting away. They didn't have any illness, but they were pale, gaunt, sickly. The slightest noise made them jump. And especially poor Louise, who'd been so pretty—she was like a recluse. He father had forbidden her to go back to the doctor, and Jean had often begged her not to; she'd promised to obey; but when the hour of the witches' Sabbath came she always managed to escape. It was usually around seven o'clock in the evening. Once her father locked her in her room; but the poor girl was so possessed that she jumped out the window, which luckily wasn't very high, and ran immediately to Doctor Lussay's. When old Jacques came home—Jacques is Louise's father—at first he was furious that his daughter had escaped; then the poor man began to weep because she was possessed by a demon. It raised a scandal, and old Jacques wanted to go complain to the priest and get him to exorcize his daughter; but Doctor Lussay gave him some money, and the witches' Sabbath went on as merrily as ever.

"Jean—who was troubled about the whole thing, and who could see Louise growing paler and dwindling till she was almost a skeleton—Jean wanted to tear the doctor to pieces; and hell, you couldn't pay him enough money to stop him. But Louise, to whom he'd boasted about what he wanted to do, had pleaded with him so much, saying it was her happiness and maybe even her life he'd be putting at risk if he touched the doctor, that he let it drop. And yet every day he grew more anxious, because the poor girl was losing her mind; she talked to herself, she spoke nonsense, she said the doctor took her to Heaven, where there was magnificent furniture and music that made her dance all by herself. Once she tried to take me along, saying, 'Come, come, you'll taste the delights of Heaven, you'll feel pleasure entering you all the way to the marrow of your bones.' And when she talked like that her eyes bulged and glowed like candles. It frightened me."

The duchess, having listened carefully up to that point, began to laugh. "It seems to me Jean would be better suited to provide pleasures like that than the doctor. But anyway, what did he want the night he came to your house?"

"Here's what: As usual, he'd tried to keep Louise from going to the witches' Sabbath. To do that, he'd gotten her father's permission to take her two leagues away from here. They were talking calmly at the inn in the next village, while suddenly seven o'clock rang. No sooner had Louise heard the chimes than she became very anxious, telling Jean she had to leave, that the hour had come when she could hear the doctor calling her, and she added, as if she were talking to someone else, 'I'm on my way, I'm on my way.' Jean tried to stop her from leaving, he begged her to stay, but Louise could no longer hear him, and she seemed to be talking to some spirit that was tormenting her. She got up, and Jean stopped her by force. She struggled for a few seconds, but since he was still holding her she fell into a terrible fit: the poor girl rolled around on the floor, banging her head against the furniture, foaming at the mouth like a madwoman and crying out. So Jean put her in a bed and stayed close by her. She hadn't been there a minute before she fell asleep, but a sleep so deep, so deep, that she seemed dead. Jean was beginning to despair at having put her into that state, when he saw her sit up. She rubbed her eyes as if she were waking up, and yet her eyes were shut; she got up all the way, and though she was fully dressed she began to act as if she were putting on he stockings, her shoes, her skirts. Jean—who'd seen her injure her face against the furniture when he tried to stop her—let her do it. As soon as Louise was ready, I mean as soon as she acted like she was ready, because she'd looked at herself in a mirror as if to arrange her scarf and her bonnet, off she went, straight to the door of the inn, and opened it, and went out into the street, all that with her eyes still shut. Jean followed her, not daring to touch her, he was so surprised. The storm had come, the rain was beating down, there was wind and thunder—horrible weather. Louise didn't seem to notice, and as soon as she was in the street she turned toward our village, still with her eyes shut. Though she was so weak and so thin, she walked so fast that Jean could barely keep up. Several times he approached her and called to her, but she didn't answer. Night had fallen completely, and the little paths that cut through the fields were all flooded and had practically vanished. That didn't stop Louise; she recognized them by night and followed them as if it were broad daylight, and a lovely dry day. Several times Jean tried to take her hand, but she began to cry out and shake like an epileptic. So he let her do what she wanted, still following her, though no longer knowing where they were, the night was so black. That went on for a good half hour. Suddenly Louise stopped at a wall that blocked their way, opened a little door that Jean couldn't see, went through it, and closed it behind her. He tried to force it open, but he couldn't. Finally he went around the house, and realized it was the doctor's. They'd walked almost five miles in three quarters of an hour. No matter how much Jean shouted and knocked, no one answered. So, not knowing what else to do, he climbed the wall and got into the garden. Approaching the house, he heard a strange noise: it was the voices of a dozen men and women, some laughing, some singing, some crying out loudly, others whimpering, all of it mixed with a kind of humming like someone praying. Jean had the idea of smashing the windows or breaking down a door; but the shutters had bars and the doors were padlocked. That's when he thought of the underground passages that lead to the doctor's house, and he decided to come to our place—because in going around the house he could tell the cries came from some kind of cellar; and when he put his ear to the basement window he could the noises more clearly, and he could recognize Louise's voice saying over and over, so loudly it barely sounded like her, 'Again! Again! Again!'"

At that word the duchess burst out laughing. By some strange chance, just then there was a gentle knock at the door to her room. Honorine, who'd been terrified by her own story, threw herself toward the Duchess of Avarenne with a cry and collapsed at her feet. She'd gone white and was staring around her wildly. The rain lashed the tall windows; the wind moaned and howled through the corridors of the chateau; the light from the single candle was lost in the enormous room. Seeing and hearing all that, the duchess herself grew pale and cold. She heard another knock, louder this time, that made her start. But whether it was courage, or whether it was just that the habitual word slipped out unintentionally, she called out in a strained voice, "Come in!..."

33

A man appeared, covered in a long cloak that dripped with rain and carrying a broad hat that he took off as he entered the room. It was Jean d'Aspert. "I've come to receive the duchess's orders."

The duchess and Honorine had been so frightened that neither one of them could recover, even after they'd recognized the miller, and they couldn't answer right away. The entrance

just at that moment of the hero of the strange story about Louise gave him some romantic, adventurous quality that made the duchess study him curiously and attentively. He was truly one of the handsomest men she'd ever seen. He'd taken the powder out of his hair, and his black locks lay in curls across his high forehead. He wore deerskin trousers and gaiters, and a leather belt, from which hung a brace of pistols, snugly encircled his powerful lithe waist.

Without taking her eyes off him, the duchess said—without the casually insolent tone she normally used toward people so far beneath her—"We were just speaking of you, sir."

"You were expecting me, ma'am. I beg pardon for my lateness. But the courier will wait for me till eleven, and it's only ten now."

"Oh, good," said the duchess, completely forgetting the reason Jean had come. "You can tell me the end of your story."

"My story?" said the miller in surprise.

"Louise's story," said Honorine. "I was in the middle of telling it to madame when you came in."

"Alas, ma'am," said Jean, "it's an awfully sad story."

"Up to this point it certainly doesn't lack for interest," replied the duchess. "But the night's grown cold. Stir up the fire a little, Honorine, and light a few candles—it's like a tomb in here. And go to the kitchen and have them send something up for me: now that I'm not listening to you talk anymore I feel like eating something ."

Honorine left, and Jean remained standing before the duchess. She'd turned her big armchair toward the fire, taken off her black mules, and set her beautiful white feet on a cushion before the hearth to warm them. Jean said nothing, and the Duchess of Avarenne, surprised at his silence, turned and saw Jean, standing still, his eyes fixed on her delicate feet with a look of desire. Caught in the midst of his admiration, Jean blushed and lowered his eyes.

The duchess gave him a wink, and a slight smile crossed her lips, a smile we might translate thus: "Well, sure, they're lovely and white, and your peasant girls aren't rich in beauty of this kind."

Then, after that little monologue in a smile, the duchess began to laugh properly—a muffled laugh, to be sure, but that certainly said, "It'd be amusing to drive this boy out of his mind."

She turned to him, and saw that his eyes were aimed boldly beneath the loose collar of her dressing gown and were pressed like a kiss on the satin of her beautiful shoulders. It was now the duchess's turn to blush. She put her feet back in the velvet mules and gave Jean a look—and this time he didn't drop his gaze till his eyes had met hers. They were both silent. She found him, at a minimum, very bold.

She had a wicked thought, which was to have fun at the handsome miller's expense, and to make him say something stupid and awkward. So, eying him up and down over her shoulder and addressing him in her haughty duchess's manner, she said, "So, I hear you do as you please around here?"

"Well, ma'am, you do what you can."

"But there have to be better things to do than run after all the pretty girls to seduce and abandon them," the duchess added bluntly.

Jean took the reprimand seriously, and he replied seriously, "I've had lots of girls, and I didn't seduce any of them. I've never been either the first or the last lover of the girls I've had. By that measure, you can't say I either seduced or abandoned them."

The duchess was surprised at Jean's reply, both for its simple eloquence and for its speaking directly to the point. She'd expected some kind of big, dumb smile, with halting words, and his hat awkwardly shuffled in his hands, like the rustics in the king's brother's theater. Still, she kept up her moral inquisition, and looking the miller in the eye she went on sternly, "That's not all. I hear you've even aimed as high as bourgeois women."

"Ma'am, I don't know whether it's that I've aimed as high as them, or that they've aimed as low as me; but it seems to me you can only get into a woman's bed on a basis of equality."

"And you'd apply that principle to a high-born woman if she stooped as low as you?" replied the Duchess of Avarenne sharply.

Jean grew pale, and a spark of anger glowed in his eye. His bit his lips, as if to block the answer he wanted to make, and—in a voice whose change in tone he couldn't quite disguise, but in which he affected the most reverent respect—he said, "Allow me to remind the duchess that the courier awaits her orders."

The duchess was sorry to have missed the insolent retort Jean had been on the brink of delivering, if only so she could laugh about it later. But she was stunned by both the miller's command of words and his restraint. To understand this young fellow completely, she moved abruptly to another kind of question, which in a manner of speaking contained her entire train of thought in the ellipsis.

"Where did you get your education?"

"From the Jesuits in Toulouse, ma'am."

"Did you know my uncle, the Abbot of Auvergne, when you were there?"

"I saw him, ma'am."

"He's another one who does what he pleases, isn't he?"

"In a different way, ma'am," said Jean curtly.

"Yes," said the duchess haughtily, "like a gentleman and not like a peasant." As she spoke the duchess looked the miller scornfully up and down.

Jean lowered his eyes and replied, with poorly disguised impatience, "I await your orders, ma'am."

"But you scarcely await them," said the duchess, "since you ask for them every minute."

She fell silent and became agitated, like a woman who sees she's not gaining the point she was aiming for. Her sudden movements undid her dressing gown and revealed the top of a fine, elegant, smoothly rounded leg. Just then the duchess was lost in thought; a minute later she noticed the nakedness of her legs; she took hold of the skirts of her gown to hide them— but then she stopped in that position, and looking to one side she sought Jean's eyes.

His eyes were lowered and his face was solemn: either he hadn't seen those new charms, or he hadn't paid attention to them, or he scorned her. The duchess found him much more impudent now than the first time he'd let his eyes rest on her. She felt angry. Why? Against whom? For what reason? She couldn't say. Resolving to send Jean away, she rose and carried the prince's note and her reply back to the fireplace to see if her answer was adequate. To make sure, she reread the prince's note—which only made her angrier than she already was; and when she reached the phrase, *You're in such an awful place that I won't ask you to be faithful as proof of your love*, she couldn't contain an exclamation of anger and contempt. She shrugged, crumpled the note between her fingers, and went back to thinking in silence.

A new moodiness, a new source of agitation, a new disarrangement of her dressing gown: it had opened at the top, and the silk of the robe, sliding smoothly down the silk of her shoulders all the way to the top of her arms, revealed that pure, lithe, endless line that started at her head and descended along her slender, graceful neck and her pure, flowing white shoulders till it ran beneath the folds of her gown and vanished so gently, so gradually, that it seemed as if the eye could keep following it and complete it.

The duchess's train of thought lasted long enough for Jean to lift his gaze and see her perfect white bosom—long enough that, after he'd turned his eyes away from the intoxicating sight, they went right back to it regardless; then, forgetting that the direction of his glance could be noticed, he let himself go in an admiration that made his brow redden and his body tremble.

At the sound of his panting, the duchess turned; but now Jean's eyes no longer fell before hers: on the contrary, they looked straight into hers, and poured all their fire into hers, and this time it was the Duchess of Avarenne who closed her eyelids. She no longer wanted to reprimand him; and at the moment when she could've turned serious, she made the mistake of wanting to laugh, and she said graciously, "So, my good fellow, you've had lots of pretty girls?"

"Pretty in a different way, ma'am."

"You use that answer for everything. When I said the Abbot of Auvergne does as he pleases, you answered, 'In a different way'! I understood, and I got angry, though you were right: the abbot is a very low, coarse man. But now when I ask you if your lovers are pretty, and you answer again, 'In a different way,' I confess I no longer understand."

"And yet I meant it in the same way as about the abbot."

"Meaning those pretty girls are low and coarse?"

"Yes, ma'am," said Jean with a sigh, giving the duchess a shy look, but one that was so like a gentle caress that she smiled inwardly—no longer the smile of a woman mocking a man in her triumph but that of a woman taking pleasure in her triumph. Still, she pulled her dressing gown back up around her neck, but slowly, as if she only did it reluctantly. And Jean's gaze—which had been divided between those lovely shoulders and those ivory breasts, and had gradually narrowed along with the damask collar as it tightened around her neck—now focused on the duchess's face, and then her eyes. He, filled with burning admiration, and she, filled with a triumph that unwittingly flattered her vanity, gazed into each other's eyes a long time. Their line of sight, as they crossed, mingled and melted together like rays of light, growing warm and intense enough to burn the two of them...

Till Honorine bustled in, saying, "Isn't that a terrifying story, ma'am?"

Jean gestured angrily, the duchess gestured impatiently. "Oh, he forgot to tell me the ending."

Honorine stared at them both in surprise; if she'd dared, she would've said out loud what her looks expressed only mutely: "So what've you been doing here together for the last half hour?"

Though he was still shaking, the miller fell back on the words that had already served him twice in his attempt to extricate himself from his position: "Ma'am, it's getting late, and I'm at your orders."

The duchess might perhaps have gotten angry, if the feeling in Jean's voice hadn't expressed, louder than any words could possibly have, "Dismiss, me, ma'am! I'm going mad, dismiss me!" Without answering, she shook her head. What could that mean? Presumably her refusal to send him away didn't imply that she intended or foresaw everything that followed; but the duchess still had something she wanted to hear from Jean. She'd been left with her feelings incomplete. If Honorine hadn't come in, perhaps the handsome miller, transfixed by the look that had consumed him earlier, would've said something to arouse all of the duchess's arrogance; she'd have driven him away, and that would've been the end of that. But perhaps, in spite of his agitation, he would've kept silent, and lowered his eyes, and allowed his delirium to fade, and then the duchess would've had a good laugh over the miller's amorous ecstasy; but chance had saved both of them from either one or the other of those two awkward resolutions to their interview, by interrupting it abruptly and leaving in each of their hearts the allure of an emotion experienced but not completed, like the mere taste of a fruit in the mouth.

Jean took the duchess's gesture as nothing more than stalling, but still it pleased him. Meanwhile Honorine put a small table beside the duchess and set on it a lady's supper: a chicken wing, a biscuit, a few preserves. The duchess said nothing, and neither did Jean. Honorine had forgotten something; she went out again; the duchess watched her close the door, and as soon as they were alone she said, "Who taught you to see that those pretty girls were pretty in a low, coarse way?"

Why had she waited till they were alone to ask him that simple question, which Honorine could certainly have heard? Because the answer she hoped for or expected couldn't be uttered before the chambermaid, and no doubt Diane didn't want Jean to have any excuse not to say it; perhaps she wished to hear it. But he was an indescribably awkward position. He was certainly not a shy fellow; when the attractions of conversation with so great a lady as the Duchess of Avarenne had practically given him the right to walk side by side with her, then his mind, his heart, his feelings thrilled fast enough for him to close the distance between them. But when an accidental circumstance broke the spell that had carried him along, he had to go back to being plain old Jean, the miller facing the great lady. So, when he heard the duchess's question—a question he would've answered gratefully and passionately a moment earlier—he was taken aback, and didn't dare speak his thoughts, and tried to lie, and couldn't, and ended up saying something stupid: "That's what I heard."

"Oh," said the duchess, disappointed. "I thought you'd seen it for yourself…"

Jean realized his mistake, and stamped his foot. Neither one of them knew what else to say; both, stuck in their roles, no longer knew how to regain equality. But—though they both felt regret in their hearts for the mutual position they'd lost—Jean, gone back to being a miller, still found the duchess beautiful enough to admire or to rape; yet he was in despair. The duchess, gone back to being a duchess, no longer felt his masculine gaze igniting her feminine feelings; but the great lady lusted for the handsome miller. They remained silent.

Honorine returned, and once again she allowed her glance to express her astonishment at finding them there, silent and unmoving. "Well, tell madame your story!" she said, elbowing Jean, as if to warn him he was acting like an idiot, but certainly with no inkling why he seemed like an idiot.

"Yes," said the duchess carelessly, making use of that pretext for keeping Jean there. "Yes, do, tell me the story."

"He'd better hurry up," said Honorine, "because eleven o'clock has already rung, and Jean won't have time to get to the market in Clermont tomorrow morning."

"Oh," said the duchess, "you're going to the market in Clermont?"

"As you can see, ma'am, he's got his belt on with his pistols."

"Oh, so there's a reason to be afraid on the roads?"

"No," said Jean, "but since I have to carry fairly large sums of money with me, I take a few precautions."

"Unnecessary, I assume," said the duchess.

"Unnecessary!" cried Honorine. "Jean's been attacked twice, and if he hadn't killed one of the four robbers who fell on him, he'd have left his bones there."

"You're very brave," said the duchess, giving Jean a look.

"I was just defending myself, ma'am, that's all," said Jean with a confusion that had all the graciousness of noble modesty.

It didn't matter whether Jean was brave or not: it hadn't mattered a few minutes earlier. But that new quality, which earlier would've passed unnoticed, was revealed just in time to interest the duchess and make her see Jean as special. After a moment of silence, she added, as if regretfully, "Well then, leave, since your business summons you."

"I thought," said Jean, "the duchess wanted to hear what happened to Louise."

The Duchess of Avarenne understood that he wanted to stay, and she was delighted. And, since all feminine vanity grows more demanding the more it's fed, she wanted Jean's sacrifice to be as complete as possible, and she made him feel its full impact. "But I don't want you to miss the market at Clermont. I believe it's the season when you grist millers do your buying."[21]

"Oh, no, ma'am," said Jean, "that's not for a few months yet. And even if this market was more important than it is, I wouldn't go if..."

"Well then, stay, and you can tell me your story," interrupted the duchess quickly, for she'd noticed an expression on Honorine's face that she assumed was wiser than in fact it was. Then she added, "Take off that cloak; good God, it looks wet through. Come closer to the fire... Have a seat, sir... I'm listening."

Jean obeyed, but he didn't begin his story. The duchess didn't prompt him to start; she turned to the small table, cut herself a slice of chicken, put it on her plate, poured herself something to drink... But she neither ate nor drank.

Honorine said to Jean, who was watching the fire dance with no thought for the reason he was there, "I stopped at the point where you came to the house to ask me for the key to the cellars... I told madame everything that happened before then."

"My God, you're losing your mind tonight!" said the duchess angrily. "There's nothing on the table—you forgot the wine!"

"Madame never drinks any," said Honorine.

---

[21]By "grist miller" was meant a miller who, besides grinding grain, also bought and sold flour. (Soulié's own 1834 footnote.)

The duchess bit her lip and answered, "Of course not, but here's Monsieur Jean, soaked through by the rain; maybe he needs…"

"But, ma'am," said Jean, stung at being offered a glass of wine like a laborer, "I'm not accustomed to it…"

"Even so," said the duchess impatiently, "go get me some wine."

Honorine went out.

"It's neither for you nor for me," added the duchess quickly. "But that girl is unbearable. She means well, but she's so indiscrete!… She won't go away!"

The Duchess of Avarenne was moving fast. First she'd waited to be alone with Jean to pick her conversation with him back up; now she wanted to send Honorine away so they could be alone again. Finding out what had happened to poor Louise was a good excuse; it would be difficult not to talk about her, but there was a way of going about it; and here was how it was done:

"That Louise," said the duchess, pretending to be busy with her supper. "Was that Louise also a low, coarse girl?"

"Oh, no, ma'am," said Jean. "Louise was a very elegant girl. She had small, slender hands…" Then, looking at the duchess's hands, he added, "But they were rough and red, because she worked, just like all the other farm girls."

"Perhaps she had pretty little feet too?"

"Yes, ma'am, small—but malformed by clogs and misshapen by fatigue."

"Was she fair-complexioned?"

"The sun had burned and blackened the skin on her face and neck, and I never saw further than that."

The duchess looked at Jean with a smile, then examined herself: she was completely covered up, and there was nothing she could do about it, worse luck. She went on, "Based on what I've heard, I'd say you loved Louise because she seemed more distinguished than the other girls. That shows good taste, and you should be happy to have found in a peasant girl what can usually be found only in women of higher social rank."

"And which is a great deal more attractive there!"

"Oh," said the duchess, setting down her fork and leaning forward with her elbows on the table, "have you had occasion to notice that?" And she gave Jean a look and a smile full of indulgence for whatever answer he'd dare give.

Jean was stirred, and he trembled. Some vague instinct told him to advance, but he also felt an urgent fear of going further than he ought to go. He avoided answering her question directly; turning his head, he said in a muffled voice, "Yes, ma'am, to my misfortune."

"To your misfortune!" said the duchess, throwing back the collar of her dressing gown, which revealed her white shoulders.

Jean, who no longer dared look at her, didn't see that.

"To your misfortune!" repeated the duchess, in a voice that shook seductively.

"Yes, ma'am," replied Jean, "for it's a misfortune to have seen, involuntarily, something you wouldn't dare look at again."

He lifted his head slowly and gave the duchess a look of despair—a look that showed him she was exposed, and ravishing. He drew back with an expression in which fear and supplication were mingled; but he could no longer take his eyes off her. The duchess lowered her own eyes to let herself be admired, and when she lifted them they were so languid, so veiled, so steeped in a sweet expression of indulgent satisfaction, that Jean was carried away and cried out, "Oh, ma'am, you're so beautiful!"

The blow had been struck, and it was hard to respond to. But a new interruption saved the Duchess of Avarenne from embarrassment. Honorine returned.

Jean thought all was lost, but the duchess saved them both. "That story is truly incredible," she said, "and since you've decided not to go Clermont, I'd happily hear it to the end."

"He still didn't finish?" asked Honorine.

"Not yet," said Jean, thereby boldly making himself complicit in the duchess's lie.

"That's too bad," said Honorine, "because they're closing the gates, and then they'll give the keys to the marquis, as they usually do when he's here at the chateau."

"Are the gates the only way out?" asked the duchess.

"Oh, ma'am, of course there's the little door. But they're going to release the hounds. And that door leads to the woods, which aren't exactly safe."

"Well," said the duchess, "Jean is armed, like a knight in search of adventure, and you just have to tell your father not to release the hounds."

"But to go see my father," said Honorine hesitantly, "you have to cross the entire grounds, and at night, all alone…"

"Don't you go home every night?"

"The problem isn't going, because Pierre, our apprentice, waits for me in the kitchen and walks me home; it's coming back, so I can undress madame and help her to bed."

"Oh my God!" said the duchess. "I don't need help. Go to bed, child; you must be very tired."

"But I'm worried, ma'am… It's not that Jean doesn't know his way around the chateau and the grounds; but I wouldn't want to abuse madame's goodness and fail in my duty to her."

"But since I'm giving you permission… Here, take this wine to your father. It'll do him good, the worthy fellow."

"Oh!" cried Honorine, "madame is so good! Thank you ma'am… Goodnight, ma'am, goodnight…"

"Goodnight, Honorine."

The girl left. Jean and the duchess were alone.

Since the duchess didn't hear the end of Louise's story that night, our readers will be forced to do what she did, and wait for another occasion. We can also make it clear that her letter to the prince wasn't sent the next morning, and the one that was sent wasn't the first one she'd written.

II. THE EXILES IN ROME

(1798)

I've never seen Rome, but I'll go see Rome. I want to find out for myself what the prevailing feeling is in the enthusiasm everybody brings home from that city. I have a terrible fear that all the Roman excitement—which for some takes the form of half a dozen ancient ruins, for others the intact majesty of the Christian monuments, for a few the ragged beggars at St. Peter's—is just the merchandise you feel obliged to bring back from Rome, the way you wouldn't dare leave Strasbourg without a pâté, Mainz without a ham, Périgueux without truffles, Tours without prunes.

The cogitators (may I be forgiven the word) who've restored the city (like architects) in their imaginations, while seated on the pedestal of a column as the wind moans under the arcades of the Coliseum, and who, on some summer night (very unhealthy in Italy) have seen Rome rise intact before them; have heard Antony and Cicero at the rostrum, have seen Spartacus at the circus, Clodius[22] at the baths, Messalina at a brothel; who, because of all those thrilling memories come alive in that dead city, have felt their souls overflowing and their enthusiasm being captured—those same cogitators who, at home by their fireside in Paris, have never thought to read a page of Mirabeau,[23] who'd get sick to their stomachs just passing through the city gate at the Place du Combat, who bathe in a bathtub, and who think the police aren't doing enough against prostitution—those gentlemen disgust me. They're plagiarists of noble feelings who've degraded those feelings so far that before leaving Rome they pick up an order of emotions at so much a sheet—because emotions are still for sale. Those rascals who haggled over the price of a Mass said in memory of their father, and to whom the vastness of St. Peter's, the scarlet spectacle of the cardinals, and the ancient children's voices of the castrati, revealed, they claim, the power of the Christian religion, strike me as even more despicable. As for those who find that the dense shade of the trees at the Tuileries doesn't protect them enough against our feeble August sun, but who,

---

[22]Publius Clodius Pulcher (circa 92-52 BCE): a Roman politician and demagogue best known for his opposition to Cicero.
[23]Honoré-Gabriel Riqueti, Count Mirabeau (1749-1791): a writer, orator, and statesman prominent in the lead-up to the Revolution.

beneath the parched trees on the Via del Corso, have soaked in deeply the hot showers of burning rays from the Italian sky, they fill me with pity and scorn. All of them make me want to see Rome: not to catch a fever on some lovely summer night, nor to be converted by the Pope saying Mass, nor to get a sunburn like a luggage porter, but to tell them they've almost all lied about it.

I know only one man who, in my opinion, made the trip to Rome in a new and productive way. He was an old friend, the son of a regicide who fell on hard times after the Restoration, and who brought back from Rome the bones of St. Peter, bought for seventeen or eighteen francs, and presented them to the priest in his village—which was good enough for him to be married without going to confession and to have dinner with the deputy department prefect. Besides that, he never said a word about his trip to Rome. I hardly need add that the man is perfectly intelligent and distinguished.

Now, here's the reason for all these reflections: If we acknowledge that it's in very good taste not to talk about Rome when you've seen it—as a result, by the law of contraries, it must be logical and sophisticated to talk about it when you haven't seen it. And I haven't seen it, and therefore it's sophisticated, and it's fair, and it's necessary that I talk about it; and there's no one besides me with the right to talk about it pertinently, and therefore I'll talk about it. That, in my opinion, is what's known as using reason. My right, my privilege, my monopoly having been indisputably established by that triumph of logic, I mean to take advantage of it.

Everybody knows enough history to know that in 1798 the good Revolution, known as '89, and the Terror, known as '93, were over and done with. And for that not to sound too obvious, I'll add that most people know it only because the events of those two periods have been named after the years in which they happened. Because if I ask my readers directly, "What was going on in Europe in May of 1798?" I'd bet a hundred to one they'll scratch their heads and begin to list the events they know about so they can connect them firmly to their dates. I'll do it for you.

In 1798, to atone for the assassination of General Duphot, Rome had been proclaimed a republic.[24] A few months earlier Cardinal Doria, incited

---

[24]Mathurin-Léonard Duphot (1769-1797) was assassinated during an anti-French riot in Rome, which gave Napoleon a pretext to occupy the city, abolish the Papal States, and proclaim a republic.

by Acton,[25] the British ambassador, had cleverly set up a kind of revolutionary movement whose repression gave the cardinal a chance to rid himself of several fervent republicans. But, unluckily for him, his success against the very people he'd brought to the fore led him to insult the French nation in the person of its ambassador, Joseph Bonaparte. The ambassador's residence was stormed, and the Papal troops despicably killed brave Duphot at the ambassador's side. In those days offenses committed against France weren't left to slumber in some ministerial file, and the Roman government paid with its life for the French general's death. The Roman Republic was established a few months after the assassination.

The Romans no sooner had their liberty than they thought of revenge. At the time, liberty meant nothing besides the power of the lower classes, and power and its abuse are happy to walk along hand in hand, no matter from what height they're carried out. Among the wrongs to be avenged, the first to be satisfied was the one prompted by the most recent grievance, and what came to mind immediately was the trap into which Cardinal Doria had lured the republicans of Rome, and the punishment he'd inflicted on those he'd turned into criminals. Among the accomplices in that plot the people singled out, as the most influential, a few French exiles who worked everywhere, by every means, to incite the enemies of the French Republic. At first people grumbled about their presence in the city; then they were met with threats in the streets. Almost all of them left Rome. The populace was sorry its insults had unwittingly given the exiles warning, and now concentrated all of its hatred of aristocrats on the few who remained.

One morning in the Piazza Navona, very near the Pantheon, a group of men and women was speaking loudly of the joys of liberty. An orator standing on a curbstone was babbling about a revolutionary leaflet in which, two years earlier, he'd improvised a song of joy. In a niche in the wall behind him was carved a Madonna, on whose head someone had set an enormous tricolor cockade at a jaunty angle. The Baby Jesus seated on her lap sported one just as large; and even the Holy Spirit, hovering over the sacred family, had its feathered head decorated with a barely noticeable tricolor. Just as the orator had reached the point of proving to his listeners that the liberty of the common people meant neither more nor less than the enslavement of the mighty, a woman passed that little gathering,

---

[25]Sir John Acton, 6th Baronet Acton (1736-1811). He was the grandfather of the more famous Lord Acton, a historian and politician.

considered it for a moment, and went on her way with a gesture of anger and disgust.

"Santa Maria!" cried someone in the crowd. "That woman passed the Madonna without saluting the tricolor cockade!"

"She's a noblewoman, an aristocrat!" responded the first people who heard that remark. "She's defying us! She's insulting us! She looked back at us over her shoulder! She made an insulting gesture toward the Madonna! She murmured something between her teeth! She's treating us like scum! She called us despicable! She threatened us! It's people like her who'd have us all hanged if they ever got back into power! And who've already done it! And are we going to take it? No! No! No! Revenge! Yes, revenge! Death to aristocrats! Into the Tiber with the aristocrat! Into the Tiber with her silk dress! Into the Tiber with her lace mantilla! Into the Tiber with her velvet hat!"

All those cries, in which the need of each person to top what had just been said had led the last people to speak of murder, had followed each other quickly enough to retain the flavor of thoughtlessness and violence that almost always turns what's called popular justice into public crime—justice that's always criminal in the sense that it reaches its verdict passionately and carries out its sentence ferociously—justice that's almost always unjust, because it rarely touches anyone but the innocent. But all those cries, each conveying an opinion, each a verdict, had nevertheless taken the time needed for each opinion uttered to sink into the heart of the mob, so that each verdict could give birth to the resolve to carry out the sentence. That had given the woman thus condemned to death enough time to get away and vanish around a corner.

"Where is she? Where'd she go? Where'd she run off to? Where's she hiding?" came the cries on all sides as soon as they lost sight of her.

"That way! That way!" replied a few voices.

The mob immediately rushed off in that direction with a great unceasing cry that served as a summons to all those who'd neither seen nor heard anything, but whose rags put them in solidarity with whatever happened in the public square, and who responded, "To the Tiber! Death to the aristocrat!" with all the enthusiasm of idlers who've found a way to pass the time. The first people to turn the corner saw, far down the street, the silk dress, the lace mantilla, and the velvet hat. "There she is! There! There! Stop her! Stop the aristocrat!" came the cry on all sides.

Their victim, who'd neither sped up nor slowed down as a result of those cries, turned onto a street going left. Seeing that, the mob split in two: half followed the woman, while the other half ran down a diagonal street that intersected the other end of the street she'd taken—making sure, by that means, to block her progress from the front, while the first group would keep her from retreating. The two groups, running at the same speed, reached the two ends of the street at almost the same time; but among the few pedestrians going along it there was no silk dress, no lace mantilla, no velvet hat.

"She went inside somewhere... She's on this street... She's in one of these houses... We have to check them... Let's start here... Who are you?"

"I'm a dealer in pottery who makes antique lamps for the excavations at the Campo Vaccino."[26]

"Did you see a woman go by wearing a velvet hat, a lace mantilla, and a silk dress?"

"No, I was at the back of my shop."

"Say, 'Long live the Republic!'"

"Long live the Republic!"

"All right, you're a loyal citizen."

"Now for this place... Why are you shutting your shop?"

"Well, milord..."

"There are no more lords. He's a partisan of the aristocracy! Hang him if he won't confess!"

"Alas, brother, I know nothing."

"He called me 'brother'! He's a Vatican spy! A flunky of the monks!"

"But, citizen, I'm Jewish."

"And you dared call me 'brother,' you dog!"

With a kick in the stomach, the poor man was flung to the back of his shop. No doubt it would've gone even worse for him, if another group hadn't been heard crying, "It's here! It's here!"

They all ran there, and those who'd called out first now cried to those just arriving, "It's this one! It's this one! They refuse to open the door! She can try all she wants, she won't escape our vengeance! To the Tiber with the aristocrat! Open up! Open up! To the Tiber!"

Since no one answered, they set about breaking down the door. They broke it down! They went in. The house was deserted: not a single person,

---

[26]The Campo Vaccino (literally cow pasture), on the site of the ancient Forum, was heavily looted for antiquities till it was closed off and turned into an archeological site during the Napoleonic occupation.

48

not a single piece of furniture—no one to kill, nothing to throw out the window.

"It's treason! This house is a meeting place for conspirators!"

"You live in this neighborhood?"

"Yes."

"Whose house is this."

"This used to be the house of the lawyer Glacetti, who died a month ago. His heirs had all the furniture taken away two days since."

"Why didn't you say that right away, you idiot?"

"How was I to know what you were looking for?"

"We're looking for a woman. Do you know her?"

"What woman?"

"A woman! A great lady, an aristocrat, an enemy of the people. She's in this street, she lives on this street."

"I know lots of women like that."

"Where do they live?"

"Well, first, there's the Marquis de Daguesta's wife, that way, at the end of the street, in the house with two columns."

"A marquise! That's right. A woman about thirty…"

"Thirty! I don't know. Her grandson, whose tailoring I do, jut turned twenty-five."

"Idiot! We're asking you about a woman aged thirty."

"Well, there's my wife…"

"She's a great lady, you animal!"

"Ah, I have it, I have it! It's Countess Despont, who just had a baby yesterday."

"She was walking in the Piazza Navona this morning!"

"Then I don't know, I wasn't there."

"Sweet Jesus! Tailors are stupid! She came down this street after she left the piazza!"

"But you said she lived here."

"Whether she lives here or not, she's here. Did you see her go by?"

"I've seen lots of people go by."

"A woman wearing a silk dress, a velvet hat, and a lace mantilla?"

"Could be. I didn't see her."

"Merciful heavens! You animal! If they made me security minister I wouldn't hire you as a spy."

"I wouldn't want to be one."

"Not good enough for you?"

"I'm a Roman citizen."

"You? You're a bad tailor! Go back to your shop, and try to do a better job on the clothes people buy from you! Go on, get out of here!"

"Don't touch me, I'm a free man. Long love the republic!"

"Will you shut up and get out here, you vagabond?"

The tailor, shoved around, called names, went back to his shop.

That scene was being repeated more or less simultaneously outside every door on that street, with only minor variations. Having lost the scent, the mob came and went; everybody questioned whoever he met, and nobody got a satisfactory reply. Lots of people were at the windows, trying to learn what was going on in the street. One woman, dressed like the one the mob was after, sat at the window of a house of modest appearance. The mob, busy questioning the shopkeepers, had yet to lift its eyes in the air, and hadn't noticed its victim delivering herself to them so complacently. She seemed very calm, because she was unaware that it was she the furious mob was after. She pointed out all of the crowd activity to an old man who stood next to her, and they both followed the stir with more curiosity than anxiety.

On the street across from that window, among the people who'd been drawn to the scene by that same curiosity, stood a man whose clothes easily gave him away as a Frenchman; he wore the uniform of an army surgeon of that period. He studied the woman carefully, and more than once he murmured, "It's her, it's obviously her."

At first he seemed uncertain what to do. He crossed the street to enter the house in which he'd seen the woman; but then he paused, turned the other way, and spoke to a dealer in plaster figurines who stood at his door peacefully watching what was going on.

"Who's the woman who lives across the street?"

"What woman?"

"That woman, at that window, in the velvet hat and the mantilla," said the surgeon, pointing.

"That woman…"

The plaster sculptor had no time to reply before a terrible cry suddenly rose above the din on the street. "There she is! There she is! There she is!"

When the surgeon pointed, a few eyes had followed the direction he was indicating, and the guilty party from the Piazza Navona had been recognized. The entire mob converged on the spot where the cry had started. Then the howls for death rang out with horrifying violence; and before the woman understood she was the object of all that hatred—even as she was sharing with the old man her astonishment at the threats she heard—a roof tile thrown at her window struck him in the head. She cried out, and, pulling the old man away from the window, she disappeared into the room.

The cries of "To the Tiber with the aristocrat!" continued, and the mob began to break down the door.

The surgeon repeated his question to the plaster sculptor, who replied, "I believe she's a Frenchwoman."

"An exile, perhaps?"

"Could be."

"Ah, it's her!" cried the surgeon. He threw himself into the crowd to get to the door and keep them from breaking it down, but he was pushed back and even threatened. Realizing he was powerless against the infuriated mob, he hurried to the barracks of a French army company. He hoped to be in time to alert them and to bring them back to clear the street; but in spite of all he did, in spite of his running as fast as he could, he was unable to prevent the misfortune he feared. He hadn't even reached the end of the street before a collective shout of joy, followed by even more furious cries, told him the door had been broken down. Still, he kept going, hoping the people's rage wouldn't be sated in a moment.

As he'd guessed, the door had been broken down, and the mob had rushed into the house. The most fanatical of them reached the room from which the woman had shown herself at the window; she was still there, beside the old man, whose face was covered in blood, which she was bandaging. Seeing her, the first howls of the fanatics invading the room were, "To the Tiber! To the Tiber with the aristocrat!"

However, they didn't seize her right away, but went on shouting at her, accusing her of her crime, which she seemed unaware of: the mob was conforming to a kind of barbaric instinct for justice, wanting its sentence to rest on some pretext, even in the eyes of its victim. The woman's astonishment was so complete, so unfeigned, that it stopped even the most infuriated of the mob. But when she was asked if she hadn't just walked through the Piazza Navona, and she said yes, they all cried out in rage, "She admits it! She admits it! To the Tiber! To the Tiber! To the Tiber!" Some came forward to seize her. Terrified, the old man stood in the way, saying, "What crime has she committed?"

"She insulted the colors of liberty! She's an aristocrat, and you are too! Step aside, unless you want us to treat you the same way as her!"

"As if I'd let you murder my daughter before my own eyes!" cried the old man.

"She's his daughter! He's protecting her! He's a traitor! Kill him! To the Tiber!"

"That's right!" cried one voice. "But first, they have to make honorable atonement. Take them to the Madonna, and let them kneel before the cockades they insulted!"

At that point the young woman, who'd walked by that spot with her head held high, and the old man, who hadn't even left his house, were equally guilty in the eyes of the fanatics. They were seized, and separated, and rushed down the stairs, and dragged out into the street, where it was announced to the mob what the vanguard had decided to do with the two criminals: first to the Piazza Navona, then to the Tiber! As if death had to be intensified by humiliation.

Those two unfortunates, father and daughter, were so dazed by the unexpected attack, the sudden calamity, of the anger that had acted so quickly against them, that they let themselves be pushed along, neither thinking nor resisting, already dead, and with no other concern than not to die the way they were intended to, but to fall, piece after piece, sigh after sigh, agony after agony, beneath the canes and the knives that threatened them.

They'd reached the first corner when suddenly the mob fell violently back on itself, and the cry went up on all sides, "The French! The French!" They turned, dragging their victims with them; but at the other end of the street they could see another triple line of bayonets—and the whole mob found itself trapped by the same maneuver they'd used against the woman they were pursuing. Closed in like that, the crowd lost nothing of its fury; but they tried to get through, and—hoping to get the soldiers to make way by flattering them—they began to cry, "Long live the French! Long live the republic!"

An officer on a horse pushed his way into the crowd while trying to calm them with his hand; but he couldn't be heard over the shouting all around him. He moved forward gently, aiming to reach the poor people the mob held in the middle of the street. The crowd let him advance, but with every step they closed in behind him, without ever stopping their cry of "Long live the French! Long live the French general! To the Tiber with the aristocrats!" The general was only a few yards away from the prisoners when they first saw him. Carried away by the irresistible hope for rescue, the old man began to cry, "Help! Help!"

That word provoked a terrible movement in the dense crowd pressing around the father and the daughter: a single sharp but isolated cry was heard, and the old man—whose bloody head the general could already make out—vanished. A hundred voices answered that single cry. The general guessed what was happening; in a sudden burst of anger he spurred his horse, drew his saber, and struck indiscriminately at whatever blocked his way.

The crowd parted and pressed itself back against the walls, revealing the old man stretched out on the ground, his daughter kneeling next to him, and a man holding her around the waist and trying to drag her away. At the sight of the general hurrying up, the man let go of her; but when he realized he'd been robbed of his vengeance he turned, drew a knife tied at his belt by a small cord, and raised the blade over the poor woman. One final effort brought the general close to the murderer, and with one terrible swing of his saber he dropped to the ground both the knife and the hand that held it. The wretch ran off howling, and from the crowd that had formed a circle around the general came a thousand furious insults. He approached the woman, who knelt on the cobblestones, searching for some sign of life in the face of the corpse lying at her feet.

Yet still the crowd grumbled, and, impelled by those furthest away, it tightened slowly around the French general and the woman he was trying to protect. He, intent on comforting her, didn't notice the crowd's movement. Now that, under his protection, she no longer had her personal safety to worry about, she gave way to her grief and wept. When the general bending over her had finally persuaded her to move away with him, he realized they were being pressed in by the boldest of the mob. He stood up straight, and that gesture and the look in his eye that accompanied it were enough to make the crowd draw back. Looking around for his horse, he saw it lying dead on the ground: the most fanatical of the mob had in a manner of speaking sharpened their daggers for murder on the body of the noble animal.

The general then realized the danger he was in; seeking to get out of the crowd before the collective excitement had overspilled the bounds of respect and fear inspired by the name of France, he called to the poor weeping woman to follow him, but she didn't seem to hear him. Finally, not knowing how else to tear her away from the corpse whose head she cradled on her lap, he said to her in French, "Diane, follow me."

At that word she rose, and the body of the old man fell back on the cobblestones. She looked at the man who'd called her by that name, searching his face for some memory—which presumably she found, because she replied with a nod.

"You must follow me, or you're done for," said the general.

"I'm following you," she replied. Turning to look at the body of her father, she extended her hands over it; then, raising her eyes, she appeared to call on heaven to witness the vow she was making to herself.

The general took her by the hand and advanced a few steps, but the crowd barely made room for them to pass. The general didn't have enough eyes to watch all the hands holding knives that appeared and disappeared in the folds of a shirt or a coat, though his glance was still enough to stop them. But the murmur was growing angrier, and a few voices cried, "To the Tiber! This woman is ours! To the Tiber!"

By now the hands holding weapons no longer hid, and as the mob gestured the knives shone and flashed like lightning around the woman and the general. He'd reached his horse; determined to open an escape route by force, he bent down and searched for his pistols in his saddlebags. The murderers took advantage of that movement; one of them leaped toward the woman the mob had sentenced and raised his dagger over her. She ducked to avoid the blow, and the dagger sank into the general's arm. A murmur of delight rewarded the brave man who'd struck the blow. But the wounded officer straightened up; a new circle formed around him, and the man who'd struck him stood in the front row, still holding his bloodstained dagger. Anger drove the general to get revenge; he advanced on his attacker, saber in hand. But no sooner had he taken a step away from the woman he was trying to save, than behind him another murderer closed in on the chosen victim. A cry rang out, the general turned, and with one backhand swing of his saber he laid the wretch out at his feet.

At that sight the crowd gave a muffled roar, like a mastiff when you try to take away the bone he's gnawing. The mob was stirred, agitated. People pointed out the general with their fingers, their stares, their knives. He gave a terrible look around, and in a voice that rose over the roar of the entire mob he cried out, "Grenadiers, advance!"

A clash of steel answered his call: the sound of rifles being lowered from shoulders at the order, "Mount bayonets!" The soldiers rushed forward from one end of the street; the crowd fled before them, but the flood threatened to carry along the French general and his companion, who'd fallen to her knees on the cobblestones once again. So, instead of standing in front of her and using his body to shield her, he positioned himself behind her. But above her head he extended his arm, holding his saber, with

54

the point aimed at the crowd rushing toward them. Like the end of some jetty that divides and thrusts aside the roaring current of a river, that saber, extended and immobile, divided and thrust aside to left and right the flow of the crowd. Finally they were all gone, draining away in a murmur till the grenadiers arrived. The general handed over the young woman he'd just saved to the army surgeon, and ordered him to take her to the general's residence.

Meanwhile the crowd, driven to the far end of the street, tried to get by; but the troops standing there blocked their way, and a desperate struggle began at that spot. The French staggered back, because those at the front of the crowd, pushed by those who followed them, were impaled on the bayonets that faced them; and the mob, hurling itself unceasingly forward by using the corpses in the front rank as a shield, finally broke the dam and fled, howling in fury. And those men, robbed of their prey and now escaped from their prison, immediately scattered through the streets of Rome, calling the people to arms.

Only a few minutes had passed. The general had barely had time to step into a house to wash the blood off his wound before he heard the alarm being rung from the nearest church bell. He went outside and placed himself at the head of the small group of soldiers who remained with him. Soon the alarm had spread from bell tower to bell tower, leaping, calling, replying, in an instant covering the city in a vast thundering in which the repeated blows of each bell rang out indistinctly, the way a few white flames stand out against the blood red of a bonfire. At that terrible sound Rome thrilled to the depths of its most secret entrails; the lairs of vice and misery vomited their denizens into the sunlight; the thunder of voices echoed the thunder of bronze; the riot was kindled, and soon it had spread to the entire city.

By order of the general, a few officers hurried back to barracks to rally all the troops at a single spot, while he himself marched to his residence. In spite of the uproar all around him, as he crossed the city with his grenadiers he found the streets deserted. Only now and then, as he turned a corner, he glimpsed at the far end of the street a head that vanished with a shout. He marched toward the cries that rang in the air; but the sounds that guided him seemed to flee at his approach as if by magic. Finally he decided to return to his residence. Two battalions were already guarding its approaches. Yet nothing seemed to suggest there was any risk of an attack; no rebellious mob had appeared, but the alarm still rang out, and beneath it the city still murmured: the explosion was inevitable.

The general gave a few clear orders and entered his residence. He summoned the surgeon; and while the latter cut away his sleeve and used strips of adhesive plaster to bring together the bleeding edges of his wound, the general said, "Well, Lussay, you're right: it's her."

"Still as beautiful, isn't she?"

"Still as beautiful."

"Still as proud?"

"I don't know. In all the uproar she showed neither extreme boldness nor extreme terror. It's not how I expected a woman like her to act. Anyway, I've found her, and she'll tell me what I want to know."

Doctor Lussay shook his head. "I don't know what you want from her, but the danger has passed. She'll keep silent, if she thinks it's in her interest. Did she recognize you?"

"I don't think so. Where is she now?"

"In my apartment, where Louise has given her new clothes."

"Your wife is an angel, doctor. How is she doing?"

"All the noise frightened her a little—especially because when the riot started she was out on a walk with no one but Henriette."

"A woman going out alone with a child of three in a city in which our soldiers barely dare go out by threes or fours! It's a folly you shouldn't have allowed."

"Oh," said Doctor Lussay, "You know how capricious she can be! When she wants something, how can you stop her? The slightest contradiction throws her into a fit."

"Isn't that partly your fault? And if all your experiments with mesmerism haven't driven her mad, I don't know why."

"Let's say no more about that," said the doctor impatiently. "You and I will never agree on that subject, nor on many others. For you the French Revolution is a renewal of the social order, while I see nothing in it but anarchy and misery. For me mesmerism means the regeneration of the human species, while you consider it charlatanism and unrest. If I know nothing about politics, you know nothing about medicine."

"Could be," replied the general, like a man who hasn't been listening. "I have to go see the duchess."

He walked out and, accompanied by the doctor, went to another apartment. The Duchess of Avarenne was standing before a lit fireplace, and seemed lost in thought. You'd never have believed she'd just escaped from the hands of an angry mob, so calm and cool was her manner.

"Ma'am," said the general, "I've come to inquire about your condition; I was worried that the emotions…"

The duchess smiled scornfully, and her haughty look froze the words on the general's lips. He expected at the very least her polite thanks, if not her gratitude. But the duchess's first words were, "Have you given orders, sir, for my father's body to be removed in a decent manner appropriate to his rank?"

The general was taken aback both by the question and by the tone of command in which it was asked. Nevertheless he replied politely, "Those orders were forgotten, ma'am, and it would be impossible to carry them out given the state of ferment that currently exists in the city."

"Ah!" said the duchess. "The murderers are still thirsty, and they're calling for more blood. Yours, perhaps, for having saved me."

"Mine! They've already tasted it, ma'am, as you put it, and perhaps they'd like to have the rest."

"Quite right," said the duchess in a tone of awful sarcasm. "Your turn, General Jean d'Aspert."

"Diane!" cried the general, coming toward her with delight, "Diane, you recognized me!"

"Who are you talking to?" she said, motioning to him with the back of her hand to keep away, while she retreated haughtily.

D'Aspert glanced around in irritation. Seeing Lussay and his wife in the room, he attributed the duchess's reticence to their presence; he motioned to them to go away, and they left the room. He went on, "We're alone, ma'am, and we can explain ourselves…"

"There is no explanation I need have with you, sir, except to ask you for a safe-conduct so I can leave Rome."

Jean had reached the end of his patience, and he replied with a harshness to match her haughtiness. "But I have other explanations to ask of you, ma'am."

"Are you my judge, and are you in a hurry to hand me over to the executioner?"

"Diane," he said gently, "you're putting on an awkward act with me. You know very well what I want to talk to you about."

"About my father, whom your people murdered?"

"No," replied Jean bitterly. "About my son, whom you made disappear."

The duchess turned pale, and ground her teeth in anger; she said nothing.

"Do you understand me now?" went on the general. "Here before you is no longer Jean the fool, the madman, who loved you the way one loves God, whom you could've asked to commit a crime and who would've done it for a single one of those nights of love in which you sought nothing but pleasure."

The duchess eyed him with contempt.

"Here before you," he went on, "is no longer the wretched peasant snatched up by a recruiter and destined to go off and die in India when his lover grew tired of him and worried about his despair. This is a man who knows what he's worth and what you're worth. This is a father who's asking you again for his son and who wants him."

The duchess stood straight, pale, unmoving. D'Aspert fell silent, waiting for an answer; Diane said nothing. He waited another moment, feeling anger stirring within him, but he suppressed it. Coming toward her, he said with a kind of respectful submission, "Well, ma'am, let's forget the past; let's say no more about it; I'll erase it from my memory. But I have in fact just saved you, torn you from certain death. For that service, for the blood I shed defending you, give me back my son."

"Fo the blood you shed! Is that worth twenty sacks of flour?" she asked with astonishing contempt.

Any other woman would've trembled to the roots of her hair at the terrible expression that now filled Jean's face. But she brazenly endured his gaze, and didn't drop her eyes at the spark of rage in his own. He ground his teeth in fury: he'd have given up half his life for this woman to be a tiger, which he would've attacked unarmed, body against body.

"Is your soul home to every vice?" he answered, choking with fury. "You who gave yourself to me like..."

"Throw me to the mob, sir," said the duchess coldly. "They at least would cut my throat without insulting me."

The general fell silent: he was crushed, routed. He began to pace around the room, reviewing in his mind all the circumstances of his life. He'd been this woman's lover right up till her pregnancy could no longer be concealed. At that moment he'd been abducted and put in a regiment that left for India. Returning to France three years later, he'd found out that just before it was time for her childbirth the duchess had gone away, taking Honorine with her; and Honorine had written from Spa that the duchess had given birth to a son. Since then the Duchess of Avarenne had reappeared at court; but nothing more had been heard either of Honorine or of the boy born in secret.

The Revolution of '89 had broken out. The Duchess of Avarenne and her father had been among the first to go into exile. The Duke of Avarenne had died on the scaffold. Jean, despairing of ever finding any trace of his lost son, had continued his career in the army, and had risen rapidly, as was common in those times. Finally, after eleven years, he found himself face to face with this woman whom he'd loved, who'd been his, who was the mother of his child, whose equal he'd become, whose life he'd just saved: and silence and contempt were his only reward. He thought she must be mad—or rather he thought he was mad, for only he was emotional, only he felt his heart bursting and the blood rushing to his head and ringing in his ears and beating like a hammer in his head. The duchess was calm, her gaze serene, her manner proud; she knew exactly what she was doing.

Tired of pacing and of the turmoil of his thoughts, he came to a stop before her. He studied her for a long time, hoping his stubborn examination would disturb her or soften her, and that some word spoken in anger or pity would come to enlighten him. But the duchess's impassive expression outlasted the persistence of his stare, and the general spoke again. "So you have nothing to say to me?"

He waited a moment for a reply. The duchess said nothing.

"Is there no feeling in your heart I can appeal to?"

Again he waited, again she said nothing.

"Not one?"

He was addressing a statue made of ice.

"Don't you realize you're in my power," he cried with a fury that knew no bounds, and seizing her by the hand, "and I only have to say the word, I only have to let it happen, and you'd be torn apart piece by piece?"

The duchess smiled ironically.

"I'm telling you, I'll do it... I'll do it, you hear?" As he spoke he squeezed her arm violently, then left her and threw himself into an armchair.

The duchess smoothed her cuffs, which he'd crumpled, and replied coldly, "You could've made your fortune as a luggage porter too."

"Oh!" cried the general, and he stood up, seized her by the arm, and forced her to her knees. "Then so be it! Answer the luggage porter!..." Then taking her hands in his, he squeezed them hard enough to break them.

"Ah!" she cried. "Just murder me right away! You're torturing me!"

"Then answer the murderer!" he cried. "Because you have to answer: what've you done with my son?"

"He's dead," said the duchess in a dull voice.

"Dead?" echoed Jean d'Aspert, releasing her and hiding his face in his hands.

"Dead," repeated the duchess, standing up and giving him a look that shone with cruel joy.

The general turned his face aside, wiped away a tear, and sighed deeply several times. A moment later he turned back to the duchess and said with great sadness, "Please tell me where you'd like to go, ma'am; and not only will I give you a safe-conduct for that place, but I'll provide you with an escort."

"I'd like to go to Naples, where I hope to get a ship to London."

The general bowed and was about to withdraw, when Doctor Lussay returned in a hurry. "The governor of Rome, Signor Canzini, wishes to speak with you immediately. I believe it's about madame."

"Have him come here," said the general. "I'd like madame to know what'll be decided about her."

The governor entered, followed by two officers, one of whom carried a strongbox. The duchess rose at the sight of that box, but she contained herself when she noticed the general watching her.

Addressing the governor, the general said, "Well, sir, what is it you want?"

"General, I've come to demand the Duchess of Avarenne, so that she can be handed over to the courts and judged on the merits of her crimes against the republic."

"Judged!" replied the general haughtily. "Judged because she wasn't murdered! You're moving along too fast in your republic, sir, and the time of the Convention[27] has passed. If you really want to judge something, find the murderers of the Marquis de l'Étang, find whoever gave me this wound, and judge them on their merits."

"By this time they've already been arrested," said the governor. "Those who attacked the Marquis de l'Étang will be brought face to face with madame; the man who stabbed you will face you; and as soon as madame's testimony has been heard, their sentence will be read out."

"That's fine, sir, but madame is in no condition to deliver that testimony on the spot."

"Indeed," replied the governor, "that's not why we've come to demand her: it's to hand her over to the courts herself, for having conspired against the liberty of the Roman republic."

---

[27]The National Convention was a revolutionary assembly that ruled France from 1792 to 1795, a period that included the Reign of Terror.

"Conspiring against liberty is an awfully vague charge, sir," said the general, "a charge that has severed many an innocent head. Madame is French; in that capacity I owe her my protection, and only after very clear proof will I allow her to be charged."

"Madame is an exile," said the governor with a look of greedy impatience, "and in that capacity she shouldn't find such an eager protector in a general in the Republican army. As for the proofs you ask for, here they are."

He opened the strongbox, which the officer had set on the table. As he drew out some documents the governor went on, "The strongbox belongs to madame. When we put a stop to the looting of her house, the officer commanding the company we'd dispatched found this strongbox. Hoping to find information about the people who lived in the house, the head of the household having just been murdered, he opened the box and read a few of the letters it contained. You decide, general, whether they constitute sufficient proof."

The general glanced at the duchess with concern; but she, with her eyes fixed on the box, closely following every one of the governor's movements, didn't notice the look of pity on Jean d'Aspert's face. The general approached the governor, who handed him a document, saying, "Read that."

The general took it, and glanced at the duchess once again; but she seemed to have eyes only for the strongbox in the governor's hands. Jean read the document: it was a letter from Acton, containing the plans for an insurrection intended to break out in Rome and in all of the Papal States, with the support of significant armaments from the government of Naples and reinforcements from Austria. The correspondence following that letter gave more specific details on the plan, naming its leaders and the locations for its rendezvous and enumerating the troops, the weapons, and the funds. The proofs were overwhelming. As he read each letter, Jean couldn't help glancing up at the duchess's anxious face; and each time he was surprised by her indifference to the contents of those letters, and her complete focus on the governor's physical examination of the strongbox itself. He could clearly see that the danger she feared wasn't from the exposure of the conspiracy: something else worried her. Yet what had already been revealed was enough to put her life at risk; what could possibly be of more compelling interest to her? Her honor? The Duchess of Avarenne's honor was an enigma to a man like Jean, though she herself might have a very strong conception of it. Someone else's life? But her father was dead, and anyway the duchess wasn't a woman who'd care about anyone else's life when her own was in jeopardy.

Without wanting to dig any deeper into the duchess's secrets now, Jean resolved to save her. But first he needed to be sure that nothing more remained to tie them to each other. He approached her and said in a low voice, "So, that child is dead?"

"Dead... yes... dead!"

"The day he was born?"

"Yes."

"In the same place where he was born?"

"Yes."

"In Paris?"

"Yes."

Jean paused. The answer to every question had been the same: affirmative, precise, automatic, delivered with the impatience of someone who wants to dismiss the question rather than answer it. As a result the duchess hadn't noticed the trap d'Aspert had laid for her. He knew only two facts about his son: that he'd been born at Spa, and that he'd lived for a few months—and about both of those points the duchess had lied. It was almost a certainty that she'd lied about the principal fact; presumably his son wasn't dead. The general considered: he thought about the duchess's stubborn silence, which could only arise from an irrevocable decision to leave him in ignorance about his son's fate. He recalled that only shameful violence had extracted the answer the duchess had given him; that answer was presumably just a way of escaping from further questions and further extremes.

After a moment of silence Jean said the governor, "Allow me to question madame myself, sir. I'll vouch for her; leave those documents here, I'll need them. I'll share the results of that interview with you."

"I'll wait for it in the next room," said the governor. The Italian had guessed that Jean wasn't indifferent to the woman he'd saved—not because he had the least inkling of the intimacy there'd once been between the duchess and the general, but because it struck him that she was still a woman well worth saving. She was then thirty-three, and was in the full bloom of the beauty of that age: a beauty less innocent, less delicate, less rosy than the beauty of sixteen; a strong, bold, regal beauty that particularly suits great ladies and noblewomen. The governor thought Jean wanted to save the duchess on one condition; to him she seemed beautiful and the general seemed preoccupied with looking at her. The governor was wrong only about what the one condition was, and it was that assumption that prompted his response. So he withdrew to the next room.

The general was too caught up in his own thoughts to draw a single one of the conclusions we've just described; he therefore let the governor do what he wanted, without taking offense at a gesture that in any other circumstances he'd have found insulting. As soon as he and the duchess were alone he stood before her and looked her in the eye and said, "My son isn't dead."

The duchess couldn't help looking disconcerted.

"My son isn't dead," he repeated. "He didn't die where he was born, and he didn't die the day he was born, and he didn't die in Paris!"

The duchess saw that her careless answers had undermined her lie. Inwardly she resolved to keep up the stubborn silence that had initially made Jean angry.

He understood her; but he'd gained advantages over her that enabled him to stay calm, and he went on, "Now you have to tell me the truth, and give me proof of that truth. Where's my son? You won't answer? Then listen carefully: here's an accusation that hangs over your head. That accusation is justified; that's lucky for your judges, no doubt; because, justified or not, it'll lead you to your death. I've already saved your life, and you didn't acknowledge it. I'm not offering to do you that favor again, I'm offering to sell it to you. Don't give me that look of scorn, ma'am: you're only worth a cold, hard bargain. You've insulted the general who offered you his arm and his sword; now here's the miller, who's offering you his sacks of flour. Are you willing to buy back your life?"

"What'll it cost me?"

"A single word."

"What word?"

"The name of the place our son is living."

"Our son! Do I know you?"

That stunned Jean d'Aspert. He thought he was dreaming. But he recovered quickly, and picking up the thread of his speech he went on, "Be careful, don't be reckless for both of us. A single word can doom you, and doom you without a later retraction being able to save you. Look at that clock. In five minutes your fate has to be settled. In five minutes I have to say to the governor, 'Take this woman away,' or else I have to refuse to hand you over. I'm still enough in control of myself not to say they can take you away, but once I say that word, neither you nor I will be able to hold back the consequences. Nothing you could offer me from a prison cell would save you, anything I tried to do would only hasten your death. The people of Rome need victims. They think they're not keeping up with our Revolution: they want dates they can throw back at the aristocracy, so they can tell them over and over, the way we will someday, 'Don't forget the second of September, remember the twenty-first of January.[28] Once you leave this house you're dead. Do you want to live?"

The duchess didn't answer. Instead she picked up a pen and wrote a few words.

"What are you doing? What are you writing?" asked the general, coming forward.

She handed him the piece of paper. He read as follows:

My son: General Jean d'Aspert sent your mother to the scaffold.

"And the morning of my execution I'll add the address to that note—an address that I assume you'll soon discover. Hurry up, sir; I'm ready."

D'Aspert dropped the note; he felt like a monster. He watched the duchess stand up and walk to the door of the room in which the governor was waiting. He threw himself in her way. She stepped back haughtily. He stared at her wildly for a few moments. Suddenly a look of tenderness crossed his face, and he fell to his knees before her. He was weeping, and the words he spoke were painfully broken by the sobs he tried to choke back. "My child! Ma'am, my child!... Oh, for pity's sake, my child!" he cried.

The Duchess of Avarenne smiled at the sight of this man on his knees. "You're mad! You're ridiculous!"

Why can't you beat a woman? Not kill her, but beat her, hurt her, rip her skin with your nails, with a whip, with the sole of your boot. The miserable wretches! They take your heart, they squeeze it, bite it, torture it, slice into it, cauterize the open wound, scratch off the scar as it forms. And those women have a soul that nothing touches, neither shame nor pity. And because they're women, and fallen women, there's no vengeance you can have without being a coward! It's idiotic.

Jean had fallen too far down into agony for the duchess's words to pull him back at one leap to the terrible fury that had made her tremble earlier. He rose, and considered her with horror. A thousand phrases came to mind to move her, appall her, seduce her. He'd threatened, he'd wept. He no longer knew what to do, what to say, what to offer. He thought of making himself her slave, of telling her he loved her, of becoming her

[28]The September Massacres, the mass killings that launched the First Terror, began on September 2, 1792. Louis XVI died at the guillotine on January 21, 1793.

lover again. He could've suggested cutting off one of his arms, or resigning his rank. Across all of the turbulent storm of thoughts running through his head, he asked himself, "What's in her mind? What does she want? If only I could understand her!"

He was so disoriented he'd forgotten why he'd wanted to be alone with her. The five minutes had expired.

"Well, ma'am, decide."

"It's up to you to decide."

"You want to die?"

"If you want to hand me over."

"Then you'll go away," replied d'Aspert, who'd decided to save her, if only to hold onto the chance of finding her again, of softening her or terrifying her...

"Very well."

"But not without my having made sure of you. I'm keeping these documents."

"Keep them."

The duchess picked up the strongbox and asked, "Where will you hide me?"

In a flash the general was enlightened: he reached for the strongbox and tore it from the duchess's arms. "Not so fast!" he cried.

"What do you mean?"

"Ah! Ah! Ah!" The general uttered those three exclamations as if the weight of all his uncertainties were escaping by means of those excited sighs. He set the strongbox on the table, set his hand firmly on the box, and, trembling with terrible joy, he gave the duchess a look of triumph and said, "Now, ma'am, where's my son?"

"Sir... sir... you're a villain... My strongbox... Oh, you'll pay for that!... You struck me... You're despicable... That box... That box is mine... Give it back!"

"Where's my son, ma'am?... Where is he?"

"Oh! Oh, I want it back! Help! Help! Help me!"

At the Duchess of Avarenne's cries, the governor, his officers, and Doctor Lussay all entered in an uproar. The duchess was kneeling on the floor. When she saw all of them, she rose quickly and said to the governor, "Sir! Sir! Save me from this wretch! Save me from his violence! Yes, sir, this is my strongbox. I took part in a conspiracy, I'm guilty, take me away, have me tried, execute me. I'm placing myself under your protection."

The general's manner was so threatening that the governor and his officers drew their swords. Jean d'Aspert began to laugh in scorn. "Lussay," he said calmly, "go fetch a corporal and a couple of men to escort these gentlemen back where they came from."

"General," said the governor, "you'll be responsible for what happens. The people await us, but they don't expect us alone. They know we came here to demand a woman, a French exile, who conspired against them, and they expect her."

"So they can cut her throat," said the general. "Take her away."

"You're insulting me," said the general. "This woman will be tried, and fairly tried. I'll protect her from the people as well as from your violence."

"Take her away," repeated the general. "Here are the proofs of her crime," he added, handing the governor the papers that had been pulled out of the strongbox.

The Duchess of Avarenne was defeated; she knew neither what to say nor what to do. Finally she rose. "Sir," she said to the governor, "take those papers, take the strongbox, and let's go."

"I'm keeping the box," said the general.

"It belongs to me," said the duchess. "General d'Aspert wants his share in the looting..."

"That strongbox is probably worth one louis; here's ten."

"Did I ask you to buy it?" replied the duchess. "And do you know if it's for sale at any price?"

"Is what it contains so valuable?"

"Is there some secret to that box?" asked the governor.

"If you'd like," said the general, "we'll find out together."

"No, no!" cried the duchess, throwing herself at the governor. "They're family secrets, nothing that would interest you, I swear."

"They might be new instructions about the plot," said the governor, sheathing his sword. "Please excuse my haste, general. We'll proceed with the inspection of those new papers."

"General d'Aspert," said the duchess quickly as she turned to him, "Jean, oh my God! Jean, I beg you, save me from this humiliation!"

"Sir," he said, "I believe I'm safe in saying that those papers concern only madame's private family interests, and perhaps mine. It's a matter just between us. Allow us to be alone for a moment. I'll be at your orders In a minute."

As he spoke, the general had moved away from the table on which the strongbox lay, and he was walking to the door with the governor. The latter insisted on staying; the general, half politely, half brusquely, was forcing him to withdraw, when they heard a slight noise behind them. When they turned they saw the duchess throwing a packet of letters into the fire in the hearth. They all rushed there. The general reached for the letters; and the duchess, with a boldness and strength only fury or despair could've given her, fought to stop him.

"Pull those letters out of the fire!" he cried as he struggled with the duchess.

But she was so determined in her defense of the fireplace that it was almost impossible to get near it. Finally d'Aspert got his arms around her and lifted her aside, and the governor was able to pull out of the fire only a few scraps of paper, the remains of no more than half a dozen letters. D'Aspert handed the duchess over to the officers and took possession of those scraps.

The duchess, her eyes fixed on every one of his movements, anxiously followed Jean's minute, breathless search for the few words he found at the edges of the pages:

... growing...
... as handso...
... the prince wants hi...
... Charles asks me questio...
... his mother and of his fath...
... nothing. He makes me sa...
... sir. He understands...
... and in spite of the old...
... his intelligence and his discre...

That was all that was left of the first letter. There was no date, and no place indicated. The letter had been burned across its middle; only the beginnings of the lines remained. The disappointment on the general's face was matched by the anxious satisfaction on the duchess's. They exchanged a look of hatred.

Jean picked up a second letter. Of this one, only the very beginning remained:

London, 15 October 1796
Duchess...

He angrily threw the letter aside, and picked up another, that seemed more intact than the others. He opened it: all of it had been burned, except one word and a few letters:

... respect...

... ge...

The duchess heaved a great sigh, as if the danger had passed. But, seeing the delight on Jean's face, she turned pale and trembled again. The general had found a letter in which two whole lines remained intact. He read eagerly:

... When he saw his son, he wept as he embraced him. He was on the brink of revealing his secret, but he...

And in one corner of that page had also been preserved:

Ghent, 17 June 1797

Jean d'Aspert's hopes were a terrible agony to him. Only his guess that the duchess's fright, assuring him that these letters concerned his son, brought him joy. Two letters remained to be examined; he shook with anticipation at opening them. He went back to the strongbox, hoping there might be something left inside, but it was empty. With inexpressible fury he picked up the box and flung it onto the floor. Everyone was silent.

The general returned to the two letters. One of them preserved a date:

... 1 November 1797...

The other, a location:

... Verona...

Nothing more. He examined every scrap of paper once again with the most careful attention, but not a single word had escaped his first inspection. He paced vigorously about the room, muttering quietly. The fateful strongbox lay in his way, and—in his fury at being unable to take his feelings out on anyone—he kicked it aside with astonishing violence. The strongbox flew past the hearth, and the gust of air it caused made the ashes fly up. Those ashes were all that was left of the burned letters. The general watched as a few fragments floated for a moment before him and settled at his feet. Mechanically, he bent down to pick them up: one flew away just then, the other dissolved into dust as he took hold of it. That metaphor for his hopes angered him. He went back to pacing, furiously grinding beneath his feet the bits of burned paper scattered around the room, in his despair destroying the last traces of what could've enlightened him and what had eluded him so quickly.

He stopped and sat down, and with his elbows on the arms of the chair he stared at the floor. There'd been silence in the room for several minutes, when suddenly the general's face lit up with incomprehensible joy.

The governor came forward. "Well, general, what are we going to do?... What have you decided?"

But Jean remained seated and motioned to him to stay still. Then he slid slowly out of his chair onto his knees on the floor, leaned down, and seemed to be devouring with his eyes a fragment of black dust on which the ink had left a few letters in white. He held his breath. His outstretched hands seemed to command silence and immobility. His lips moved, like those of a man who's spelling something out. He smiled, and his eyes lit up. But his breath, which he'd been struggling to hold back, made the cinder he was examining fly a few feet away. He followed it on his knees. It came to rest, and he resumed his dubious reading, and put together a whole word. Then in a low voice he repeated a phrase... His joy grew unbounded; carried away, he made an incautious movement, and the cinder flew off. Again he followed it, it settled, he approached it, he was almost there, it a little further, he slid gently along the floor, afraid of stirring the air. Finally he got there, his eyes always fixed on that cinder of paper that held everything for him. He was about to resume his reading—but with a sharp stamp on the floor the cinder dissolved into dust and vanished beneath the duchess's foot.

At that moment Jean could've stabbed that woman with his dagger. But he held himself back, and returning her look of triumph with a look in which menace and joy were mingled, he said without addressing her, "Today's the twentieth of February, isn't it?"

"Yes, general."

"Ma'am," he said, rising proudly, "I'll decide your fate the day after tomorrow."

On that black cinder Jean had read, in ink that had turned white, the words:

... We'll be in Rome with your son the twenty-first of February...

III. EXPLANATORY COMMENTARY

We've placed on stage what was once known in theater terms as the backstory. There are so many people with a completely rigid idea about the right way to construct a work of any kind, that perhaps the reader won't be sorry to meet an author who has none. Perhaps I'd have done better to leave in a drawer the first two chapters you've just read, and to explain in a brief preamble how the different characters stand in relation to one another. Perhaps I'd have done better to save the whole explanation for the final chapter, and to steer the entire drama of this novel through a mysterious destiny that would've exploded at the end, like one of Monsieur Ruggieri's bombs,[29] and shone a sinister light on all the characters and all the intrigues of this plot.

You can find men everywhere who are always ready to criticize furiously whatever literary choice you've made, for a thousand reasons you hadn't thought of. First, because you didn't conform to their politics, or you don't share their religion. We still see that in 1834. There are some who treat you with contempt because you're nearsighted, and you didn't notice them one day when they had a new suit on. Others consider you a writer of obscenities because one night you recognized them in the street, drunk, attacking the walls while imagining they were beating up the night watch. That man hates you because you know he has a false tooth; that one because you're not aware he's a gentleman; that one thinks you're a plagiarist, because you had an idea before he did, which he could've had; that other one calls you ignorant because unluckily you already knew something he thought he'd teach you; I know some who'll tear a book apart because the handsome cab you were riding in spattered them with mud; and there are those who'll call you an idiot because you wear yellow kid gloves.

I'm not talking about myself—my God—I who don't wear yellow gloves or ride in a handsome cab, who knows nothing, who goes home early, and who doesn't write about my political opinions. But there might

---

[29]Claude Ruggieri (1777-1841) was a French pyrotechnician and innovator in fireworks design. His sons and grandsons created fireworks displays for Napoleon and Louis XVIII and Charles X, as well as for George II of Great Britain. Soulié may be referring to any of the family.

still exist a reason I'm not aware of, that might arouse the dormant bile of some Aristarchus[30] that'll earn me some lofty lesson in literature, some stern reprimand on my work. Perhaps there'll be someone who'll ask me (if anyone notices this book), there'll be someone, as I say, who'll ask me why I wrote this novel the way I did, why I chose this way over another. If I told them I have no idea why, no doubt they'd think even worse of me, and yet it would be true.

For who knows anything in the era in which we live? Who can say whether a thing is good or bad? Who'd dare write beside some road, *This is the true path*? And what I'm saying doesn't apply only to literature; I'd say the same about politics, laws, morality. For half a century so many ideas have been tried, and have failed to produce anything powerful or lasting, that there isn't a single thing that's been destroyed that we don't occasionally have reason to regret. The insolent aristocracy of the middle, which for the last three years[31] has managed to monopolize power over legislation and criminal justice and regional administration—that nobility based on rent, which is the sole deputy and jury and member of the departmental council—doesn't it sometimes make you miss, deep in the bottom of your heart, the arrogant aristocracy of the Old Regime?

And yet would you dare go back to that? The venality of the tax burden is absurd; but the venality of the king's men, who served at his pleasure—wasn't that odious? The exemptions granted to the clergy, their wealth, their demands—weren't they unbearable? But the rejection of all religion, and the existence of that shifting cult, changing once a year and voted on every session, like the funds for a bridge or a sewer line—wasn't that just as deplorable? Weren't the trade guilds contrary to any spirit of progress? But doesn't the law against trade unions reduce civilized man to his individual strength? Didn't the eternal indissolubility of marriage wreak awful havoc? But hasn't the right to divorce led to terrible scandals? The rule of the three unities produced tragedies by d'Avrigny and Royou; the neglect of that rule brought us *Charlotte Corday* and a thousand idiotic plays.[32] Racine's poetry, with its strict meter and its purity of expression,

---

[30]Aristarchus of Samos: a grammarian in ancient Alexandria, famous for his edition of and commentary on Homer; by extension, any severe, quibbling critic.
[31]Meaning since the bourgeois July Revolution of 1830.
[32]The principle of the three dramatic unities, attributed to Aristotle, dictated that a play should consist of one action (no subplots) in one location during one continuous time, preferably a single day. Charles-Joseph Loeillard d'Avrigny (1760-1823): a poet and comic opera librettist of no great repute or distinction. Thomas-

had as its heir the poetry of Viennet;[33] and Molière's fast pace was invoked in the creation of *An Armchair Play*.[34]

So where does that leave literature, morality, the law? What's the social utility of all that? At the happy medium, perhaps? Ugh! A curse on the happy medium! The sample we've been given is enough to make you throw up. What can we do? What can we say? What path can we follow? Alas, to do what I've done: to toss your pen into the wind and follow the path it leads us on; chance is wiser than men. Besides, make no mistake, we will be neither the builders nor the architects of the new social edifice. Encumbered as we are by the ruins of past centuries and fallen institutions, we build a few shacks haphazardly out of their debris, wretched hovels that'll last no longer than we do; we select a few materials, we try to build a few institutions that last only a day, with no trust in our work, because we still feel the ground trembling, and we're afraid we'll be buried in the collapse of what we put up. If a few men, here and there, still have or already have powerful and unshakeable convictions, they're the exceptions: our century doubts, searches, feels its way, tries things out. That's why I began this novel the way I did.

Now let's return to our heroes.

The day after the scene we've just written, a man and a woman entered Rome by way of the Porta del Popolo. The man was arrested and brought before General d'Aspert. He was some kind of servant, who, finding himself face to face with a republican general, imagined he was going to be eaten on the spot. As a result, the general didn't have to wait long to make him confess everything he wanted to know. Now he understood the duchess's resistance; but not wishing to be a party her plans, he went to her, and this is the explanation they had together.

"Now, ma'am," he said, "I know your plans, and I know why you wanted so badly to hide my son's existence from me. Your right-hand man has told me everything, or rather he's allowed me to guess everything,

---

Marie Royou, also known as Abbé Royou (1743-92): an anti-Enlightenment philosopher and writer. Charlotte Corday assassinated the Jacobin leader Jean-Paul Marat in 1793. No play or opera of that title published before 1834 has been identified, though in 1807 an American playwright, Sarah Pogson Smith, wrote a verse drama about Corday called *The Female Enthusiast: A Tragedy in Five Acts*.

[33] Jean-Pons-Guillaume Viennet (1777-1868): a soldier, politician, playwright, and poet, widely disparaged as a writer.

[34] *Un Spectacle dans un fauteuil* (1832), a volume of verse by Alfred Musset, imagines that the reader is attending a theatrical performance in multiple genres.

since he's completely taken in by your tricks, and he truly believes he's bringing you the prince's son. Indeed, to leave your lover in Paris, to take another lover six days later, and to make the first lover believe the second lover's son is actually his—none of that's impossible, and it could succeed, and in fact it did succeed. I also understand how that trick would be strongly in your interest when the prince occupied the highest rank in the nation; but now that he drags from one court in exile to another, why should you persist in an undertaking that deprives me of my son without satisfying your ambitions?"

For a moment the duchess was silent; then after brief reflection she replied, "Listen to me, sir. You've uncovered a secret that I assume now has no more confidants, because Honorine, the chambermaid who accompanied me to Spa, was arrested soon after I left France, and I have no doubt the crime of serving me has sent her to the scaffold. The truth about Charles's birth—Charles is the name I gave your son—is a mystery to everyone; but the supposed story about his birth is known to lots of people. The prince doesn't doubt it, and even my father believed it. As for the child, he knows nothing. I have enough respect for you, sir, to be candid with you; the shameful way I treated you yesterday is, believe me, the greatest proof of that respect."

That made the general smile.

The duchess went on, "Yes, sir, it's the greatest proof; because when I was heaping scorn and contemptuous insults on you, not for a moment did I doubt I was safe in your hands; not for a minute did I fear you'd have the thought of delivering to the scaffold the woman you'd loved, the woman who'd given herself to you."

The general blushed, either because his heart hadn't been filled with quite all of the generosity attributed to it, or instead because he realized how well-equipped the duchess was to dominate him by her boldness of her spirit and the audacity of her decisive character, and he was ashamed of that domination. That thought prompted the idea that he should be on his guard against anything the duchess might propose.

Since he remained silent, she went on, "I'll be candid, I said, and to show you how candid I wish to be, I'll ask you straightforwardly to let me keep your son."

"For him to go on playing the role in which he debuted?" asked d'Aspert.

"For that, sir."

"Don't count on it," said the general sternly. "To make me oppose that plan there are reasons the least of which would make me the most despicable of men if I failed to heed it. And first of all, that child is my son, and I won't give him up."

"Give him up!" said the duchess impatiently. "Are you dropping him off at the foundling home? You're giving him a better life, that's all."

"My son should owe nothing to anyone besides his father."

"What a fine gift you're giving him! Let's see, let me take on your thinking and put myself in your place. I'm married, I love my child, I have all the bourgeois affection possible for him. I'm asked to let him pass for a prince's bastard. I have strong ideas about morality, and I refuse: I want my child to have a legitimate name, humble as it might be. Nice, very nice; I can conceive of that if I really try. But this boy is a bastard: he'll be your bastard, just as much as he'd be a prince's. Would he be happier being your bastard? Let's see: you're a general, granted. But with you people your field marshal's staff of discipline is the guillotine, or you could simply be killed by an Austrian bullet. Do you have a fortune to leave to that child? You had a small one, I know. What a fortune! A fortune that's liable to seizure, that'll be disputed by other collateral heirs. You have no gold, no silver, you haven't stolen anything… Aren't the people on your side looters? But you yourself must not be one. What would become of that child if you died?"

The general didn't know quite how to reply to all that reasoning. He wasn't in the habit of discussing honest feelings; he just acted according to their dictates, believing that all that was good must be reasonable and even profitable. He didn't feel strong enough to rebut the duchess's arguments one by one. In his soul there was just a single cry, which seemed to him the peremptory answer to everything, and that cry was, "But, ma'am, he's my son, and I love him!"

The duchess gestured impatiently and went on, "You love him for your own sake; you're dressing up your personal satisfaction with the name of paternal love. Oh, for God's sake, don't act so startled; do you really think that pious sentiment is very often anything besides patriarchal egotism? That feeling is just a fallback for people who have nothing else left. For example, I'll always remember the Marquis de Bréfort: he was thirty, he was as rich as a Dutch merchantman, he was good-looking, he'd had some success as a wit, he'd had lots of women—including some who were hard to get—he was a brave man, and he'd had success in several duels… And he was a used-up man, weary, worn out by the world. One day he saw my steward hugging his son, and he cried out to me, 'Ah, that's happiness! That's the genuine goodness that makes life precious!' He got married. Why? To create happy beings? No! To have something to love and protect and raise; for he loved his children, and he raised them perfectly He paid attention to them, but for his own sake, so as not to be bored. He became a father so as to be something in this world. Well, you're acting like him, worse than him—because he gave his children a name, a fortune, a position, whereas you want to take all of that from yours!"

D'Aspert was hearing language so disorienting, so subversive of all of his beliefs, that, not knowing how to defend himself, he chose to go on the attack—which is, whether in war or in debate, always the easier course. "What, ma'am! You speak of egotism, of selfish sentiment! It seems to me, if that reproach can be directed at anyone, it's you, who are using that child as a tool in your intrigues, and who are planning to turn a profit from him, I don't know how, but with some goal that undoubtedly is in your interest more than in his."

"Undoubtedly," said the duchess. "But I don't parade my maternal love. I don't strike tragic poses and say, 'He's my son, I want my son, I must have my son! Instead I tell you: here's what I want to do for Charles. Is it better than what you can do for him? Yes. So I'm the one who loves him more."

The general felt even more entangled. Instead of sticking to his unassailable rights as a father, he seized eagerly on an apparently debatable point, and replied, "However, ma'am, even conceding everything you said earlier—I mean everything that's the real core of your argument, that it's good to renounce your son if he'll gain something by it—there still remains the question of knowing whether he'll gain that something. Didn't the Revolution destroy all of the advantages he might once have found in passing for the son of a prince?"

"The Revolution!" cried the duchess, delighted to have drawn the general onto that terrain, where between them, in a manner of speaking, it was only a question of comparing balance sheets. "The Revolution has raised that child's expectations higher than they could ever have risen before. Your crimes have opened the way to the throne to a prince who would never have reached it. You've left only one head between him and the crown of France. That head is strong, no doubt, but it governs a sickly body that will quickly be worn out, and then Charles will no longer be a prince's son, but a king's son."

"When will that be?" said d'Aspert bitterly and disdainfully.

"When Europe will have overthrown the party of blood that's decapitating France. When legitimate kings will have retaken the power they lost only through the weakness of Louis XVI."

What the Duchess of Avarenne thought would win the debate for her instead caused her to lose it. She attacked the general at a place where he was stone and steel. She'd said the party of revolution could be beaten, and that royalty would return to France. The Republican general was stronger at reasoning and in his feelings of love for the Republic than the father had been for his son, and he replied, "Can you, of all people, ma'am, still hang onto such illusions? The return of kings to France! You might as well call for the resurrection of the dead. That you thought so for a month or two after your exile, sure; but by now can't you see everything that stands between us and them? There's too much hatred, watered with blood, for France and its old masters ever to be reconciled."

"What!" cried the duchess. "You, of all people, are still stuck in that foolishness? You, in 1798? My God, can't you see the Republic is finished? There's not a single man of good sense who still wants it. Poor people who thought you were establishing liberty by killing and looting the aristocracy, and who didn't see you were just building a new aristocracy from the remains of the old one! General, there isn't a single corporal, risen to adjutant general, who isn't tired of being at the mercy of popular whim; there's not a single farmer, become the owner of his old master's property, who isn't calling loudly for a stop to the disorder that made him rich. Is it the Directoire[35] that's going to bring about that order, that calm? No, general, no. But the existence of the Directoire is the surest symptom of returning royalty: they're lackeys having fun in the chateau till the masters get back. Don't you see they're already wearing silk stockings and embroidered coats? They have a palace, they receive, they have their circle, they hold court. But people laugh at them, because they're artificial and awkward. Ridicule will kill them, and France will need better actors, lead actors, genuine royalty in all its greatness. You can see it, you can smell it, you can breathe it."

Presumably d'Aspert didn't believe the duchess's prophesies, for he shrugged without answering.

After waiting a moment, the duchess cried, "What! You don't understand that? Oh, I didn't think you were so common!"

---

[35]Governed the First Republic from 1795-1799 when it was overthrown by Napoleon Bonaparte.

That word angered d'Aspert. Nowadays, when equality has made enough progress in society by pushing down the great and raising up the small, that word doesn't seem offensive enough to trigger the anger of a man like d'Aspert. But at that time the nobility's insults were still thrashing around in the deluge of blood in which people thought they'd been drowned; and when a few of them floated back to the surface and began to swim around in view of the newly powerful, they set a foot on them to push them back under and finish them off.

"Common!" retorted the general. "Yes, ma'am, I'm a commoner, and I'm proud of it. And it's because I'm common and you have contempt for me, that I don't want my son to be raised to have contempt for his father."

"You're crazy, Jean," said the duchess, softening a little. "What I'm proposing is for his benefit."

"Benefit or not," replied d'Aspert, sticking stubbornly to his idea so as not to have to defend it, "benefit or not, he's my son, and he'll remain my son and a commoner."

"But he's mine first, sir," said the duchess haughtily, "and no matter what your rights to him might be, mine—though I can't admit to them publicly—are at least recognized by long possession, and by many witnesses. Yours, sir, can only be rights imposed by violence."

"Well then, ma'am, we'll go to court."

"Go to court! Can you even consider it? You'd dishonor me!"

"Dishonor you? In what sense? Because people would learn the truth? Then why did you do it?"

The duchess was silent. She attached too much importance to the plan she'd conceived to jeopardize it through anger or impatience. She tried another tack. "Listen, Jean, don't get carried away. Well then, I'm asking you for a favor, and expecting a sacrifice on your part: leave me your son, and I'll repay you for that favor however you choose. If you're blind enough to think things as they are now will stay the same, what remains of my fortune is yours. If, on the contrary, what I predict comes to pass, the fastest rise in the career you've chosen..."

The general hadn't understood right away, because otherwise he'd have stopped the duchess after the first phrase; but when he saw what she was driving at, he cried out violently, "First you wanted to steal my son, and now you want to buy him! What do you take me for, ma'am?"

She could see he was in the saddle astride one fixed idea, that of keeping his son. She felt she had enough strength of will to force Jean to admit he that was wrong, that he didn't love his son as much as she did, that it was better for the boy to do what she proposed; but after all that was said and the point was won, he'd wreck everything by saying, "He's my son! I want my son!"—driven by an instinctive sense of what was right, stronger than all of the duchess's skillful sophistries.

D'Aspert's heart was like those young turtles a traveler carries far away from shore: he separates them from each other, he puts them down with their heads pointing inland, and as soon as they're free they turn around and, by some mysterious instinct, they head back to the ocean, their home and their refuge. As many times as he wants, the traveler can pick them back up, carry them even further inland, set them down facing another direction, spin them in circles twenty times... The poor creatures don't defend themselves, but as soon as they're neither in his hand nor under his hand they head back to the ocean with their tiny but unceasing steps.

That's how Jean was, and the duchess gave up trying to win a victory that brief reflection on his part would undo. Being a deliberate, capable woman, she resolved on the spot to make the sacrifice in the most advantageous possible way. She said, "Well, sir, if you want your son, have him! But I assume it's your son you want, not mine: he'll be a milkmaid's son, whom you'll love as much as if he were the son of a queen!"

"Of course," said Jean, thinking that answer would convey a lofty sense of what he understood by paternal love and the dignity of the common citizen.

"All right. Then give me your word of honor that you'll never tell him his mother's name. Remember—or learn if you didn't know before—that I later had a daughter by the Duke of Avarenne, and I rely on that mystery to protect her future and her reputation. Swear to me that Charles will never know his mother's name."

"I swear it," said d'Aspert, happy to concede something to this woman to whom he'd refused everything. "I swear he'll never know he's your son. Believe me, I have no desire to injure your reputation, and I'll do everything you wish to protect it."

"Fine, fine," interrupted the duchess impatiently. "But the disappearance of my child—whose death I'll have to announce to those who think he's the prince's son—that disappearance, I say, if it coincides with your discovery of your son; the matching ages of the two boys; the death of my son immediately followed by the resurrection of yours; all of that might give rise to suspicions and lead to conjectures that might produce enough comment at l'Étang to open lots of people's eyes. The dates would be compared, and soon all would be discovered. Promise me, therefore, not to tell my son what he is right away, and to confide your secret to no one. Treat Charles at first as an orphan you've taken in and raised. Later, when you'll have managed to make him a couple of years younger, as if he'd been born in India or during your travels, tell him only who you are to him. As for his mother, she must be dead to him, for he's dead to her. It seems to me I'm asking awfully little, considering how much you're taking away from me. Will you do it?"

The general didn't answer right away. For a long time he reflected; he thought the precautions the duchess wanted for her own sake would serve to protect his son. He understood that, in the nomadic life he led, he'd often have to be separated from his child; in those circumstances, just knowing Charles was his son would make him too easy a target for people who might want to kidnap him to give him his first starring role—or just make him disappear completely. He consented, saying, "I give you my word, ma'am, to pass Charles off as the son of a friend killed a few months ago. That friend had a son the same age as ours, and it'll surprise no one that he confided him to me. In any case, Charles will learn nothing about himself till he reaches an age at which he can defend himself against ambushes set against him."

The duchess bit her lip—proof that she still retained some hopes for that child, or had made some plan for him or against him. "Let it be as you wish," she said, "as long as I play no part in his life, or in yours. And now, what do you want me to do?"

"In a week you'll be in Naples, ma'am, and you'll be safe. Allow me to wish you all the happiness you desire."

The general tried to take her hand, but she pulled it away and gestured to him to withdraw. He bowed and left the room. She watched him go, and as soon as she was alone she couldn't help saying, with an angry, violent gesture, "Ah! How could I have slept with that!"

The libertine had been extinguished; the schemer had begun.

The next day, just as the duchess was leaving secretly for Naples, the general was ordered to report immediately to Terracina to explain his conduct, about which the Roman authorities had felt it necessary to complain to the general in chief. Lussay accompanied him, and his wife followed. Before they left, d'Aspert confided his son to Durand, his most trusted servant. "Here," he said. "This is the son of Captain Dumont, who was killed a few days ago."

"Say!" said Durand. "That's the same boy who was arrested, along with an elderly servant, at the Porta del Popolo, on your orders!"

"Yes, I took that precaution because those wretched Romans have it in for the French, and a child and an old man would be prey worthy of them. Listen carefully: you'll pass him on to Sergeant Bazil, who'll come get him tomorrow to escort him back to France."

"That's funny!" said the servant. "They say the poor captain's son disappeared at the time of his father's death."

"As you can see, he's been found again."

The general knew about that disappearance. He had reason to believe Dumont's son had been killed by the partisans; and that occurrence tied in too neatly with what he wanted to do for his own son for him not to take advantage of it.

We'll learn later how the general's plans unfolded, and what became of Captain Dumont's real son, and of the boy d'Aspert substituted for him, to whom he gave a name that didn't belong to him.

IV.

(1815)

One evening in March of 1815, three people were seated by the fire in a fairly fine apartment on the rue Saint Honoré. Complete silence reigned in the room, presumably because there was also a sick person present: a woman lay in the bed, fast asleep. Still, a careful examination of the behavior of the people by the fire would suggest that they were silent because each of them preferred to engage with his or her own thoughts than converse with the others. Those three persons were Lieutenant General Count d'Aspert, Surgeon Major of the Army Baron Lussay, and Henriette Lussay, his daughter. The sick woman was Madame Lussay—the same Louise whom d'Aspert had loved, and whose strange story Honorine had once told to the Duchess of Avarenne.

General d'Aspert was somber and concerned, like a man who's fallen from a magnificent past into a worrisome present, and for whom the future offers no hope. Lussay stirred the fire, smiling into the flames, like a man who sees himself holding forth in public, pontificating, proving his point, carrying the crowd with him, convincing them; and congratulating himself on his victory and on the skill required to bring it about. Henriette was anxious and lost in thought. One idea in particular had hold of her, but she seemed to be afraid of it, for several times she shook her head as if to drive it away, and several times she rose to rearrange the china and the bottles on the mantelpiece, and several times she went to her mother's bedside and watched her sleep. Still, no sooner had she set eyes on that suffering, mask-like face than her own expression became fixed, frozen, lost, as if bound to some ghost that stood before her always and everywhere. Then she tore herself away from that obsession with her own thoughts by some new abrupt gesture full of fear.

Finally she resolved to seek refuge from that strange persecution in some occupation that wouldn't leave her free to think. She went to a glass-fronted bookcase that stood in one corner and read the gilt lettering on the spines of the volumes, set her finger on a few, then moved on. She touched

Clarissa Harlowe, Paul and Virginia, Estelle and Némorin,[36] then pushed them back one after another. Finally she stopped in front of a volume by Racine. She opened it at random. It was *Phèdre*, Act I, the scene between Phèdre and Oenone in which Minos's daughter, obsessed by the divinely inspired love that consumes her, speaks unthinkingly about all those in her family who experienced a fatal love: her mother, her sister—like her, victims of some implacable fate more than of human love.[37] Henriette skimmed the scene and almost angrily discarded the book.

Finally in a corner she found Levaillant's *Voyages*.[38] She seized it eagerly. Detailed accounts of journeys by sea, of treks, of battles against savages and wild beasts, tales in a sense devoid of any of the concerns of the civilized world—that was presumably what suited Henriette. She went back to her seat by the fire and began reading at the first place the book fell open. The contents didn't have much interest for her, but she followed the words and forced herself to pay attention. Suddenly her eye was drawn to the page. She devoured a fairly long passage, her mouth half open; and when she'd finished reading, both her hand and the book dropped into her lap. She let slip the words, "So it's really true!"

And she sank back into her deep thoughts.

However, if you'd been able to read that passage over the girl's shoulder, the way our painters enjoy depicting Mephistopheles watching and spying on Marguerite's daydreams, you'd look in vain for what had provoked that attention, those words, that preoccupation. The passage in Levaillant was the one in which he describes how, hearing pitiful, desperate cries, he drew near a bush and saw a mouse struggling under the eyes of a snake, spinning around, retreating, shaking, but drawn back as if by bonds of steel to fall into the reptile's gaping mouth. In that passage Levaillant reports that another time, when he was following the edge of a swamp, he

---

[36]*Clarissa, or The History of a Young Lady* (1748), a novel by Samuel Richardson. *Paul et Virginie* (1788), a novel by Jacques-Henri Bernardin de Saint-Pierre. *Estelle et Némorin, ou Les Bergers de Massanne* (1816), a pastoral play in three acts by J.-B. Hullin. All three works, famous and highly influential in their time, would've been considered morally improving.

[37]In Racine's play *Phèdre* (1677), Phèdre, Minos's daughter and wife of King Theseus, falls in love with Hyppolytus, Theseus's son by a previous marriage. Though the play is a classic, the obsessive incestuous passion it portrays is the opposite of wholesome.

[38]François Levaillant (1753-1824): an explorer, naturalist, ornithologist, and writer. His accounts of his travels in southern Africa, beginning with *Voyage dans l'intérieur de l'Afrique* (1790), were published in multiple volumes.

felt himself being drawn out of his way as if by magnets; surprised by that phenomenon, which he took for dizziness, he looked in the direction in which he was being drawn, and saw an enormous snake whose round, wide-open eyes were fixed on him. Levaillant, warned of their power by the earlier fate of the unfortunate mouse, only broke the spell by shooting the snake with both shots from the double-barreled gun he was carrying.

While we were reporting on all of that, the silence had continued; and Henriette's meditations, turning on themselves, had presumably excited her thoughts greatly—for when a bell rang quietly she shuddered in every limb and couldn't keep from saying, in a muffled, desperate voice, "It's him!"

Soon Baron Premitz was announced, and a man of about thirty came in. This Baron Rhodon de Premitz was a German, who'd followed the foreign armies here; he claimed to be a native of Prague, and a descendant of the great Count Premitz who founded the city, and one of whose shoes is carefully preserved in the old royal castle. Baron Premitz was tall and robust—more from the vigorous way he was built than from his weight. His hair was a charming shade of blond. His cleanly drawn features, taken together, suggested gentleness when his eyes were lowered; but when he lifted them, the savage light that escaped from his large gray pupils seemed to illuminate that face like a new day, and to reveal in it a new quality, and that's when he assumed the inquisitorial, dominating expression that overwhelmed the weak and disturbed even more decisive men, who often overcame their embarrassment by quarreling with him.

Henriette, seeing Baron Premitz come in, turned icy cold and lost the strength to stand up.

"Well, good day, or rather good evening," said Lussay. "It's already nine o'clock. I'd given up expecting you."

Premitz bowed to the general and to Henriette, and replied, "I was with my protegee, and I didn't want to leave her till I was sure she'd have a restful night."

"Speak more quietly," said the general. "Madame Lussay is asleep, and you'll wake her."

"Wake a woman I put to sleep with my own hands!" laughed the baron loudly. "No, general, no. I ordered her to sleep for three hours. She still has thirty-five minutes to go, and all of Buonaparte's canons, even those from Moscow, wouldn't wake her, rest assured. By the way," he added, "How's Madame Lussay doing?"

"Just as I wish," said Lussay. "Between my wife and me, it's no longer a matter of chance. I hold the mesmeric attraction over her in all of its power. She's a somnambulist to the highest degree of clairvoyance, and I know her illness as if I could see it."

"She's no better for all that," said d'Aspert.

"Ah," said Lussay, "there's our skeptic. I warn you, my dear Premitz, our general isn't among those believe without seeing... He's rather among those who see without believing—a useful quality for someone getting married. If you can believe it, a long time ago, twenty-five years ago... no, my word, it was twenty-eight years ago, it was in '87, and he'd convinced himself I was a sorcerer and Louise was possessed by a demon. In fact there were certainly reasons for believing that: at the time we were still quite backward, we used tubs, we made everybody link arms and make a chain, we still had the steel wand. All of that mesmeric apparatus made it look something like a witches' Sabbath, especially because a gathering of dozen or so people, far from weakening the mesmeric force by dividing it, only amplified it by multiplication. But better focused studies, and especially your excellent advice, my dear Premitz, have restored me to the right path."

"Yes," replied the baron, with his eyes fixed on Henriette's brow, "yes, direct personal influence is both more powerful and less disorderly; that way you can achieve results that would horrify the imagination, if they weren't simply and precisely explained by the presence of magnetic fluid, which is no less powerful than electricity. Since the gentleman refuses to believe in that power, he should do us the honor of observing the demonstration I'm going to give tomorrow at the home of a worthy woman who for twenty years has suffered from a kind of madness that makes her think she's always facing the scaffold. Several doctors from the Academy of Medicine and people of the greatest distinction will be present; the Duchess of Avarenne will be in the audience."

"The Duchess of Avarenne!" cried the general.

"You know her?" asked Premitz.

"Yes and no," said the general. "She owns some land in our department, and sixteen or seventeen years ago I met her in Rome."

"In Rome," said Premitz, "where her father was murdered by the republicans, along with a child she was raising, and where only by a miracle she herself escaped from the fury of the soldiers."

"What soldiers and what republicans are you referring to?" asked the general angrily.

"The French Republican soldiers, of course," replied Premitz. "If it hadn't been for an elderly servant in her household, who saved her from their claws for a certain mount of money, she probably would've been killed like her father and that child."

"And you repeat that story, sir!" said the general.

"My word," said Premitz, "I've very wrong to repeat it, because she herself tells it often enough for the whole world to know it!"

"Well!" said d'Aspert to Lussay. "Behold the people to whom you've given yourself, body and soul. What do you think of them?"

"What can you do, my dear general? The duchess suffered so much during the Revolution! It's certainly her right to be unfair and to complain now."

"She can complain, but she can't spread slander," said the general. Then he went on with a touch of sadness, "Let's stop talking about it. We'll never agree on that subject, any more than we do about mesmerism."

"If the count's skepticism is only a question of lack of proof, he should come tomorrow at two o'clock, and be convinced by his own eyes."

"I thank you," said the general. "Tomorrow at that time I have an appointment with the Minister of War, and I can't miss it."

"Do you still have some hope?" asked Lussay, taking advantage of the general's answer to turn aside their first subject of conversation and introduce another.

"I don't know. They've announced that tomorrow they'll release the final list of officers being held prisoner in Russia; and if poor Charles's name isn't on it, I fear he must've succumbed during the terrible retreat of 1812."

"And after all that, you still miss that vile Buonaparte!"

"Whoa there, Lussay!" said the general angrily. Then he went on, "You're right, I'm the one who started it... Poor Charles! Battalion commander in the Guard at twenty-five, he'd have won his colonel's epaulets in 1814, if only..."

"Was he your son, count?" asked Premitz.

D'Aspert started. "I'm not married, baron," he answered curtly; being addressed as "count" was as annoying to him as a wisecrack.

"He was at the very least his adopted son," said Lussay. "He took him in in Italy, where the boy's father, the valiant Captain Dumont, was killed. But I've always been surprised by that child's turning up, after people said he'd been kidnapped or killed after his father's death, and while he was on his way to Rome to ask for your support."

"He escaped from the clutches of a few Austrians, and showed up the same day we were forced to leave Rome on account of that business with the Duchess of Avarenne. That's what kept me from telling you about it at the time."

"Ah, Mother's waking up," cried Henriette.

"What did I say?" cried Lussay excitedly. "It's five after ten: three hours of sleep—neither a minute more nor a minute less. You have to be prejudiced to an astonishing degree not to concede on matters like that."

D'Aspert went to Madame Lussay's bedside and asked her gently, "Well, how do you feel?"

"Oh! That sleep exhausted me! My legs are worn out, my head feels heavy!"

"It's nothing," said Lussay. "We'll clear all that up."

Putting his hands on his wife's forehead, he drew them away several times in succession while shaking his fingers. Then he moved his hands from her head to her feet, keeping them an inch above the bedspread, and shaking them in the same fashion, even after he'd passed the tips of her toes. Finally he said, "That put her at ease, I think."

"Yes, it did," said Madame Lussay. "I have a great sense of well-being now. It's like a warm breeze carried away all that heaviness. I feel good, very good."

Lussay gave d'Aspert a look of triumph, while the latter turned away with the invincible resolve of a mind that refuses to believe. To Henriette he said very quietly, "He'll end up killing your mother."

"Alas!" said Henriette, leading the general into a corner. "My mother's wasting away day by day. But since she always feels a few hours of relief after the help my father gives her, she believes that's her salvation. You have to admit, it's an extraordinary power."

"Henriette," said the general, "don't forget you promised me not to get involved in your father's foolishness. With your delicate constitution, he'd drive you insane in days."

"Insane!" said Henriette, with an anxious and almost horrified expression. "You're right, there are times when I don't know what to think."

"Well, Henriette!" called Madame Lussay. "Aren't you going to give me a kiss? Oh, general, you're courting Henriette, I'm sure of it, and I won't allow it!"

"Fifty-two years of age, twenty-seven years in the army, nineteen campaigns, ten wounds, and gray hair—that's not the way to please a girl," said General d'Aspert, smiling at Henriette.

"Nor is it the way not to please a girl," said Henriette, with the boldness of a young lady playing games of the heart.

"Besides," said Lussay with a laugh, "when you've been the handsomest man in the army there's always something left."

"Just like with slander, according to Figaro," interjected Premitz.[39]

The general was the only who took note of that reply, which surprised and wounded him without his being able to attach any precise meaning to it, for in fact the reference was fairly inapt. He was about to ask for an explanation, when someone rang loudly at the door to the apartment.

"A visitor at this hour!" said Madame Lussay. "I don't wish to receive anyone. Go see who it is, Henriette, and tell them I can't be seen."

Henriette left, but soon they could hear several voices in loud discussion from the next room.

"No, no, child," a woman was saying in a clear, elegant voice. "There are no instructions concerning me. I know Baron Premitz is here, and I want to speak to him. The mission I'm charged with is too important to entrust it to someone besides myself."

Upon which Madame Bizot entered the room. She was a woman past thirty, short, brunette, well-rounded, with a rosy mouth, sparkling teeth, a joyful eye, lovely hands, lovely feet, amply endowed in all the projecting parts of her body, and sparking desire by the lithe, supple way she carried herself: one of those appealing women that the eye is eager to undress. Greeting no one as she came in, she went straight to Baron Premitz and said, "I'm very indiscreet, very inconvenient, am I not? But between people who are pursuing the same goal, there's a kind of ready-made acquaintance. Tomorrow your going to give a demonstration on mesmerism which is being talked about as something that'll be miraculous. I have to see it, for it interests me more intensely than you can imagine."

"Is madame involved in mesmerism?" asked Premitz, looking at her seriously.

"In being mesmerized, sir," said Madame Bizot with a cheerful, open smile.

"Yes," said Monsieur Bizot, who'd come in behind his wife. (Monsieur Bizot was one of those husbands who come in behind their wives, who walk down the street behind them, and who, in a handsome cab, ride up front with the coachman.) "My wife had terrible migraines, and she underwent a treatment that did her the greatest good. It's been going on

---

[39]*The Marriage of Figaro* (1786), an opera with music by Mozart and libretto by da Ponte, based on Beaumarchais's play, includes an aria for Figaro about slander.

for a month now, and she's unrecognizable. She no longer has those raging agonies that sometimes made her bad-tempered."

"What! Bad-tempered!" cried Madame Bizot.

"Yes, my dear. Now you can be told. You were becoming unbearable." He turned to Lussay and his wife. "Good evening, Monsieur Lussay, good evening, ma'am. How are you? Good, very good, I'm delighted." Then he turned back to Madame Bizot. "Unbearable, that's the word, and I bless that good Monsieur Drisson for undertaking to cure you. He's an excellent young man. Good evening, pretty Henriette, good evening."

"Who is this Monsieur Drisson?" Premitz whispered to Lussay.

"He's the head clerk of the lawyer who lives across from here." Then, turning to the general, he added with an air of mystery, "Well now, look at how plump and rosy Madame Bizot is. Can you still deny the positive effects of mesmerism?"

The general couldn't help laughing in Lussay's face, and even Premitz turned away to maintain his serious demeanor. But, wanting to put an end to all these smiling confidences, he hastened to tell Madame Bizot he'd see her with pleasure.

"And me too, right?" said Monsieur Bizot, snorting in a large measure of tobacco. "Because I've never seen mesmerism done, if you can imagine that. No, devil take me, that's the truth. Monsieur Drisson isn't yet expert enough to practice in public, it disturbs him. And when I'm around it's all more of a struggle, and the migraine gets worse, and I have to leave. One day I wanted to watch through the keyhole."

"What!" cried Madame Bizot, rising from Madame Lussay's bedside, where they'd been chatting. "You looked through the keyhole! And what did you see?"

"I saw the address of Monsieur Drisson's hatmaker, because he'd hung his hat from the key in the door."

"Oh," said the general, looking Monsieur Bizot straight in the eye, "that's because mesmerism requires great precautions to arrive at its results. Here, take Madame Lussay: she's far from feeling the same benefits as Madame Bizot, because her husband isn't taking all the precautions Monsieur Drisson takes."

Monsieur Bizot looked at Lussay and at Premitz to figure out what that meant. But Madame Bizot cut short her husband's pondering and said, "Baron Premitz knows I can't go before such a large gathering alone, and he'll agree to let you in."

"And besides," added the general, "it's a good idea for Monsieur Bizot to make sure mesmerism is something very respectable."

But d'Aspert's joke was in vain: Monsieur Bizot had already given up wanting to understand. He was a man who'd become rich thanks to a distinguished business career. He'd gone to work at fifteen, and promised himself that at forty he'd retire. At forty he found himself the possessor of three hundred thousand francs; and, though he was in a position to increase his fortune quickly, he'd stopped, in spite of all of his wife's complaints—she who could already picture her carriage and her chateau. He'd dedicated himself to relaxation since then: he relaxed stubbornly, allowing not so much as a single idea to enter his head—not because he had enough but because he didn't want to have any. He had no children, and it didn't bother him. Still, he'd subscribed to a political magazine that, containing not a single idea, suited his tastes perfectly.

Ten thirty had just rung, and the relaxation of his bed beckoned; Monsieur Bizot told his wife it was urgent that they go to sleep, and they went back to their place. Madame Bizot, who'd sensed, without guessing at the cause, that d'Aspert had almost given her away with his jokes, whispered to him in a tone of gentle reproach, "General, Monsieur de Lussay told me you weren't always an enemy to women!"

D'Aspert realized that, out of his hatred of mesmerism, he'd come close to being disagreeable to a woman who'd never offered him anything but the warmest welcome. He took her hand, and answered so only she could hear, "There are mesmerists who make me feel pity, like Monsieur Lussay; there are those I despise, like Baron Premitz; and there are those I envy, and Monsieur Drisson is one of them."

"Well, who knows, general?" laughed Madame Bizot, showing off her white teeth all the way to the rosy gums and making her eyes sparkle as they caressed d'Aspert's face. "Who knows?"

A moment later the general left, and Henriette withdrew, and Lussay and Premitz began to talk. Premitz led the conversation around to the connection between d'Aspert and the Duchess of Avarenne, and Lussay told him what people in the country had said long ago: that the duchess found d'Aspert to her taste; but beyond that he knew nothing. He also told him about the incident in Rome, meaning what had taken place during the riot, and the scenes he himself had witnessed, which showed there existed some secret between the duchess and d'Aspert, but a secret he didn't know.

Premitz seemed barely to be listening, and he withdrew at an early hour. But instead of going home, as he'd said he was doing, he stopped at a house on the rue Saint Honoré and walked up to the sixth floor. He knocked at a door that took a long time to open, though he'd knocked urgently and repeatedly, and he seemed anxious not to be found at that hour, in that house, on that floor, and at that door. Finally someone opened the door, and Premitz entered.

V. A SOMNAMBULIST

The room Premitz entered was a kind of antechamber. The servant who'd opened the door had a face that suggested she was a borderline idiot. Premitz stopped in that first room and asked the girl whether her mistress, Madame Divon, was asleep. Before she could answer, a hoarse voice from the next room cried, "Come in, come in, Baron Premitz. I saw you."

He was surprised, because the door was closed. In spite of the strange phenomena he witnessed every day, some things were such a surprise to his reason that every now and then he was frightened by the effects he himself had produced. Going into the room from which he'd been called, he said to an old woman who lying in the bed, "Oh, so you saw me?"

"Of course," said the woman, "and you passed the porter's lodge as fast as if you'd seen the executioner in there."

She spoke those words with a stumbling, or rather a heaviness, that suggested some kind of stupor.

But what she said was true, and Premitz was so surprised that for a moment he couldn't speak. After a fairly long silence he said, "Well! Do you think you're strong enough to appear before a large audience tomorrow?"

"Oh," said the old woman, "they'll guillotine me. All right, all right, let's dance the *Carmagnole*..."[40] She still spoke like a cretin whose thick tongue didn't have enough room to move in her mouth.

"Listen to me," said Premitz, watching her. "Tomorrow lots of people will be there. Will you recognize them from the descriptions I've given you?"

The madwoman began to sway vigorously, marking time with her head and singing very softly,
Madame Veto[41] *had promised*
to butcher everybody in Paris.
But her plan went awry,

---

[40]The *Carmagnole* was a wild dance, accompanying a song of the same name, that was performed by the crowds at many events during the Revolution, especially bloodstained victories over the nobility and the monarchists.
[41]In the *Carmagnole*, of which this is the first verse, Queen Marie Antoinette is referred to as "Madame Veto."

Thanks to our artillery.

"Enough," said Premitz. "Look at me."

He himself began to stare closely at the madwoman, and the power of his gaze brought her wandering eyes to focus on his. Then he said, "Would you like to sleep?"

"Very much."

"Well then, sleep!" he said, raising his five joined fingers to her forehead. The old woman's eyes closed, and Premitz said to her, "Do you remember the names of those who'll be in the audience tomorrow?"

The sleep of the body acted like the awakening of the mind. The somnambulist recited twenty names with remarkably clear enunciation.

"Do you know who those people are?"

Madame Divon reported fairly intimate details, relating to each of the persons named, with a precision Premitz himself presumably lacked, because he had to check what she was saying against a sheet of paper to make sure she wasn't getting confused.

When she was done Premitz added, "There'll be a few more people: Monsieur and Madame Bizot," and he told the somnambulist what he knew about them. Then he said, "Above all don't forget this: the Duchess of Avarenne and her daughter will be present at the demonstration."

At that name the madwoman started and cried loudly, "What did you say? The Duchess of Avarenne? Ah, the Duchess of Avarenne..." Then she became anxious, sad, and upset.

"Do you know her?" Premitz asked her peremptorily.

"Ask me nothing, don't ask me that," said the somnambulist, struggling under the terrible spell that bound her.

Premitz repeated his question in a solemn voice. Then, when he placed his hands on the top of her head, the madwoman suddenly became calm and submissive, and replied slowly, in a low voice, "Oh, the Duchess of Avarenne! The Duchess of Avarenne! She'll be there with her daughter, you say? And her son, won't he come?"

"What son?" asked Premitz, who in the several months since he'd met the duchess had never heard mention of a son.

"Well!" said the somnambulist. "Her son by Jean, Jean d'Aspert, the miller at l'Étang. The son she named Charles, the name of his supposed father, who wasn't really, the name of Count d'A..."

"Silence!" cried Premitz quickly.

The somnambulist stopped talking, and Premitz fell into deep reflection. He matched up what he'd learned from Lussay, and what he already knew, and what this woman had just said; and a vague, ill-defined, shifting idea leaped up from the depths of that chaos of events like a shining spark of fortune and future prospects. But Premitz had made other plans, and before dropping them like a madman to pursue opportunities that suddenly offered themselves to him, he insisted on long reflection and on time to bring those plans to fruition. Still, he wanted to find out right away by what means this woman knew anything besides what he'd taught her.

Within that lost, debased being there were two distinct persons: the half-witted, half-mad, half-dead old woman, and the lucid, powerful somnambulist. As soon as that woman was under the influence of the mesmerist, her intelligence returned; and the powers of her mind, raised to an extraordinary degree, acquired a prodigious delicacy of perception and range of analogy. Premitz knew that; but what he hadn't yet discovered was the power of the memory when the mind was stimulated that way. He'd often noticed that the somnambulist remembered his words and could repeat them back easily and with great accuracy; but he couldn't be sure he could also command old memories that weren't about him. So he made her tell him how she knew the duchess's secrets, and once he knew that, he could force her to talk or silence her at will.

But how did that woman know all those things? Our readers will have figured it out easily: she was Honorine, Honorine gone mad, with no intelligent existence except under the stimulation of mesmerism, a sleeping mind that woke only at one man's voice, and therefore was his possession: a frightening slavery of the mind, due to the power of some unknown force, or to the overstimulation of the nervous system, whose effects—no matter what the cause—appall the reason.

What Premitz had just learned left him plunged even deeper in thought. He realized he was the possessor of a secret, which the person who'd just told it to him didn't really know—a secret that might turn out to be worthless, just as it might be of the greatest importance. Besides, there were circumstances Premitz didn't know, because Honorine didn't know them. What had become of that child? Was he alive? Was he still a link between d'Aspert and the Duchess of Avarenne? Premitz resolved to wait, to act with caution, and to seek information.

A moment later he said to Honorine, "All right, wake up!"

He passed his hands a few times across her forehead, and the old woman opened her eyes. Premitz, who was always disturbed by his own powers, always proceeding on tiptoe in the enthrallment he exercised without knowing the secret of that enthrallment, feared that memories of the past would become accessible to the wretched old woman when she was awake as well as when she slept. So as soon as she was awake he said, "So you know the Duchess of Avarenne and Jean d'Aspert?"

But her mind had fled, and Honorine began to mumble quietly, "Good morning, Monsieur Sanson.[42] It's my turn today. Guillotine me with one stroke... let's dance the *Carmagnole*."

Relieved, Premitz went away and left the house.

We've said something about Baron Rhodon de Premitz; but we spoke of his appearance, and we've said nothing yet about his mind, nor about his past, nor about his fortune. If a novelist weren't required to know everything, we'd remain silent on all those subjects; for the truth is, Baron Premitz's mind, his personality, his principles, were rather hard to define. Though usually serious, he had moments of mad, noisy delight that surprised those who knew him. He was so indifferent to most things in life that it seemed he was interested in nothing, or that he had no willpower; yet about other things he was unyieldingly stubborn, and would yield to no one. There was no reason to doubt his honesty or his courage, and yet he didn't give off the air of frankness and decisiveness that would lead one to expect those qualities. His conversation was bold about things and reserved about people. He was willing to be known as an atheist, and disliked stories about ghosts and hauntings. As for his past, it was completely unknown, and his means of existence weren't openly visible. In other words, he wasn't known to own any property, and he didn't claim to. Neither did he speak of an income from the State funds, or a government pension; and yet he lived comfortably. He moved at all levels of society, from the highest to the most mediocre. What could've allowed him to pass as a man of good taste was that he didn't hide on the right so he couldn't see the left, nor did he boast on the left of being on good terms with the right. Besides that, he was a great advocate of mesmerism, which was his career. He was a fanatic on the subject; to the point that, if someone had seen him give Honorine the instructions we've just described, he might think Premitz was fooling people sincerely, for the benefit of a cause he believed was a good one—the way long ago a few priests, who meant well, would arrange small miracles to win souls for heaven who might not have followed the righteous path without that: all of it done with good intentions.

---

[42]Charles-Henri Sanson (1739-1806): royal executioner under Louis XVI and high executioner under the First Republic. He personally executed nearly 3000 people, including Louis XVI. He was the first to use the guillotine professionally.

The middle of the next day was devoted to the demonstration of mesmerism whose audience would include most of the characters in this story. It was past noon when the first spectators arrived at Madame Divon's attic apartment. Premitz was already there. People sat in the armchairs or on the chairs that had been arranged around the parlor. A few of those who'd been admitted to the demonstration had an air of mocking solemnity, of fake mystery, that foretold they'd be hostile to Premitz. But he wasn't worried about those people: he had it in his power to astonish them and to impose silence on even the most determined heckler. He would've been more concerned to meet some cold, resolute observer, one of those people who neither reject nor accept anything without examination.

Monsieur and Madame Bizot soon arrived, then Lussay and Henriette, and finally the Duchess of Avarenne and her daughter Julie. Lussay bowed to the duchess like a man who knows the importance of the person he's addressing. The duchess returned his bow with the casual graciousness that was used toward people who'd taken part in the Empire and who now supported the Bourbons. Henriette and Julie sat close to each other. They'd gone to the same boarding school, and were bound by a friendship of the heart rather than by the intimacies of girls; they didn't confide in each other. They'd almost never talked of the hopes and dreams that had excited each of them separately; and yet they loved each other. They would confidently have asked each other for support, but perhaps without confiding their sorrows, perhaps without understanding them, because their feelings weren't the same, they didn't see life the same way.

Finally Baron Premitz announced that he was about to start the demonstration. He left for a moment, and returned with Madame Divon. At the beginning of this book we didn't describe Honorine, a fresh-faced, charming girl. Madame Divon had nothing of Honorine in her appearance. The name she bore had been given to her in the prison in which she lived in '93; it was the name of the prison warden, a wretch who'd saved her from the scaffold by making her what he insolently called his wife. Since he was as ugly in body as he was in spirit, he'd only obtained the price he demanded for saving her by constantly filling the poor woman's ears with talk of the executioner and the guillotine. He made her go down into the courtyard when the condemned climbed onto the tumbril; he made her watch them primping over their final toilette; one day he asked one of the executioner's assistants to tease Honorine by praising the whiteness of her neck; then he would come offer himself as the alternative to those dangers and that death. He managed it so well that she accepted him and went mad.

That's when the prisoners gave her the name Madame Divon. Finally, one day when he'd grown tired of her, he fulfilled all of his promises; and after saving her life her gave her her freedom: he threw her out the door.

Then she begged in the streets, and was sheltered by a few priests in hiding, by a few royalists who, having learned her history, passed her on from one to the next like a sacred repository of the miseries of their side. Then came the Empire, in which stability and order opened the way to the pursuit of private interests; everyone thought only of himself; suffering lost its poetic charm; once you could make your fortune no one wanted to be a martyr; and Honorine rotted away in a dumping ground for beggars, near the border on the Rhine. The invasion of 1814 opened the doors of that establishment, and the madwoman found herself once again responsible for her own misery without even being aware of it, with nothing but the instinct of need that made her ask for food and drink, and which preserved in her the memory—present in almost all of the kinds of madness that coincide with poverty—that you can get a piece of bread for a piece of copper. Ask certain madmen what money is, what it's worth, what it's good for, and they won't understand you and won't answer; but give them a sou, and they'll go off right away and buy tobacco or bread.

So in that manner Honorine arrived in Paris. Chance put her under Baron Premitz's care, and he'd achieved such astonishing results with her that he withdrew her from the asylum in which she was staying and found her lodging in Paris. That was her entire history. And now she entered the room in which she was awaited, and which contained people for whom her existence was of such great interest. She was unrecognizable to them, because of her age, her sufferings, her illnesses; she was thin, sallow, her eyes changed, her body spasmodic, her lips drooping, her limbs pendulous, her muscles and nerves slack. Her appearance, devoid of strength and reason, surprised everyone; the skeptics thought she was faking madness, others felt a twinge in their hearts. Her eyes wandered indifferently around the audience, finding nothing on which to fasten. On Premitz's instructions she sat in an armchair; with the baron's invitation several people questioned her. She did no more than murmur a few disconnected words, looking at those who spoke to her with eyes so empty of all thought that her madness seemed real to even the most skeptical. But they expected to regain ground once they got to the tests of mesmerism.

Finally the demonstration began. At the stage Premitz had reached, all of the mimicry of somnambulism—the sweeping passes over the body, the massaging of the thumb, the laying on of hands to the head or the stomach—all of those preliminaries were unnecessary. It was enough for him to stand before the madwoman and say, "Would you like to sleep?"

"Very much."

"Well then, sleep!"

He reached out a hand to her forehead, she closed her eyes, and without moving he addressed his audience, delivering the following little prepared speech: "This woman is the most extraordinary subject of all those on whom mesmerism has exercised its power. The state of somnambulism produces in her a physical and mental transformation, such that it frees her of the excessively acute physical senses that make the slightest noise or the faintest smell unbearable, while it restores her lost reason and rekindles her buried intelligence. The cause of that return to her normal condition is the reestablishment of equilibrium in the magnetic fluid accumulated, while she's asleep, at the extremities and in the external organs—which produces both the oversensitivity of those organs and the insensitivity of her mental perceptions. So, touching a pear can make her pass out, and the scent of a rose is unbearable to her, while she remains without mental understanding of either the past or the present. Enough people who are present here have witnessed that state of physical irritability for us to have judged it unnecessary to repeat experiences that cruelly fatigue the subject."

"It's true," said Lussay.

"It's true," added several other people. "We've all seen it."

"It's a fairly common condition in asylums," said another voice. "We'll accept the statement as true."

"Since I hear no objections on this matter," said Baron Premitz, "I will ask you to follow the explanation that I feel it necessary to give you of the phenomena you're about to witness. The displacement, the disturbance of the magnetic fluid, which has invaded the sense organs and led to their extreme irritability, can only have taken place at the expense of the sensitivity of the brain, which, starved of what it needs while the other organs gain a superfluity, remains inert and insensitive within this body whose senses are so active and acute. The first result of mesmeric somnambulism will be to reestablish equilibrium, to remove the excess magnetic fluid from the extremities and send it to the brain. Then you'll see reason and intelligence returning, the subject will understand what's said to her and will reply clearly and directly, like a waking person."

"But in your system," said someone, "where is the immaterial, immortal soul? Is the soul just magnetic fluid?"

Premitz reddened, a few people murmured, and Julie whispered to Henriette, "That gentleman's right: how can a man claim to dispose at will of that divine attribute? Ah, my uncle told me all of these stories were just a ridiculous way of attacking religion. But my mother wanted to come."

"Listen to Baron Premitz's answer," said Henriette.

"Oh," replied Julie, "there are some things it's a crime even to discuss. I'm very cross I came."

The murmuring had died down, and Premitz had recovered. He replied loudly, "I'll answer the question I've just been asked with the same question: where is the immortal soul of this woman when she's in her normal state? Where is the soul of any lunatic? If the question I was asked was an objection to the existence of the soul, it wouldn't be my place to answer."

"He's right," Henriette whispered to Julie.

"It's not good to touch on matters like that," she replied.

"Besides which," said Lussay, rising, "there's a very simple answer for the gentleman. The soul exists in all cases. The soul, being the superior agent of life and all of its operations, produces its effects by means of the organs it works with, the way an engine makes a machine function by means of the gears that compose it. If the gears are sound, and mesh well, the machine will work easily and produce good results. If the machine is out of order, nothing good will be produced—though the engine will be no less powerful, no less existent, no less intact. The soul is the engine. If the organs are in good order, the actions of reason will be easy. If some accident has paralyzed them or left them in disorder, the soul will still exist; but, acting on unsound organs, it will produce only disorder and madness."

"The gentleman is right," said several people.

"Very well," said the original questioner. "But that means it's not the soul that's intelligent, reasoning, or sovereign. As a result, goodbye to the morality of human actions; and as another result, goodbye to all right to reward or punishment in this world and the next. Goodbye to all religion."

"Oh, mother, mother!" said Julie. "All of these people are ungodly."

"Does this have anything to do with your religion?" asked the duchess. "Have they said a word against priests or Jesus Christ?"

Julie fell silent. Premitz, who was visibly annoyed by what was happening, replied sharply, "We're not here to do metaphysics, but to do experiments. I will therefore continue."

"Yes, yes!" said Madame Bizot. "That's much more entertaining."

"One last word," said Premitz before beginning. "The system I've explained to you is so real, that once I've managed, by means of somnambulism, to reestablish the lost equilibrium, to remove the excess sensitivity from the organs and restore its dormant activity to the brain, I can, by sending a superabundance of fluid to the brain, lend it prodigious sensitivity and perception, while leaving the limbs completely insensible. The experiment will show you that astonishing result better than I can explain it."

After that digression he approached the subject and, placing his left hand on her head, he passed his right hand a few times across her forehead. Turning to the audience, he said, "Now, as soon as I wish it, she'll hear, she'll understand, she'll be able to respond to whatever she's asked: equilibrium has been reestablished."

"Ah," said the first questioner with a snicker. "That's very good. But is that woman really mad? That's what you'd have to prove first."

"That, sir," said Premitz, "is a matter well known to the inhabitants of this house. This woman came out of the Salpêtrière.[43] Here's her certificate from the administrators of that institution, with a description detailed enough to forestall any mistake. Let the gentleman read it, since he appears to be familiar with medical terms, and let him examine the subject."

The stranger approached, took the paper the baron handed him, and read aloud, "We the undersigned do attest that the individual named Honorine Radon, so-called Mother Divon..."

"Honorine Radon!" cried the duchess quickly. "Honorine Radon! Oh!" Then, after a moment of silence, she added, addressing Premitz, "She's mad? She remembers nothing?"

"In her normal state, certainly," said Premitz, stressing each word. "But when she reaches this level of lucid somnambulism, everything is restored, her intelligence and her memory."

"Her memory!" said the duchess. "Well, may I question her?"

"By passing your questions to me, it's easy. Because right now she's only in contact with me and would hear only my voice."

"Well!" said the duchess, hesitating. "Ask her where she was born."

The baron asked the question. Honorine remained immobile and replied in a loud, clear voice, "I was born in the village of l'Étang, in the Auvergne region."

"Till when did she live there?"

Again, Premitz repeated the question.

---

[43]The Salpêtrière, founded in 1656, was a women's asylum for the mentally ill, the learning disabled, and epileptics, all living in terrible conditions.

"Till 1788," said Honorine.

"What did you do at that time?" asked Premitz without waiting for a question from the duchess.

"I was in service with the Duchess of Avarenne."

"That's true," said the duchess quickly. "I remember this girl, I recognize her now. There's no need to question her further," she added quietly. "I don't want to be a spectacle for other people."

"So," said the stubborn questioner who'd raised all the objections, "this woman is really Honorine Radon?"

"Can you doubt it?" asked the duchess haughtily.

"I'd like to doubt it," replied the stranger. "For if this woman is truly the one described in this certificate, then she is or was truly mad: at the time she lived in the Salpêtrière she remembered nothing, and now here she is, remembering very well. Only one thing can be true: either she's been cured of her madness, which no one claims; or mesmerism produces the effects Baron Premitz has described, which I cannot admit."

"And why can't you admit it?"

"Because it's absurd."

"And why is it absurd?"

"Well, by god, because it's absurd! I maintain that this woman has been medically cured of her madness, and she's putting on an act."

"Oh, as for her being mad, and mad to the point of imbecility, I can attest to that," said Lussay to the stubborn man. "Struggle as much as you want, doctor, but you'll have to concede it."

"Oh, it's you, Lussay," said the stranger. "By god, I'm willing to believe it, since you guarantee it. Let's not interrupt the baron anymore."

While everyone was getting seated again, the duchess turned to Henriette and said, "Is your father right, miss, and that woman is truly mad?"

"Oh, ma'am," said Henriette, "I could guarantee it even more than my father, for I've come often to help him out. No matter when I've come in, even when I've surprised her a few times in a way that she couldn't have been prepared to put on an act, I've always found her in the state of imbecility she was in earlier."

Meanwhile Lussay was saying to the stranger, "How can it be that you—a man who's always been a passionate proselyte for new ideas—how can it be that you're so obstinate in denying the effects of mesmerism?"

"Oh, it's not mesmerism I'm suspicious of," said the stranger, "it's the mesmerist. This fellow is a schemer of the first order, and he doesn't realize I know him."

Finally Premitz thought he should begin what he called his experiments, to prove to what degree the mesmeric force had acted on this woman. For the first few seconds nothing extraordinary—mesmerically speaking—happened. A few people asked the somnambulist questions, and she responded fairly lucidly about their personalities and the illnesses they faced.

One unexpected incident added some interest to that demonstration: Monsieur Bizot, delighted by everything he was hearing, whispered to Lussay, "Well, we'll find out what this mesmerism is all about. I know Madame Bizot's illness—migraines and palpitations. I'll find out if the somnambulist knows something about that." Turning to Premitz, he said, "Sir, would you be so good as to submit my wife to your somnambulist's inspection?"

"With pleasure!" said the baron.

Madame Bizot resisted for a moment; but, realizing it would be ungracious to refuse, she gave in.

Bringing Madame Bizot closer, Premitz put her hand into Honorine's. Having thus established a connection between them, he said to Honorine, "Do you see madame?"

"I see her very well," said Honorine, who still had her eyes shut.

"Can you tell us what madame suffers from?"

"Madame experiences nausea, heart troubles, and dizzy spells."

"Oh," cried Monsieur Bizot scornfully, "it's really migraines and palpitations!"

"Yes, indeed!" said Madame Bizot with a forced laugh. "The somnambulist is mistaken."

Premitz seemed disconcerted, but he went on, "Tell us the cause of madame's symptoms."

"That's easy," said Honorine. "Madame is pregnant."

"Pregnant!" cried Bizot with a start. "Pregnant!" he repeated, stunned. "Pregnant!" And he almost began to weep for joy.

Madame Bizot turned as pale as death. Premitz couldn't keep from smiling. There's a remarkable instinctive intelligence in any gathering of people. No one knew Monsieur and Madame Bizot's story; her pallor had barely been noticed. But everyone began to laugh loudly, and on all sides and in every tone of voice people mockingly repeated, "Pregnant! Pregnant!"

"And why not?" said Monsieur Bizot, drawing himself up like a man.

The laughter redoubled. Delighted, he approached his wife, paying attention to no one, drunk at the news. "Is it... is it true? Charlotte, is it true? After ten years of marriage!"

"Alas!" stammered Madame Bizot. "I suspected as much, but I wanted to wait till I was sure..."

"Well!" cried Bizot. "It's since she began having herself mesmerized!"

The laughter exploded.

Bizot led his wife away in triumph; whereas she, embarrassed, could guess, with her feminine intuition, at the inappropriateness of his delight. As for Bizot, he held his head up like a victorious athlete.

The foreign doctor couldn't help asking him, "Is it Baron Premitz who mesmerizes madame?"

Premitz hastened to answer, to forestall some foolish husband's blunder that Monsieur Bizot would've delivered without fail. "No, sir, I don't have that pleasure!"

The word "pleasure" seemed delightfully inappropriate to the whole gathering. Bizot thanked Premitz with a smile. It occurs to us to mention to our readers that Monsieur Drisson, the lawyer's clerk you've already met, had not come to the demonstration.

After that incident the demonstration resumed a more serious tone. Baron Premitz, bringing the attention of the gathering back to the somnambulist, sat down facing her, put her knees between his, her hands between his, and once more began his mesmeric gestures, passing his hands over his face, setting them sometimes on her head, sometimes on her stomach. A look of contentment and joy spread across the poor woman's features; and soon that expression, growing gradually more intense, reached a state of excitement that gave that pale old face an uncanny aura—the look you could imagine on the face of a martyr as he entered the Roman circus or went to the stake.

At first that state provoked surprise and almost admiration in the onlookers; then the rigid expression on the woman's face, its suggestion of delirium, made the gathering feel a certain horror and discomfort: it was like a face ready to burst into exalted praise for the Lord, into exclamations of joy, into fanatical cries. Everyone felt the tiresome wait, like the wait in the hearts of miners who've lit the fuse, who are watching it burn, and who await the moment when it'll reach the gunpowder packed into the rocks, to shatter them and make the pieces fly. But her state of extreme exaltation led to nothing.

Finally Premitz addressed the general tension as he announced some new phenomena. "Now this woman's condition has been reversed: not only has she recovered her intelligence, and lost that excess acuity of the senses that made all physical sensation unbearable; but now she's reached the point where she can perceive—without the mediation of the sense organs—the most subtle and distant objects, while those same sense organs have fallen into complete dormancy."

That explanation was obscure enough that it was difficult to know exactly what Premitz meant. But what happened next showed more clearly than words the incomprehensible power of the mesmeric instinct, which leaves scientists no option but to deny what they didn't see or what they refuse to see. At that point the enslavement of the somnambulist reaches its peak; he wants what the mesmerizer wants, and he can perceive beyond his actual intelligence.

Anyway, here was the first test attempted: After calling for a glass of fresh water, Baron Premitz asked the somnambulist whether she wanted a drink; when she replied yes, he asked to say what she'd like to drink. Honorine asked for a glass of lemonade. Premitz took the glass of water, blew on it, and handed it to the subject, who drank it and declared it to be excellent lemonade. That experiment made a few people smile, but the foreign doctor grew more attentive. Honorine said she was hungry and would like to eat a piece of fruit, a peach. Premitz handed her a chunk of lard; she took it and ate it with complete satisfaction. The onlookers felt surprise mingled with disgust. Whether this woman had overcome natural repugnance to play that scene, or whether mesmerism had the power to trick the senses to that degree, the fact was that what had happened was quite extraordinary.

But an even more curious experiment awaited the spectators. Premitz asked for someone to write down a few words, and the foreign doctor took charge of doing so. While he was writing out two or three lines in large letters, Premitz asked someone to blindfold the subject. When they were sure she couldn't possibly see at all, Premitz put the piece of paper under Honorine's elbow, and she read it with that part of her body just as if the paper had been placed before her eyes.

Each of those demonstrations produced varying reactions among the people present. The most foolish, determined to believe nothing, tried to

find the conjurer's trick behind the performance. A few others were astonished without analyzing their astonishment, thinking that once they were
out of that room they'd have other things to worry about than mesmerism,
and not wishing to get involved in a dissection of phenomena they couldn't
pursue to the end. But of all the people present, the most struck by those
demonstrations had been three women: the Duchess of Avarenne, her
daughter Julie, and Henriette Lussay. The duchess was perhaps less interested in the marvels of science than in meeting Honorine, and in that dead
memory brought to life at the will of a man. Julie, keeping her eyes lowered, didn't dare look at Baron Premitz, and deep in her heart she resolved
to go to confession as soon as possible to say what she'd seen. As for Henriette, she'd reached such a state of terror that she was almost unaware of
anything besides the bizarre spectacle. She couldn't take her eyes off
Premitz, and there's no doubt he could've made her do awful things at that
moment, if he hadn't been careful to avoid looking at her.

Soon the baron showed the gawkers around him things every bit as
astonishing. The somnambulist's physical lack of feeling was so complete
that she didn't respond to even the sharpest pain: her arm was pierced with
an awl, several people pinched her till the blood came, and yet she didn't
seem aware of anything that was happening. Finally the unknown doctor
approached her, saying he knew how to provoke some reaction by brush-
ing her lips with a feather. He stood behind her, and just as he was bringing
a feather near her lips he secretly drew a pistol from his pocket and fired
it close to her ears. Everybody cried out in fear and surprise; but the somnambulist didn't move, and her face showed not the least sign of startle-
ment.

"Come on!" he cried. "It's catalepsy!"[44]

"But if it's catalepsy," said Premitz, "how can it be that this woman
remains responsive to me, whereas she isn't for you? You can torture her
all you want, and she won't feel a thing. You can shout as loud as you can,
and she won't hear. But if I touch her or talk to her, she'll feel the slightest
pressure of my hand, and she'll hear my voice no matter how softly I
speak. The same would be true for you, if you'd like me to put you in
contact with her."

"All right, let's do it," said the doctor. "I'm willing to try the experiment."

---

[44]A malady in which physical insensibility and lack of response of the sense organs have frequently been observed (Soulié's own footnote).

Without using any hand waving, Premitz established contact between the somnambulist and the doctor, and told the latter he could now speak to the subject. The skeptical doctor asked her a few questions, which Honorine answered using a vocabulary that surprised him a great deal. But his astonishment turned to a kind of stupefaction when Premitz told him he could address her in any language he knew. The doctor agreed, and first asked Honorine a question in Latin; she replied unhesitatingly, but in French. Honorine might know Latin; so he asked her a new question in Italian. She understood the question and replied clearly. A woman! A woman of the common people! A woman of the people reduced to such a state of conjuring—if what he was seeing was conjuring—a woman like that who knew Latin and Italian, was already extraordinary enough. But the doctor went further, and, pulling together all of his knowledge of foreign languages, asked the somnambulist a question in English. She understood it, and didn't hesitate before replying.

At that point the doctor began to be suspected of the same deceit of which he suspected Premitz: seeing him speaking to the subject, and seeing her reply so lucidly, others imagined he was just Premitz's accomplice, that his skepticism was part of the act, that the pistol shot he'd fired had been planned. Someone stood up and handed the doctor a piece of paper, saying, "Would you please ask the somnambulist this question? Read it right now, without stopping, just read it as best you can."

The doctor read half a dozen words, and the subject remained silent. "Do you not understand me?" he asked her.

"No," said Honorine, "because you yourself don't understand. When you speak in a language other than French, it's not your words I hear, it's your thoughts I read. And you have no thoughts about the words you just read, because you don't know the language you've been speaking."

That answer stunned the doctor, because she was right. But it only aroused the incredulity of the people who believed he was conniving with Premitz. The person who'd passed him the paper cried, "But it's just as good German as this gentleman's English was. It seems to me she could've understood it."

"But for that," said Premitz, "the questioner has to know what he's asking. I'll take the paper and read it."

He hadn't even finished reading the German words before Honorine replied, "You're asking me if the reign of the Bourbons will be long-lasting. In a month, there'll be no more Bourbons in France."[45]

The boldness of both the question and the answer caused such a sensation in the gathering that the scientific point was lost as people focused only on what had just been said. Premitz protested that he didn't know the person who'd written down the question, and that the somnambulist's answer was madness. The Duchess of Avarenne rose and withdrew very angrily. Everybody scattered, and the demonstration ended without exploring any further the vast question as to whether there might exist, between a somnambulist and someone in contact with him or her, direct communication of thoughts without the mediation of the sense organs.

As for everything we've just reported, we declare we were an eyewitness to it. We're not writing a work of theory here, nor a textbook on mesmerism; but we saw the results we've just described. And if all the people involved weren't still alive, and desirous of avoiding negative publicity, we could name every one of them. Was it charlatanism, was it the truth, was it the presence of some genuine fluid, some invisible agent that caused all of those perturbations in the natural order? Was it, as some claim, a delirium of the imagination, a wild over-excitement of the mind? We wouldn't be able to say what we think. But that's what we saw, and that's what time will presumably explain.

---

[45] In early March 1815 (the time of this chapter) the war was over, Napoleon was in exile on Elba, and the Bourbons seemed securely restored to the throne of France. But by the end of that month the Bourbons had fled once more and Napoleon had returned to power for the start of the Hundred Days that ended with Waterloo.

VI.

The evening following that demonstration, Monsieur Lussay was at home, seated by the fire. His wife lay in her sickbed. Henriette, seated next to him, embroidered with a care that proved she had to force herself to keep her mind on her work. It was still early, and yet the newly ennobled baron seemed impatient—till they heard the doorbell ring. "Ah, that must be the general!" he cried. "I fear he has bad news, else he would've brought us word sooner."

He rose to go meet him, but was quite surprised when the Duchess of Avarenne was announced. She entered quickly, bowed to Madame Lussay and Henriette with gracious condescension, and immediately began to speak. "You're astonished at my visit, Monsieur de Lussay. I'll make no excuses for intruding, and you wouldn't want any, I feel sure, if you knew I've come to ask you for a favor."

"From me, ma'am?" said Lussay. "You're doing me a kindness, and bringing me news—because I was far from imagining that poor Baron Lussay could do a favor for the Duchess of Avarenne."

"I can't tell whether I should take that as an epigram or a compliment," said the duchess with a smile. "I know people think I have some influence, but the source of that influence seems to be so high up and so long ago that I'm reluctant to make use of it, unless I'm truly driven to it, as I would be if you asked me to do so."

Lussay bowed.

"But I must give the impression of bargaining for the service I want of you by offering my own services," the duchess went on. "Let me start by owing you something, and later I'll pay my debt, if people would only understand that we poor exiles have to be given what we need so as not to remain in debt to everybody."

"It's true," said Lussay, "nothing has yet been done for the true friends of the Bourbons: a few appointments in the army, that's all, and even then the men of the Empire still fill all the spots."

"Oh, we'll see, we'll see..." said the duchess. "But let's come back to the reason for my call. Do you know the woman we all saw today?"

"I've seen her mesmerized several times, but it was only today I learned who she was."

"She's a girl who worked for me for a while. It was her devotion to me that drove her to the state she's in, and I'd like to make sure she's cared for now."

"I understand your benevolence," said Lussay, "but if anything can restore her reason, it's Baron Premitz care; and it would truly be a loss for science to deny him such a precious subject."

"Come, come," said the duchess with a smile, but while studying the doctor's expression to find out his real thoughts. "Come on, do you want me to believe that everything I saw was something besides a well-performed act?"

"Is that what you think?" said the doctor, almost offended. "You consider Baron Premitz capable of such fakery?"

"Baron Premitz," replied the duchess impatiently, "is a man whose livelihood isn't so solidly established for a suspicion about him to count as an injustice... And as for Honorine..."

"Honorine!" said Madame Lussay. "What? That somnambulist is Honorine? The duchess's former chambermaid?"

"Yes, yes," said Lussay with some embarrassment. "You must've heard us talking about it."

"But she was my friend," said Madame Lussay, "my dearest friend!"

"Yes," said Lussay, "I know you used to look out for her... in the old days..."

The duchess winked at Lussay and said, "Yes, Baroness Lussay is quite right. A long time ago Honorine told me a story involving Jean d'Aspert in the village of l'Étang."

"There are lots of stories about Jean d'Aspert at l'Étang," said Lussay dryly.

"Well, first of all there's the story about you and Mademoiselle Louise," replied the duchess. "I only ever heard the beginning of it. I was told about the time Monsieur d'Aspert caught you in the cellar of your house."

"Yes, it's true," said Lussay, "and it almost had terrible consequences, but for me they were changed into true blessings."

"How so?" asked the duchess.

"He interrupted me in the midst of my proceedings. At that time we were using Mesmer's tub, which, by means of steel wands radiating out from a common center, enabled us to act on a large number of people at once. Jean's sudden appearance, and the angry argument I had with him, kept me from moderating the action of the magnetic fluid. Some terrible disturbances resulted: a few of my somnambulists fell into violent convulsions, and Louise, who was the most sensitive subject of all, almost died. Honorine, who'd followed Jean, was so terrified that she fainted, and we had to carry her home. The next day d'Aspert came to see me; he wanted to kill me."

"Kill you! Why?"

"Well," went on Lussay, "d'Aspert, who didn't believe in demons, and who believed even less in mesmerism, thought I was using my influence over Louise..." He paused.

"For what?" asked the duchess.

"Well..." he said, glancing at his daughter to suggest to the duchess that he couldn't really explain while Henriette was there. "Well... well..." He stopped again.

Presumably the duchess understood, because she said, "Is such a thing possible?"

"Very possible!" said Lussay.

"Presumably if you consent?"

"Without your consent, without your even knowing, without your having either awareness or memory of it."

"Did you try it yourself?"

"Henriette," said Madame Lussay," go get me some water. I'm terribly thirsty."

The girl went out. Madame Lussay went on, "Monsieur Lussay, you forget your daughter's here; perhaps you also forget I'm here."

"All right, all right, my dear," said Lussay. "Does Henriette understand any of it? Still, it makes you angry, so let's drop it... Well, ma'am, d'Aspert, who knew nothing about mesmerism, made clear to me the insulting rumors about Louise and even more about me. He brought them up, and we discussed them. I'd compromised Louise; I married her; that's all."

Henriette came back.

The duchess went on, "So, this power Baron Premitz has isn't some empty charlatanism?... You swear that on your honor?"

"I swear it, and I can offer you proof more indisputable than my word."

"It's a terrible power!..." The duchess pondered, then resumed, "No, it's impossible! You yourself have been fooled."

"Fooled!" said Lussay with a smile. Then he went on very quietly, "You'll see. I normally put my wife to sleep at the same time every night.

It's still fifty minutes till the usual time. Well, all I have to do is say out loud that the hour is chiming, for the power I have over Louise to be shown instantly." Then, raising his voice, he said casually, "What! Is it already eight o'clock?"

"Eight o'clock!" murmured Madame Lussay.

Lussay motioned to the duchess to approach his wife's bedside; she was fast asleep.

The duchess stood there, flummoxed. "In any case," she resumed quickly, "Baron Premitz has to give me back Honorine. He can come treat her at my house. I'll witness her progress."

"Oh, in that case I'm sure he'd agree."

There was a loud ring at the door.

"This must be him," said Lussay, "because I expect him this evening."

D'Aspert came in without being announced; he was agitated. "Well, Lussay, here you are calmly, while all Paris is in an uproar!"

"What's happened?" asked Lussay

"The Emperor has landed at Cannes and is marching on Paris."

"That butcher?" cried the duchess.

D'Aspert turned. He hadn't seen the Duchess of Avarenne in almost twenty years, but he recognized her instantly. Without answering her, he quietly asked Lussay, "What's the duchess doing here?"

"Oh," said the doctor, "it's a strange story… I'll tell you about it. But are you sure about the news?"

"This morning," said the general, "I suspected something at the minister's audience, because he seemed rather embarrassed…"

"By the way, what did you learn about young Charles Dumont"

"I can no longer have any doubt that he's dead."

"Who's dead?" asked the duchess.

"A child I adopted in Rome, seventeen years ago, a few days after I had the honor of meeting madame there."

"Ah!" said the duchess in surprise. "I beg your pardon, sir, you're General d'Aspert." He bowed, and she went on, "And Charles… your adopted son… is dead?"

"Dead!" said the general. "He's on none of the lists of prisoners brought back from Russia, though several officers from his regiment are listed."

The duchess said nothing. After a moment of silence she rose and said casually to Lussay, "You won't forget my message to Baron Premitz. I'll leave you now; I'm going to the palace to find out how reliable these rumors about Bonaparte are… I can't believe the audacity of that wretch!"

"Ma'am," said d'Aspert, "the man who ruled France, the hero of Italy, deserves another name!"

"A cartridge with epaulets, that's all!" said the duchess. "A brigand who ought to have been shot at the foot of a tree. Farewell, gentlemen!"

She left, and d'Aspert got ready to do the same.

"Where are you going?" asked Lussay.

"I'm not sure… everywhere… I've got to see, to find out… Ah, Lussay, Lussay! All is not lost! And those crooks from the old regime, that insolent aristocracy!"

"Oh, d'Aspert, you don't mean that about the Duchess of Avarenne!"

"The Duchess of Avarenne! That woman's a monster! You didn't see how calm she was when I said…"

"What?"

"Nothing! Nothing!…" said d'Aspert, stopping himself. "I'm so worked up… I wasn't thinking about her… I'm going out; I'll bring you back news."

"By God!" said Lussay. "I'm coming out to learn the news with you!"

"Aren't you expecting Baron Premitz?" asked Henriette.

"Oh! He probably won't come tonight. Like us, he'll have gone in search of news. Goodnight; don't be alarmed if I come home late. Keep watch over your mother; when she wakes up, give her the medicine she ordered for herself the day before yesterday, and tell her why I went out… "Oh!" he cried suddenly, as if struck by an idea. "Do you remember, Henriette, how this morning Honorine said that in a month there'd be no more Bourbons in France?"

"Yes, father."

"It's incredible!"

"What are you saying about Honorine?"" asked the general.

"Yes…" went on Lussay, pondering, "yes, it's possible… Bonaparte will be victorious… She announced it… It's terrifying, it's sublime… The future! Seeing the future!"

"Have you gone mad?"

"Come, come! I'll show you something that'll astonish you."

They started out. The excitement that the news of Napoleon's landing had prompted in Paris had so thoroughly spread to every corner that as they crossed his apartment Lussay found no one: the servants had all gone down to the porter's lodge and were discussing the great event. Henriette had been left alone; the poor girl was in a state of agitation whose cause was quite different from the typical reflections of young ladies. Born of a mother whose nervous system had undergone violent attack by Lussay's ignorant experiments, Henriette was thin, sickly, and extremely impressionable. Surrounded since her childhood by theories of mesmerism, which constantly presented her mother to her as a creature subject to a supernatural power she couldn't escape, Henriette had grown accustomed to thinking that some powerful will could impose the same effects on her.

And yet her father had never tried, and he'd even said repeatedly that he didn't think he was the one who could produce mesmeric results from his daughter. Henriette had therefore escaped from the danger of letting such things fill her imagination... when Baron Premitz was introduced to her father. She interpreted the strong impression the newcomer made on her heart at first sight as her fear of falling in love with him. Indeed Henriette, who couldn't see Premitz without feeling some agitation, remained fairly calm about what she felt, thinking she'd met the man she was destined to love, and being neither surprised nor concerned, to tell the truth, at falling in love at the age all the novels proclaimed was the right one for doing so.

But one day, when mesmerism was being discussed in front of her, and her father said Premitz was one of the leading men in that science, achieving astonishing results, she reconsidered in horror the impression Premitz created in her, and since there was an element of fear involved, she refused to believe it was love as soon as she was able to imagine it was something else. From then on, Premitz became for her the man who was going to act on her will the way she'd seen her father act on her mother's, the master who'd make her a slave, the fate that would dominate her life. Often, when he was caught up in the excitement of his research into mesmerism, Lussay had asked Premitz to mesmerize his daughter. She'd refused with desperate intensity—Premitz himself had refused—but still the idea had struck her imagination. Premitz had become a figure of unspeakable horror to her; she turned her eyes away from his, she trembled when their hands met, she shivered at the sound of his voice. She felt like one peremptory word, one gesture of command, would make her fall to her knees, no matter what she did to defend herself. The most powerful torture device that could've seized her limbs to confine or break them seemed no more irresistible than the voice or the hand of that man; and she'd reached the point that if he'd placed his finger on her brow and stared at her with his savage look and told her to die, she'd have died.

So Henriette was alone with her mother, who was sleeping the mesmeric sleep in which her husband had left her. The girl contemplated her for a long time, and sank deep into her contemplation. The strangest ideas rose and whirled around her head like a phantasmagoria of the spirit. Could that power of one man over another, of one will over another, really be a physical manifestation, some invisible tenuous substance that intoxicated the soul and the mind like wine vapors? Wasn't it rather something supernatural, one of those fallen divine powers now drifting among men but belonging to another nature? In fact, why were all the stories from the past filled with sorcerers and vampires and fairies and demons? The cynicism of the nineteenth century denied those supernatural influences, but didn't prove their falsity. What were the familiar spirits from those old stories doing, now that they had as their slaves all the souls that had been bargained away to the powers of hell?

All those thoughts coming and going, flying away and returning, had made Henriette cold. When she arrived at the suspicion of a soul bargained away to hell, she got so scared she cried out, and that cry brought her back to reality. She saw she was in her mother's room; she saw her mother; she understood that her own mind was driven by fever and out of control. She grew afraid of herself, and wanted not to remain alone. She called to her mother, but the artificial slumber that bound her would end only at a given command, at a given time; her mother didn't answer. Henriette felt her heart pounding, her throat constricting; an icy veil fell over her brow and hung to her feet, like a shroud. As if against her own will, she spoke aimlessly: "Oh! No... no... I'm cold... I've gone mad... My God!"

She dragged herself to the bell and rang it, and waited. No one came, because all of the servants had gone downstairs and were discussing the great news. Henriette was no longer sufficiently in command of her reason to think of that explanation for their absence. She seized the rope again and pulled it violently; in the silence of the apartment the sound of the bell seemed to reply like some infernal laugh. She cried out and fell into a chair. An attack of nerves came over her: her fragile arms stretched out as if they would break; she moaned and panted; she ground her teeth; her open, glazed eyes no longer saw; she fell down and rolled around, choking; her disheveled hair dragged across the floor, got tangled in the chair legs in the convulsions that shook her, and was torn out; she broke her nails in the cracks in the parquet; she bumped into the corners of the furniture and injured her face and tore the skin on her forehead.

Finally nature prevailed in the struggle: the spasms eased, and a kind of bodily rest followed those terrible convulsions. Henriette remained sprawled on the floor, though broken and unmoving, and full of an awareness of vague aches. Her reason had returned, but it was tentative, confused, divided: each of her limbs felt like it had a separate existence, that bothered and weighed on her. In both body and mind the torrent of convulsions and ideas that had borne her along had come to an end. It was like the agitation of white water reaching a deep spot where it had to stop, and where the waves, driven back by the banks, turned in on themselves and rose up, dancing, balancing their foaming crests. That's what both her body and her mind were like.

After those extreme exertions came a soft trembling, a few inarticulate cries, a few painful efforts. And across her mind ran memories, genuine but disconnected: Honorine as a madwoman, Honorine seeing the future; then Honorine stretched out on her mother's bed, who was also Honorine and who was going mad... Premitz, the Duchess of Avarenne, Napoleon, all whirled around, appearing, vanishing, returning. Then came a terrible nightmare, and then sleep, deep but troubled, against which she fought. But it seemed to her that someone was speaking near her, she was being lifted up and carried. With an effort she opened her eyes: a night light burned by itself in its porcelain cylinder, but by its light she thought she saw a man, a man standing before her and laying one hand on her brow and another on her heart and saying in a grave but irresistible voice, "Sleep."

Henriette fell back in her chair and slept.

It was midnight when Lussay returned. Henriette was still asleep. Madame Lussay, who'd been awake for a while, had called her in vain. Lussay woke his daughter; but for a long time sleep resisted before letting her go. Seeing the dishevelment of her clothes, he questioned her. She searched her memory, and recalled everything that had happened to her up to the moment she'd rung the bell. Lussay thought he understood the cause of her state: he concluded that his daughter had been frightened and had an attack of nerves. He ordered her to rest, prescribed a few sedatives, and sent her to her room. And he himself went peacefully to bed, after swearing to his wife that he would no longer speak about mesmerism in front of his daughter, nor make her witness experiments that upset her so badly.

VII. A PACT

The day after that extraordinary vision, a gentleman—whose name is too well known for me to record it—called on the Duchess of Avarenne. He'd been announced almost with scorn; and as long as the servant, who'd set a chair for him near the duchess's armchair, remained in the room, the visitor had maintained an air of deeply respectful contrition and humility. But as soon as he was alone with the duchess he became angry and said, "I assume you must have some compelling reason for summoning me; because you know very well every moment is precious, now that the news of Bonaparte's landing has forced us to guess which way everyone's leaning, to the point of studying the expression on every face."

"I know you're at my orders," said the duchess. "I also know you're making a big fuss about Bonaparte's escape to inflate your own importance. But I have more serious things to tell you. Did you get the information I asked you for?"

"Here it is," said the gentleman sullenly.

The duchess glanced at the sheet of paper he handed her. After reading it she said, "So you're sure General d'Aspert never had a child?"

"Never."

"And didn't that young Charles Dumont he adopted die in Russia?"

"We can't assume that."

"But that's what General d'Aspert was told, and he believes it."

"That's because it might be true."

"So he's been misled?"

"Or he's misled himself."

"Sir," said the duchess haughtily, "answer directly, plainly, but not stupidly. What happened to that Charles Dumont?"

"News came today," replied the gentleman incredulously.

"So he's alive?"

"Yes, ma'am."

The duchess reflected, then went on, "What's his family?"

"Here's what the civil records say: Son of Pierre Dumont, captain in the seventeenth half-brigade and of Anne Lépaulier, his spouse; born the 23rd of April, 1787. Here's his baptismal certificate."

"His baptismal certificate?" said the duchess in surprise. "So this child isn't the one General d'Aspert adopted in Rome sixteen years ago?"

"The same one."

"That's impossible."

"Impossible!" replied the gentleman. "Yet it must be possible, because otherwise it would be a case of stolen identity. The individual Charles Dumont was educated at the lycée as the son of an officer killed in battle; he was admitted to the Academy at Saint Cyr in that capacity, after which he became a battalion commander in that capacity."

"Have you found the man who brought the child here?"

"Yes, ma'am. He's a retired sergeant in the Army of Italy, who's now a police sergeant."

"What did he say to you?"

"Here's his written report."

"Give it to me." The duchess took it and read as follows:

In February 1798 General d'Aspert ordered me to collect Captain Dumont's son at the general's palace in Rome and to escort him to Paris, where I would leave him at a boarding school the general named. We were then at Terracina; I set off and reached Rome at daybreak. I went to the general's palace. But when I got there I learned it had been sacked by the mob, which accused the general of having saved an aristocrat; that the servants who'd remained there had fled; and that the stables had been looted. Not knowing what to do, I was about to return to the general, when I noticed a child sitting at the base of the portico; he looked sick from exhaustion and hunger. I asked him if he knew anything about the palace.

"Alas, no," he replied, in tears. "I came here looking for General d'Aspert. My father told me as he was dying, 'Go to Rome and find d'Aspert, tell him you're Captain Dumont's son, and he'll take care of you.' I came; but I found the general gone and the palace deserted."

"By God!" I said. "My little fellow, it couldn't have worked out better. The general sent me to find you. I assume he thought you'd already reached the palace, because he told me I'd find you settled in, and Durand, his servant would hand you over to me."

Upon which the little fellow followed me. I took him to Paris and left him at the boarding school the general had named.

"And since that time?" asked the duchess.

"The general scrupulously paid all of young Dumont's expenses."

"What happened to that Durand?"

"He'd been killed in the attack on the palace."

"And what became of the general himself? I want to hear about his travels and the places he lived."

"For a short while he stayed with the Army of Italy. Then he moved to Corsica; later he was part of the Saint Domingue expedition,[46] and he was one of the last to leave."

"Such that he only saw young Dumont again after an absence of several years?"

"It was at least six years, starting from when he took charge of him."

"And during that whole time he was alone? He didn't have a child with him?"

"No, ma'am."

The duchess didn't know what conclusions to draw from that report. Was Charles Dumont d'Aspert's son? Was he genuinely the captain's son? Was the peculiar way the sergeant had found the boy just chance, or a precaution taken by d'Aspert to reinforce his lie? She didn't know what to think. Finally, carried along by her train of thought, she said aloud, "If this one is truly Captain Dumont's son, what did he do with the other one?"

"What other one?" replied the gentleman.

"What other one!" cried the duchess, angry that the man had overreached his job to the point of spying on her thoughts. Then, using the words that had escaped her to refer to someone quite other than she'd originally meant, she added, "The one I wrote to you about this morning."

"Ah!" said the gentleman whose name I haven't given, "that's Baron Premitz."

"Well, who is he? Where'd he come from? What brings him to Paris? What's he after? Will my orders be carried out?"

"To all those questions I have only one answer, ma'am, the answer given to me by our department chief himself, who knows nothing more, because he showed me the register where it's written."

"What does it say?"

"Look here: *Baron Premitz, no age or country of origin given. Explicitly forbidden to investigate him.*"

"Who could've put such a note in that register?"

"It seems to me the duchess must have some inkling."

"None whatsoever."

---

[46]In 1801 Napoleon sent a military invasion to Hispaniola to try to reconquer the French colony of Saint-Domingue (modern Haiti) after the slave uprising and declaration of independence led by Toussaint Louverture. The French expedition was defeated and withdrew in 1803.

"That's odd, because that's word for word the same note that's attached to the duchess's name."

"To my name!" said the duchess, reddening with embarrassment. "My name is in a register like that one?"

"All important or dangerous names are listed there."

"Have the police no respect for anything?"

"On the contrary, ma'am, you can see there are persons the police is forced to respect, no matter what."

"Is that answer stupidity or insolence?"

"It's simply the naive truth, ma'am. Because the note I've just shared with you was attached to Baron Premitz's name following a report filed against him by the ordinary police, a report that concluded Baron Premitz had had communications abroad, especially with the Roman court."

"That's enough... I don't need you anymore... You may go..."

The gentleman withdrew. Left alone, the duchess wrote a note to Baron Premitz, asking him to call on her. He arrived a few hours later, and here is the conversation they had:

"Sir, have you any idea why I asked you to come see me?"

Premitz gave the duchess such an arrogant, irresistible, dominating look that she could only shrug. She hastened to respond, saying, "My God, baron, there are only two kinds of people you can look at that way: little girls whose senses you want to arouse, and silly old women whose imagination you want to strike. I'm no longer in the first group, and I have yet to reach the second. So don't dress up your eyes like a vampire or a sorcerer; I'm neither gullible nor easily frightened. I need to speak with you: will you answer me according to the ordinary rules of conversation?"

"Ma'am," said Premitz, still in a tone of solemn mystery, "I know why you summoned me."

"Well then, since you know, what do you intend to get out of that secret?"

"I haven't thought about it yet."

"And yet you still need to make your fortune, I assume, sir."

"Perhaps at this moment my fortune is made."

"In what way do you think it's made?"

"In this way: I'm in a position—under threat of scandal and perhaps dishonor—to force a wealthy family, one with some power, to accept me as a son-in-law."

The duchess, outraged at a threat she thought was directed at her family, cried angrily, "You, to become my son-in-law, sir! Oh, we haven't reached that point yet."

The surprise on Premitz's face showed her she'd been wrong. She was about to recover her error, when her daughter Julie came in quickly and unannounced.

"Mother, mother!" she said emphatically. "May I go out, to go see Mademoiselle Lussay, Henriette? She's dying, and she asked for me..."

"Dying!" cried Premitz, rising suddenly and turning very pale. "Henriette dying!"

"Yes, sir," said Julie coldly. "She's very ill. But perhaps her imagination is even sicker than her body, and I hope to calm her down."

"Go... go..." said the duchess, who'd noticed how upset Premitz was by the unexpected interruption. "Go, and send me word how she is."

When she was alone with Premitz, she put together the baron's ambiguous words earlier, and Julie's news, and the baron's fearful reaction, and said, "So, sir, you were saying you'd forced Monsieur Lussay's family to accept you as their son-in-law?"

At that vile insinuation, anyone other than Premitz might've let slip the secret the duchess had hit on so squarely. But, as short as the moment had been for him to think, it had been enough, not necessarily to change his plans completely, but at least to inspire him with the idea of pursuing the new direction the duchess's earlier reckless outburst had opened to him. So, rather than reply to her insidious question, he said, "The duchess is mistaken to be angry at a claim I haven't explicitly stated, and that might be far from my thoughts. For I spoke of a wealthy family, and the duchess's fortune is entirely at the mercy of the court's generosity. And I spoke of a powerful family, and the duchess's power, like that of the people on whom it depends, is subject to events whose outcome no one can predict."

The duchess, balked in her hope of catching out one of Premitz secrets in turn, no longer wanted to pursue a conversation whose faulty basis left her at the discretion of a man who seemed skilled at drawing advantage from every unplanned moment in the dialogue. To keep from giving him another foothold, she retreated all the way and said, "For a quarter of an hour, sir, we've been speaking ambiguously. Come now, let's explain ourselves openly. What do you know?... And if you know something, what do you want? There's a bargain to be made."

"I know everything."

"That's exactly how all those letters begin, the ones from jealous lovers who know nothing and who'd like very much to learn something."

"Well then, ma'am, here's what I know. I know from Honorine that you had a son, that your son was by Jean d'Aspert, and that you passed him off as the son of... I know the prince believes it, and that it's to that memory you owe whatever credit you enjoy. I also know that son disappeared, and that you managed his disappearance skillfully enough to be able to make him reappear again, if ever you find him, or if you found someone else who'd do."

That last idea had never occurred to the duchess; and perhaps Premitz had included it merely as an add-on to his list of unprincipled actions, one last brushstroke in his portrait of the duchess as a schemer. But no seed falls on fertile ground for nothing. The duchess filed away the idea to consider seriously; and to do so to her profit she asked Premitz, "How old are you?"

The intelligence of plotters is remarkable. Premitz smiled and replied right away, "Exactly the right age: twenty-eight."

The duchess was embarrassed at being so quickly and so completely found out. She realized she had nothing to gain by trying to play games with a man like Premitz, and she replied straightforwardly, "Let's drop that idea; it's absurd."

"No idea is absurd in the hands of skillful people. From Genesis to the Charter,[47] people have been made to believe so much nonsense that I no longer think there's anything they can't be persuaded of."

"People, sure, but one single man is another matter. Crowds are remarkable: while they can sometimes multiply their intelligence so that they're wiser than the greatest minds, they can also multiply their ignorance so as to be more gullible and stupider than the stubbornest brute."

"But didn't the prince fall for that lie?"

"Of course, but what a difference! That was a child of mine which could perfectly plausibly have been his too. Whereas now you'd need a man with no past, a man about whom no one could make claims relating to his birth, his youth, his life; about whom no one could say, he was there at that time, he was using that name, he belonged to that family, he came from that place. Such a man..."

"Is not impossible to find. When we've agreed on our facts, I'll have to tell you my history."

---

[47]The Charter of 1830, following the July Revolution, deposed Charles X in favor of Louis Philippe, who became "King of the French" rather than "King of France."

"What do you mean by agreeing on our facts, sir?"

"This: you need my silence, and I need your influence. Let's make a pact. I'll be quiet, which is to say I won't tell the prince, 'You're the victim of a well-played confidence trick. You owe that woman neither the regard due to her usurped status as a mother, nor the gratitude a noble heart maintains for an affection he believes was sincere. On the contrary, you should hate her and banish her, for as a lover she deceived you in the arms of a provincial peasant, and as a prince she deceived you by imposing on you the duties of an alleged father.'"

"Sir!"

"Don't be angry, ma'am. I won't say a word about all that, I'll be silent; for starting today I'm you're accomplice. But let's be clear, it's to share in the profits of the crime."

"And what would you rate them at?" asked the Duchess of Avarenne with ill-concealed fury.

"As I was saying, ma'am, that depends on what your secret's worth."

Just then a servant entered and handed a note to the duchess. She was surprised and very alarmed. "Come on—is this Bonaparte business serious? The prince is leaving for Lyons."

"I fear it's more serious than you think," said Premitz.

"But what'll become of our plans?"

"The future alone will show. That's why I told you I'd wait to tell you what I demand of you in turn."

Baron Premitz withdrew, and the duchess thought about nothing but the new political events agitating France.

VIII. SECRETS
(1816)

Time passes quickly in our century: great epochs are contained in the span of a few years, and history is cut up into discrete blocks, each with its own color and spirit and name. At the time I'm writing this, anyone older than thirty[48] can remember the dying remnants of the Republic gathered into a sheaf in the hands of the Consuls; and the Empire, that sublime sunny day, brought to an end by the storm of 1812, beneath which France struggled for three years—a genuine storm, in fact, in which the thunderclaps were battles, in which the floods were the entire population of Europe poured in fury against France; then a magnificent day that seemed to waken again in the false light of the Hundred Days; then the Restoration, the Restoration that lasted twice as long as the Empire, and which, as it recedes into the distance, seems to shrink to the eye, like those uniform plains where no outcropping gives a sense of distance; then the Revolution of 1830, those three days as high and isolated as the Pyramids of Egypt, pointless monuments that attest to what the united effort of a whole people can do, but which are lost in a desert where nothing has sprouted, where nothing else has been built nearby. And amid all those complete memories, so many years with their own distinct character! So many days that shine with a particular light!

Among those years there's one that in my memory remains under a cloud of sadness and despair. Am I the only one who sees it that way, the only one whose personal feelings wrongly paint the character of that year so dark? I was young; I was at the age when you're almost done being a child. I'd just stopped wearing my lycée clothing, that precocious uniform in which we'd fought so many hopeful battles in campaigns in which we quickly won our veterans' stripes, the sooner to become young soldiers. I was very young, and twice already I'd seen the drummer boy flee before the warning rattle, drill replaced by Mass, and religious stories usurp the place of bulletins from the Grande Armée in the daily paper. I wasn't yet sixteen, and the whole future I'd built up in my dreams had already collapsed. I dreamt of the army; my father, one of the paragons of our glory,

---

[48]*Le Magnétiseur* was written in 1834; Soulié was born in 1800.

had promised to get me into battle before I was of age. But there was no more army, and a death sentence pursued General Clauzel from one refuge to another.[49]

I wanted to take up my father's honorable career; but the most outstanding abilities and the most irreproachable probity hadn't saved him from dismissal. All my life I'll remember the lesson in misery that made me so angry then: suddenly being abandoned by all our friends, an abandonment that came in the *Moniteur*, an abandonment without ceremony or subtlety. It happened at nine o'clock in the morning, in the office: people greeted my father, obeyed his orders, listened to him, flattered him. Then the paper came, and they read the news of his dismissal; in a flash we had not a single friend, not a single acquaintance; the visitors vanished, and the clerks became almost insolent. The fact is—and you can believe me—it wasn't a desertion carried out at length, carefully spaced out over a few months or weeks; it was simply people picking up their hats and leaving without a word. And that evening, that very evening, my father wanted me to experience something: we went out onto the public thoroughfare, which was full of people we'd received, who'd received us, who were our intimates as we were theirs. Well, here's the literal truth: when we appeared on the street, the crowd of passersby parted before us. As far away as they could spot us, people ducked down alleys or looked off to one side or into the air, at a bird's nest or a gnarled branch; everybody seemed very preoccupied; people spun in circles to keep warm—anything not to have to greet a man who'd been dismissed.

Doesn't what I'm writing, what you're reading, seem like nonsense? Isn't it an exaggeration? Certainly not. But it's hard to conceive the terror that followed the Restoration of 1815. At that time the fear was all the greater for the danger being unmeasurable. We trembled at the massacres in the South of France: there weren't many victims, but the murderers were fanatical and numbered in the thousands. Only Ramel was murdered in Toulouse,[50] but he was murdered for three days running, stabbed in every

---

[49]Bertrand Clauzel (1772-1842): one of Napoleon's generals. For his actions against royalists during the Hundred Days, he was condemned to death in absentia by the newly restored Bourbons. He fled to New York, and later to a Bonapartist colony in Alabama, and returned to France and a successful military career after he was pardoned in 1820. He was Soulié's uncle.

[50]Jean-Pierre Ramel (1768-1815): a former officer in the Grande Armée who'd been given a government position by the Bourbons, and who was assassinated by royalists who suspected him of retaining secret Bonapartist sympathies.

part of his body. The army—that remnant of ten years of victory and three years of defeat—was discharged, and it didn't utter even a murmur.

I'll always remember, and always with tears, how we traveled with my father during that year, 1816. It was a year of disasters: the rain spoiled and damaged everything; the harvest lay down flat and rotting in the furrows; the country roads were nothing but long smears of mud. As we went along, wrapped up in out greatcoats, at every step on the road we met miserable soldiers and even more miserable officers, gaunt, beaten down, unable to face an hour of rain and an hour's walk—the same men who'd marched from Madrid to Moscow, who'd endured the Cairo sun and the frigid Dvina! They were often seated by the side of the road, ten paces apart, but unknown to each other, not wishing to be known, stopped and inspected at every village like freed convicts; finding among their fellow-citizens no courage beyond that of insulting them; and letting themselves be insulted, since it seemed to them that nothing could touch their hearts after they'd been through Waterloo and their regiments had been disbanded. In that sad time, for us young men, the future opened onto disappointment and despair.

It was an evening in September of that year, a few days after the order to dissolve the Parliament of 1815—that Thermidor of the royalist terror, which, with its enthusiasm for banishment and penal servitude, put an end to the excessive devotion of the extremists. A man and a girl, Lussay and Henriette, were seated by their fireplace, both of them upset—he angrily, she with resignation. They didn't speak: a misfortune stood between them and kept them apart. Some misfortunes bring people together and meld two souls in the same regrets; the most powerful of those is usually the loss of a shared loved one, a heart with bonds of affection reaching in both directions, bonds which now connect one to the other. Madame Lussay was dead. Why didn't Henriette and her father weep together? Because another misfortune had arisen: one blamed the other, who didn't admit guilt; the wrong couldn't yet be erased by forgiveness. Each of them thought of their own situation, without considering that of the other: sunk in that egotism of reflection in which the mind reviews one by one all the hopes that have fled, and cherishes all of its own misfortunes without noticing whether the other person has their own share. It was a cruel separation of a father and a daughter, in which both, turned in on themselves, refused each other forgiveness in one case, repentance in the other.

A man arrived who brought distraction from those personal preoccupations, a man who was a friend they'd not seen for a long time: d'Aspert.

He'd hesitated at first to come visit Lussay, knowing he supported the government in power. But he'd learned of Madame Lussay's death, and he counted on that grief to be made welcome. As he came in he could see at a glance the disharmony between the two, as they threw themselves warmly into his arms—but without embracing or even touching each other. D'Aspert noticed that Henriette was pale, her smile slow to appear, her eyes close to tears, and her whole being full of a pure dignity that didn't belong to a girl, nor to a happy woman. A resigned soul is certainly something sublime: in that passive strength used only for suffering, in that martyrdom of the heart, endured without complaint or resistance, there's a charm I consider more deeply touching than the fiercest struggles of the emotions.

That's why I want to describe for you old d'Aspert's affectionate astonishment when young Henriette, now twenty, pressed the soldier's rough, saber-calloused hands in her slim white hands and said, "Hello, my friend! Oh, I'm so happy to see you! I'm so happy!"

A tear came to d'Aspert's eye, but he didn't dare kiss Henriette the way he used to. Without knowing anything, without understanding anything that could be put into words, without her having asked him for help, without him knowing she needed any, he replied with an inexpressible sympathy from one heart to another, "Well, here I am, here I am. Don't worry."

Then they conversed.

"I admit," said the general, "I was afraid I wouldn't find you in Paris. I was told in Poitiers you expected to be appointed to the prefecture in Vienne."

"No," said Lussay, "it's Baron Premitz who got that. He left a few days ago. He'd followed the king to Ghent, with the Duchess of Avarenne."

"And you weren't considered pure enough?"

"It wasn't that," replied the former doctor. "It's I who turned it down—I, to whom all ambitious prospects are closed. Not that I wanted it for myself, but for Henriette I wanted..." Then he stopped, and started again quickly. "And you, d'Aspert, what's new with you?"

"I've been assigned to the fourteenth level of officers. I might as well have retired. On top of that, I've been ordered to go live in the department where I was born."

"You're not happy either," said Lussay bitterly. "And you look sad."

"Oh, it isn't that which makes me sad: I saw so many men who out-ranked me fall in battle that I don't have the right to complain. Anyway, we're no longer the men of France, just as it's no longer our own France. I was resigned to go and bury myself in Tremblay, on the little bit of land I bought near l'Étang. What makes me sad is a misfortune of my own, a misfortune that's mine alone, because it's so awful I can't even share it."

"Yes," said Lussay, "but it's not so awful that it can't be guessed at someday, and once it's found out it can be a source of shame and infamy."

Lussay's tone was somber; his head was lowered and he looked at no one. But there was such bitterness in his unhappiness that it could only arise from a father's heart, and d'Aspert looked at Henriette. She didn't seem embarrassed, but she was crying, and she nodded to suggest to him, "Yes, he means me."

D'Aspert held out his hand to her; turning to Lussay, he said, "Well! What exactly has happened?"

"What's happened! What's happened!" said Lussay, rising angrily. "How would I know? It's a crime, you see, d'Aspert, a terrible crime, not because of what happened, but because of a stubborn insistence on playing innocent, because of an unbearable refusal to say, 'I'm guilty... Father, forgive me... And since you're here, d'Aspert, you see, I can say it... I can admit it...' I would've forgiven her... I would've wept with her... But she didn't want to... She told me fairy tales... She told me... It's impudent madness! She told me... But, come now, let's say no more about that. It drives me mad to think about it... To say to me, 'I'm innocent'... To tell me, with her head high, 'I'm pure'... To tell me..."

At that moment they heard the cry of a child, and Henriette rose. D'Aspert let her hand drop as he withdrew his own, and she said, her voice full of tears, "Oh, general!"

"Where are you going?" asked Lussay angrily.

"To care for my son," she answered with sudden and almost scornful firmness.

The two men remained alone. D'Aspert, more embarrassed than he'd ever been, sadder than he'd been when he came in, felt a deep sorrow at the news he'd just learned. After all those fallen glories, after all those sublime spirits scattered in exile, after that great nation confined once again in the old borders of France and bordered by enemies who insulted her—after all that, this lost child, this young flower now withered made him weep. Deep in his heart, with the profound despair that takes hold there so firmly that it becomes second nature, he said to himself,

"Everything perishes, my God! Is there really nothing left to believe in? Poor France, and poor girl!" Then aloud he added, "But surely this isn't something without recourse. There's a guilty man, some debased man who, with the law on your side, can be forced to… You must already have tried that."

Lussay shook his head.

"A man you can force, with your sword in your hand. Lussay, would you like me to…?"

Lussay began to laugh sarcastically.

"And that man can be killed!" said d'Aspert.

"There's no one," cried Lussay. "You're looking at me… I look like a madman, don't I?… No, there's no one."

"She refuses to name him?"

"No, no," said Lussay furiously. "No, there's no one… You don't understand… Look, I told you, when I think about it, it drives me mad."

"Come now, calm down… Pull yourself together and tell me the truth."

Lussay's expression was odd. Clearly he wanted to tell the story he was being asked for, but it seemed as if he couldn't figure out where to start the tale. His mind lit on one idea, then gave it up, jumping to another idea only to drop it immediately. What he had to say was so incoherent that he was unable to express it.

Just then Henriette returned.

"Ah, there she is," said Lussay. "She'll tell you herself, if she can, if she dare… Goodnight… Listen to her… I'll see you again tonight if you have enough patience to wait for me, or tomorrow… Whenever you like… Goodnight."

He picked up his hat and left. D'Aspert and Henriette remained alone. The beautiful, unhappy girl had followed her father with her eyes, but her look was cold and resolute. D'Aspert was surprised, and asked reproachfully, "How can you have no pity for your father's despair?"

"General," she said sadly, "I have barely enough strength for myself. My father didn't understand me; I don't know if someone else will." Then with a deep sigh she added, "I'll tell you everything: My mother loved you, general, and perhaps she kept you in her heart as long as she lived. I know that, having often seen her crying. I'm going to speak to you the way I would if she were here. I've expected you and hoped for you for a long time. You'll decide what's to become of me; but I'll ask you for your word, as a man of honor, to tell me, when I'm done, what you think of me. If you deny me your absolution, I'll wait for God's. But don't deceive me, general: no false pity for the child you saw born, no ambiguous expressions, no disguised hopes. Don't count on some improvement the future will bring. If what I'm going to tell you isn't everything I know, if you have any doubt, any suspicion, that I mean to trick you or hide something from you, tell me... I won't hold it against you. It might make me more unhappy, but at least I'll know what I'm up against. I'll prepare myself for the wretchedness of my life—for I don't even have the consolation of being able to die voluntarily, and I'll let time take its course. It'll either kill me or toughen me. In fact I think that's already begun."

Henriette was standing while she spoke. The general watched her with an almost fearful astonishment. Never had a woman appeared before him in the holiness of sorrow that makes her so beautiful and so moving. He could say nothing, and he motioned to Henriette to have a seat. She wiped away a few tears, sat down, and began thus: "When you left Paris, eighteen months ago, I was ill. The worries that my illness caused my mother completed the destruction of her health. In spite of what my father called his care, she died."

Henriette had spoken those last words with a noticeable sarcasm that was unusual in her. She dried a few tears that clung to her eyes and went on:

"The loss of my mother was a severe enough blow for me to have attributed to that grief my habitual state of suffering. That suffering was manifested in symptoms my father explained by highly plausible medical reasoning and by common examples drawn from a condition identical to mine. I imagine I've said enough: if you knew all I had to surrender in terms of modesty, I who'd never received so much as a lover's kiss, you might be surprised at my restraint. But I'm wandering from the point; let's resume. My condition, which was a very natural one, seemed to my father and to his friend, Doctor R..., a dangerous condition that must be brought to an end. One day, when they'd tormented me with remedies capable of killing me in my condition, I was undressing for bed, I was standing before a mirror, my nightgown dropped from my hand, and I saw myself naked... You're blushing, general, you're blushing at what I'm telling you so boldly! Oh, this is nothing; listen. I saw myself naked; I'd already lost my slim figure; and I couldn't help saying to myself, what an odd illness I have—here's another symptom that indicates a woman is going to be a mother! That idea crossed my mind like an aimless, pointless thought. I concealed neither that symptom nor any other from myself; I had no reason to feel alarmed. Meanwhile my father questioned me with his eyes. Sometimes I could see him observing my figure and my demeanor with concern. He said nothing, but I was wounded by his suspicions. But there was plenty to justify them: spasms, heart palpitations, dizzy spells. Anyone else in his place would've condemned me. One evening, when we were sitting together, I cried out in surprise. He asked me what was wrong. I replied, with an innocence that baffled him, "That's odd, I feel like something just moved inside me."

My father grew pale and cried, "So, it's a certainty!"

"What is?"

"What?" he echoed. Then he stared at me as if I were mad, or as if I were insolently mocking him. His arms shook; he eyed me with a terrible look.

I understood him. I rose and said confidently, "Father, this has to end. Up to now I've put the care for my health in your hands, for good or ill, it didn't matter. But today it happens that you suspect me of a sin I shouldn't even understand. I beg you to send for a doctor who's a stranger to us."

"A stranger!" he cried. "Must the whole world know..."

"Oh, father!" I interrupted indignantly. "Not even the barbarians deny an accused man the means of defending himself."

The next day a doctor came whom I've never seen since. I met him with such a strong desire to bring it all to a conclusion that I barely noticed the immodesty of the questions he asked or the examination he put me through.

"Well?" asked my father anxiously.

Well!" said the doctor confidently, "madame is pregnant."

My father said nothing; but he gave me a look that could've killed me.

As for me, I began to laugh as I looked at them both. "Pregnant! You must be mad!"

My father took both of my hands in his, and made sign to the doctor. They both observed me attentively. Finally the doctor responded to my father's inquiring glance. "No, there's no sign of insanity. It can only be that she's chosen to play it off with audacity."

Now I grew troubled with an inexpressible fear, for my child was moving in my womb. "Pregnant!" I cried. "Pregnant! But to be pregnant you have to have..."

"For shame!" cried my father violently. "She's keeping up her impudent act!"

I despaired, and fell to my knees. "No, father, I swear, never was I guilty of that sin."

I thought my father was about to beat me. The doctor whispered a few words to him, then had me sit next to him and spoke to me gently. It's impossible for me to repeat that conversation, general. Now that I'm a mother, now that I can speak to you as a mother, the memory of it still makes me tremble. Imagine a girl of twenty, who's assumed to be as ignorant as a child, being questioned about what's believed to have happened to her. Imagine all the details I was asked about, the descriptions I was given, the medical sketches of the act of love that were drawn for me verbally and with gestures; all of that, ending with, "Is that what you saw, what you felt, what you endured?"

And I answered, "No... no... no..." always and to everything. I—a poor girl dishonored by a terrible misfortune, disgraced by a horrible examination, dirtied by an interrogation uglier than the crime, if I'd committed it—I didn't give in, because my feeling that I was innocent made me strong. Now it's your turn to look at me in astonishment, general. You reason, you look for answers, you try to explain... But there's nothing to explain. On my soul, I've never had a lover... On my life, I've never belonged to a man..."

"And yet you're a mother!" cried the general.

"And yet I'm a mother," said Henriette. "Listen carefully: I have nothing to say to defend myself. After all, I don't believe in miracles. I've searched my memory; there's nothing in my memory, not a caress, not an intention, not a look exchanged with a man, not an hour of solitude. So then..."

"So then," said the general, "there must have been a crime."

"Ah! Thank God, thank God! You think so, you who are not my father, you think there was a crime..."

"And that crime, it seems to me, is not so difficult to explain for your father, especially, not to have thought of it."

"Or for him not to have admitted it," said Henriette in a voice in which terrible despair and terrible anger were mingled.

"Admitted!" cried the general. "Admitted!... What, Henriette, you'd dare to..."

"Well, what do I know?" she replied like a madwoman. "Because I'm innocent! I've said so on my knees, while beating my brow against the floor, while begging for mercy and pity, and he hasn't listened to me. I've appealed to heaven, I've appealed to my mother's ghost, I've offered to die, I've prayed; and he's never replied with anything but sarcasm, contempt, accusations... He hasn't been willing to believe me... Well! Why would you expect me—all by myself, you understand—to believe other people? Rejected, insulted, scorned in the heart of hearts of my innocence, what respect do I owe anyone? What guarantee do I have that the crime I'm accused of isn't in fact their crime?"

"Henriette!" cried the general.

"Sir!" she replied with growing intensity. "Oh, I've learned a lot, I know a lot, I've taken advantage at least of the outrages being hurled at me to listen to what I once wouldn't have dared to hear, to search for what I once would've fled from. Yes, sir, there are villainous fathers who seduce their own daughters. They exist, and I know some... I've had them pointed out to me; and they didn't have the sinister power that could explain my crime and my innocence. In the end..."

She stopped. Falling to her knees before d'Aspert, she shed a few tears as she went on, "Oh, general, general, forgive me! I don't believe what I'm telling you... I don't believe it... But I'm innocent, and I'm being accused, and I'm succumbing to it, and I'm doomed, and I'm being cursed... Well then, I too will accuse and curse and hate and despise: I've been given that right. Forgive me."

"And why would you accuse you father rather than someone else?"

"Someone else," said Henriette sadly as she got up. "I've certainly thought about it, for you can understand that every hour of my life has only one goal, which is to find some evidence, whether externally or within myself: a gesture, a look, a memory that would illuminate me and put me on the right track. That someone else, the only one you could be thinking of, and who's often been the subject of intense interrogation in my thoughts, that someone else we both understand without having to name him, has never been alone with me. Not once have I ever left my father's house alone; in all the times I've been out, there hasn't been a single encounter with that man, nor a single blank in my memory—for you can't imagine the way constant tension can resurrect trivial details and unnoticed circumstances in your memory. Within our house, he couldn't have taken me by surprise in my sleep, crept in to me in the night, without the servants knowing, and I've questioned them all. Yes, general, I've done everything, I've even sunk to that... Why should I be careful? What could happen to me that wouldn't be to my advantage?... And if nothing can take away my faded complexion, at least I can defeat that accusation of boldfaced lying, which is perhaps the more despicable: for if it's true that there's forgiveness for the sin I might be guilty of, there's none for the impudent hypocrisy with which I would've tried to deny it."

And how do spend your days now?" asked the general. "What do you do? What's to become of you?"

"I live in this room... I watch over my child... Yes, that's the word, I watch over him. For in his first transports of anger my father spoke of the foundling home; and sometimes his anger flares so abruptly, and is so extreme, that he could profit by a moment's absence on my part to take my child away from me. And that child must never leave me. Alas, I'm a miserable wretch, lacking my mother, alienated from my father's love, banished from humanity's respect, destined to live alone without friendship or love ever to comfort me. It must be my right to raise some hope of tenderness and affection, to seek, within the misery in which I've been isolated, some consolation that might elude me, but that's still the only one on which I can build a future. Yes, general, perhaps my son won't despise me and won't curse me. Perhaps he alone will believe me when I tell him the truth... For I can tell by your thoughtful, preoccupied look that even you are reconsidering the impulse of pity that led you to believe in my innocence. You draw back from the idea of accounting for it by some incredible crime. You look for commonplace explanations for something that might be supernatural. You too are abandoning me... Already you're accusing me..."

"Henriette," said the general after a moment's silence, "Henriette, would you be my wife?"

At that word Henriette's face lit up with sudden astonishment and inexpressible joy. She placed her hand on her heart and then on her brow, as if she wanted to hold in her thoughts and her happiness. She fell to her knees; resting her head on the general's lap, she let her soul dissolve in tears and sobbing. She tried to speak, but the sobbing always got in the way of her voice. She tried to look at him, but the tears constantly veiled her eyes. All she could do was to take his hands, cover them with kisses, and squeeze them violently, with muffled cries.

The general helped her back to her seat, and she calmed down a little. "So," he said, "you accept."

Henriette smiled sadly. Shaking her head gently, she replied in broken fragments, "No... no... general... I can't... I mustn't... I have everything I wanted... a friend who believes me, finally, who forgives me for my wretchedness. Now that you think I'm innocent... I can lower my head and tell you... I know I'm a fallen woman... it's a misfortune... an irreparable misfortune in the eyes of the world... You can't take me just out of generosity... I don't want that, I can't allow that... No... Oh, I wish I were as pure as the angels in heaven, so I could kneel before you and say, do you want me?"

"Henriette, all of us have our own miseries, our own sins that make us suffer cruelly, and which we'd like to pour into a friendly heart. I too have a terrible misfortune in my life... I have a sin, a crime I'm guilty of, and which I wouldn't like to carry to the grave without having someone tell me what I have to tell you: I pity you, and I want to comfort you."

"Oh, tell me, tell me," cried Henriette. "I can't offer you comfort, though only misery can understand misery. But I can suffer along with you."

"No, no... I can't tell you anything... There's only one person I can confide in... that's the person who'll share my life, my future, my name... To her, I'd tell everything... Come now, Henriette, answer me: do you want to know my secret?"

"I'll be your daughter," said Henriette with a heavenly smile in which the joy in her soul still shone. "I'll be your daughter... Speak to me, father."

"My daughter!" said the general bitterly. "No... that position would bring you misfortune... it can't be... I beg you, in return, to have pity on me. One word, one single word, and I'll tell you."

Two large tears fell from Henriette's eyes. She held out her hand to d'Aspert and said, in a voice that contained all the gratitude in her heart, all the devotion of a life given unrequited, "Well then, speak, speak, my friend. I want to listen to you." She drew her chair closer to the general's and, raising her serene, confiding eyes to his, she said again, "Speak, speak..."

"Henriette, what I have to say is a solemn secret."

"Yes, a solemn secret that belongs to you, a secret you can do what you like with, that you could forget tomorrow without my holding it against you, or that you could remind me of without my fearing it... Yes, I'm yours, to be your wife... or your friend... You've told me something that binds me to you forever without expectation of return: you said, 'I believe you're innocent!'"

D'Aspert collected his thoughts for a moment, then said, "Well! Here's what's given me the sadness your father noticed, and which will be the torment and eternal doubt of my life. I have a son, or rather I had a son, for now I no longer know what to believe. That child was taken away from me by his mother. There's no need for me to tell you her name and the reasons that made her decide to steal him; that's a secret that isn't mine to share, and that I've sworn to be silent about forever. I found that child again and resolved to keep him. But, as much to obey his mother's intentions as to protect him from future attempts to steal him from me, I decided to raise him under an assumed name. At the same period a friend, a captain serving under my orders, was killed. Dumont was a decent man, but so strict that everyone feared him. That strictness, constrained by the eye of his superiors when it was directed at his soldiers, became the most unreasonable cruelty when he was dealing with people who had no one to protect them. As a result, in a little village near Rome, he'd come to be hated by the Italians, to the point that one evening when he walking at some distance from the village he was attacked by the inhabitants and had his throat cut. Captain Dumont had a son, and that son…"

"Is Charles Dumont, isn't he?"

"Listen," went on d'Aspert. "This story is so fatally complicated that I no longer know what to hope nor what to think. Dumont's son disappeared while he was on his way, in accordance with his dying father's instructions, to ask me for protection and support. Various reports assure me he'd been kidnapped by the same men who murdered his father, and I assumed he was dead too, like his father a victim of their hatred. That's when I had the idea of giving my son the name of that lost boy. For reasons I've sworn to keep secret, my son had been raised in ignorance of who he was; he knew neither his mother's name nor mine. I told him he was Dumont's son, and he believed me."

"So Charles Dumont, that gallant young man, is your son? Oh, you must be proud of him."

"Don't interrupt me, Henriette; I wouldn't know how to answer, and you'll judge for yourself. By a series of incredible circumstances, the day after I'd found my son and introduced him under the name Charles Dumont, the day I was to hand him over to a worthy sergeant to escort him back to France, an order from above required me to leave Rome: it was no less than a capital charge of having helped an exiled woman escape from the authorities. I didn't want to take my son along on a journey in which my freedom might be at risk; so I left him in Rome, with my servants, with orders to hand him over to Sergeant Bazil. I found Bazil at Terracina, I gave him my instructions, and I reported to the general in command.

"The difficulty of justifying my actions, and the disgrace I suffered as a result—and which later got me assigned to the Saint Domingue expedition—kept me from returning to France. I learned from Bazil that in Rome, at the gates of my palace, which had been sacked by the mob in my absence, he'd found a child who said he was Captain Dumont's son. The rest of my instructions had been faithfully carried out. Since I was convinced the captain's son had been murdered, Bazil's report satisfied me, and I had that child raised in Paris under the name Charles Dumont.

"I didn't return to France till 1804; six years had passed. I'd only seen my son for twenty-four hours; his face wasn't so indelibly traced in my memory that I couldn't be mistaken; and anyway, between the ages of ten and sixteen a child's features go through so many changes that they're almost completely different. I saw the boy again. Was it my heart? Was it the pride I felt at being the father of a young man whose talents and fine character everyone praised? I thought I recognized my son by the affection he inspired in me; I had no doubts. The gratitude he expressed to me distressed me. I wanted to tell him he owed the care I lavished on him to something other than an old friendship with his father. I couldn't do it, for a reason that was the source of my worries from then on.

"To a friend who'd kept an eye on my son in my absence, and who was a lawyer, I confided the secret of his birth and my intention to restore his real name to him. My friend was appalled at the news. Without meaning to, I'd committed a crime, and I'd made him my accomplice. Believing I'd sent him Dumont's real son, he'd taken all the steps necessary to have him acknowledged as such. He'd summoned a family gathering; a guardian had been appointed; Dumont's estate, small as it was, had been settled on the boy, at the expense of Dumont's nephews. He'd been placed in a lycée using a birth certificate that gave him his name. In short, it was a true identity theft.

"That's when my friend put a terrible fear in my mind: if Dumont's son wasn't really dead, then we'd consigned to a life of misery and abandonment a child whose modest inheritance from his father would've been supplemented by the Emperor's generosity, since the imperial recommendation by itself had given the child who was passing as him a full stipend at a lycée. I trembled at the thought; but I was so convinced Dumont's son was dead that I reassured my friend. Then he said the most prudent course would be to carry on as in the past. As for the inheritance, under the guise of settlements and shares we turned it over to the rightful heirs, and I was treated as the most generous of friends. I was ashamed, but I had to keep quiet."

"Well!" said Henriette. "Is that a serious enough crime to keep you awake? Whom did you harm? No one. And aren't you convinced, in your conscience, that if Captain Dumont's son had lived you'd have done for him everything you appear to have done?"

"But if he's alive," replied d'Aspert in a low voice, "if in fact I've robbed him of his name, his fortune, his future... Or rather, if I've doomed my own son... If I've been punished for lying by the lie itself!..."

"What are you trying to say?" cried Henriette.

"You don't understand me!" cried the general. "And in all this chaos of events and doubts and uncertainties, I don't know whether I understand myself. Let me finish. Up to last year nothing had troubled my certainty. At that time Sergeant Bazil came to me, saying he'd been summoned by the police to testify on behalf of young Dumont. He read me the statement he'd made, and whose circumstances I knew. But what I learned in conversation with him, which I hadn't known, was that as they crossed the Roman Campagna together the boy had spoken very clearly of his childhood memories, and recognized places he said he'd been to with his father.

"Since my plan from the first was to let my son believe he was Charles Dumont, I'd never drawn his attention to his earliest years, feeling sure that, by never speaking of them, those memories would fade away completely or would become so confused he could never betray my secret by what he said. What I learned from Bazil made me tremble; because if by chance the young man really was Charles Dumont, what had become of my son? Had he been killed in the attack on my palace? Sure, the crime I thought I'd committed would be erased, but I'd have lost my son. The dilemma was awful, and the more awful because I couldn't get out of it. My son, or Dumont's son—anyway that young man whom I no longer know what to call—was a prisoner in Russia, and I believed he was dead."

"So he isn't?"

"No, thank God!" cried d'Aspert. "Whoever he is, he's alive, and he'll be coming back to us. I'll question him, I'll search his memory for the fatal truth. Fatal no matter what, because I have other reasons to suspect that Dumont's son wasn't murdered as I'd believed."

"And how did you receive that new information?"

"Like this. After my palace was looted, I filed suit against the city of Rome to compensate me for my losses. I won that suit, and my lawyer handed all the documents over to me, but I never examined them. A few days ago, being required to present my credentials to the war ministry, I was going through all my papers when I came across the police report that had been drawn up the day after the mob looted my palace. It stated that a child had presented himself, bearing a letter from Captain Dumont, recommending his son to me; that since the captain's real son had been caught in the palace and recognized as such by an individual named Durand, the newcomer had been chased away as a little vagrant; that the other boy had been set free on his own demand, to wait, he said, for the sergeant who, in accordance with my orders, would take him to France. The anger the Roman authorities felt at my conduct, and their hatred for the French, can explain, if not excuse, their casually abandoning unknown children who were connected to me.

"In any case, that's what happened, that's what I learned, that's what makes me despair. For now who was the sad, weeping child Bazil found sitting at the gates of my palace? Was it my son who'd come back and who was reciting the story I'd taught him? Was it the real Charles Dumont, whose abandonment and despair had brought him back to the deserted gates of the place where he'd found shelter? I don't know. My mind struggles to unravel all those circumstances and explain them. The one thing that stands out, clearly and horribly, is that I've disinherited a child of his name or his fortune, which is a terrible crime; or that I've lost my son, which is a misfortune no less terrible. And now that he's coming back, I don't know how to decide. I don't know if I'll have the courage to question that young man. Either I have to give up the sweetest illusion of my life, or I have to take on a terrible remorse; either I have to learn that I have no more child, or I have to know that another child paid with his future and maybe with his life for the future and the life of my son. The uncertainty is awful. On both sides there's crime and misfortune... So you can see, Henriette, I too need a heart that pities me, that consoles me, and above all that supports me in what remains for me to do to repair the wrong I've done."

"Alas!" said Henriette. "Based on everything you've just told me, you're more unfortunate than guilty; because everything seems to suggest that the child you thought was your son bears the name that really belongs to him."

"You're right. And if I remain uncertain, it's because paternal love speaks louder in my heart than honor; it's because I'm afraid to see the truth; it's because I'm not so horrified at having doomed a stranger as I am at having lost my son. Sometimes I've wanted to question the duchess..."

D'Aspert suddenly fell silent.

"Who were you speaking of?" asked Henriette.

"Oh, someone who was in Rome, who might've heard what happened. But I neither want to, nor should, confide in her. That's the thinking of a man who clings to the feeblest glimmer of hope he sees."

Henriette could easily see he was hiding something from her. But she didn't feel she had the right to question him. She said nothing, and the general pursued his train of thought about the Duchess of Avarenne. He pictured his son, wandering the streets after the palace was looted, being found by some servant of the duchess's and taken to his mother and raised even more secretly than he'd been before. He'd constructed an entire narrative, and was perhaps on the point of resolving to confide everything to the duchess, when Lussay came back. He was gloomy, and seemed ashamed at being seen again by d'Aspert.

The latter rose as he entered, and, going to meet him, said solemnly, "Lussay, on my honor, your daughter is innocent. Are you yourself as sure you're not guilty?"

"What do you mean?"

"I'm certain that someone infamously violated her, and that that violation was perpetrated during mesmeric sleep: which leaves no memories when you wake, which makes the sleeper, body and soul, the slave of whoever imposed it, and which is within your power."

"So!" cried Lussay, his whole face turning white. "She's accusing me! Abomination!"

He threw himself like a madman at his daughter, but d'Aspert stopped him. "She's not accusing anyone. She's saying, 'I'm not guilty.' Can you say that with the same confidence?"

"Ah, that was the only trick missing!" cried Lussay. "This new accusation will be her last crime!"

"She's only looking at you till you can point her to someone else," said d'Aspert, eyeing Lussay steadily.

"Someone else!" said Lussay, struck by an idea that seemed to him to illuminate the past. "Someone else... Yes, someone else... That could be."

His daughter listened eagerly. Lussay questioned her anxiously, but nothing came of it... not a single clue... not a single memory... That didn't surprise him. But after a moment of silence he cried, "Well then!... I'll find out!... I'll find out!... He'll have to answer me!"

"Will he be willing to?" asked d'Aspert.

"Oh, I'll force him to."

"In that case," replied d'Aspert, "I claim the right: I'm more accustomed than you are to weapons."

"Weapons!" smiled Lussay. "That's not how I'll make him talk... I have a much more certain way, one that will deny him all avoidance, all lies, all subterfuge."

"More nonsense!" said d'Aspert.

"General," replied Lussay, "it'll be a terrible struggle, but I believe I won't fail. If what you call my nonsense caused my daughter's fall, at least allow it to be used for revenge. And if that goal seems insufficient to you, above all let it be used to justify me."

"That's no longer necessary. I don't know the secrets of your so-called science, but I know that in a man's tone of voice there's an unequaled power that attests to the truth louder than words. That power was in your daughter's voice when she told me, 'I'm innocent.' It was in your despair and your anger when I tossed out my accusation against you, on the off chance. I'm sure someone else is guilty."

"Thank you, thank you," said Lussay. "I believe you too... You've brought light to a very dark day, and consolation too, since it makes me see Henriette as unfortunate, but stainless... Come, my daughter, come. Forgive your father... Forgive him... If you only knew what it's like to believe in your child's shame!"

Weeping, Henriette threw herself in her father arms. She stayed there a long time, as to recoup all the embraces she'd missed.

Finally d'Aspert said to Lussay, "And now won't you allow her to embrace her husband?"

Lussay didn't understand, and the general explained completely. They were happy that night, happy for a moment, during which they forgot the past and had no thought for the future.

IX. DESCRIPTION

That's the most honest chapter title in the world. It warns the reader of the danger he faces, and allows him to hop right over it or to tackle it voluntarily. That's a rarity these days, in which titles are a very commonplace fraud in modern literature. Of course, I have less right than anyone to moralize on the subject: it seems to me that at some time or other I enclosed, in a collective title that announced an almost maritime book, *Créteil Harbor*,[51] a dozen short stories in which I can't recall the slightest harbor or the slightest boat. I don't even know whether there was a drop of water in all those stories, unless one or another of my readers went so far as to shed tears over the depravity of authors and booksellers. And on the subject of that depravity, I could tell you, in the form of a reflective commentary… But allow me to open a parenthesis here.

(I'm gathering my thoughts for that commentary, which I intend to replace the preface. Nobody reads the preface anymore, I know. Readers don't like that rumination at the front of the book, explaining the philosophical idea the writer had, and the goal he set for himself in writing: an admirably useful precaution in a literature like ours, devoid of either goals or ideas. Readers—well warned that such and such a book, in which humanity is condemned in the form of its most deplorable anomalies, is just a way of making them love virtue—eager for what they've been told to expect, search for the promised moral, wait for it, pursue it, and finish the book without having found it; which they certainly wouldn't have done without that warning. The preface has another purpose, which is to tell readers, "Notice that this is a serious and deeply considered book, and on pain of being taken for an ignorant, superficial person, you can't admit it bored you."

(The preface has been a place of vengeance for all of the author's failed works; the preface has been a substitute for critical analysis; the preface has been the author's life story; the preface has been a speech in defense of leftist opinions that once were rightist; the preface has been

---

[51]*Le Port de Créteil* (1833), a collection of short stories by Soulié, came out only a year before *Le Magnétiseur*, but in that interval he wrote at least three plays and two novels.

something sublime; but in the end the preface has outlived its time. Readers dread it, flee from it, loathe it almost as much as the dedication. So I want to replace it with the reflective commentary. The commentary, as I see it, is in fact nothing but the preface dispersed, the poison diluted in a greater quantity of liquid, which the reader will drink without resistance, and without the disgust he feels for the preface concentrated. If this isn't a new idea, then too bad for the public; because in our day the public is a devouring and quickly sated monster. The monster needs two new volumes to absorb every morning; and yet at the fifth or sixth iteration of an idea he doesn't want it anymore, he finds it cold, worn out, thin as dishwater, and he rejects it. Nowadays the eel pâté wouldn't last till the third day. I'll close my parenthesis here, because that last thought leads me directly to the commentary I wanted to write on the depravity of writers and booksellers.)

I could tell you that their depravity—the one at least by which they mockingly use the titles of their books to lie openly to the public—is not of their making. Observe indeed the infatuations and the disgusts of our world. Let an English book appear, labeled as a "historical novel": everyone with the patience to read old histories, and the power to dramatize them, rushes to construct historical novels, because the historical novel is much in demand, much appreciated, much sought after. "Blech!" says the public at the third example, "drive away those pale imitations, the *servum pecus*[52] of Horace (whom they've never read), I don't want any more! Shoot them! Shoot them! Their books are everywhere!"

Are they writing tales of the fantastic in Germany, which are eagerly received in France? Let's all rush to tales of the fantastic. "What's that?" (pronounced "wuhzzat") cries the noble public. "What! That man who's out for a stroll and who just had dinner writes tales of the fantastic! That other man wearing gloves and eyeing that dancer writes them too! That's indecent! A tale of the fantastic requires the soul of a dreamer and the manners of a poet. Down, down with tales of the fantastic!" And the sea tale, that fine sea tale that luffed and reefed and stowed and furled, look what kind of welcome it gets today: we've had it up to the hatches, we don't want any more of it. There are readers who'd rather see the entire French Navy sink than swallow one more page of a sea tale.

The same goes for fairy tales, for short stories, for chronicles: people wanted them at first, to the point that the booksellers never had enough.

---

[52]Literally "slavish cattle"; used by the Roman poet Horace to refer to fawning flatterers.

141

"Write more fairy tales, you gentlemen of the pen!" The publishers, delighted, commissioned them by the handful, like fresh eggs. Writers were so pleased, they willingly waived their four percent. But then—Bam! Bif! Poof! Pow! Crash!—while the in-octavo sheets were still at the printer, the fairy tale, the short story, the chronicle, all tumbled into the abyss of public boredom. It was a book doomed in advance, pushed out of the reader's family like a posthumous child born after the tenth month. So the publisher and the writer got smart: they thought up a title that didn't give away the fairy tale, the short story, the chronicle; and with a little imagination, they called one *The Such and Such*, another *A So and So*, et cetera, et cetera. Do you have any idea how many titles have fooled you? Well, in good conscience, is that the fault of the trade or of the public? That of the public, of course, for not understanding that working in a genre doesn't mean imitating works in that genre; and for rejecting books based on their title, which means they get fooled by titles and they deserve it.

There are stubborn people who, rather than admitting their own responsibility, tell us, "Well, gentlemen, why don't you invent something original, some new form, bold, unexpected, that doesn't come from abroad and isn't reused from some old tome?" But just between us, and without addressing the question of whether there's anything new in literature, since we're speaking frankly now: are the thousand or twelve hundred readers or reading clubs that buy a novel worth taking the risk of being original and innovative? No, my word! "Oh, the impudent, insolent author!" cries the reader. Even more impudent and insolent than you know. Foremost and above all, there aren't enough of you, you who love literature simply for itself, for us to write you a good, purely literary book. The masses spend their time in ideas applied to things; and there's neither profit nor glory except in politics and industry and business. And besides, there's no nation less receptive to original ideas than ours. We don't have a single man of any distinction who hasn't been mocked almost to death the moment he stepped off the beaten path.

Don't you remember that Chénier,[53] making a literary report to the Institute, couldn't find enough ridicule for the author of *Atala* and *The*

---

[53] Marie-Joseph Chénier (1764-1811): a poet, playwright, and Revolutionary politician. The "report" Soulié mentions here is probably his 1808 *Tableau historique de l'état et du progrés de la littérature française depuis 1789 jusqu'à 1808* ("Historical overview of the state and progress of French literature from 1789 to 1808"). The "Institute" refers to a national literary body established by Napoleon.

Genius of Christianity,[54] and didn't even mention Madame de Staël,[55] who was as forgotten in that report as if she'd died, or rather as if she'd never lived? Wasn't Lamartine[56] rejected before his friends passed him off as some kind of lesser Byron? I won't speak of Hugo, who's still fighting; nor of Dumas, who's being torn apart—proof that he's alive, no matter what they say in the *Journal of Debates.*[57]

So what is it you want? People to jeer at them when they've worked hard? Might as well be jeered without the hard work. That's why you get so many bad books... That's why you have this book. I added that last part to save readers the trouble—those readers, sparkling with wit, who add their thoughts in the margins of a book they borrowed for four sous, which ruins the book and is therefore not an act of scrupulous decency.

I feel like I can see the reader's anger or scorn as he reads all these reflections. Most of all, I can see his indignation against an author who boasts of the honesty of his chapter title on the first line of this chapter, only to fall short on the next line. Well! That was one last excusable trick, not to make you read these grievances, but to keep you from reading them. At that title, "Description," most readers will have skipped this chapter and continued the book with the tolerance it needs; and the author will be able to indulge the small boast that he told the public the truth without any harm coming to him.

So now I'll continue; and believe me, if I describe anything, it's not to keep the promise of my chapter title, but because it's part of the plan I've drawn up—for this book is following a plan, though you may act like you doubt that.

THE FORGE

---

[54]François-René de Chateaubriand (1768-1848): a writer, politician, diplomat and historian. His *Génie du christianisme* (1802) was a defense of Catholicism at a time when atheism was prevalent in intellectual circles.
[55]Germaine de Staël (1766-1817): a prominent philosopher, writer, and political theorist.
[56]Alphonse de Lamartine (1790-1869): a poet, prose writer, and statesman.
[57]The *Journal des Débats Politiques et Littéraires* was the most widely read newspaper in France in the 1820s and 30s.

When the ballet entitled *Vulcan's Nets*[58] was put on at the Opéra, there was an explosion of admiration—spoken, shouted, written, printed—for the stage set representing the forge of Jupiter's lame son, who was so exquisitely performed by Mérante. Well, those speakers, shouters, writers, and printers should all have been sent to Charenton, not to be locked up in the insane asylum there, but to see the forge built by Messrs Mamby, Wilson, and Co.[59]

My God! Those cast iron columns poorly reflecting a reddish light, those metal caves where a pot on the fire was meant to represent a furnace, and where a rod burning with a violet flame represented an iron bar about to be forged—what a weak, miserly effect! Surely that was the time to go big, to go spectacular, to go beyond nature! The workshop of a god! It needed to be at least as good as the workshop of some provincial locksmith. Alas, it was and still is beneath a farrier's smithy. Imagine that that was where lightning was created; the only people who'd believe it would be members of the public you're familiar with.

But O beautiful and magnificent forge at Charenton! Vast, sublime creation of industry! Nothing retains an image of your infernal appearance; not even painting has attempted to recreate it. Imagine a dark night—if people whose nights are lit by the glow of streetlights even know what a dark night in the country is like, when everything is the same color, trees and houses, foliage and brilliant flowers, when distances can't be reckoned, and a bush six feet from you looks like an enormous oak tree far away, whereas a tower that stands out on a hill looks like a leafless tree trunk by the side of the road.

On a night like that, if you'd gone to visit that forge at Charenton, you would've thought you were seeing a hundred enormous roaring bonfires in the distance. You'd have seen its fourteen fire pumps with their hundred-yard-tall chimneys, from which the flames rush out with a furious whistling, hurling pillars of dark smoke into the sky, which the breeze spreads out over the countryside like a black curtain; then its sixty furnaces with their gullets of fire below and the plumes of fire at the top of their brick chimneys—all of that fire roaring around you and lit by stars so white

---

[58]*Les Filets de Vulcain* (1826), a ballet and pantomime by Jean-Madeleine Schneitzhoeffer.

[59]Aaron Mamby, an English engineer, and Daniel Wilson, a Scottish chemist, created the *Companie Englaise*, whose ironworks at Charenton pioneered the production of steam engines and heavy machinery in France after the Restoration. In 1822 they won the concession to provide gas lighting for Paris streets.

they burn your eyes where the bellows inject moist air into the flames to be consumed.

And iron everywhere, molten here, hammered there, but everywhere red and flaming, poured like lava into immense molds in which it becomes the roof of a house or the hull of a ship, or poured into the tilted grooves of a rolling mill, which, starting with a flaming block of iron, turns it into a six-foot cylinder the size of a man, then a tree trunk like a squared-off poplar, then a branch as slender as a Gothic column, then an enormous flexible cord that emerges in serpentine curves from the terrible pressure of the rollers, then a bar already as thin as an arm, then a rod, then a ribbon, and always glowing red, with flames from white to cherry red.

And among all those machines at work, colossal men move around those blocks of fire with six-foot-long pincers and throw those fiery masses either into the roller or under the steam hammer that beats endlessly in perfect time, under which they turn over the iron to make anvils, plowshares, metal blocks; while others, attached to or suspended from the immense levers of the machines, ride along with great crucibles in which molten iron boils, so as to pour it boldly into the yawning mouth of a mold; and all that on a ground black with slag, black with the coal that other men hurl incessantly into the famished mouth of the furnaces.

Yes, it's truly beautiful, and no sight has ever surprised and terrified me as much; for in that awesome array there wasn't a single machine that wouldn't have consumed or crushed in less than a second anyone who got too close. My God! The ancients—who created the Corinthian column after seeing a palm tree, and myths of giants based on Mount Etna, and the mask of Jupiter from the human face—they would've made something fine out of the forge at Charenton!

But there are forges and forges, and the one I owe you a description of didn't resemble that one in any way.

"Then why describe the forge at Charenton?"

"To entertain myself."

"But we're not entertained."

"Do I care?"

By the side of a road bordered by woods, turning right on your way out of the village of l'Étang, you followed a lane wide enough for two carts to pass but narrow enough for the branches of the trees to meet overhead. At the entrance to that lane there was a wretched inn, with a bundle of holly as its sign. You followed the lane for about two and a half miles, without seeing any other habitation than some shabby charcoal burners' huts next to their smoldering pits; the density of the forest limited the view to a distance of a few yards. Suddenly, at a bend in the lane, you could see a wider horizon: it was a funnel-shaped valley, whose elliptical bottom was filled by a beautiful lake. On all sides of the lake the forest rose in the form of an amphitheater, except at the foot of the lane, where the lake, held back by a narrow dam, escaped into a ravine, flowing out by way of a dozen waterfalls through a dozen immense wheels, which turned the machines in the ironworks raised on pilings above the dam.

At one end of the dam stood a steep-roofed house with a tower in one corner for the spiral staircase that seemed to have been forgotten in the original design of the building. A short distance away, in three or four clearings made in the wooded slopes, stood small brick forts of some sort: those were the furnaces for the forge. Here and there were carts loaded with wood, with iron ore, with pig iron; and women, children, a few watchdogs—a world of people, but a world apart, shut off in this narrow space, counting the days till they could leave the woods that cut them off, and even more the days till a stranger should come all the way to them.

You had to go down the cinder-covered lane, which seemed to fall steeply toward the lake, turning only a few feet from the dam, with no railing or hedge to protect a reckless cart that didn't make the turn carefully. Then you crossed the dam, which you could feel shaking from the water wheels and from the force of the water hurling itself through the dozen openings, and you reached the other side of the lake. To the right, next to the factories, stood a cluster of boilers, home to the blacksmiths; to the left, without a fence, without a yard, without a flowerbed, without a lawn around it, was the house with the tower: the owner's house, General d'Aspert's house.

Going in, you entered a vast hall: there was no antechamber. That was the dining room, paved with gray flagstones. A large glistening oak table always occupied the middle of the room. Around it stood open-work cane chairs, whose seat and back cushions were attached with cotton ties. On the walls hung two barometers, a pendulum clock in its case, a few maps—almost the whole of Europe, printed under the Empire, with the naive and sublime title of *Theater of War*—engravings from paintings by Greuze,[60]

---

[60]Jean-Baptiste Greuze (1725-1805): a painter of portraits, genre scenes, and historical tableaux.

Prud'hon's *Child*,[61] Charlet's first lithograph,[62] of two grenadiers defending their flag. In the corner was a passageway leading to the kitchen. A door opening onto the garden, across from the front door, was flanked by two large buffets that projected prominently up to shoulder height, then narrowed as they rose to the ceiling. Here and there stood serving carts with their deep tin wells for holding bottles. And finally there was an enormous walk-in fireplace with a mantelpiece of carved oak, flanked by two benches and a double rack of oak on which lay four or five hunting guns, a rifle, and a blunderbuss.

If you crossed the length of the room you'd reach a door similar to the one you entered by, leading to what was called the garden. If you turned to the right you'd find the parlor. The vast fireplace recurred there, but more elegant and more richly sculpted. All around it was gray paneling, with a wide baseboard and a projecting chair rail, marked off in squares or oval frames surrounded by carved flowers. Magnificent wallpaper covered the room, showing scenes from the life of Alexander the Great; it was said to be a gift from Louis XV to the previous owner of the forge, for his remarkable manufacture of the ironwork for the locks on the Languedoc canal. The furniture, normally covered in protective draping, came from the same source; it was much spoken of in the area, and had made familiar the name of Gobelins.[63] In the middle of the parlor stood a square table covered with a lace cloth with a fringe; two console tables with splendid copper inlay and with yellow marble satyr's feet; two enormous armchairs, not matching the other furniture, in green velvet with gold marbling, with bolsters for the back and wings for the head; an ebony pedestal table; card tables inlaid in black and copper; and a tortoiseshell backgammon board inlaid outside and in with rosewood, ivory, and mother-of-pearl.

On the fireplace stood a clock with spiral columns and gilt trim; several candelabra, whose elaborate stems spread out into twelve or fifteen tulips to hold candles; and mirrors whose joins were concealed under flower garlands. The ceiling was painted in oils, showing Cupid parading

---

[61]Pierre-Paul Prud'hon (1758-1823): a painter of portraits and allegorical scenes. The reference is probably to his popular *L'enfant au chien* ("The boy with the dog").

[62]Nicolas-Toussaint Charlet (1792-1845): a painter and printmaker, specializing in military subjects.

[63]The Gobelins factory in Paris was founded by Louis XIV to produce furniture for the royal palaces and government buildings.

around with doves; from it hung a chandelier with gilt ornaments and pendants of rock crystal. Finally, in the midst of all those luxurious furnishings were a few rackets, shuttlecocks, hoops, some needlework in progress, and in one corner a small writing desk, which, when it left Paris, must've been the only presentable piece in the house, and which now, amid the riches and the splendid relics of our parents' luxury, looked cheap and shamefaced, like a music-hall couplet in a tragedy by Pierre Corneille.

One more room and I'm done. Beyond the parlor, reached by a low door covered by a curtain, was a boudoir—but a boudoir of that period: a sofa with large cushions, wall hangings of embroidered muslin against a background of Marie-Louise blue,[64] a cheval glass, a Roman console table, a vanity table with columns, a piano by Érard, gondola chairs, an Aubusson carpet, and gold-framed mirrors everywhere they could fit.

That's all the detail necessary for our story. The rest of the house was also luxurious in a style different from that of today, but we won't take our readers on a tour. There were half a dozen bedrooms on each upstairs floor. The garden, properly speaking, was just a half acre of flowerbeds. No trees had been planted for shade, since the forest was right there. Nor was there a pond with a few goldfish; they made do with the lake. Ten yards away, to one side, stood another building, containing the offices of the forge and a few decent lodgings. Then came the warehouses, and beyond them the forest began again. That's where the drama took place.

[64]Marie-Louise, Duchess of Parma (1791-1847) was Napoleon's second wife, and Empress from 1810 till 1814.

X. CHARACTERS

That's where a number of people important to this book lived: d'Aspert, Lussay, Henriette; and later that questionable person, who has yet to appear in these pages except by name, the Russian prisoner, Captain Dumont. However, though only a year had passed since their move to the Tremblay region, at least the first-named of them were no longer the people we knew; or rather they no longer showed the lack of character that used to confuse them in all of that Parisian world, among all those people of the Empire, upon whom some of the great man's stature, his brilliance, his grand ideas had rubbed off.

When an emphatic stamp is put on a century, when a strong will guides it, it becomes cloaked in a uniform color, a general manner under which individuals who don't have the power to resist it disappear. Consider the century of Louis XIV: all of his generals, his courtesans, even his literary men, have a demeanor, a family resemblance, that makes them all look like their master. Go back to the century of that Sardanapalus Henri III; beneath its lecherous failings you'll see such original characters, such strong individuals in history and drama! Go forward, and notice how later the strength of Henri IV's reign eclipsed the prominent figures of the Catholic League; then see how they returned under Louis XIII, a weak prince fought over by courtesans and ministers; and how those characters teemed again during the Fronde; and how they finally disappeared under the Sun King.

The great emperor was like the great king: during his impetuous reign he absorbed the already feeble remains of the Revolution; other than him, there were no prominent figures except those who were the most like him, either by their courage or by the boldness of their luck. So most of the generals under the Empire, marching to the beat of the drum that set the pace for France, shared a uniformly brave, devoted military character, following the flag as long as the flag was upright. But as soon as it fell, there was an utter rout; they were no longer the men they'd once been. The great feeling of being the conquerors of Europe, which wrapped them in some strange power, disappeared with their master, and each of them became himself again, and himself alone.

Remember also how those whose luck was worth more than they were had little self-esteem and sold themselves for very little; and how all those who'd grown unexpectedly great on the soil of France let themselves be scattered at the Restoration by the call to dismiss: true obedient soldiers, to whom it didn't occur that with the Army of the Loire, their old army of a hundred and twenty thousand men, they could've fought back and prevailed. Three noblemen from the Vendée had begun their uprising with a hundred and fifty peasants.

A few of them survived the universal disappearance, in which so many men returned to the shadows once the torch that had lit them had gone out: those few were the ones to whom the speaker's platform or banishment offered another field of battle and action. Almost all the rest, reduced to themselves, went off to live or die in obscurity—to live or die indifferently. When the supernatural stimulation that had sustained them for twenty years was used up, they subsided into bad-tempered regrets, into mercantile occupations, into laziness, into boredom, into the *Constitutional*.[65] They felt their wounds and their rheumatism. They were finished.

D'Aspert was one of those men. When he was a general of the Republic, free to act and to command on his own responsibility, he seemed like one of the great spirits that were transforming Europe. Under the Empire, reduced to understanding and obeying—but understanding a genius and obeying sublime orders—he was one of those minds of steel that chance seemed to have created for Napoleon. But under the Restoration he became Jean d'Aspert once again; he put away his epaulets, he hung his sword from the head of his bed, and he became the master of a forge. He'd bought the Tremblay forge and had taken Henriette there, after marrying her in Paris. He still had the childhood sensitivity that made him resent the superiority of aristocrats, and the soldier's courage, which might not have faced down the sight of the scaffold, but which, with a sword or a gun in hand, considered death no more than an ordinary enemy, met a hundred times and beaten a hundred times. From lack of activity he'd gotten gout, and he often spent months at a time in his armchair. He was neither bitter nor a scold, but he was sad and bored.

One thing made him despair: the malicious, hateful slander that had welcomed him on his return. For those of his generation who, having been

---

[65] *Le Constitutionel* was a newspaper with a liberal, Bonapartist, anti-clerical slant. It was suppressed several times in the early nineteenth century, though by the 1840s it strongly supported Louis Napoléon and eventually the Second Empire.

born poor, hadn't become rich, he was a thief; for those who'd only managed to become clerks or lawyers, he was an idiot or an ignoramus who'd risen by trickery. There were some who said he didn't know how to read, especially two merino farmers who subscribed to the *Mercury*. Those people, far from being proud of their brother having risen to be a count of the Empire, only referred to him by that title derisively. Only the peasants and laborers, many of whom had been soldiers, adored him and were grateful for his benevolence, which the greedy landowners of the area saw as impertinent ostentation. The familiarity with which he'd greeted them had been taken as insolent condescension; and they preferred being looked haughtily up and down by the Duchess of Avarenne, when she visited her chateau at l'Étang, to having d'Aspert extend his hand for them to shake at Tremblay. As a result, he received no one, except for Monsieur Bizot and his wife. Partly ruined by the stock market collapse of 1814 and 1815, they'd had to withdraw to the country, and they'd chosen a place where they knew people. They lived about two miles away, in a town that had a lawyer. The mesmeric child had died; people said Bizot had been happy about that.

Lussay lived with his son-in-law, but he wasn't much company for him. Lost in thoughts he shared with no one, he lived in solitude with what family he had left. Silent, already an old man but a brusque, pale, nervous, energetic one, he still maintained his passion for mesmerism; and since d'Aspert loathed the very name of that alleged science, Lussay never spoke to him about it. The ennobled doctor therefore went out to the cottages, mesmerizing, studying, experimenting, without d'Aspert even wanting to know the reason for his frequent absences. The general was reduced to looking forward to Bizot's visits—Bizot who would listen, who shared his beliefs, who was a liberal, who played piquet and trictrac well enough and with enough enthusiasm for the game to be exciting.

When the fervent sentiments of youth and the vigorous battles against the world have passed, solitude has the effect of fastening itself on the puerile things that remain in life. If the profusion of interests available in Paris doesn't spare worn-out people that passionate taste for trivial things, how much more powerful must that impulse be in the country, how much more for someone who's withdrawn to a country house! Alas, in one village backwater I knew a man who'd been chief of police under Fouché and Rovigo,[66] and who in the evening talked to us about nothing but forced quinolas[67] the night before at the priest's or the tax collector's. We had a colonel who'd been in Egypt and Russia, and who remembered nothing but a game of trictrac by correspondence, won empty-handed, in which he'd taken forty-eight points on a single return run. For some it's hunting, for others it's fishing; I've known some who raised canaries: O misery!

But if solitude has that effect on old souls and closed minds, it also animates to an extraordinary degree those who have something left to give in their hearts and minds, and especially those who are rich in unspent youth. And such were Henriette and Charles Dumont.

Henriette, removed from the world, innocent at heart though with a disgrace on her brow, without ever having loved, having burned through neither her soul nor her emotions, was twenty-three. It was now 1818. She'd come to the solitude of Tremblay with her whole life to live, even to begin. Caring for her child, and the gratitude she felt for d'Aspert, had kept her busy at first and had been enough. The novelty of the general's occupation—she often accompanied him to the ironworks—had interested her for a while. But when the general became gouty and sedentary, all those days spent by his side, staring at the wallpaper, her mind empty, felt long to endure. The thousand things she tried, in an attempt to fill them, showed how heavily the time weighed on her.

Till the start of 1818, Dumont, desperate to keep up a career he'd begun so brilliantly, had stayed in Paris looking for work. He'd only reached the capital after d'Aspert and his wife had left, so that he was essentially unknown to them. Still, one day the general, feeling he was unable to continue managing his property, said to Henriette, "For several days I've had a plan I'd like to carry out, and about which I want your advice. I need someone to take my place here. Charles is wasting his youth sitting around in waiting rooms in Paris; I want to bring him here. Whether or not he's my son, I love him as if he were. He'll have not only my affection but yours. I'll will him half my fortune and keep the other half for your child. And when he's here I'll try to clear up a mystery that obsesses me."

---

[66] Joseph Fouché (1759-1820): a zealous and much-feared minister of police under the Directoire, the Consulate, and the Empire. Anne Jean-Marie René Savary, Duke of Rovigo (1774-1833): Napoleon's minister of police from 1810 to 1814.
[67] In the card game reversis, the jack of hearts was called the quinola; to be forced to play it resulted in a penalty paid to the other players.

So said the general; but there was in that speech much more in the way of conventional expressions than of real need for affection or a desire for answers. He needed a man; he preferred that it be his adopted son; that was all. There was a mystery about that young man's birth that nagged at him; he couldn't pretend indifference to that, and so he spoke about it; again, that was all. But it was no longer the painful anxiety it had once been, that fear of having jeopardized the fate of his son or that of a stranger's. Gout had filled up a great deal of the general's thoughts; piquet and trictrac had diminished his interest in his son.

Still, Henriette happily agreed. She spoke enthusiastically of the need to uncover Charles's real identity. She was clear about wanting him to be d'Aspert's son. Perhaps, without being conscious of it, she'd noticed her husband's lack of interest in matters of the heart, and she'd realized they were no longer in the same place they'd been the day she agreed to marry him; and that, if he considered dispassionately his position relative to Charles, he might well reconsider with displeasure his position relative to her. Indeed sometimes, when the general reflected, which didn't happen often, he was vexed by his odd position, between a young man who might or might not be his son, and a child whose father was unknown. He recalled Lussay's promise; and, seeing that Lussay let his resentment as a father remain dormant, he told himself he was wrong to worry about things that could only bring sorrow. Then he wanted Bizot, and sent for him, and in a game of six-king piquet he recovered the equanimity he'd lost for a moment.

So Charles was sent for. He announced his arrival at some distant time, and they waited patiently, with little concern and no hurry. Only Madame Bizot asked if he was friendly, if he was good-looking, if he could play the guitar. No one could answer her questions. D'Aspert said he was brave, and Henriette, who'd read the letters he sent her husband, said he seemed very educated. Lussay, who'd seen him a few times between his leaving school and his joining the army, remembered him as some kind of Hercules, upon whom mesmerism would probably have no effect.

While they waited, the general's illness grew worse; he was reduced to never leaving his armchair, and his business suffered. He was almost angry with Charles; he found him ungrateful, and he wrote him a letter he would've thought harsh a few years earlier, telling him to choose clearly, either to accept to refuse his offer, almost in the tone you'd use with a clerk. The letter was sent, and the next day, his mood growing worse along with his gout, he agreed with a factory manager's suggestion that Charles

153

was a Parisian who'd refuse to come. It was only at Henriette's insistence that he waited long enough for a reply. But he still had an apartment prepared for the manager, while he grumbled about young people, barely recalling the interest he'd taken in this particular young person.

One night—it was already September, and the equinoctial wind blew hard, rushing into the hollow of the Tremblay valley—it was ten o'clock. Bizot and his wife were visiting. The evening had wrapped up early, because they'd talked instead of playing games, and they'd all withdrawn to their rooms. The general, in great pain and sleepless for the past few days, on Lussay's advice had taken a grain of opium to help him sleep. Opium has such a reputation as a soporific that d'Aspert had agreed, even though it was Lussay who suggested it. The latter had returned to his own room, dropping from exhaustion, because he'd spent the whole day going around the nearby shacks and villages. Monsieur and Madame Bizot slept side by side, bored with one another.

Only one light was on in the house: it was in Henriette's room. The conversation had left some residual emotion in her; but on the surface it had been nothing that ought to have agitated a beautiful young woman: the deadline for Charles's reply had passed that same day, and the general had announced angrily that he'd settle matters in the morning with the manager. They'd also talked a great deal about a muted disturbance among the workers and the charcoal burners in the forest. It seemed they were reading the *Constitutional* out loud in the nightclubs, with the orators, meaning the readers, standing on the tables. Lussay had cried out against revolutionaries. D'Aspert—whose business was doing worse every day, whose factory output had diminished noticeably, and who never managed to complete his orders on time—had said there was nothing surprising about the idea of rebelling against a government that was ruining industry. They'd gotten worked up, and exchanged some sharp words. Lussay had gone so far as to say it wasn't surprising that people who owed their promotion to the chaotic times of the Revolution would welcome even minor signs of another one. The general had replied that every man had risen according to his talents. Lussay had shrugged, and d'Aspert had said bluntly that the only disappointed people where those who confused absurd dreams for talent. Lussay had answered, "Absurd for those who don't understand them." D'Aspert had said bitterly, "Their results attest to their greatness." A look from Henriette had made them both stop. Meanwhile Bizot had been calmly cleaning his teeth with his toothpick; Madame Bizot had been

154

yawning, for she hadn't said anything, and she liked to keep busy. They'd all parted, if not angrily, at least eager to be separated.

In her room Henriette thought about what had just happened. She couldn't put her reflections into definite words. She wasn't analyzing to its full extent the unpleasant change that had come over her husband. She didn't see their little disagreements as the seeds of a split. But she was worried; and she longed for some new event, unconnected with all of their concerns, which could absorb everyone's attention, including her own, one of those dramas that can be added to rain and sunny weather to avoid conversations that could only be excessively dull or dangerously interesting.

All of that, plus perhaps the autumn wind that stirs the blood in the heart, had agitated Henriette so much that she'd opened her window in search of calm from the cold night air. The wind ruffled her hair and drove across the surface of the lake the leaves that flew through the air like living beings. Gradually her mind had become absorbed in contemplation; she watched the clouds and listened to the wind whining. Her head had grown heavy; she felt sleep gaining on her, but she had neither the strength nor the will to go wait for it in bed: she'd have had to leave that spot, that wild harmony, that spectacle.

Suddenly she started: she thought she'd heard a horse's hoofbeats near the house. She listened, but heard nothing more. The wind whirled in the valley, and now the rain, which she hadn't noticed, was falling soft and cold on her head. She was about to go in, when a strong, continuous gust of wind, coming from the direction of the forest road toward the house, brought once again the sound of hoofbeats—distinct, hurried, ringing on ground hardened by the slag that was used to cover it. It was a traveler: a traveler at that hour could only be a charcoal burner returning to his cottage. But it was the vigorous step of a lively horse, not one of the wretched beasts that carried charcoal from the forest. Perhaps it was one of those men who secretly roamed the countryside to foment rebellion.

The wind shifted in another direction; the sound stopped, and the roaring of the forest filled the air. Henriette decided to go in. She closed her window and the double shutters that protected it. She went to lie down, and undid her robe; but the wind rushing down the broad chimney brought the sound of those hoofbeats once again, but even closer now. They appeared to come from the top of the rise; and that seemed likely, because they slowed down like those of a horse being cautiously reined in. There was no doubt now that it was someone coming to the forge. She was about the reopen her window to see who it could be, but the storm intensified and burst, and the trees groaned; she could hear nothing besides a steady roar. Perhaps it was an illusion: more than once the wind had brought noises in the night that came from a couple of miles away but that seemed to start only a few steps away! She'd finished undressing and was getting ready to climb into bed, when a terrible cry, followed by a muffled impact, rose above the roaring of the storm.

"God! My God!... The traveler has missed the turn!"

She opened her window. The night was very dark, and the noise of the storm was horrible. She could hear nothing more. She waited for a cry, a call for help, but nothing came through the storm. She tried to remember what she'd heard: it might've been a tree that split and fell into the lake. From time to time the wind dropped, but no voice took advantage of the lull to call out. She reclosed her window, lay down, and went to sleep.

She'd been asleep for half an hour when the fierce barking of the watchdogs woke her with a start. This time there was no mistake: the horse was stamping at the door to the house. Henriette got up, reopened her window, and asked shyly who was there. No one answered. She tried to figure out what could cause that silence, and finally decided the horse was alone: presumably his rider had been drowned. The idea of going to his rescue had no sooner come to her than she decided to carry it out. She put on a robe and her slippers, threw a coat over her shoulders, and went downstairs to wake someone.

She was in the dining room we've already described when she heard a voice that seemed to be addressing the horse at the door. She had no doubt it was the traveler. With her own white hands she undid the iron bars that protected the door from the inside, and immediately opened it. The wind, rushing suddenly in through the open door, blew out the candle she was carrying; Henriette found herself in the dark, facing a man who was leaning against his horse.

She felt almost afraid, but she said right away, "Who's there? What do you want?"

Instead of answering, the stranger said aloud in astonishment, "It's a woman!"

"Yes!" said Henriette quickly, frightened at his words. "But there are other people awake. I'll call for someone."

"No," said the man, reaching out to stop her, "don't call. It'd be better if I went away, if I didn't come in."

He spoke those words sadly. Alongside the coldness of the hand that held her, Henriette felt large drops of some warm liquid flowing. She started. "Were you coming here? Who are you? What do you want?"

Once again the stranger didn't answer. He considered, then said, "Perhaps I'm mistaken. Is this the house of General d'Aspert?"

"Yes, it is."

"Is this where a window was opened and closed twice?"

"That was my window."

"Then farewell. I'm leaving. I won't enter here... This is a house of misfortune."

"Oh!" cried Henriette, who'd been upset by that entire night and who was frightened by this strange conversation. "Why are you cursing this house?"

"This house has long been cursed," said the stranger. "Cursed, not for those who sleep under its roof, but for those who want to get in, in spite of so many warnings."

As he spoke he leaped onto his horse. Henriette, frozen with inexpressible horror, stepped forward to go after him, saying, "Who are you, sir? Who are you? In heaven's name!"

"Be careful," said the stranger. "Don't follow me. You'd slip in my blood and you'd fall."

He rode off at a rapid trot. Henriette, who hadn't moved, heard him going away into the distance. She reclosed the door and felt her way back upstairs to her room. After she'd relit her candle at the lamp that was still burning, she looked at her hands... They were covered in blood.

XI. A NEWCOMER

When dawn finally came, Henriette, broken by her emotions, let herself go to sleep; she slept fairly late. Eventually an unusual noise in the house woke her; amid the loud voices she recognized her husband's, calling to her with a kind of happy impatience. She sat up. Retrieving her still muddled thoughts, she wondered if what she thought had happened in the night had been reality or a dream. She looked at her hands, which were clean and white. She ran to the basin where she remembered washing them: nothing. She recalled that, in her horror at that blood, she'd thrown the water she'd used out the window. She looked down at the spot, and also at the place she believed she'd held that conversation; but she noticed that, as was common practice at other forges but rarely done at Tremblay, workers had dried up the ground soaked by the rain by spreading charcoal cinders over it. She might've undertaken a more detailed investigation of her memories, but she was called once again. She went downstairs, convinced she was being haunted by a terrible dream.

As she entered the dining room, her husband cried, "Henriette! Henriette! It's Charles Dumont! He's finally here!"

Charles Dumont was thirty. His whole being had something poised about it that was neither serenity nor coldness. That demeanor wasn't natural; it was the result of a deliberate choice not to let the actions of his heart show in his face. Nothing about his lithe figure suggested the brute strength Lussay had spoken of. His face had nothing remarkable about it besides the beauty of his eyes and the sparkle of his teeth. He bowed to Henriette, and with great ceremony she returned his greeting.

"Well!" said d'Aspert. "Is that how you make his acquaintance? You're receiving Charles like a stranger, after urging me so strongly to have him come!"

"Oh," said Charles, "madame was so good as to wish for my coming?"

"Your coming would be a pleasure and a benefit to my husband. As such, I must wish for it."

"Fine, fine!" said d'Aspert. "You can deliver all those compliments some other time. When you came in, he was telling us how he got here.

158

He traveled through the forest all night. He got lost, and when he finally found the forge he was as soaked as if he'd fallen into the lake."

Henriette started, and looked at Charles Dumont. She noticed nothing particular in his expression, though he was observing her just then.

"And where did the gentleman spend the night?" she asked.

"When I arrived, ma'am, everyone here was asleep. I found a work-man who was awake. He asked me if I was the new manager they were expecting, and I said that was me. He called a servant who took me to a building where I found an apartment all ready for me."

"That wasn't for you!" said Henriette. "It's not suitable for you. There are bedrooms here in the house."

"In the house!" said Charles, in a slightly different tone. "That's not necessary. I'm fine where I am—better accommodated than I've ever been before. Besides, to keep an eye on the workers, that'll be more convenient for coming and going at all hours, especially when they're working at night."

"As you wish," said the general. "The business certainly needs super-vision: everything's going wrong; half the days go to waste."

"I thought I noticed that," said Charles, "and I've already issued a few orders."

"Ah!" said d'Aspert. "If the weather hadn't been so awful yesterday, I'd have tried to go out to show you the workshops myself. But in this terrible country, as soon as it's rained for fifteen minutes you'll sink into the mud up to your ankles."

"Not at least in front of the house," said Charles. "I tried to make that bearable. I had them spread several cartloads of cinders and slag there."

"So it was you who had the ground covered in cinders?" asked Hen-riette quickly.

"It's awfully black, isn't it, ma'am?" replied Charles, as if he were saying something profoundly true. "But it's better than..." He paused, looking at her. She had her eyes fixed on him. "Better than mud."

For a moment Henriette had thought that sentence would end with, "Better than blood."

"Much better," said Madame Bizot. Not having contributed to the conversation for two minutes, she thought she'd given sufficient proof of her discretion and left enough room for familial effusions. She added, "Let's take advantage of that to go for a walk before lunch."

"Oh," said d'Aspert, "Madame Bizot, Madame Bizot, don't take Charles away so soon... Later, later, you can do with him what you like..."

And he began to laugh. Monsieur Bizot, her husband, laughed along with him. "Come now," went on the general. "Henriette, give me your arm. You too, Charles. I'll try to drag myself as far as the door."

They helped him up. He handed his wife the cane he used both for support and for signaling, for he beat the floor violently with it when he wanted to summon help. Supported by the two arms he'd requested, he left the dining room. At the door he let go of Charles's arm; held up only by his wife, he pointed out the various workshops that could be seen in all directions emitting smoke around the house. Charles listened closely to his descriptions. D'Aspert, energized by his account, had let go of Henriette's arm and had taken a few steps forward without help or support.

Henriette, deeply preoccupied, was using the tip of her husband's cane to dig around at the place where they were standing. Charles, while listening to d'Aspert, had stepped closer to her. He stopped her with his hand and asked in a low voice, "Why dig up those cinders to discover secrets in the ground?"

"So it was you?" said Henriette, looking at him in surprise and almost in fear.

"Why ask a man for his secret?" said Charles. "The man and the ground might reveal to you only a secret of blood."

Henriette was stunned. Charles moved away to return to his place beside d'Aspert. Madame Bizot, who'd been waiting for the right moment to share secrets, took hold of Henriette's arm and whispered, "He's really very handsome. There's something distinguished and decisive about him, and he has lovely feet and elegant hands. He seems to have injured his right hand, because it's wrapped up in black silk."

Henriette had a sudden thought, and looked at her arm where Charles had just held it: she saw blood there. She cried out and dropped her husband's cane. He turned at her cry; Henriette was white and shaking.

"Well! What's the matter with you?" asked the general. "Madame Bizot, Charles, help her… She's as pale as death… Look, look, she's going away, she's taking my cane with her. I can't take a step to go to her. Bizot, give me your arm… You're the only one who's taking care of me!"

What casual words to the ears of Lussay and the Bizots! What burning, caustic words to Henriette's heart! To her they appeared to have a sinister meaning: that husband, abandoned and left without support, seemed like a living symbol of the future. She was frightened; she wanted to resist, to contradict him. She picked up the cane, approached d'Aspert, and held out her arm to him.

"You have some blood on your hand," he said.

"It's nothing. I must've cut myself or pricked myself," she replied, furtively hiding her hand in her apron pocket.

She was lying—poor woman, who thought that by walking next to her husband she could be close to him, she could put herself under his protection against an astonishing emotion, against a feeling of curiosity and horror that overmastered her and made her tell a lie! The split between them had begun. She'd created a secret between the stranger and her, without her husband's knowledge. What secret, you might ask? Casual words, drawn from the imagination, that seemed to be connected to a dream; a bit of foolishness she'd have been ashamed to recount a moment earlier. It was nothing; but it was something powerful she was hiding. It was something, because it was no longer shame that kept her from speaking, it was fear, and perhaps it was pity. My God, that woman so deeply wished to be alone! What a blessing solitude would've been! Henriette was still at the stage in which solitude brings good advice.

The announcement came that lunch was served.

They went inside, they sat at the table, they talked a great deal. During the conversation Charles's face lost the odd color that had struck Henriette. He shared the news from Paris with perfect grace, described the current fashions to Madame Bizot, reported to Monsieur Bizot the exact number of subscribers to the *Constitutional*, gave Monsieur Lussay an account of several new books, and told the general about the current positions of his former classmates. With the ease of good manners he carried out the thousand duties of reciprocal civility that are owed to people seated at the same table. He struck everyone as charming and distinguished, but Henriette found him no more than commonplace.

Finally the general, delighted, said, "Tell us the story of your captivity."

"It's a sad story, replied Charles, "a series of miseries, with cold and hunger playing the lead roles."

"Well then, the story of your youth, because we barely know it," said d'Aspert, giving his wife a wink of understanding.

"That's a wretched tale," answered Charles once again, "the tale of a schoolboy."

"Well then," said d'Aspert, giving his wife a look to show her the skill of his timing, "tell us about your childhood."

"My childhood," said Charles, growing thoughtful. "My childhood is a story almost forgotten. I've always been surprised by my lack of early memories. A few scattered events, a few names whose identity I'm not sure of. I really believe childhood memories, which are said to be so strong, endure so long and are etched so deeply in the memory only because they're constantly being refreshed. The conversation between a mother or a father and their son, or that with a childhood friend, by returning so often to the past, remake the impression that would otherwise be erased, and allow it to endure. But I, as a wandering orphan, had neither mother nor father not childhood friend. I've forgotten... forgotten."

As he spoke, Charles had softened. Everyone listened to him in gentle silence. There were two hearts that pounded as they followed his look into the past, as if into an abyss where he could see nothing. Realizing that he was being watched, Charles went on effusively, "I've forgotten so much! Except that you took me in and protected me, general, and may God curse me," he added forcefully in a voice that made Henriette shiver, for it was the voice she'd heard in the night, "may God curse me if I ever forget that I owe you the same respect I'd owe my own father!"

D'Aspert held out his hand to him, and the last heartfelt tear that had survived gout and a provincial backwater ran from his eyes. The Bizots found his gesture sublime. Henriette thought it was overdone, if it didn't conceal some hidden intention. Why did she think that?

"It's all right, it's all right," said d'Aspert. "We'll help you a little, and we'll all review our memories. Who knows whether we'll find some odd, unexpected, bizarre occurrence?"

"Oh," said Charles, "my life is a plain one. Nothing has happened to me that hasn't happened to everybody, especially to a soldier."

"What!" said Henriette. "Nothing?"

"Nothing, at least, that I can describe. For if there've been moments of destiny in my life... they don't belong to me, and I can't share them with anyone."

"Maybe there's something a long time ago," said d'Aspert, always returning to his goal.

"Or perhaps something very recent," said Henriette, giving Charles a look.

"Who knows?" he answered. "Perhaps I'm a fool and I've believed in ghosts. Don't laugh, Madame Bizot; I believe in ghosts, I've seen some... You've all seen some; you might be seeing one now. Wasn't I considered dead? And here I am. Who knows where I've come from? Perhaps from the grave, where I was believed to be, where I assume I'm still thought to be. And if you had any idea what the dead know!..."

"My God!... My God!... What's wrong, Madame d'Aspert?" cried Madame Bizot. "How pale you are!"

"It's nothing... It's nothing," said Henriette with a pained smile. "I'm not well. I spent such a bad night!... An awful night!"

"Besides," said d'Aspert, who'd been shaken by Charles's words, which seemed to allude to that child who must've disappeared, "what the devil are you doing talking to us about dead people and ghosts, here in a region that seems like their native land, and in a house with ceilings eighteen feet high? Now, now, tell us instead what kept you from coming right away."

"Oh, business," said Charles.

"Business important enough to keep you there? I know your business affairs, and I don't know of any whose nature could delay the pleasure of seeing us."

"Really, general," laughed Charles, while he eyed Madame Bizot, "you don't know of any of that nature!"

"Very funny! Very funny!" cried Bizot, who hadn't spoken yet and who now burst out laughing. "Ah, you joker, you!... That was good... very good... Youth must have its day."

It was the first witticism Bizot had understood. He'd laughed, d'Aspert had laughed, Madame Bizot had managed to blush, and Henriette felt hurt. Why? The joke in no way concerned her. The bold look Charles had given Madame Bizot showed that he didn't treat her and Henriette the same way. Still, she found the joke crude, and even more she found it unseemly. It changed something in Henriette's mien: perhaps the profile of a person that had to be redrawn. It was like a disillusionment.

After lunch the conversation continued for a long time around the table. They drank an unusual amount of champagne. Charles was delightfully cheerful, and displeased Henriette more and more. Four hours after his arrival, she considered him one of those men, distinguished for their coarseness, who are the toast of salons. "He'll be good for nothing here," she said to herself. "He'll soon get bored in our solitude. He needs balls, soirees, the endless exchange of ideas that refreshes them in the emptiest heads, of which Paris is full. Here, where we all have to rely on our own resources, he'll soon come to the end of his supply, and he'll become... who knows what?" Henriette looked around her, and still resisted lowering Charles right away to the level of d'Aspert's gout or Bizot's stupidity.

While Henriette was lost in thought, the general had had the forge's account books brought in; he was showing them to Charles, who examined them carefully. Henriette was surprised to hear him speak with a very mercantile ease about the books he was looking at: the daily register wasn't up to date, the logbook and the general ledger and the daily ledger were in chaos, bookkeeping items were wrongly entered—unexplained expenses had been scattered carelessly under both profit and loss. D'Aspert listened admiringly without really understanding. As for Bizot, he was hopping up and down with satisfaction, crying, "That's right, that's right!"

Madame Bizot murmured to Henriette, "Well, he's an invaluable man!"

"Yes," she replied, in a tone of voice perfectly suited to the Parisian style of mockery, "he's an amiable soldier and a good accountant!"

Madame Bizot, brimming with admiration, didn't understand her, and went on, "And perhaps he plays the guitar!"

"I swear he does," cried Henriette with sarcastic gravity. "I swear he plays the guitar—he has to!"

If she'd dared, she'd have asked him if he did. It's remarkable how much women dislike men with a broad education, and especially how much they detest useful men. Whether women's more subtle understanding tells them right away that a mind that encompasses too many things is superior in none of them, or whether their acute but narrow intelligence gets tired of following those men through everything they know, they usually prefer men who have one distinct specialty, one transcendent talent, one quality carried in isolation to its highest degree: as if their love, lacking in breadth, can only rise to the level of the admired object on condition that it addresses one single thing.

As for their hatred for useful men, it can be explained like this: usefulness carries with it a host of activities, ideas, and projects in which women play no part. So they can only amount to half of the man's life; and to be only half is not be loved, according to women. The egotism of love—I don't dare say the egotism of women—considers an enemy anything that doesn't interest it, and believes women would prefer a man who devotes an hour a day to a rival lover, to a man who'd devote four hours a day to business that interests him. You can go to battle against a rival, you can hurt her or ruin her or kill her, but anyway you can deal with her; but a bail of indigo or a spreadsheet, that's fatal, and there's nothing you can do.

Notice also how women pick and choose among the vices. Nothing repels them like a miser; they'll forgive a gambler who drags them into poverty, whereas a miser would condemn them to nothing worse than austerity. No matter what they say, it's not because there's something dramatic, a certain grandeur, about the vicissitudes of gambling; it's because that vice carries with it a chance of returning their lover to them through ruin, of returning him submissive and repentant and entirely theirs. That goes for the majority of women, those who conform to the egotism of the sex. Then there are those who follow fashion in choosing lovers: women who've loved abbots or musketeers, women who've loved Encyclopédistes, who've loved Jacobins, poseurs, second lieutenants, hussar captains, half-pay colonels. The second lieutenants date from Michu's time, the hussars from Elléviou's, and Monsieur Scribe brought success to the colonels.[68] How many women with lovely blonde hair and rosy complexions have turned away in scorn from a handsome young man and toward some colonel's perky mustache, inspired by a couplet at the Gymnase Theater! How many of those men married good providers, and should owe a commission to Scribe or Gonthier![69] There are women with lots of imagination, who want a man like the one they've dreamt of, who'll consider no other as a possible lover, and who, never finding what they imagined, end up giving themselves to some boor, whom in their heads they dress up in all the qualities they demand: a scoundrel who, at the first setback, slips through their fingers.

I couldn't tell you which of those categories Henriette belonged to, but I believe she had in her a little of all three kinds of women. Firstly, she was ready to give herself entirely over to her feelings at every moment of her life, and she hated the idea of occupying a lover's thoughts only in his leisure hours: still a virgin in her heart, she couldn't treat as an equal a man who spoke lightly about matters of love. Secondly, the fashion for military men having passed, it wasn't rational that with a general for a husband she should notice a gallant captain. That was a leftover from the Empire, and the days when the aide-de-camp was triumphant. At the time we're describing now, Lord Byron was tossing out into the world *The Corsair*, *Lara*, and *Parisina*, in short all of his fatal poetry: pale men with large trembling eyes were rising in value. Charles had first entered Henriette's consciousness with something of that supernatural aspect; but that illusion hadn't lasted more than an hour, and Henriette had come to the brink of

---

[68]Louis Michu (1754-1801): an actor and comic-opera singer. Pierre Elléviou (1769-1842): a singer, actor, and librettist. Eugène Scribe (1791-1861): a dramatist and librettist known for writing "well-made plays."

[69]Gonthier, or François-Pierre-Gonthier de Biran, usually known as Maine de Biran (1766-1824): a sensualist philosopher.

doing two things she would've drawn back from doing before: the first was to tell her husband about her encounter in the night; the second was to have her son brought to her immediately.

But before we go any further, what kind of woman, you might ask, could this Henriette be who thought all those thoughts, who was infatuated and then disgusted by a man at first sight, and who weighed him so exactly for what he might be to her? The thing is, Henriette didn't put a single one of those thoughts into words; no part of all that was in her heart, unless in the sense that a large, showy flower is contained in its seed. That seed, which we've grown prematurely, might not have fallen into her heart; or we might've recklessly forced it to bloom, when perhaps it was destined to die there. No, Henriette had calculated nothing, reasoned nothing. She'd felt happiness and unhappiness in turn, but without knowing why, without seeing or suspecting the cause, and yet always a little afraid of that happiness, feeling safer in her ill humor. In spite of all of her instincts, the instinct for peace and the instinct for duty required that Charles be displeasing to her, so he displeased her. And at that very moment her actions resumed their natural, habitual course. As we've said, she decided she'd have her son brought to her, and she decided to tell the general that very day what had happened in the night.

She stepped out for a moment, and soon returned, holding a charming child by the hand. The entrance of a young woman's child is almost always a happy moment for her. There's no lout so uncouth that he doesn't find the child sweet, and want to pet him and kiss him and frighten him with his red sideburns and ask him to smile. But when Henriette came in everyone was filled with a terrible embarrassment. Lussay, who barely noticed what was going on around him, became somber and had to suppress a gesture of anger. D'Aspert blushed with ill humor. As for Madame Bizot, she was too much a woman to come to the rescue of a friend in the presence of a man who could choose between them.

Only Bizot acted appropriately: there was sometimes real feeling in his foolishness. "Well, well!" he cried. "My big Henri, how splendid you look in your red shoes! What? You're not saying hello to your papa?"

Henriette had been astonished at the effect produced by her entrance. All of her unhappiness had been evoked in the embarrassment of her father and her husband, and in Madame Bizot's treacherous silence. She hoped Monsieur Bizot's exclamations would give a natural direction to the conversation, and that the child would be embraced without further hesitation. But Henri had his eyes fixed on Charles and hadn't responded to Bizot's question; he hadn't gone to kiss the general. He wrapped himself in his mother's dress, and, pointing at Charles, he trembled and cried out, "Who's that, mama? Who's that?"

Henriette, upset, embarrassed, red-faced, her heart aching, felt close to fainting. She looked pleadingly around her; seeing no one come to her assistance, she found within herself the strength God often sends those who've been abandoned. She lifted her head and replied to the child's question more for the others present than for him: "That's your brother, Henri, that's the general's adopted eldest son."

As she said those words she gazed, with a sad but powerful dignity, at Charles's face, which she hadn't dared look at before. He was watching the child as eagerly as the child was watching him. Two tears—of the kind that come stealthily into your eyes and run down your face before you can hide them—two tears ran down his cheeks. He felt them, and with his injured hand he tried to wipe them away. To hide them better, he picked up the child and embraced him. But his wound, which had opened with his gesture, had also run onto his face; and when he put the child down he was smeared with blood.

"You've marked my son with blood!" cried Henriette, taking him back with inexpressible horror.

"Me?" said Charles, appalled. "Me?... Yes, it was me..."

"It's nothing, it's nothing," said the general, taking the child and wiping his face, then kissing him to calm him down.

"Oh, general, general," said Charles with touching warmth. "You're the father of orphans... Curses, curses on the one who's ungrateful! Curses on the one who forgets what he is and what you are!"

Lussay had left. Madame Bizot bit her lip and looked troubled: Charles's sentiment was beyond her, and besides it seemed favorable to Henriette. The general was moved. He took the child on his lap, and was no longer ashamed at being an honorable man. Bizot was crying. And Henriette no longer wanted to confide in her husband as she'd resolved.

XII. A CHARACTER TRAIT

That day, so full of conflicting emotions, was followed by days that were peaceful and uneventful. For the first two weeks after he arrived, Charles concentrated on restoring to the forge the productivity it had lost. He told the workers the day would begin at five in the morning and end at seven at night, for those who only worked the day shift. He gave them a two-hour midday break, set the daily wage, started an attendance log the workers had to sign on entering and leaving, or that a foreman had to sign for them, and announced that hours absent would be deducted from the daily wage. As for those who worked both night and day, instead of having them work twenty-four hours straight on alternating days, he divided them into crews that would relieve each other every six hours.

At first that made the workers grumble: they worked very little at night, when the shops weren't supervised, which then gave them a whole day off. But one of them, a furnace chief, famous for his strength and his courage (he'd been a soldier and a fencing master) and valuable for the brutal fearlessness with which he undertook the most dangerous work, calmed them down by telling them it was just a young man's zeal and it wouldn't last a week. So they pretended to submit; and the first day they were on time, the second day they were a few minutes late, the third day they'd shaved off a quarter of an hour in the morning and again at night, and by the end of the week things were back to the way they'd been. As for the workers who had to relieve each other every six hours, they were careful to let the furnace fires go out about an hour before quitting time: the incoming crew lost an hour getting them relit, and the output after two weeks was pitiful. Charles said nothing. Payday came.

The workers were accustomed to getting a round sum for their days of work. They were very surprised when one found he'd been docked five sous for two hours he'd spent sleeping, another for a half-day he'd spent digging over his garden: none of them got the sum he was used to being paid for not working. There were some remarks, but they were timid. Charles, who was doing the payout in person, confronted them sternly. The workers said nothing, but they lingered in a clump at the door to the office. They were talking intensely among themselves in low voices when their hope, their leader, the fencing master, appeared. He found out what was going on, shrugged at what he heard, and entered the office, his old police bonnet on his head and his old briar pipe in his mouth.

Charles eyed him steadily and said, "It seems your tobacco is good."

"Not bad," replied the insolent worker.

"In that case you'd do better to keep it to yourself. I don't like pipes."

"That's right," said the old soldier. "Officers out of the training academies didn't like smoke, whether it came from a pipe or from a cannon."

"Here's your pay," said Charles, who seemed not to have heard.

The workman took the wages, glancing out at his comrades to show them the success of his boldness. He counted the money, then set it calmly back on the counter, saying, "That's not the right amount."

"Let's see. Your name?"

"Pierre Aubert, known as the Spadroon," replied the furnace chief, waving his arm as if it were a sword.[70]

"Well then, Pierre Aubert, known as the Spadroon, twelve days at forty sous…"

"Makes twenty-four francs, twenty-four good francs, or I can't count."

"Minus sixty hours of absence, which is to say five days, adding up to ten francs. Here's fourteen francs. That's your total."

"That's your total," said the rascal, "but it isn't mine. I want my twenty-four francs. I'm not used to being treated like a nobody."

"We're not going to argue about it. Here's your twenty-four francs. You're done working at the forge."

"We'll see about that," growled Aubert as he pocketed the money. Outside the office he said, "Well, you imbeciles, I got my total."

"Sure," replied one of the workers, "but you don't work at the forge anymore. You got fired."

"Fired! Me, fired, by some greenhorn?" said the Spadroon with an oath. "If you believe that, go have a drink of water. Come on, we'll get the better of him. Let's go to the bar, and I'll tell you how you break a clothes horse like him."

Charles had overheard, but he went on calmly issuing wages. The Spadroon had gone away. It was now the turn of the night crews, and their pay was reduced even further: Charles docked them not only for the time lost, but for the charcoal they'd wasted. There was a general outcry. Charles said simply, "Take it or leave it."

---

[70]Spadroon: a kind of sword used in French fencing.

"We'd rather do like the Spadroon," said a few of them, "get our full pay and quit."

"You'll quit, but you won't get your pay. Aubert harmed no one but himself by not working; you harmed the business. If I paid you, I'd be robbing the general."

"But you paid Aubert when you fired him."

"I gave him a handout as charity when I fired him. And you can tell him not to set foot in here again."

The workers, intimidated and now without their backup, took their pay and ran off to join their comrades at the bar. They told them what had happened, and what Charles had said about the Spadroon.

"Holy God!" he cried. "That whippersnapper! Charity! Charity, to me? I'll have his guts for dinner rather than take his charity. Oh, by God, we'll see!... As I'm a fencing master, I'll tear off his red stripe[71] if he even looks at me when I show up to work on Monday!"

"So you're going back?"

"Am I going back? Ha! I'll be there early! By God, I don't know what's keeping me from slashing him across the face with my hammer!"

Charles didn't think he needed to inform the general about that little incident. In any case, he spent almost the whole of Sunday bringing the accounts up to date and answering correspondence. During that entire first two weeks he'd rarely appeared at mealtimes, nor had he often stayed in the parlor to read or to play chess with Lussay. The romantic impression he'd made on Henriette the first day had faded little by little. He was gentle, polite, considerate; he'd recovered a calm, easygoing manner that made him no more than an amiable companion. He said nothing with a hidden meaning, gave Henriette none of the significant looks he had at first, made no effort to avoid a private conversation with her.

They found themselves alone together almost every day. The first time she'd trembled to think what he might say, feeling sure he would take advantage of the situation. But he chatted about commonplace things. The second time she found it extraordinary that he made no reference to that peculiar first night, or to the mysterious words he'd spoken to her. After that she thought less about it, and finally she decided she'd been mistaken. She looked for some other explanation of the mystery that preoccupied her. After two weeks, Charles seemed to be very last man to disturb her equanimity. The Bizots had gone home, but they were due to return: it had been agreed that they'd all spend the winter together.

---

[71]In the Imperial army a red stripe designated someone of officer rank.

Monday came. All the workers were there at dawn. Charles was at the workshop door himself, marking down their arrival time. The Spadroon showed up, but he went by without looking at Charles, whistling impudently. Charles let him pass. As he settled in at his furnace and began to work, he said to the others, "He caved in! You're all a pile of weaklings who don't know how to get your own way!"

After the workers had come in, Charles moved around the shop floor. With a care he'd never shown before, he'd attached his red ribbon to the boutonniere of his coat. The workers looked at him curiously, some of them insolently. Finally he came to Aubert's furnace. As if by magic, everyone within earshot stopped work and turned toward them. The Spadroon had begun to whistle when Charles was still in the distance. When he reached Aubert's own shop floor, the rascal began to sing, in a stentorian voice, a song of the volunteers of '92 that began like this:

There was a battalion
Whose name was Ariège,
A little band of fighters
who could hand out a thrashing...

Charles stopped him, considered him for a moment, then asked calmly, "What are you doing here?"

Aubert pretended he hadn't heard, and went on the next verse of the song. Charles repeated his question.

"Seems pretty obvious, I'd think," replied the workman.

"I told you you wouldn't work here anymore."

"Maybe so, but I didn't believe you."

"Come now," said Charles, who'd resolved to prevail over him. "Enough insolence. Leave."

"And who's going to make me leave?" asked the Spadroon, looking around at the workers who were gathered at the doors.

"Well," said Charles, "all of these good men if I order them to."

"Maybe," replied Aubert, "as long as I don't tell them not to."

Charles knew very well that the man's insolent behavior was a deliberate choice. But he got carried away by his own hot-headed nature, crying, "Come on, now, throw this man out of here!"

The Spadroon picked up an enormous pair of pincers and shouted, "The first one who moves, I'll break him in two!"

None of the workers moved.

Charles eyed them with scorn and said, "So it'll be me who throws him out." And he advanced on Aubert.

"Don't touch me!" said the workman, backing up. "Don't touch me!"

"I'm happy not to, but leave this minute!"

"I won't!"

"Oh, you won't!" said Charles, advancing again.

"I told you not to touch me!" cried the Spadroon, raising the pincers in both hands.

But before he could finish, Charles had grabbed the pincers and torn them from Aubert's grip.

"Will you leave?"

"No, by God, I won't leave!" replied Aubert furiously, thinking he'd only been disarmed by surprise. "No, no one's going to say a greenhorn made me back down!"

Charles came closer still. Looking him full in the face, he said in a terrible though muted voice, "Listen, I'm telling you to leave. And I warn you not to say another insulting word, because if you do it won't be to fire you that I'll lay hands on you."

"Well, what is it I said? I said greenhorn. I'll say it again, you're a greenhorn!"

"And I'll say it again as well: now it's no long a matter of you leaving."

"Then what?"

"Of apologizing."

"Oh, apologizing!" said the Spadroon with a loud laugh. "Apologizing! Apologizing to the gentleman!..." He became more and more excited. "Apologize! Apologize! I tell you what: I swore I'd rip off your ribbon. Here you go, here's how I apologize!"

He finished neither his words nor his gesture. Charles grabbed him by the throat and forced him to the ground. Aubert tried to get up, but he was caught under an iron buttress.

"Apologize!" said Charles.

"No! No!"

"Apologize!" the young man repeated furiously.

The workman struggled. He tried to bite the hand that held him down. He straightened his arms to push back against the arm that weighed on him like a mountain. He could do nothing. He roared and foamed at the mouth.

The workers were terrified. A few cried, "Aubert, Aubert, apologize... He'll kill you."

To which he replied, "I'd rather be killed than apologize to a bastard!"

The cry of anger that burst from Charles's lips made all the worker's tremble. "Well, so be it!" he replied. "You called me a bastard! Well then, I'll crush your tongue so it can never again speak that word."

And in a transport of wild rage, he dragged Aubert toward a hammer, powered by one of the channels of water, which pounded its colossal anvil with a weight of six thousand. A general cry of horror warned Aubert what was about to happen to him. He struggled, he wriggled like a snake, he hung onto every bump on the floor. But he was held by a hand that was stronger than steel, and step by step they drew closer to the terrible machine.

"Beg for mercy!" came the shouts from all over. "Mercy! Have mercy on him!"

Aubert responded only by struggling harder.

Finally his feet were touching the edge of the horrible machine. With one gesture, Charles turned him around so his head was closest. Two steps away from him, the wretch could see the hammer rising and falling with a noise that shook his skull. He began to cry, "Murder! Murder!" in a voice so piercing that it rose over the sound of the hammer and filled the workers with emotion.

"Well!" said Charles, lifting him off the floor, "will you beg for mercy?"

At the moment the crowd of workers parted and Henriette appeared. "What's all this noise?" she asked. "What's going on?"

Charles relaxed his hand and let Aubert go. The wretch got up slowly.

"It's an insolent worker whom I'm punishing," said Charles calmly.

The crowed murmured. Aubert tried to move away, but Charles stopped him. "Not yet. It isn't over between us. Ma'am, this worker insulted me, and he has to apologize."

"Apologize," Henriette said to Aubert.

The workman, still held by Charles, had noticed the latter's will falter briefly a moment earlier, and he replied coarsely, "Anyone can get angry when you see your bread being taken away."

"Say, when you don't earn it."

"Well, all right," said Aubert. "Excuse me, if what I said offended you."

"Enough!" said Charles. "Take your clothes and leave."

The Spadroon obeyed, smacking his head in despair. He pushed aside several workers who were in his way.

"I'm asking you to forgive him," said Henriette.

"He doesn't deserve it," replied Charles. "Let him leave! As for the rest of you," he added, eyeing the other workers sternly, "as for all of you who didn't obey me earlier, you can see I know how to deal with a man who won't obey. Let this be a lesson to you!"

He left the shop floor with Henriette. She had the solemn, brooding look of a woman who's just had a request refused.

That brutal scene, in which a man who had the right to expect his orders to be obeyed had to use force to obtain obedience, is more common than you'd think in the interactions of masters and workers, especially in situations where an appeal to the law and official support is slow to obtain. I've said above, and I'll say it again here: all power, no matter how it's exercised, no matter how highly placed it is, must have an extraordinary ability to intoxicate; for there's almost no one who isn't tempted to abuse the power he has. I don't know if human nature is fundamentally good. But if there's some wickedness within reach that a man can do with impunity, he takes hold of it so fast that I begin to agree with those who say our nature is wicked, and who, unable to deny the existence of good actions, give them a wicked motive and claim that egotism is the source of all the virtues. One of those moralists said to me one day, "Pity—the sentiment that more than all others, uniquely perhaps, seems the least selfish, the sentiment that makes us feel another's pain—isn't it just, as La Rochefoucauld said, a calculating act of self-regard? It's the instinct of self-love."

Throw a wounded man, calling for help, onto a road with lots of passersby. Some of them will help him, and lots will avoid him. Take the most callous man of all those who avoided him, lock him into a room with the wounded man, and let him go on crying out for help, and by the second day the callous man will help him. Is it because he's become more pitying? It's because, for his own comfort, he needs to make the tedious noise stop. Well! Those who would've helped him right away did it to ease their frightened consciences, which had absorbed the sublime and ultra-egotistic precept of Christian charity: do unto others as you would have them do unto you.

For now imagine that instead of a man crying for help, it was a pig, with its ghastly squealing; and lock it up with it the most soft-hearted woman, the kind who can't bear to watch a dead chicken being plucked; and after the fourth squeal she'll say, "Comfort this animal, or finish it off!" Why the choice? Because she's protecting her nerves under the pretext of pity. Perhaps—if it weren't for the moral lessons we've been taught, the penal code, the judge, the gendarme, and the executioner—the same thing might've been said about the man, if he'd cried out for help as loudly and disagreeably as the pig. Do you think the barbarians who smothered the insane between two mattresses felt pity for the madmen and their heart-rending convulsions? They were afraid of being bitten, that's all.

In the same way, much as I respect morality, I don't look down on the executioner, especially when I remember that the same hand struck Louis XVI and Robespierre, monarchy and anarchy, those two great enemies of the people. Besides, the abuse of personal physical strength is the one the common people, constrained on all sides by social bonds, gives way to with the greatest joy when it has the chance; for that's perhaps the only area in which they have the advantage in fighting back against the bourgeois masters who oppress them. The rascal in a tilbury carriage runs over the beggar on foot who didn't get out of the way; but the cart driver in his enormous vehicle happily runs over not only the rascal in a tilbury but the respectable man in his carriage as well! The greengrocer who gives way to you in the morning in front of the police chief's door—if you meet him again on a road five miles from any gendarme, where a whip handle can settle the question, it won't matter how elegant your phaeton is, how fine your English horses are, they'll wind up in the gutter if you don't have good fists. The truth is, there's no power so small that those who possess it aren't tempted to misuse it; so that I understand lots of people's hesitation to give power to those who don't have it, and the indifference of so many to the quality of those who exercise power, caring very little whether they're governed by a White rather than a Red, and then letting themselves be guided by a Tricolor.

Anyway, the workman Aubert's behavior in this business is the best proof of what we're arguing. No doubt his plan was malicious; but if that malice hadn't believed it could act with impunity, it would've raged secretly and hated mutely. It expected to triumph by means of strength that's rarely found in gentlemen in society; and perhaps it would've gotten the advantage if it had confronted someone with a less decisive temperament and a weaker arm. And in fact what would've happened if Charles had been a man of ordinary strength?

That's what Henriette was asking him as they returned to the house together. "No matter how rebellious the man was, sir, was that the way to force him back into obedience? Couldn't you have ordered his comrades to throw him out?"

"I believe I already told you ma'am, they refused to obey my order."

"You could've gotten your order confirmed by my husband."

"Really! And I would've come back with a servant as a guarantee of my authority?"

"Oh, if it's a matter of pride, I have nothing more to say," replied Henriette curtly.

"No, ma'am, it's a matter of prosperity or ruin for you—I beg your pardon, I mean for the general. That man intended to keep up the chaos that prevails here, ma'am; so if he'd disobeyed the general's orders as well as mine, what would your husband have done?"

"I assume he would've called on the local authorities."

"You think a man like him, confronted by a wretch like that, would've waited for the authorities?"

"What else could he have done, as ill as he is?"

"In his illness he'd have done what I'd have done if I were weak and disabled: he'd have blown out the man's brains."

"That's what you would've done?" asked Henriette, looking at Charles in terror.

"Yes, ma'am. Please listen, because you're angry with me, and I offended you by refusing your request, at a time when I knew I was going to need your support."

"My support?"

"Yes, ma'am. The general is going broke. It would be easy to give you detailed proofs of his imminent ruin. To prevent that will take a strong hand and sustained effort. I'm not boasting about having those qualities: I was born with them, and it's easy to nurture them in a soldier's career. But for them to be of any use to the general, they have to be met with prompt and unconditional obedience. For a long time the general had that obedience, first of all because the authority he was exercising came naturally to him and admitted of no question, and secondly because he had all the qualities needed to exercise it: a decisive character, and a name he always made people respect, which is more important than you might think to the lower classes. Perhaps he also had the advantage of needing only to maintain an established order, while I have to fight against disorder that people have made into a habit and a source of profit. And who am I to do all that? A stranger."

"A stranger!" said Henriette, in a tone of polite but unaffected reproach. "You, my husband's adopted son!"

"Yes, ma'am, a stranger who's only the custodian of an authority that's not his own, an underling whose orders can always be appealed to someone superior—which'll certainly happen today—a young man whose willpower they wanted to test. If I'd given in, that wouldn't been the end of my well-meant intention to serve you... to serve the general. And I'll say again, ma'am, there's no time to lose: this business's clients are abandoning it; they'll make other arrangements, and soon it'll be too late to get them back."

"You might be right. Those are reasons you didn't need to tell me for me to know their power. But speaking frankly, sir, your love of command, which is no doubt justified, went so far that you forgot that my position as the wife of the owner of this forge could give me some rights; and that, having substituted my plea for those rights, I could at least expect it would be honored."

"No doubt, ma'am, and in any other circumstances..."

"Yes," said Henriette bitterly, "in any other circumstances in which your pride weren't at stake, you would've deigned..."

"No," said Charles with dignity, "in any other circumstances in which the preservation of your fortune... of the general's fortune... wouldn't have been compromised."

Henriette sensed that she'd been unkind and unfair; she felt guilty toward Charles.

He hastened to go on, "Let me finish explaining my behavior to you, ma'am, and telling you what I expect of you. If I'd granted your plea, the harm might not have been irreparable; but it would've led to an eternal struggle between your pity and my strictness. I couldn't have punished a single wrongdoing without them appealing to you to intervene. To soften your heart they'd have sent their wives, their children, their ailing old people. You wouldn't have resisted: there's no such thing as wrongdoing before a woman who's talking about bread for her children, before little blond weeping heads. I had to deny your plea: instead of holding it against me once, you'd have held it against me almost every single day. We're destined to live in too small a social circle not to fear the wretched causes of friction that a fuller social world would erase... It would've been an irritation to you, and an unhappiness for me."

The word made Henriette look at Charles in surprise, as if she were astonished to hear him say he'd be unhappy to see her irritated. But he quickly made her repent that feeling by adding, "Yes, ma'am, an unhappiness for me to have to give up my care of the general's affairs later; which, however, I might have to give up tomorrow, if you won't help me."

"How so?"

"Because they're going to try with him what they tried with you. I've argued the justice of my cause with you; I won't do so with him, if his natural fairness, perhaps more biased or more easily duped than yours, or an enlightened sense of friendship, don't persuade him to stay out of this business and declare that he supports my decisions and can't exercise powers he's delegated to me. That would provoke another struggle I won't expose myself to. I'll leave this house. And it's to you, ma'am, that I appeal to prevent that misfortune."

"A great misfortune indeed for us, sir, the misfortune of losing you, " said Henriette, who in relation to this business found everything about Charles annoying: his words, his ideas, his manner, his diction. Never had she found him so displeasing. She thought he was speaking regally and learnedly about something trivial, and she looked for a reason to get angry. Essentially, Charles's last statement, if put into the mouth of someone like Bizot, would come out like this: "Just between us, your husband's an old man, whom I love and respect a great deal. But he's declining, he's becoming credulous." (The excellent expression "stupid old man" didn't exist yet.) "Stop him from doing something foolish."

Henriette understood that. But Charles's words dressed up his thoughts, and protected them from any reproach; and she began to compose a witty reply in place of showing her indignation—for she felt some shame at seeming to share with a stranger, and especially with Charles, an opinion expressed about her husband.

Charles irritated her even more when he said, with a frankness so lofty it did away with any sense of smugness, "Yes, ma'am, at this point, in the current state of your affairs, it would be a misfortune to lose me. If this called for great talent or for deep expertise, I'd give the job to anyone who came along. But it calls for integrity and loyalty, and I believe I possess the first of those as much as anyone, and the second more than everyone. Therefore I beg you, ma'am, protect me. I'm appealing to your affection for your husband, as well as to your reason."

"And presumably also to my self-interest?" asked Henriette.

"Ma'am, ma'am," said Charles coldly. "Neither my words nor my thoughts contained that insult. No matter what I've been told about you, no matter what I might have believed, I already know enough to see that my cause is lost if that were the only motive that could lead you to support me."

With those words he bowed and withdrew, leaving her fairly uncertain what she should do or say.

If anything seems odd in the tone in which those two conversed, it should be remembered that, whenever Charles spoke even slightly seriously, the events of the night in which Henriette thought he'd first appeared to her immediately came back to her mind.

Finally she returned to her husband. And in fact, the whole incident had already been brought before its tribunal: he was listening to the terrible Spadroon, who stammered when he saw Henriette—proof that he was lying.

"Yes, general," he was saying, "he tried to force me to apologize on my knees—an old army veteran like me—because I told him I could only be fired on your orders. Upon which he struck me, and if it hadn't been for mercy…"

That was when Henriette came in, and the Spadroon stopped.

"Well!" said the general, "if it hadn't been for mercy, you'd have struck him back, is that it?"

"I'm not saying that,"replied Aubert, disconcerted. "It's just…" Finally he got out of it fairly skillfully by saying, "In fact, madam was there. She was kind enough to plead for mercy for me, and he refused her… quite firmly."

"You were there, Henriette?" asked the general. "What happened? Come, you must know who was in the right and who was in the wrong."

Suddenly Henriette found herself on the spot, forced to commit herself on a question, about which her opinion had practically been dictated to her. She vacillated for a moment between her reluctance to obey that demand and what she felt to be its justice and its correctness. Hoping to dodge, she replied, "I was passing near the workshops. I heard a great noise, I went in, and I found Aubert in Monsieur Dumont's hands. That's all."

"And Charles was beating him?"

Henriette didn't hesitate to answer, seeing that what she was going to say was true, though it was contrary to Charles's interests: to hinder without lying is the very least an honest woman can do to her own satisfaction. "Oh, it had gone much further than that: he wanted to smash this poor man's head under his steam hammer."

"To smash your head! And you were letting him?"

"Oh, that's to say…" said Aubert, trying to chuckle.

"It appears that Monsieur Dumont is tremendously strong," added Henriette quickly, seeing that Aubert was preparing another lie and not wanting to have to contradict him.

"But you don't kill a man for something he said! This is serious," replied the general. "You didn't call him anything?"

"Nothing."

"No insults?"

"Hell, no."

"Then I'll put an end to these excesses."

"And you'll be doing the right thing," said the Spadroon, delighted, thinking he'd won. "With that gentleman, in a week you wouldn't have a worker left."

Hearing that, Henriette understood how right Charles had been, and the spirit of justice immediately prevailed in her. The terrible consequences of her own weakness or her ill-humor became clear to her, and she added, "It also must be said that this man insulted Monsieur Dumont."

"Insulted him!" said the general, to whom, as an old military man, that word had a bad ring. "What did you say to him? Come on, out with it!"

"Hell, general, us old veterans... you know..." said the Spadroon, stroking his army mustache. "The thing is, general, when you're fifty... in a moment of anger, you'd have said the same thing I did... We said it all the time about youngsters, in the army..."

"Well?" cried d'Aspert impatiently. "Come on, what did you say to him?"

"Hell, I guess I called him a draftee."

"You called him a draftee?" said the general, who didn't seem angry.

"That's not true," said Henriette, outraged at the man's lies and his servility following his insolence.

"Then what was it?" asked d'Aspert with a frown.

"Well, general," said the workman, who thought he saw a way out of his tight spot, "I was beside myself. I was wrong, I admit. And anyway, what people say about him around here isn't his fault, it's not the young man's fault... Well! I called him... a bastard."

Henriette didn't know that insult. She'd overheard the workers saying amongst themselves that Aubert had called Charles a greenhorn and had threatened to tear off his medal, and she'd expected that Aubert would admit to that. She and her husband looked at each other in astonishment.

The Spadroon had preferred confessing to this insult, knowing that in the eyes of an old soldier the other word would justify anything in response.

Suddenly the general's expression changed, and his cheeks practically hung loose. In a voice that choked in his throat he said, "You called him a bastard!" He rose from his seat. "Well!" he went on very loudly, "he's a coward not to have finished the job of killing you! You called him a bastard!" he repeated furiously, advancing on Aubert with his cane raised.

"My dear!" cried Henriette, throwing herself in his way, "what are you doing? This man is capable of anything! Don't go near him! He raised his hand against Charles: he wanted to rip off his medal."

"Rip off his medal!" cried the general. "Rip off his medal!" And turning away, he hurried to the fireplace and took down a rifle. Henriette let out a terrible cry. The door opened, and Charles barely had time to rush over to the general, who struggled against him, crying out like a madman, "And you didn't kill him!… And you didn't kill him!"

The wretch Aubert left, but he was saying to himself, "All right, but this isn't over."

When the general had calmed down a little, he asked Charles to tell him the whole story. He told it truthfully, but without speaking as explicitly as he had with Henriette of the urgent need to reestablish order, without telling the general about the appalling state of his business affairs, and especially without mentioning the word "bastard." Both d'Aspert and Henriette noticed, but neither one nor the other dared point it out. They understood too well that if Charles refused to say the fatal word, no one could force him to hear it. It would take another occasion, a more deliberate conversation, to arrive at a complete account. They were simply surprised, in their own minds, that the word had been spoken and that it had struck home.

Finally d'Aspert ended the conversation by saying, "Well! Without Henriette, I'd have taken that man's side!"

D'Aspert withdrew, and Charles said quietly to Henriette, "I thank you, ma'am, for not having abandoned my cause."

That woman persisted, God knows why, in not wanting to appear to have rendered any service to the young man. She replied curtly, "You haven't forgotten that it's also my husband's cause?"

"I believe, ma'am," said Charles in the same tone, "you were the first to point it out."

He withdrew, and she remained there, lost in thought.

XIII. A WINTER EVENING

The Bizots arrived two weeks later. They came partly in a carriage, partly in a wagon: Monsieur Bizot in his hat and with all of his things, in the German calèche he'd bought; Madame Bizot next to him, by herself, with almost all of her appurtenances and seductions in immense boxes in the wagon. When Henriette saw all that luggage, she glanced at Charles, who stood next to her. There's nothing like a woman for understanding, all at once, another woman's plans against her, contained within the six crates that filled the dining room a minute later.

No sooner had the first greetings been exchanged than Madame Bizot seized Henriette, and, rushing to confide in her, said very quietly, "My dear, I'm very cross with Monsieur Bizot. Since we left here we've been on fairly bad terms. If it weren't for my friendship for you, I certainly wouldn't have come back with him. For a while now we've fallen out of the habit of..."

Henriette didn't interrupt her, though she'd dragged out that sentence in such a way as to announce that she wanted to be understood without being forced to say everything—and it was exactly because Henriette did understand that she didn't interrupt. So Madame Bizot was obliged to come to her question by herself, and she added, "Instead of giving us our usual room, could you arrange...?"

"Two separate apartments?" said Henriette with noticeable speed. "With pleasure. I'll give the orders right away."

"Oh, Lord, no!" said Madame Bizot. "Two rooms in the same apartment. Or even, if it's more convenient for you, the room with two beds."

Henriette was almost sorry for her suspicions about Madame Bizot and the plans she imputed to her based on her request. But in this case the tactful woman was fooled by the cheap flirt: instead of pushing her suspicions too far, she'd fallen short of Madame Bizot's aim. Because of the plans for seduction made sufficiently obvious by all those boxes, Henriette had thought the separation from the husband was a way to facilitate trysts, but that wasn't Madame Bizot's motive. She had too much experience not to know that, when you've reached the stage of a tryst, it's not a room here or there that's the problem: the oddest and the riskiest rooms are the most amusing. But to reach that tryst there are a thousand paths that Madame

Bizot knew better than Henriette. So she knew there are men, of whom Charles seemed to be one, who consider love, even carnal love, something refined enough for them not to be particularly attracted to a woman who "sleeps" with her husband—especially when the husband is a Bizot who says every night at ten o'clock, "Come along, wife, come to bed, and don't do like last night, don't take up three quarters of the bed. But that's how my wife is: she settles in, she pushes me, hard too!" etc., etc., etc.

Unless you're a bachelor Bizot, you leave that woman to her Bizot husband. The beauty knew that; almost all women who put a little elegance into their flirtation, or a little flirtation into their love affairs, know that. It's only the most vulgar loose women, and the souls ruled by violent passions, who aren't aware of it: the former, because of their vulgarity, the latter because for them the act is the smallest part of love. I've known women who would've killed themselves for their lover, and who wouldn't bother to bathe for him. There's a woman in Paris, the only one I know of, who writes sublime love letters with her fingernails black with dirt. God knows where that got her.

Soon began the winter evenings, those evenings that are so difficult to fill, even in Paris, even with the help of balls, concerts, theaters: a time when intrigues are formed and unformed in the turns of a contradance, when a waltz and a galop turn heads and steal hearts, when the blood boils under the lash of a violin, in the midst of that hot, humid, steaming air that already oppresses the chest like a desire filled with the scent of women and flowers. That's where passions are kindled and flare up, steeped in voluptuous desire, but a desire that's sweet and delicate and ready to evaporate by morning, to be renewed the next evening.

In the country, at a chateau, in the isolated home of a wealthy rural gentleman, how different those evenings are! And what a different and much more dangerous delight they concentrate on the few who pass those evenings together! If I may put it this way, it's an incubating atmosphere, in which everything germinates to extraordinary proportions, in which nothing evaporates to the outdoors, neither words nor memories nor glances; in which everyone returns the next night with everything they took away the night before, without having lost any scraps to another social world, to the pleasures of another salon. It's fertile ground, where everything that falls germinates, like in the virgin forests of America, which are fed by their own fallen leaves, their broken branches, their own exhalations, where everything they give off returns to them—so grandly and magnificently superior to our civilized forests, which lend something to everyone: to the passerby a path, to the owner his regular cuttings, to the hunter his game, and to the poor man his deadwood.

There, if two people are destined to fall in love, if a man and a woman must risk everything for each other, they have to succumb. Not a day is lost; every day they see each other again, with no distractions to separate them, no interests to engage in to restrain them, no time to devote to fashions or the latest play or other people's intrigues or the requirements of propriety. All of their thoughts and all of their time belong to the same thing.

Charles and Henriette were destined to fall in love. Destined why? God knows. Was it that both of their lives held something unusual and bizarre that made them seek each other out? Was there in their personalities, in their inclinations, some similarity that attracted them to each other, or some difference that for each of them made the other's presence necessary? Was it their superiority to everything around them, their youth among older people, their isolation, that threw them together that way? No, it had nothing to do with any of that. They had to fall in love, because. You who are reading this aren't surprised. It's not a printing error, the sentence is complete: they had to fall in love because. Only a popinjay or an academician would be capable of adding anything to that sublime reasoning of love.

Anywhere they could've exchanged a glance or a word, anywhere they could've sensed the other's presence, they would've fallen in love. For each, the other's name spoken by a stranger, a name belonging to so many others, the name they might've heard the night before addressed to a servant or a streetwalker, that name—when it meant them—would've struck them instantly. Oh, presumably they wouldn't have mutually invaded each other at that speed nor to that excess. In the world, the world retains its rights: a marked inequality in their social positions, or a great physical distance between them, would've cost them some time. With separation would've come delays, and the path would've been longer, and they'd have had to overcome or get around obstacles. But the result wouldn't have changed, and they'd have reached it just the same.

They'd guessed all that: they'd guessed they'd fall in love. Not that the word "love" came right away to illuminate the future of their meeting and their first encounter. They'd calculated nothing, analyzed nothing, predicted nothing; but they'd tried to hate each other. The adopted son of a benevolent man, and that man's wife, who try to hate each other—that's a premonition of the crime of loving each other. And it was a crime to them, a terrible crime, for the first requirement of their falling in love was ingratitude. And beneath all that lay a shadow still darker and more terrible, a shadow that, if it ever came to light, could leave the word "incest" etched across their lives.

Poor young hearts, who when those winter evenings began were far from having any of those gloomy ideas! How satisfied they were with themselves! How protected they thought they were against each other! To Charles, Henriette was exactly the woman he'd had described to him in Paris: a sly hypocrite who'd taken advantage of the general's goodness; later we'll know whose hand it was that had drawn that portrait. How he laughed now at his hesitation in coming to the forge, because a mocking voice had told him, "You'll court her, and when the old man's dead you'll marry the widow with the child found in a cabbage patch!" How absurd he now considered that prediction—a prediction made more frightening through half-revelations that had been magnified by Charles's imagination and by a kind of witchcraft at work on him, whose secret slumbered in his heart. How childish his fears now seemed to him! She was an utterly ordinary woman, lacking even the scope of a talented schemer, a little girl who'd made a child and found a husband to take on the responsibility.

For Henriette, Charles was certainly no longer the distinguished young man who, when she was a child and even in her girlhood, had so often earned her mother's delighted praise. He was no longer the young second lieutenant decorated on the battlefield, winning new epaulets with every campaign, one of those fearless soldiers who, as quickly as they rose, could've fastened every mark of their fortune in a wound hole. He was no longer the poor prisoner wandering across the frozen wastes of Russia, nor the young man with the uncertain identity whose very existence might mean another man's arrest. He was just a fairly decent young fellow, tidy, meticulous about his duty, with a sense of honor and a fist of steel and a few notions—more brutal than well thought through—about order and discipline, well brought up, polite, a man alongside whom you could live in complete security.

Two months had passed since Charles's arrival. The general's business was so clearly going better that they'd added more workers. D'Aspert, delighted by everything going on around him, found there was not a moment in his long days when he wished to disturb the tranquility in which he lived. He dreaded any change. The clarification of Charles's identity that he'd wanted so badly now seemed to him one that could only have unpleasant results, and he pretended not to think of it anymore, which is to say he thrust aside the thought when it came to him.

Of course, someone had been sacrificed: a child had been consigned to misery in that business in Rome. But since Charles could be one or the other, he seemed to be both the one and the other; and since d'Aspert didn't know whether it was his son or Captain Dumont's son he should pity, he took advantage of his uncertainly to pity neither of them. He didn't risk his pity.

Lussay remained unchanged: almost always absent; become indifferent to all subjects of conversation, though he followed them with the ease of a man who's seen much in his life, and he contributed his share of learning and wit, but never of joy or carelessness. He was nurturing something within himself. It was the kind of silence of the soul that had to explode sooner or later. Nothing suggested whether the explosion was imminent or far distant. He was a man set apart from that little world.

As for Bizot, he "Bizotted." What could the verb "to Bizot" mean? I don't know, but look, just between us, I knew Monsieur Bizot. I saw him in Paris, I saw him in the country, and we all found no better way to describe his manner of being than to invent the word "to Bizot." He got up, he dressed, he came downstairs, he ate breakfast, he went for a walk, he looked around, he answered questions but he never asked any, he never said no to anything, he read when others were reading, he chatted when they chatted, he got warm when someone else felt cold, he played all sorts of jokes, even when he was driving his carriage, he took care not to frighten anyone, he learned from someone with interesting information, he kept silent with someone who had nothing to say. He acted as a kind of echo of everything that went on around him, having no gift except that of being like everybody else: he could run away with a coward, advance with a brave man, voluntarily give back everything he received, whether in wit or good manners or consideration. He spent time with those who spent time with him, neither fleeing from nor seeking out anyone, very happy in company, very happy by himself. I've seen him speak adequately on politics and dancing and beans. In short, to sum him up in a word, he was Monsieur Bizot. But, since nothing is perfect in this world, he had one quality that was his own, a quality that distinguished him: he was a bit of a musician. He had to be a little bit of a musician, as a matter of course, but here was where he fell short of lacking all individuality: instead of playing the violin a little, or the flute, or the cello, or even the bassoon, he played the lyre. Yes, Monsieur Bizot played the lyre, that sort of bastardized guitar that forces you to extend your arms and stick out your hips—an invention of the Empire for making women assume a Greek pose.

That leaves Madame Bizot. Madame Bizot took care of herself in mind and body. She was always tightly corseted and tightly shod, and she spoke tightly and laughed the same way; whereas she'd have been better off letting her lovely white teeth show, and allowing her fiery glances to do their teasing work, and showing off her fine legs and her swelling bosom a bit. She wanted to act distinguished; and though she was too much a Parisian and too elegant to be awkward, she was constrained, and she'd lost the opportunity that delivers the most refined men into the hands of an appetizing woman some morning, by chance, when they first get up, or in some corner in the evening when it's dark. Sometimes her true nature surfaced, especially when d'Aspert laughed, and Bizot returned the ball to him by laughing even louder, and Henriette let herself go, and Charles followed her, and Lussay unclenched the corners of his narrow lips.

That happened one day, when the general, feeling spry, announced he wanted to have supper served in the parlor. The wind was howling outside, and a cheerful fire burned in the fireplace. They had champagne, and drank a lot, by the glassful, d'Aspert urging everyone on. He told old army barracks stories, and Bizot responded with traveling salesman stories, the kind of stupid stories that end up going off on a tangent or finish with a dirty joke, and which everybody laughs at far more than their wit deserves. Then, when the table was cleared, the general wanted to dance; he recalled that he'd been a fine dancer. They were only six, so Bizot and Henriette had to double up as the last couple; but Bizot could only be the gentleman with Henriette after he'd been the lady with the general, and then he faced his wife, who was dancing with Lussay. (Lussay was dancing!) So with charming dexterity Bizot put on or took off a lady's bonnet, depending on which role he was playing, and at every costume change the general laughed out loud. Bizot danced normally as a man, doing his leaps and forward steps; but then he simpered and wiggled as a woman. It was delightful, it was hilarious. Madame Bizot laughed so hard she almost made Lussay collapse, since she was leaning on him. Then they waltzed. Henriette went to the piano. They'd sung the contradance; now they waltzed, Bizot with the general, Madame Bizot with Charles. They spun around, they grew animated.

"Look at my wife," said Bizot. "That's the way to let yourself go. Dear friend, dear general, you have to lean into it, you have to get excited!"

And he made himself graceful. His wife—to imitate him, she said—leaned on Charles's arm, brushed his face, looked deep into his eyes, made her waist supple under his hand, and allowed her moist half-open lips to tremble. The general, noticing, laughed like a madman, and Bizot laughed even louder, till they both collapsed onto a sofa. Henriette stopped playing. The two other waltzers also stopped. But Madame Bizot, finally carried away by her excellent amorous nature, squeezed Charles's hand before letting it go, and said very quietly, in a changed voice, "Oh, Charles!"

Then she went and dropped into an armchair, without arranging either her dress or her hair, flinging her feet out before her, loosening her collar to get some fresh air, her eyes bright, her color high—so lusty, in short, that the youthfulness in Charles couldn't help noticing all that, nor looking at it closely, looking at it a long time, so long that Henriette observed it. Then Charles noticed that Henriette had noticed, and they both became very serious. Luckily it was midnight, or the evening would've ended badly.

I've said that Charles and Henriette allowed themselves to please each other; here was how. You don't take pleasure from things that move you, which is to say things that involve affection or tenderness and that cause strong emotion. You take pleasure in trivial things. If the source of love is a mystery, the source of pleasure is not. Some women give pleasure by their looks, their beauty; others by their wit or by some chosen talent; almost all by some happy mix of all those qualities. And since the result of pleasure is the same as that of love, lots of people take one for the other. So that Charles and Henriette pleased each other as soon as they became candid and natural, and they allowed themselves to listen to each other without guarding their words, to speak neither pompously nor bitterly.

It happened that the two of them could talk easily about anything. Henriette had accurate judgments about things as they are; Charles had strong, naive judgments about things as they ought to be. She had a charming, exquisite appreciation for the world, for books, for ideas; he had scorching criticism or fiery praise, but never within conventional bounds. To others he seemed to contradict Henriette's opinions; to herself—she who had perfect taste—his mind held something she could never have dared to have: ideas different from the world's, bolder and more original, an attitude that doesn't suit a woman but is always an asset in a man.

He wasn't a storyteller, but when a story moved him he could bring others to tears by retelling it. All those fine manners, which on the first day had defanged the vampire Henriette had created in her mind, become so many virtues for a man in a salon. He sketched with distinction, he was an excellent musician. But his deference placed those talents at Henriette's command, without making a show of them, without forcing the whole world to notice what he did well. It was a touching story that taught them all how he'd become a musician.

The question was whether music pleases us by acquired habit or by a natural power agreeable to our senses: if a song with neither a clear meter nor a clear melody would give us pleasure if we lacked the conventional meters and modes we've learned. Charles believed meter was something innate to the ear, the thing that gave order to music, and he considered order to be the first prerequisite of all beauty. To back up his opinion, he told them that when he was in Russia, he was one of several hundred prisoners being led through a vast desert of snow in a line that stretched for a mile, flanked by a hundred Cossacks who galloped back and forth from the head to the tail of the line like sheepdogs, badgering the men with the handles of their lances to make them march faster. He told them they'd reached a village where they were supposed to rest for a few hours.

Charles had entered a house that was cleaner than the others; it was a dependency, like the whole village, of the manor that could be seen in the distance. In the room that contained the stove, where everyone was gathered, there sat in one corner an odd group, made up of some kind of Russian soldier and a fairly elderly peasant and a strikingly beautiful girl. When Charles came in, the girl was sitting in the floor, weeping; the soldier was grumbling and ordering the old man to hit her; and the old man said nothing, neither refusing nor obeying. The soldier drew his sword and threatened the old man; the old man struck his daughter, for she was his daughter. The poor child stood up, and giving no other response, she began to sing.

What song was it? Neither Charles nor his companions could identify it. The brutal instructor cried out that she was doing it wrong; picking up some sheet music, he began to sing—without Charles having any better idea what melody the teacher's honking conveyed. The student repeated it, but incorrectly, and she had to be beaten. It was sad to watch; then, when it happened over and over again, it became awful. Through one of his companions who spoke Russian, Charles learned from the girl's mother, who was weeping in a corner, that the lord of the manor, having heard in Moscow a certain tune that he'd liked, wanted to teach it to the girls who belonged to him, so they could sing it to him every day. He'd assigned the teaching to the musician who was present, who'd been a trumpeter in a regiment; and the old man's daughter had been chosen by lot to be the first to learn it.

While Charles was hearing that account, the poor child had sat back down on the floor and was letting herself be beaten without protest. It was no longer her father beating her, it was the trumpeter. At risk of his own life, Charles stepped forward and stopped the terrible schoolmaster. The man was furious, but he couldn't escape from the young captain's grip. But imagine Charles's surprise when the father and mother begged the trumpeter to continue; and he understood through his interpreter that they were even begging him to let their daughter be beaten. They said it was because, if she didn't know the song by that very evening, perhaps the lord might kill her in a moment of anger. It was therefore more merciful to let the poor thing be beaten. So Charles released the trumpeter, who left to go make a report to the lord. Everyone trembled for the poor girl.

Charles sadly picked up the score she was supposed to learn, and that he assumed was some barbaric song from that region. Casting a glance at it, he saw it was an aria by Mozart, that wonderful love song from *The Marriage of Figaro*: "My heart sighs…" Without thinking about it, without reflecting that the girl's musical nature had refused to repeat such a beautiful melody so strangely disfigured, he went to her, showed her the sheet music, and motioned to her to sing; she shook her head without answering. So he began to sing the aria, in a voice so resonant with emotion that suddenly she listened, as if he were speaking a language she understood. She nodded her head in perfect time to the beat; and then she herself tried to sing the aria. Charles hadn't even repeated it three times before she could sing it perfectly, with a look of gratitude at her new teacher that was almost as delightful as the passionate love in the music.

Just then the lord of the manor arrived with the leader of the band of prisoners, prepared to punish both his serf and the Frenchman who'd defied the boyar's orders. But they stopped when they heard the girl's sweet voice, and saw her father and mother listening, rapt, mouths open, and a dozen prisoners also turned toward the singer, and a few heads raised at the stove on which the Cossacks were lying.

"That's my aria," said the boyar. "What were you trying to tell me? She sings it as well as that Italian woman in Moscow."

He came nearer, and had her sing it again. When Charles explained what had happened, the boyar gave the girl's father the pleasure of administering a whipping to the trumpeter who'd force him to beat his daughter.

"Well," added Charles, "if tuneless, barbarically disordered sounds aren't disagreeable to the ears of savages, why couldn't that girl, with no knowledge of music, repeat what the trumpeter taught her just as easily as she sang what I did?"

The story had interested them all. Madame Bizot—who always saw the same ending to any interaction between a man and a woman—asked Charles with a simper, "And what did the pretty peasant girl give you in payment for such an excellent lesson?"

"A chunk of bread, ma'am," said Charles coldly.

To Henriette, that answer made up for the attention Charles had paid to Madame Bizot's charms a few days earlier.

"So," said d'Aspert, "you're a musician?"

Music is a terrible thing: not so much for its intrinsic delight, for the languidness it brings to your spirit, for the rhythmic rocking with which it puts you to sleep, but also for the closeness and intimacy it creates, especially in a casual salon. A man seated at a piano, a woman seated next to him. Their knees touch. When you're concentrating, you don't notice. You play a wrong note, you hunt on the keyboard for the right note, your hands meet. And if the daylight fades or the lamp dims, you don't have time to notice. Instead you bend over the score, practically leaning on each other. Your faces are close, your breaths mix. If one of you turns recklessly, your cheeks brush, your mouth tastes a lock of hair, you're aware of a glance a thousand times beyond what you dreamt, beyond what you would've allowed your imagination to dream.

That doesn't happen to people who seek it out: by the very awkwardness with which they go about it, they give warning to avoid them. It happens to those who aren't trying; chance serves them or deceives them. So Madame Bizot, who sang and had a lovely voice, often tried to create those situations and almost never succeeded; whereas Henriette and Charles, who were innocently devoted to music, fell into a thousand opportunities they didn't notice, or which they gave no sign of noticing. They already felt so comfortable together that they hadn't thought to invent small strictures to create discomfort. And yet they weren't thinking of love; they weren't thinking of anything; they were just wonderfully well matched. If the idea of love had entered their hearts, they'd have rebuffed it. Perhaps that was still possible then; soon it was too late.

It was evening—yet another evening. Charles was never around during the day, he was always at work. And by now Henriette no longer found him unpleasant, she no longer found him ridiculous. She respected the spirit of organization and activity that drove him to rescue the general's fortunes. She respected it all the more because, before knowing Charles, she hadn't believed that spirit could be compatible with all that makes a man amiable and gives him elegant manners.

So it was another evening. They'd talked a lot about what's called sentiment: Madame Bizot was always leading the conversation toward love. She'd gone on at length about all the ways of making a declaration to a woman. In her mind, after a lesson like that, Charles had nothing more to do than choose one. The time for music arrived. That morning they'd received sheet music for a few arias from *Emma*[72]—gorgeous music to which we all were drawn, as young as we were then, weeping over its sweet melodies and pacing nervously to the dashing rondo in which Madame Boulanger[73] made the young people in the cheap seats jump: because in those days the cheap seats were young and romantic; they hadn't yet become the shop floor for wig makers and wine merchants catering to the public.

O misery mine! How young we grow old these days! No sooner do I remember than I lose myself in my memories! Alas, how the young literature of those who are twenty would laugh at the literature of those who are thirty, if they read it!

Anyway, they'd received sheet music from *Emma*. Charles, who was preoccupied that night, sat by the piano. Henriette sat at the keyboard and began to sing the cavatina:

How lovely she is! What a smile!
Such spirit! Such sweet attractions!
Alas! Without daring to say it,
I adore her, and I will forever!

The reflections that lingered from the conversation that had just ended, the beauty of the melody, perhaps also the sentiment in those first four lines, plunged Charles into a train of thought removed from his surroundings but not from what he was hearing. And when the aria was over, and everyone had applauded, Charles, his head in his hands, still repeated the melody quietly and emotionally, with passionate expressiveness:

How lovely she is! What a smile!

---

[72]Probably *Emma di Resburgo* (1819), a very successful dramatic opera by Giacomo Meyerbeer.

[73]Marie-Julie Boulanger (1786-1850): a prominent mezzo-soprano. She was the grandmother of the distinguished composers and teachers Nadia and Lili Boulanger.

Such spirit!...

Henriette looked at him, and he stopped. "Well, what did you think?" she asked.

"Of what?" said Charles, barely composing himself.

"Of that aria."

"Oh! Yes, that aria. Yes, it's good. It's for a man, isn't it? So why were you singing it?"

"No, no," said Madame Bizot, "it's the maidservant who sings it to her mistress, to tell her that that's how her lover speaks of her."

"That's too bad," said Charles. "It seems to me it would suit a man's voice very well."

"Would you like to try it?" asked Henriette.

"Yes, very much."

She got up to make room for him. As they passed they brushed each other, and Charles started. Henriette stood next to him to turn the pages. She rested her hand on his shoulder. He felt like it was burning him; through everything including the seat she'd just left, on which he'd often sat after her, she seemed to penetrate him from all sides. He played the refrain and tried to sing; he got stuck in the first measure, stammered, and couldn't go on.

Henriette, perhaps understanding him, and dreading Madame Bizot's intervention, said right away, "Well, you accompany me and I'll sing."

She began. Charles followed her with less distress, and then he matched his feeling to hers as she sang. The accompaniment mingled its love with that of the voice. They seemed united in intimate performance. Finally Charles, carried away at the moment when the cavatina returned to its first motif,

How lovely she is! What a smile!

repeated that phrase and sang it with such intense expression, so powerfully, with such feeling, that it got everyone's attention—d'Aspert, Bizot, Lusssay—who were playing cards and who now applauded loudly. Charles didn't notice, and when he was done he let his chin drop to his chest.

With an impulse so quick there was no time for thought to intervene, Henriette, her hand on his shoulder, said to him very quietly, "Be careful, we're being watched."

Ah, it's words like that that make us cling to life in spite of its sorrows, its disappointments, its torments! Those words that suddenly fill the heart, and make it melt with joy, and join it to another heart. Those words are a delight for as long as we remember them. Charles wanted to look at Henriette, but he didn't dare, he grew afraid. He stood up.

She was a woman, and braver than he was. She dared to follow him with her eyes. He was so troubled he staggered. She could no longer help him, and she was almost sorry for what she'd said, and then she wasn't sure he'd understood her. But soon she got the proof that they'd already been compromised.

Charles composed himself, and responded adequately to the compliments he was getting.

Among the musical excerpts from *Emma*, the newspapers had spoken so highly of the bouquet rondo, with its sprightly *tra la la*, that Madame Bizot looked for it and found it. She read it over in silence, picturing Madame Boulanger's teasing movements; based on the tremendous effect she'd had, Madame Bizot wanted to give it a try. She summoned Charles, who'd gone off to sit in a corner, and asked him to accompany her. He came unwillingly: she'd interrupted his joy so maladroitly! Henriette also approached the piano, and she overheard Madame Bizot say to Charles, "Let's see if you can put as much feeling into this one."

Charles was so preoccupied that he didn't hear, or he heard badly. He replied aloud, "But this number, *Fond foolishness of love*, has no chorus."

Madame Bizot bit her lip and began. The first verse went well enough. Charles's good manners took the place of his good will. Madame Bizot thought she was getting somewhere. At the refrain of the second verse she allowed herself a little movement with her head and her hip that was supple and charming. The others cried "Bravo!" but without interrupting what they were doing: the card players who were absorbed in their trictrac, and Henriette and Charles because it was well sung.

Madame Bizot was hoping for total victory. She wanted to draw Charles into the voluptuous allure of the rondo, and to make him get carried away enough to sing the *tra la la* in the third verse. She put all the flirtation at her command into her voice. Charles accompanied her with feeling. She thought he would follow her; and when she reached the place where the musical phrase doubles back sweetly to pick up the refrain she slowed down and stopped singing to let Charles's voice enter. But Charles was silent, and another voice took on the *tra la la*. It was Bizot, who was swaying to the beat in his chair; Bizot, who having lost at cards all evening, got his spectacular revenge, singing romantically, with a delightful variation in the syllables, "*Troo loo loo, troo loo loo, troo, troo, troo loo loo.*

Six four, *troo loo loo, troo loo loo,* bezet, *trou loo loo…* Carne, *troo loo loo, troo loo loo.* I take two *troo loo loo, troo, troo, troo loo loo…*"

"It's unbearable!" cried Madame Bizot. "It's impossible to sing when you're around!"

"Well, I just scored six points."

"I'm telling you you're acting like an idiot, with your swaying back and forth and your troo troo."

"Bah!" said Bizot, glancing at the general to see if it was true. "What harm did I do?"

"Your wife is right," said the general angrily. "You're keeping the ladies from singing, and you scored twice on me with your *troo loo loo.*"

"All right, all right, all right," said Bizot. "I'll be quiet. Two aces. I win the hand."

"A rubber hand?"

"A rubber hand? Sure."

And they went back to their game.

Meanwhile Charles had left the piano. Madame Bizot was tactless enough to summon him back, and he was tactless enough to refuse. She was offended and had wicked ideas, including that of observing. Henriette had gone over to Charles. Pretending to tidy something on the mantelpiece above the fireplace where he was pretending to warm himself, she asked, "Why refuse Madame Bizot?"

"Oh, that woman throws herself at all the men."

She gave him a distraught look. He didn't understand. She moved away, paced around the parlor for a minute, then left the room. She'd gone out to cry—because, no matter how much sensitivity there is in a man's heart, it's never enough to match the sensitivity of a woman's love. What Charles had said, which he thought reflected badly only on Madame Bizot, Henriette had interpreted like this: "That woman throws herself at all the men, he said… So what about me? My God, what have I just done? What did I say to him?… You wretch! What he just said about her applies just as much to me. I threw myself at him, because he seemed to be reaching out to me, and this is what he thinks of me! My God!"

Poor Henriette was saying all that to herself as she wept, sitting in a corner of the dining room, alone in the dark. Oh, what a change! Moments earlier, when Charles's distress had made her own feelings clear to her, she'd been carried away like him, sacrificing herself to save him; and now she was scorned, reduced to Madame Bizot's level! She wept, she wept bitterly. Finally her husband, surprised at her absence, called her. She stood up straight, as if she were a guilty child, and as if he'd seen her crying. She decided to go back; but to conceal her tears she went to a sideboard and found a carafe of water so she could rinse her eyes and wash away of the traces of her crying. She was so upset that she knocked over a few dishes. Charles, who was consumed with anxiety at having seen her leave, took advantage of the noise to go to the door. He opened it, and by the light shed into the dining room he saw Henriette standing at the sideboard.

"Are you unwell? What's wrong?" he asked as he came forward.

"It's nothing," she said, passing quickly by him without looking at him.

But there was love even in that "nothing," because he'd questioned her out loud and she'd replied in a whisper. Charles didn't take it that way. When you love with your whole being, when your love is topmost in your heart, you're much more attuned to sorrow than to joy. Charles saw only the cold gesture, and heard only the word by itself; it was now his turn to suffer. Still, though it seemed as if that word came between them, from then on they shared a single life. Before then each had loved the other in isolation; they got along well together, but their moods were different. That night they felt joy at the same time and sorrow at the same time, and their love was mutual. Madame Bizot deduced more than there was: that was her nature. She planned to spend that night thinking over what to do. They all retired. Henriette avoided Charles's eyes, which sought hers; he left in despair.

We've said he didn't live in the house in which everyone else in this story had their bedrooms. When he was outside he headed quickly toward his quarters, but then he stopped. He'd tried in vain to exchange a look with Henriette; now he went toward her window. Did he hope she'd show herself? It was a sharp, excessively cold night, so that wasn't likely. But she was behind the closed shutters, and he felt as if his gaze could look right through them, he felt that where she was she must be so entirely penetrated by his soul that something of him would pass right through the wood: indeed he stared at the shutters as if they were a person about to speak. And yet he could see nothing, not even a light moving or a shadow on the curtains. He sat down on a rock and stayed there, waiting. For what? Can I say what? Did he even know himself? He sat there, and he waited.

As for Henriette, she'd gone to her room upset and miserable, but already more miserable at the state in which she'd left Charles than at what he'd said to her. In addition to the sensitivity of her own heart, she had too much pride not to have realized very quickly she'd been mistaken. Before she left the parlor she was sure of it. But to comfort Charles would have required a word, a look. She was afraid for herself, afraid of Madame Bizot. She preferred letting Charles suffer; and then she still resented him a little for what she no longer called his tactlessness. She went to bed with that thought, and at first she imagined he wouldn't be made too sad by her silence. She pictured him going back to his apartment, then forgetting his sorrow in sleep.

Then she said out loud, "No, he won't sleep." And neither did she sleep.

So then her anxiety returned. Perhaps, she thought, he really meant to reject her love the way he did Madame Bizot's. And, since the mind easily completes a thought once begun, she soon persuaded herself again that she'd been scorned; otherwise he'd have found a way to beg her pardon. It was true he hadn't had a chance, it was true she'd avoided him. But after leaving the parlor he could've... what?... "If I were him, I don't know, if I were a man, I'd wait under her windows, I'd want to see her, plead with her, implore her." And perhaps he was there.

She thought that, but she didn't dare believe it. She wanted to go see, and she didn't dare look. If he wasn't there, she'd be miserable; if he was there, what would she say to him? She vacillated for a long time. Finally she decided to risk her hopes of love. But she didn't want to compromise her secret by showing herself; she went into an unlit closet with nothing but a dormer window opening to the outside. She stood close to it. In bare feet on the wood floor, she raised just the corner of the curtain that covered the window, and she saw Charles sitting there, staring up at her bedroom windows. Oh, how happy she was!!! Then her heart was filled with all kinds of pity for him. He was cold; he must be suffering. She had that thought, without noticing that her feet were growing cold on the bare floor. Twice she raised her hand to open the window, and twice she stopped. Meanwhile there he sat. Oh, it was too cruel to leave him there.

He stood up. Though it was night, she could see him as plain as day. He wiped his eyes; she wept. He moved away, but he didn't go toward his quarters. He took the path leading to the woods: he was going to use physical fatigue to ease the distress in his heart. She unlatched the little window, but he didn't hear, and he disappeared into the woods. At that moment she would've called him back even in front of Madame Bizot. When Henriette left the window, she was freezing cold, and she was ill.

XIV. THE SILK THREAD

The next morning, when they met, they were both exhausted. When he saw Henriette, Charles didn't have the courage to speak to her. She said gently, "Good morning. I didn't sleep a wink last night either."

They already understood each other more than they needed to.

Still, after that evening, which marked the start of their love, they remained at the same point for a long time. They had no rivals to spur them on, nor the fear of being separated by some chance event; they had all the future for their love. As a result, they could savor its thousand tiny delights, the thousand sorrows that are imperceptible to most men, especially to those men who fight over a woman more than they love her. It was the best time in their love affair. They knew the two of them shared a secret, but they hadn't given that secret a name, they hadn't yet written across its forehead: "adulterous, incestuous love." They could still fool themselves, telling themselves it was an exquisite, jealous, passionate friendship. They didn't spend days in alarm.

A month passed that way, during which Madame Bizot tried to learn something new. It was incomprehensible to her that, between two young people who seemed to have come to an understanding, there was nothing new to see the next morning, or the morning after that. So when she saw there was no visible progress, she convinced herself it was some little domestic secret, a surprise they were preparing for the general for the upcoming holidays. Finally she went on the attack again; and thanks to her, Charles and Henriette's love, which had paused at a sweet and innocent trust, was plunged into all the torments of desire and jealousy. Being a skillful woman, Madame Bizot retraced her steps and saw she'd been wrong in feigning prudishness: that if she tried to seduce Charles through his feelings he'd turn instead to Henriette, who had more than she did of that charm of the heart that appeals to another heart. So she returned to her candid energetic attack. Suspecting that Henriette loved Charles, but quite sure she hadn't surrendered herself to him and that she wasn't a woman who'd surrender herself, Madame Bizot decided to offer him what her rival had refused him or would refuse him. The trick was to get Charles to desire her. That didn't seem difficult; she counted on the captain's youth and his enforced celibacy. All she needed was an opportunity, and chance gave her one that she knew very well how to take advantage of.

Before describing what happened, it must be said that Charles and Henriette already felt committed to each other. Perhaps, for most people reading this story, the word "commitment" will seem awfully big to describe the tenuous bond that connected those two lovers—just a childish adventure, really. And, it must be said in passing, though Henriette was no longer of the age of youthful sentiment that gets caught up in the strands of life, still you shouldn't forget that for both of them it was their first love, and a first love is always young.

One day, a Sunday, they were all in the vast old parlor: d'Aspert and Bizot were reading the newspapers and political pamphlets by the fire; Madame Bizot and Henriette were sewing by a window. Madame Bizot was making a string coin purse. Henriette was doing embroidery. Charles, coming in, approached the ladies; having learned what they were making, he praised their work, especially Madame Bizot's, which was very elegant and which she was sewing with such lovely hands that it was impossible not to admire them. Charles allowed himself a few meaningless gallantries; Henriette contributed nothing to the conversation.

A moment later, Madame Bizot stepped out, and Henriette said to Charles, "Madame Bizot must be awfully happy you like that coin purse so much."

"Why's that?"

"Because she's making it for you."

Henriette was behaving a little like a woman who's offended: she was giving away Madame Bizot's secret and robbing her of the pleasure of the small surprise she intended for Charles. He understood that his praise had displeased Henriette, and apologized so nicely that she didn't hold it against him. So then they began to talk about the presents each of them was preparing secretly for New Year's.

"What are you giving me?" asked Charles with a smile.

"Oh, you'll see. It should get here tomorrow."

"Get here! What can it be? Some piece of jewelry, some item of furniture from Paris? Ah," he added sadly, "I'd hoped for something else from you."

"From me?" said Henriette, blushing.

"Yes, from you. Even if it were only a flower, even if it were only that piece of silk thread you're holding between your lips."

"What childishness! My present goes with the general's, but it's a present that comes just from me."

"It's very pretty, isn't it?" said Charles scornfully. "I'll have to show it off to everyone, and everyone will admire it, except me."

"Do you want to refuse it?"

"Look, give me that piece of silk thread, please; that and only that!"

"That would be going too far," said Henriette in great distress. "Let's say no more about that. Look, you made me prick myself."

She stopped the bleeding with her handkerchief and set it down next to her. Charles wanted to take it, but she quickly withdrew it and put it in her pocket. Her heart was pounding, and her lips trembled, twisting the silk thread she still held in her mouth.

"What!" said Charles. "Not even that, such a small thing!"

Henriette smiled bitterly, as if she wanted to say, "You call that such a small thing!"

Madame Bizot returned a moment later and sat back down next to Henriette, and Charles left them alone. A moment later Henriette had to go out. Getting up, she automatically set the work in her hands down on the table, along with the thread she held in her lips. Charles noticed, and she hadn't even reached the parlor door before he rose in turn to go take it. She saw him doing it; coming back, she took the thread and wound it around her finger, shaking her head, "No, no," at Charles, whose eyes were pleading with her.

In the days that followed that refusal, Charles was sad and Henriette was affectionate: she seemed to want to make up for the sorrow she'd caused him. Finally New Year's came. The presents were exchanged, with all the usual embraces. The presents were costly, like those of people who have only a couple of occasions a year to spend a lot of money. The general had taken advantage of that circumstance to thank Charles for his devotion: his gift was a fine and very expensive pair of hunting horses. The gift he gave through Henriette was a magnificent toiletries kit with gold inlay, of an almost offensive value if it had come from anyone but the general, who was clearly giving it through Henriette's hands.

When all the objects in their boxes and their morocco leather covers were laid out on the table, the general said to Henriette, "Well! Where's the key to the toiletries kit?"

"Oh!" she said, blushing and shaking as she drew it from her bosom. "Here it is."

The key was hanging on the piece of silk thread. Oh, it was certainly the same one, its luster removed by her lips, and bitten here and there. Charles's knees almost buckled from joy. He opened the toiletries kit and admired it with a childish pleasure that delighted the general. Then it was Charles's turn: for the general he'd had sent from Paris a chair on wheels that could move around the parlor by turning a very simple crank. D'Aspert rolled around in it. The present Charles gave Henriette didn't seem to evince much thought: it was a very intricate sewing basket, with Henriette's name engraved all over it.

I won't mention the other gifts, not even Bizot's peculiar presents, except for the one he gave Henriette. He gave it to her almost in secret, saying very quietly, "Excuse me for having thought of it." Then, squeezing her hand and slipping a small medallion into it, he added with emotion, "My heart isn't entirely dead, and everything's allowed when you've got white hair."

Henriette didn't know what he meant; she was tempted to think it was a declaration of love. She didn't like the mockery that was directed at Bizot; and though she was cross, she moved aside to examine the medallion: it was a portrait of her son. She gave a cry of surprise and joy. And it came from Bizot! There are women who inspire feeling and taste in everyone around them. Everyone came over, wanting to see it, but she clutched her medallion and refused to show it to them. D'Aspert was insistent.

Bizot laughed and said, "Are you jealous of me? Let it go, let it go. I've very pleased to have chosen my present well."

"Oh, very well!" said Henriette. "And I thank you for it," she added, embracing him.

Bizot took two big kisses, then, smacking his lips like a man who's just tasted a fine wine, he cried, "Hum, hum, hum!"

Henriette passed the child's portrait to the general. He was happy that day, and he held out his hand to Bizot.

"What can it be?" asked Madame Bizot. "He would never tell me what it was."

"My word," said the general, "let them work it out between them. All I know is, it's none of my business."

Madame Bizot's curiosity got her no further. Charles's curiosity was drawn so strongly that he paid no attention to what was being said. Finally it was time to withdraw, because all this was taking place on New Year's

Eve. They decided to leave all the gifts in the parlor, but Henriette wanted to take hers back to her room.

"By God!" said the general, "You'll have plenty of time to examine them tomorrow."

Henriette was about to insist, when a "Who knows?" from Madame Bizot warned her that she'd guessed at the reason for her eagerness. So Henriette replied, "You're right. We'll see them again tomorrow."

They all withdrew after they heard the clock chime midnight. Charles took away his key. He was almost sorry to be happy by himself, but what he hoped for had in fact occurred: The next day he was the first one in the parlor, and nothing had been moved. He waited for Henriette to come down, and when she appeared she held out her hand to him, and in that hand was a ring. A ring! How reckless!... How could it escape Madame Bizot's notice? As soon as she came in she examined Henriette from head to toe, and even to her fingertips. But that ring looked just like another ring she knew Henriette normally wore; except that this ring contained a word and a secret. The secret opened up the ring. The word was *nothing*. But if you looked carefully you'd find two more words off to one side: *without you*.

Charles had been right to hope. No sooner had everyone retired the night before than Henriette had come back downstairs, trembling like a criminal. She knew very well that she was already far removed from the unconditional gratitude she'd vowed to give the general the day he'd so generously agreed to take on her misfortunes. She had too much delicate feeling in her heart not to see that she was already no longer the wife who, having brought her husband no girl's dowry, owed him irreproachable behavior in its place. But she felt no anxiety at the consequences of Charles's love. He was so much her friend that she thought it would never be more than a wrong of the heart.

So she went back downstairs and searched for a long time. Finally she found that ring, so similar to the one she wore that she thought it wasn't on her finger, and she'd recovered it by chance. Then she realized her mistake, and thought those two rings could only look the same to a stranger. She looked closer and found the secret, the whole secret. She took away the ring, and the next morning she had it on. And so that Charles would be in no doubt, for a moment she took it off, opened it, and then put it back on. So she'd accepted Charles's pledge: she'd given him the silk thread he wanted so badly. You can't love each other more completely or more furtively. They were already very guilty.

XV. ILLNESS

The tranquility of Charles and Henriette's love was soon disturbed, as we've said, by Madame Bizot's carnal plans. Resolved not to contend using either her mind or her heart against the woman she saw as her rival, she no longer brought anything provocative to the evening gatherings, unless it was her physical self. Truly no one had ever been sleeker, more dewy, more flirtatious. She moved exquisitely, and when she was alone with Charles she posed so gracefully, with such voluptuous charm; but she took care not to draw his attention to it. Still sometimes his attention was drawn, and she pretended not to notice, neither stopping her teasing nor taking it any further. It didn't suit her to act demure; it didn't suit Charles to feel he was being ignored. She succeeded quite well, because he liked her better this way. He even allowed himself to pay her a few compliments. But from there to what Madame Bizot wanted was a great distance, especially for a heart that was engaged.

A mishap served her beyond her expectations. Charles fell ill and was forced to stay in his room, with heart palpitations that required absolute physical rest. Henriette visited him, accompanied by her husband, or Monsieur Bizot, or her father. But Madame Bizot visited him alone, and stayed a long time. Eventually she settled in there; she'd brought her embroidery work to his bedside. Henriette felt frustrated, then cross, then miserable—for she didn't dare say anything to Madame Bizot, and though she was disappointed in Charles himself, she couldn't hold it against him, as attentions or consideration toward another woman, cares against which he couldn't defend himself. She sat fuming in the parlor with her husband, but she didn't dare leave him. D'Aspert didn't speak to her even three times an hour when she was there, but he asked for her as soon as she wasn't. If a servant had replied twice in a row, "Madame is with Monsieur Charles," she'd have thought she was doomed.

She often found small ways to thwart Madame Bizot's private meetings with him: she'd send her father in, or more often her son; but she was tactful enough not to send Bizot. I believe that was more out of pity for him than out of consideration for his wife, for she was still grateful to the poor man for that portrait of her son.

Two days passed that way; by the third, the torment was unbearable. Henriette did nothing but enter and leave the parlor: she couldn't stay there, and she headed toward Charles's quarters. In the short distance separating his rooms from the main house, she stopped three or four times… What could she say? What excuse could she use for turning up? She found a thousand, but deep down she always felt that Madame Bizot would interpret it as jealousy—and to betray her jealousy to Madame Bizot seemed like the worst of all outcomes. Still, she wanted to know what she was doing there. Her passion must've been quite different from what she imagined: she decided to spy on them. She went to a concealed staircase, and used it to climb silently to a hidden closet, from where she could see and hear everything.

Madame Bizot was sitting on Charles's bed. "Charles," she said with a sweet smile and a caressing glance, "do you love her?"

"How can you think that? I have an inexpressible respect for her."

"That doesn't keep you from being in love, and surely Henriette deserves to be loved."

"Of course she deserves it, and it's precisely everything that makes her worthy of it that forbids me from loving her: such touching virtue, such devotion to her husband's happiness."

"Yes, yes, and on top of all that she's one of the most beautiful women I've ever met."

"She's beautiful indeed," said Charles, who enjoyed praising Henriette and couldn't foresee how Madame Bizot would take advantage of that.

"So beautiful," said Madame Bizot. "Perfect. Have you ever seen more slender, more elegant hands?" And with her own lovely hand she brushed the hair away from Charles's brow.

Feeling he should thank her, Charles said, "But yours are charming too."

"And what an elegant, lithe figure!" said Madame Bizot, swaying gently on the bed to imitate the sweet movement of the figure she was praising. And that showed off her own figure, which she could press against Charles's body, next to which she was sitting. He couldn't help noticing, and her gentle pressure stirred him a little. He was still holding Madame Bizot's hands, and he squeezed them.

Henriette didn't understand, and was just embarrassed by the praise Madame Bizot was directing at her, which she found immodest: it seemed to her Madame Bizot was exposing her shamelessly in her lover's eyes. But soon she began to understand she wasn't the one Madame Bizot was showing off to Charles; and indeed she went on, "And then how elegantly her neck is joined to her shoulders! She has this…"

And at the word "this," spoken with enthusiasm, Madame Bizot pulled a pin out of her robe and showed off her white bosom and her lovely shoulders. "She has this, with ravishing purity."

Charles couldn't help looking at the graceful illustration of what she was saying was so lovely. He sat up in bed and let his glance plunge down into the folds of Madame Bizot's dress.

"Anyway," she went on, "I've got lovely feet, and just between us I think I've got lovely legs. But Henriette's are so perfectly shaped!" She put her hand on her dress to show off her leg; posed like that, she'd exposed herself almost as far as her knee.

Charles put his hand on it. Under the pretext of removing it, Madame Bizot moved further up the bed, pretended to lose her balance, and let herself fall on him, her face against his, her breast pressing on his chest. Charles put his arms around her.

Trying to get away, Henriette took a few steps, but no sooner had she reached the top of the concealed staircase than she fainted. When she came to, her name was being called on all sides. They'd come several times to look for her in Charles's room, but had found only Madame Bizot. The two of them said they hadn't seen her. When the voices grew more distant she got away and went back to the parlor. Her dishevelment and her pallor provided an excuse: she said she'd wanted to walk as far as the woods, but she'd suddenly felt faint and had to sit down.

D'Aspert and her father and Bizot were concerned. She told them she was ill, and in fact she was. They took her upstairs and put her to bed. A burning fever took hold of her, and in less than an hour she had to be bled. Madame Bizot came running. What a torment it was! Everybody was there, and Henriette couldn't even turn away; she had to settle for silence. Lussay insisted she be allowed to rest, and she asked to be alone, so they left her. She began to weep unceasingly, without thinking about anything, without analyzing her sufferings or the extent of her misery: she just wept. She was sitting up in her bed, her head in her hands. She noticed the ring she was wearing. She tore it off and threw it angrily across the room: that was the first distinct object in her sorrow, which up to then had been only a terrible confused agony, relieved by tears, which, when her tears were exhausted, remained stark and visible before her.

"I'll never touch that ring again! Oh, if my life depended on it, if it was found there, and picked up, and examined, and they discovered what it contains, and accused me as if I were guilty—well, I'd rather face that than feel it still on my hand." That was what she said to herself at first, wiping her eyes angrily. Then she added, "But he has something of mine, and he has to give it back to me. I'll ask for it back... Will I have to tell him?... Yes, I'll tell him... Oh, no... no... never... Well, I'll ask him for it back, that's all... I'll give him back his ring... with contempt... with no explanation... Would he dare accuse me of being capricious?... And if he does accuse me, what do I care?... Yes... yes... I'll give it back to him. And my thread, my poor silk thread... to which I'd attached my life— that's all over!... My God, my God!... Oh, how he deceived me!... How I loved him!... I'm so miserable!"

She began to weep copiously again, for she'd reached the point of missing the joys of her love. So she got up, and, staggering, wiping her eyes at every step, she went over to the ring where it had fallen in the corner. There she stopped to consider it. That look contained the entire history of her love, which she recalled hour by hour. Tears and sobbing suffocated her. She fell to her knees and, picking up the ring, she murmured quietly over and over, "Farewell!... Farewell!... Farewell!"

Farewell to her love, to her life, to her trust, to everything in the world. She tore from her heart everything she'd hoped for. She would've died there, if she hadn't heard a noise. She clutched the ring violently and with one leap was back in bed.

It was Charles; he looked like a ghost. Monsieur Bizot was with him. Henriette looked at Charles. If he hadn't already suspected something serious, he would've guessed what was wrong with Henriette by the look she gave him, which contained the most indignant contempt, along with the bitterest smile. After having led Charles to the bed—for Charles could barely drag himself along—Bizot wanderer away to the far side of the room.

When Bizot's back was turned, Henriette pointed him out to Charles with an insulting mockery, and with a single exclamation, "Oh!..." She meant that to get to her room Charles had leaned on Bizot, the husband of that immodest woman. "Despicable! Despicable!" was what Henriette meant by that gesture and that exclamation.

Charles's teeth chattered, his eyes wandered, his chest heaved as if it would split, and his heart pounded. He had to put his hand on the bed to support himself. Henriette eagerly took his hand, and slipping into it the ring she was hiding, she said, "Here..."

Charles might've been expecting it, but still he drew back, appalled.

Henriette went on in a low voice, "Give it back to me." Though she didn't specify what that referred to, neither one of them was fooled: it was the silk thread, that almost imperceptible love token, she wanted back.

Shaking his head gently, Charles replied, "No... no..."

"Give it back," she repeated curtly, her voice rising. "Give it back!"

"Not like this," said Charles, calming her with a gesture. "No... to-morrow..."

"Oh!" said Henriette, clenching her teeth. "Give it back!"

This time Charles replied, his voice choking, ""No... no... no..."

"Oh! Give it back!" said Henriette, sitting up. "Give it back, or I'll call for help!"

She would've doomed herself at that moment. She would've claimed that thread back even in the presence of her husband, even if he killed her for it. Dying didn't matter to her.

Charles didn't answer. He opened his shirt—and that gesture re-minded Henriette of Madame Bizot's gesture, and she began to laugh, striking her head with her fists. Charles tore the thread from around his neck, breaking it as he did so. Henriette grabbed it, and in a blind fury she tore it with her fingers into the shortest strands she could. Then she sepa-rated them still further with her teeth, and scattered the strands on her bed. When that was done, she said in a low voice, "Nothing! Nothing left!"

"Nothing left but to die," said Charles in a terrible muffled voice. He looked at her, and two large tears dropped from his eyes, and in the same fatal and resolute voice he added, "Farewell!" And with that he turned away.

"Charles!" cried Henriette, almost leaping out of bed. But she imme-diately fell back, writhing convulsively and crying out, "Oh, my God! My God! My God! I'm so miserable!"

Seeing her like that, Charles turned back and ran to her. Bizot came too—Bizot, that good-natured man, who'd known Henriette's secret for a long time, who said nothing, and was willing to be made fun of, who had more character than all the rest of them, and played the role he played for others only because they weren't worth him playing a different role. He helped Charles put Henriette back to bed, and while Charles supported her head in his hands he made her sniff smelling salts. She opened her eyes, but they were so dull, so glazed over, that she seemed blind. Bizot went to get Lussay. Meanwhile Charles tried to say something to Henriette, but she didn't hear him. Lussay came running, and Charles had to withdraw.

The next day Henriette's crisis had passed, but Charles was in a desperate state. When they told Henriette, she didn't believe them; she thought it was just a way for him to draw attention to himself. She didn't ask for news of him from either her father or Bizot when they came from seeing him. D'Aspert had himself carried to Charles's quarters. He stayed there a long time, and sent several times to ask Henriette to join him; she always replied evasively. When he returned to the parlor he was very sad.

He was upset enough that he only reproached Henriette sorrowfully for her indifference. "It was wrong of you not to have gone to see Charles! Yesterday, as ill as he was, he got up as soon as he learned you were unwell, and perhaps it was that recklessness that's put him in this condition. Please go see him. If it's not out of real interest, at least do it out of politeness."

Henriette didn't know what to do. She couldn't think of an excuse, and the general's distress was so intense that the danger must be urgent. Just then Lussay, Bizot, and his wife came in.

"What!" said d'Aspert. "You're all here? No one stayed with Charles?"

"No," said Lussay, "he wanted to be completely alone."

"Alone!" cried Henriette loudly. "Alone! How imprudent!"

"I'll go back soon," said Lussay.

"He mustn't be left alone," replied Henriette quickly.

"There's no danger," said Lussay. "He's feeling better."

D'Aspert looked at Henriette in surprise: the sudden change, her quick transition from marked indifference to such urgent interest struck him as inexplicable.

She didn't notice, and she replied to her father in a kind of despair, "There's more danger than you think!"

"What danger?" asked d'Aspert, looking at his wife.

"What if he tried to kill himself?" she replied, carried away by her fear, by her love, by remorse for the cruelty she'd inflicted on him.

The astonishment of d'Aspert, of Lussay, and of Madame Bizot quickly informed Henriette how imprudent that exclamation had been.

Bizot rescued her: "No," he said gently, "don't worry about that. I made him listen to reason." His calm tone reassured them all, but they didn't understand. So he went on, peacefully taking a pinch of tobacco, "Just imagine, yesterday when he came to see Madame d'Aspert, he told us in a cold, resolute tone that he believed his illness was incurable, and he didn't think he had the courage to lead the life of an invalid, with all of its physical torments, and that he'd soon put an end to it. Madame took it as true, as if he'd already done it. But he listened to reason. After all, I told him, there are cures for every ailment, even the ailments of the heart. It took me a while, but I left him more at ease."

"Perhaps," said d'Aspert, "because that wish to be left alone... You should go to him, Henriette, since it was to you he said that foolishness. Go to his room, talk to him. It's an unworthy weakness, and in a man of thirty! Whereas I, my God! I suffer the tortures of the damned!"

"All right," said Henriette. "Come on. Let's go there together."

"No," said the general. "Go by yourself. He spoke to you, he confided that despairing thought to you. He might feel humiliated if he knew we'd all heard about it. Because, really, you can't be as weak as that. But some men are like that. Go on, go... Go, I beg you."

"Go on," said Bizot. "Go on."

She couldn't refuse anymore. She left the parlor, crossed the courtyard without knowing what she was going to say nor what she'd do, climbed the stairs to Charles's apartment, and entered his room.

XVI. YET ANOTHER STEP

Charles was lying on his bed with his eyes open, staring at the ceiling. His lips moved, like those of a man praying. He didn't notice Henriette had come in. She came closer and examined him. His face showed all the signs of death: his eyes were lifeless, his rigid features no longer reflected even his body's considerable suffering. She stood in front of him to make him see her, but he didn't look at her. Nothing moved, except his lips, which moved constantly. She listened to the sounds they were forming: it was neither thoughts nor words that made them twitch, it was a convulsive trembling.

Terrified, Henriette called gently, "Charles!... Charles!..."

He smiled, and without taking his eyes from the ceiling he murmured quietly, "Yes... yes..."

"Charles! Charles! It's me!" she cried in fear, taking his hand.

He lowered his eyes and looked at her, in a way that made clear he saw her only as if she were a vision. He eyed her from head to toe as if she were cloaked in some shadow through which he had trouble seeing her. Finally his gaze cleared, and Henriette could tell he recognized her. He seemed surprised and delighted. But suddenly his despair returned. He let his head, which he'd raised for a moment, fall back, and he said quietly, "It isn't you. It isn't you."

Thinking he was delirious, she said gently, "It's me, it's me."

"Henriette," he went on, looking at her. "Ah, I can see it's you, really you. Earlier I was happier."

"Happier..."

"Oh, it was dream in which I expected to die. But you were sent, and you came."

"No," she said, her voice overcome with tears, "I wasn't sent. No, I came to see you, to plead with you..."

"To plead with me? With me?" he asked, sitting up. "To plead with me? For what?"

"To be calm. Not to listen to your despair. To live."

"What does that matter to you?" he replied bitterly, turning away.

Henriette couldn't make sense of what she felt. In spite of Charles's despondency and the danger he was in, she didn't feel generous enough to say, "I forgive you." In any case, she had no forgiveness in her heart. But the thought of watching him die was awful to her, unbearable. She gave way impulsively to impatience. "What do you want me to do? Because here I am, and..."

"Oh, I don't want anything," he interrupted. "I want to die."

"To die! Oh, it's easy enough to die. But I have to go on living! And yet, am I the guilty one? Am I..." She stopped and turned away to hide her tears.

Charles seemed to come to some important decision. "Listen, Henriette. I know you were here,"—he pointed to the closet—"because yesterday I dragged myself there when I was alone, and I found this handkerchief. I was astonished. Your illness, when I heard about it, made things almost clear to me. I resolved to see you, and your behavior told me everything."

"Well! Am I wrong?"

"It would take more time than you can give me, and more strength than I have, to explain. I'm asking you to give me an hour this evening."

"This evening! No... later... in a few days, when you're better."

"You promise?"

"I promise."

"And till then, is there nothing you'll say to me?"

"What would I have to say to you? Be happy, that's all I can wish you," she replied sadly.

"Happy!" he repeated. Then he fell silent, and went on a moment later, "You've promised to listen to hear me out."

"I'll do it."

Charles fell silent again. A great many thoughts disturbed him, presumably, and pulled him away from the last thing she'd said; for he went on, looking at her, "Did you ever love me?"

Henriette considered him with an astonishment she couldn't hide. Stunned, she dropped her arms and replied with an intense outpouring of despair, "Oh, my God, what have I done?"

"You loved me!" he cried, seizing her hands in his enthusiasm.

At that word she recovered all of her dignity. "Oh, I assume it isn't me you think you're speaking to. Wait for her to get here."

She moved away from his bed. He desperately followed her with his eyes. "I'll see you again!" he said.

"I've promised, sir," she replied coldly, and she left the room.

When she got outside she was almost pleased with herself. By her reckoning, she'd forgiven nothing. All was over between them. She dared to examine her own conduct and excuse herself for her intimacy with Charles. According to her, she'd repented soon enough. She had no more secrets with him. It had been the start of an attraction that had been stopped before any harm was done. No doubt chance had brought about the break, but her honor had taken advantage of that. That was what she thought; that was what she told herself, not realizing it was because she loved him too much that she hadn't forgiven him.

She couldn't see that her satisfaction arose from two motives, both of them guilty: the first was that she'd made sure of her lover, and the second was that at the same time she'd preserved her resentment against him. How blind she was! She'd finally attached the right word to all of her actions, right up to this day that was so equivocal for her. Poor woman, who'd let herself be rocked gently by a secret attachment, in which nothing had been said to alarm her; then who'd been driven nearly to death with anger at the first hint of infidelity; who'd been asked if she'd loved him and had replied, "Never"—did she think she wouldn't forgive him? That her lover's wrongdoing was inexcusable? That nothing would erase it from her heart? No doubt she thought so, for she was honest in her emotions. But who could ever probe the depths of those complicated emotions? Who could ever trace the path by which they lead us to our doom?

XVII. ANOTHER ONE

From then on Henriette raised no further objections to visiting Charles. The first few times she acted sad; but as soon as his life was out of danger she became serious; and when he was able to take part in general conversation she pretended to be happy. Then began a whole series of petty acts of vengeance she felt it was her right to inflict on him in return for what she'd granted him. Never had she seemed so uninterested in everything around her, so cheerful, so considerate to Madame Bizot. Several times it happened that Madame Bizot came to see Charles with Lussay and Henriette. And sometimes Lussay left them, and right away Henriette left too, making a show of leaving them together. After a few days Madame Bizot stopped visiting Charles; and then Henriette almost stopped going too.

When he was nearly recovered, Charles returned to the parlor. For a long time, but in vain, he tried to find an occasion to ask for the rendezvous, or rather the conversation, he'd been promised. But Henriette always avoided being alone with him, and when he said a word to her in passing she pretended not to have heard him. Once, when everyone was in the parlor, he approached her, and thinking he could make her listen to him, he said very quietly, "For pity's sake, Henriette…"

"Excuse me?" she answered out loud. "You speak so softly I can't hear you."

In the midst of his despair Charles grew angry, and, taking no notice of her interruption, he replied in a low voice,"You lied to me, ma'am."

Henriette was humiliated: for the first time her behavior struck her as lacking the dignity she'd meant to uphold through her misery. She realized she seemed like no more than a woman who'd been hurt. She remembered the pledge she'd made; but she noticed that Madame Bizot was watching them. The vain satisfaction of getting revenge won out once again over the righteousness of her injury, and she replied mockingly, "I'm afraid of arousing Madame Bizot's jealousy."

Poor Madame Bizot! Her humiliation and abandonment were complete. She'd returned to visit Charles, but he always rang for someone to join them as soon as they were alone. She'd written to him; he'd refused her letters and returned them to her—and, so that Henriette would be in no doubt about it, he'd even pushed his brutality so far as to have Madame Bizot's letters returned to her when the two women were together. He never addressed her in the parlor; he barely kept up the minimal gestures of politeness that can't be avoided. Henriette observed it and knew it. Madame Bizot—so cheerful, so amiable—sometimes wept in secret, and occasionally her tears came even in front of her rival.

Henriette could've put an end to it with a word, a word that would've told Charles, "Enough: I've been sufficiently avenged," and he would've resumed the affectionate tone with which he could so easily have comforted a woman like Madame Bizot. Treated with a little goodwill, she'd have found it natural that a handsome young man and a beautiful young woman had noticed each other's qualities for an hour—as long as it was over by the next day. If she'd been asked, she would've have abetted their love affair. But Henriette was implacable: she demanded her victim, well sacrificed, well scorned, well rejected. And since that wasn't just out of spitefulness, she must've have had a powerful, avid, insatiable love for Charles's heart, which had gotten away from her for a moment.

She'd tortured Charles in every possible way. It took a woman's ingenuity to find another place to stick the knife in everywhere. In the parlor, if they were playing cards she'd say, "Monsieur Charles and Madame Bizot will be partners." At table, with reference to a piece of fruit, she'd say, "Offer it to Madame Bizot. You're forgetting Madame Bizot." When they were out for a walk she'd say "Give your arm to Madame Bizot." Everything led to the same place. Charles had to have a lover's patience equal to the persecution to stand it.

The evening we've been speaking of, Henriette overshot her goal, and those words, "I'm afraid of arousing Madame Bizot's jealousy," offended Charles. How often he'd felt pity for that woman, whose only wrong had been to love him after her own fashion, and to fight for him with the weapons she had, but who was fundamentally good, and lovely, and amorous! Charles had loathed her the day after his downfall; then he'd forgiven her; and finally Henriette's persecution had made her almost interesting to him, for she'd openly resigned herself to her fate. Though she was decidedly a sensual lover, she still had a kind of respect for the passionate romantic love she herself was incapable of. Henriette's crisis and Charles's desperate condition had taught her that their attraction was one of those passions you can die from, and more: for which you kill rivals, and lose your honor, and ruin your future.

From where she was sitting, she'd overheard Henriette's cruel remark, and she'd been misled by the sudden pallor she saw on Charles's face. She thought it was one of those moments of despair that often overcame him; and when he came near her she said gently, "Don't worry, I'll be leaving in a week."

"Leaving? Why?" asked Charles out loud. "Hear this, general: Madame Bizot is threatening to leave us. I assume you won't let her go. What will our evenings be like without her, since she's their heart and soul?"

"Hmm! Hmm!" said Bizot.

"What!" cried d'Aspert. "I was hoping we'd have you here for at least another month. And if she's not in too much of a hurry to see her lilacs bloom, we can offer her our own to enjoy."

"What a good thought!" said Charles. Then to her he added quietly, but loudly enough for Henriette to hear, "Oh, don't go, don't go. I have so many things to beg your forgiveness for."

Henriette was floored. Charles—whom she'd had in her grip for a month, whom she'd never even asked for all cruelties he inflicted on Madame Bizot to appease her—Charles had just rebelled. She'd studied his character: she knew that to him, even at the cost of his life, a resolution became a duty for him as soon as he'd committed himself, and she was afraid to let him make that commitment.

Make no mistake, Henriette had reached the point where Charles was constantly in her thoughts. He was hers; it wasn't for the sake of some other woman she'd asked him to go on living. She was capable of wanting to crush him under her feet, but she would've asked him to forgive her. She thought she was doomed: all of her revenge, all of her vanity collapsed at the idea that he might love another woman, and this time love her not by being taken by surprise sensually, by some act of infidelity that deep down she scorned, but by a choice of the heart, by a preference of the soul.

She came to a sudden decision, and staked her whole life on a word. She knew Charles was angry: the implacable concentrated fury on his face was the same as when he'd wanted to kill that wretch Aubert. She was taking a big risk. Perhaps he wouldn't obey the order she was about to give him, in which case it was all over, she'd never speak to him again, she'd never forgive him anything again. No matter—she gambled everything.

She rose and passed in front of Charles. "Follow me," she said quietly. And she left the parlor.

She didn't have the torment of waiting: even in the midst of his anger, Charles couldn't resist her solemn, resolute manner as she'd passed him. They went to the dining room.

"I don't want that woman to stay here," said Henriette coldly.

"Why not?"

"Am I not the mistress in my own home?" she replied haughtily.

"If you're doing it in that capacity," said Charles, moving away, "you have servants who can send her away."

Henriette, who'd left the parlor to give Charles the rendezvous she'd refused him so often, had no sooner tested his obedience than she remembered the vastness of her grievance against him, and she was unable to start on the approach she could've led off with a moment earlier. So, once again accommodating her own pride and love, and unwilling to take the first step, but still not wanting Charles to go away without an explanation, she said, almost in tears, "Oh, you can do what you want and say what you want, but you're in love with that woman!"

"I am? Oh, if you'd only been willing to listen to me..."

"But that's so difficult," she said, turning away to hide both the joy she felt at finding an opportunity to yield to him, and the shame she felt in having that joy.

"Difficult?" said Charles, whose changed tone of voice reassured Henriette fo her power over him. "Difficult! I can come back to the parlor tonight. Can't you leave your room?"

"I'll be in my boudoir at midnight." She moved toward the parlor, but before she went through the door she suddenly took fright at everything she'd made a game of for the past month. Now that she was Charles's accomplice once again, she feared his behavior toward Madame Bizot would be noticed. She said, "Speak to Madame Bizot. Ask her to stay. Let her suspect nothing."

Henriette went into the parlor, and Charles followed her a moment later. As hard as it had been for him not to talk to Madame Bizot up to then, that evening it was just as hard, even impossible, for him to say anything to her. His heart was so full, his soul was so alive, that he couldn't find any small talk. Indeed, if he'd had to speak in those first moments, he couldn't have kept his soul from bursting forth in exclamations of joy. That excessive happiness didn't arise from his having been forgiven, for the forgiveness remained uncertain, but from the idea that once again there was something secret, and avowedly secret, between Henriette and him. Whether a breakup or forgiveness followed, shared interests had been reestablished between them, and that was enough for now to account for Charles's joy.

As for Henriette, she covertly observed Charles's demeanor, and she enjoyed the reassuring conviction, which she could read all over his face, that it was once again from her that he received pleasure and joy and all of life. As for what he'd say to her that night, she'd listen to his justification, because that was why she was receiving him. But for a long time already that justification had been complete in her heart: she'd already exhausted all the explanations he might give her.

The reckless woman didn't know the power a lover's voice would grant him, and how much that voice would cause to resonate within her feelings she didn't even suspect.

Finally the time came for everyone to retire, and with it came her remorse and fear over what had happened. Henriette was on the brink of saying she didn't want to do it, but she felt she had no right to have a choice. She was on the brink of asking Charles not to come, but he gave her no opportunity to say that, and stayed far away from her. He was confident that, after the favor he'd been granted, the only risk was in having his happiness taken away: Henriette couldn't go any further, but she could backtrack.

They had to part. Charles had found some pretext to leave the parlor. Henriette was the last to go upstairs to her room. The entire time that passed between when she entered her room and when she left it again she spent envisioning vague horrors. She didn't feel a material fear, so to speak, of what she was doing—the fear of being caught by her husband or her father or Madame Bizot—she thought only of her love. She frightened herself with the voluntary casting off of the aura of virtue that surrounded her. As for Charles's feelings, she was sorry she'd lose his respect without gaining anything, for he couldn't love her any more than he already did.

That was her true torment. To be despised by her husband, mistreated, driven out, dishonored—those things didn't frighten her, once she'd decided in her heart to take this risk. But no longer to be herself, no longer to be the woman who'd inspired such a deep and respectful passion, that's what truly terrified her. She felt enough in love to excuse herself; but would Charles understand that love? Would she dare confess it to him? Wouldn't he leave their rendezvous thinking it was a tryst asked for and granted, just like in every intrigue? Henriette was too young at heart to realize that not to offer herself to him would give her an excuse: to her, the moment she went downstairs to meet Charles the whole crime was committed, the adultery was complete. She was mistaken, as you can see: she didn't know that, when we fall short of our duty, we consider sacred those people we haven't yet entirely failed to understand.

In the purity of her virtue a woman says to herself, "Never will I receive declarations of love. It's a sin to receive them—the greatest sin of all." A man speaks to her of love. She lets him, and takes refuge in resolving, "Never will I reply to him." She feels sorrow, then jealousy, then joy, and she lets slip an avowal of love. Then she retreats behind a new rampart, where she feels safe from everything: "I might've let him see I love him, but I'll never give him any encouragement, not by a glance or a word, for that's when I'd truly become a sinner. Even if you can't master the feelings in your heart, you can remain master of your actions. That's all heaven can ask, that's all people can ask of a woman's virtue. No, not a word, not a glance." She doesn't even think about a tryst, because a tryst... that would be the sin in full. But alas! The glance slips out, the word is spoken, the tryst is arranged. She feels remorse, she knows it's wrong, but she falls back on her last resource: "I love him, I know. I'm losing my mind, I can't live without seeing him or hearing his voice. But I'd die before I'd give myself to him."

Henriette hadn't reached that stage; she still considered her action a sin. So it was with terrible dread that she went downstairs. How many times had she left her room in the middle of the night to go search the house furtively for something she'd forgotten! How often, suffering from insomnia, had she gone silently down to her boudoir to find a book! But then the precautions she took weren't for her; she simply wanted not to disturb anyone's sleep. She could've been caught without it bothering her. But that night, how her heart pounded! How her knees buckled! But in fact there was no danger: it was barely eleven o'clock, the house was shut tight, no one was going to catch Charles. She could've offered a thousand excuses for having left her room, the same reasons she would've given calmly two months earlier. And yet now, if her husband had appeared before her, she would perhaps have fallen to her knees and said, "Throw me out."

When she got downstairs she went to the parlor. She unlocked an outside door, then went to sit in her boudoir. She waited there till midnight; and there, after long pondering her past life and her future, she grew calmer, for she'd finally come to a resolution. The clock rang midnight, and Charles appeared

.

XVIII. LOVE

He came in slowly. He didn't throw himself at her feet with passionate avowals, with the lover's gratitude that's practically an insult, so much does it seem to take for granted his coming happiness. Neither of them felt joyful; their consciences were burdened by the knowledge that their love would be fatal for someone, if not for themselves. Henriette was seated; Charles remained standing before her. He was embarrassed by what he had to say to her. Indeed, that encounter between two people who've never uttered the word "love" to each other, and of whom one has come to justify an infidelity, was difficult to begin.

Charles did away with the difficulty: after a moment's hesitation he turned to her and said, with his voice full of emotion, "Henriette, I love you!"

"I know."

"You know? And yet you've been so cruel to me."

"I was wrong. Why should I be angry about something I should consider a blessing?"

"A blessing? Oh, you're still pitiless, you still blame me... But you'll listen to me."

"No... no..." replied Henriette sadly. "It's you who must listen to me. Love Madame Bizot, love her. That's my advice, that's my request."

Charles was astonished, for he heard neither bitterness nor anger in her voice—just profound sadness and despairing resignation. He was mistaken about the feeling that inspired her despondency: he thought Henriette was renouncing a love she considered superficial, and which didn't meet the hopes of her own heart. He wanted to justify himself. "Henriette, I'll obey you entirely. I'll die if you wish it. I can do more: I can live— live with the condition of never speaking to you again, of being someone you're indifferent to, someone you wouldn't ask to give up his life even to spare you a tear. But I can't love another, nor stop loving you. You don't believe me!... And I've given you the right to doubt my words. But if you knew what I've done so as not to love you, you'd realize that, since I love you, there's nothing in the world that can save me from loving you."

Now in turn Henriette was surprised. She'd decided to ask Charles to forget her, and was hurt to hear that he'd tried not to love her. In a tone in which sadness allowed a little bitterness to show, she said, "Why didn't your persevere in that good resolve?"

"I persevered for a long time, for long after I'd met you. And I have to admit, even now as I speak to you my love isn't without some fear."

"Yes, I understand. It can bring you great misery. It can compromise your future."

He smiled sadly. "There's only one misery in love, and that's to be mistaken."

"Mistaken? How so?"

He seemed embarrassed; a violent struggle was going on within him. Finally he made up his mind. He sat down by her, and in the tone of a man beginning a long account he said:

"Listen to me, ma'am, listen patiently. In making this avowal I'm going to stake all the happy memories I have, all my hopes for the future, and I have the right to be heard. I'm going to show you the bottom of my heart, and tell you what no one's ever told a woman, something that might repel her, outrage her, turn her pity for an unfortunate man to hatred. But it doesn't matter: from you I must have everything or nothing. Don't withdraw; what I'm asking of you holds no danger for you. I alone am running a risk, I alone can suffer for it. For no matter what you are, I love you, and my choice is made. If you were the guiltiest of women, the vilest, I'd love you. I couldn't love you any more if you were the most virtuous woman of all. That's to say I love you like a madman, like a fool. It's to say you can make what you want of me: a great and good man, if you like; a despicable wretch, if that's your command. Anyway, I love you to the point where I belong to you more than you belong to yourself. You might have murmurs in your conscience contrary to your wishes; I have none contrary to your desires. I'm sworn to you—devoted the way someone is to God, condemned the way someone is to hell."

Charles's overblown description of his love made Henriette pay attention. She considered him with astonishment that also contained a little fear.

"Yes," he went on, "that's how I love you, and yet I'm afraid of you. I don't know you, I don't know what you are."

"Sir," she said, rising, "have you come here to put me on trial? Is this an interrogation to which I have to respond?"

"So you didn't understand me?" he asked, quickly stopping her. "I'm not asking you anything… neither about your past nor about your future. I'm asking to be yours, and for that I've come to say, behold your slave…

Behold how much I love you... Now listen to me... This is a story I've rehearsed: listen to it... You can leave afterwards without responding, without saying a word... Listen... For any love besides mine, the words 'I love you' would contain everything. For me, those words are almost empty of meaning. They'll be worth something only when I've told you all my heartbreak."

There was so much distress in his voice, in his eyes, in his gestures, that it overwhelmed her. She sat back down and remained silent. Then, when he didn't begin, she looked up at him and said, "I'm listening."

She met his eyes, which were fixed on her. He seemed not to have heard her, for he went on, while a tear fell from his eyes, "Oh, it isn't possible that I could love you so much and you might not deserve it..."

She was about to urge him once again to speak, so he hastened to go on, in a wild rush and an ominous voice, "When I came here, I was told you were a fallen woman."

"Sir," she said, rising once more, "by telling me that you're treating me as if I were. Go ahead and believe it! I have no answer."

"Henriette, I'm not asking you for an answer. I'm not asking you anything, though I have the right to, since you love me... Yes... Oh, don't turn pale! You love me. But with what kind of love?... How can I tell? Well, I have to know. I've said I don't know you; well, you don't know me either. To you, I might be one of those men whose hearts are given to a woman's charms and elegance and talents. My love for you flatters you. Well, no, it's much baser than that! It's servility, shameful servility! You have to see that servility fully exposed, and then you can decide whether there's any love in your heart to match my love. Listen, and don't interrupt anymore. Yes, when I arrived here, I thought you were a fallen woman. In Paris a few friends described the general's marriage with a kind of subtle mockery that made me curious. I asked around. The answers were bantering and repugnant: 'She's pretty. They say she has brains. She inveigled old d'Aspert.' Isn't it enough to make you tremble with rage, ma'am, to imagine I heard that about the woman I love? Isn't it clear I must've suffered a lot?"

Henriette was ashamed; never had her misfortune been held against her so coarsely. But there was a kind of fever in Charles's whole being that made her listen and wait.

He went on, "I heard all that, and I believed it. I pitied the general and felt contempt for you. I resolved not to come near my benefactor—all of that done very casually, to avoid meeting a little schemer and a respectable dupe."

Shattered by those disgraceful words, which conveyed such awful, brutal insults, she lost her strength and almost her dignity. She wept.

"You're weeping? Oh, this is nothing yet!"

"Have mercy, sir," she said sadly. I've done you no harm—at least, I didn't mean to. If, out of anger at believing my love betrayed, I sometimes treated you cruelly, forgive me… You've punished me more than I deserve. Please let me leave."

"Leave?" said Charles, as he were just coming to. "Have I offended you?"

"Sir, if you think so little of me as to doubt that, you must expect nothing from a creature like me: she's not even worth taking revenge on."

"Oh!" he cried, falling to his knees and embracing her, "oh, what have I said to provoke those tears? I can see I've offended you. You're weeping! Oh, I must be going mad! Have pity on me! Pity, pity!… No, you don't know what torments me… Oh, pity! Forgive me, Henriette!…"

"Not so loud, not so loud," she said, comforting him, for he seemed to have lost his mind. "Not so loud. I'll stay… I'll listen to you… I'm listening."

"Well!" he said as he rose, pale as death. "Well, it was a sinister plot. A few days after I arrived, a woman, the Duchess of Avarenne, summoned me. What reason did she have to see me? I don't know. But she interrogated me so minutely about my childhood that I was quite surprised. Then she asked what I wanted to do next. I replied—without knowing whether I would do so—that I meant to go live near the general. She couldn't suppress a movement of surprise and disgust. I wanted to know why. She said nothing… I gave her the reason I suspected, based on the rumors in society.

"'Oh,' she said, 'if you know no more than that, I imagine you'll go to Tremblay.' 'What else is there?' I asked in astonishment. 'Oh,' she replied, 'things so infamous you can't go near them for fear of remaining sullied by them your whole life.' I was appalled. I insisted on hearing everything. 'It makes me heartsick to speak of them,' she said. 'A girl who was her father's mistress, and who conspired with him to deceive an honest man and marry him and pass the child of her incest off on him, and who keeps up her vile behavior in her husband's house.'"

Listening to his account, Henriette had grown so pale, so cold, that she lacked both the strength and the intention to interrupt Charles. She stared at him, her mouth agape. There exist astonishments and sorrows that kill speech, and for which there are no words even if you could speak. What protest indeed could she make against such an appalling slander! What wishes for vengeance against such slanderers could come to mind that wouldn't be so inadequate to the horror she felt as to create suspicion that she wasn't truly outraged, and foster doubts about her innocence! To such things it seems there can only be one response: the death of the person uttering them or the death of the person accused. Presumably for a moment that was Henriette's wish, but her weakness saved her; she fell into a chair with a muffled, heartrending cry.

So caught up was Charles in the story that made him oblivious to what was going on in Henriette's mind, that he went on talking. "Yes, Henriette, that's what she told me. Isn't it awful?"

"Yes, awful," she said, unable to put her own feelings into words and mechanically repeating what she'd just heard.

"And then again, no!" he said. "That's not the awful part—that's not the crime!"

"Oh my God!" she cried. "What more can there be?"

"Oh, nothing, nothing more, in truth, except that what she said was corroborated by a man, a certain Baron Premitz, who said he was a friend of your father's and a regular visitor at your house. In the end they almost persuaded me not to come, though every accusation raised against you gave me an unconquerable desire to know you."

"So you believed them!" she cried.

"What does it matter," said Charles with growing animation, "what I believed for an hour, a day, a month, what might be impossible, what's beyond human powers? The light of reason dawns, and you wake from the impossible dream you suffered through; you laugh at the horrifying story you believed. So the crime doesn't lie in those ugly inventions. What's despicable, what doesn't go away, what remains like an ulcer eating away at the heart, is the casual rumors that appalled you earlier. It's the perhaps commonplace story of the girl who was deceived and who deceives in turn. It's the vulgar, scheming hypocrisy I heard attributed to you a hundred times. The real crime is a slander at a human scale, which strikes home and doesn't overshoot its mark."

"And you believed that too?"

Charles pressed his forehead in despair.

"And you still believe it?" she went on.

223

He fell to his knees before her. "I love you, you know, I love you. It's destiny. I came here in spite of everything they said to keep me from coming. And yet here's what they told me: 'When you meet her, her air of candor and her charm will persuade you she's innocent, and you'll fall in love with her.' Yes, they told me I'd fall in love with you. And they took advantage of the gloomy, fatalistic character I've acquired from my isolated life and my misfortunes, and they terrified me with magic. A woman, a madwoman, after her state of trance had amazed me, when asked about my future, replied in terms whose ambiguity made me tremble, and with predictions, some of which came true."

"Came true?" said Henriette in horror as she remembered the displays of somnambulism whose results had so long disturbed her imagination, and of which she'd perhaps been a victim. "Came true?" she repeated. "How so?"

"Here's what she told me," he said, lowering his voice. "'You'll enter that house under unlucky auspices… You'll find out you aren't what you think you are… You'll first fall in love with, and then seduce, the wife of the man you should consider your father… And then…'" He stopped.

"Then?" asked Henriette in horror.

"'Then,'" said Charles, so quietly that she could barely hear him, "'you'll cause the death of d"Aspert's son, and of the father of Henriette's child.'"

She drew back with a terrible cry. She stared at him with the intensity of a woman who sees a dagger pointed at her and who follows its every move. "Oh, why did you come?" she asked, shaking all over.

"That's what I can't answer, Henriette. That's what appalls me like some kind of fate. Everything stood in the way of my coming: advice, friends, accidental occurrences. But some irresistible force, some inexpressible desire to meet you made me overcome all of that. Do you remember the night I arrived here?"

"So that was you?"

"It was me. At the end of my journey, when I reached the neighboring town—because d'Aspert's last letter had made me decide to come, because I'd heard on all sides about his being ruined, and in spite of all the predictions that I wanted to dismiss as childish—I told myself that I was resolved to save him from you. Gratitude obliged me to do that; I invented a duty to stop you, so as to meet you. Well! When I'd reached the end of my journey, I encountered a thousand obstacles to my coming here. First it was a man I overheard saying he'd been hired to have the job at

Tremblay that I'd come for; in my state of mind, that seemed like a warning to go no further. I blushed at that fear, and the better to conquer it I left immediately, and rode into the forest.

"In the night I took the wrong path; that struck me as another warning from fate. I hardened myself against what my reason told me was superstition, and kept going. A charcoal burner put me back on the right path. No sooner had I begun to follow it than the storm broke, and I got lost again. This time I couldn't help but hesitate over what to do next. I think that if, just then, I'd known what path to take, I'd have retreated. But I met another man, and the first thing I did was to ask the way to the forge. He led me here, and I was filled with a kind of shame at seeming not to dare go to the place I'd just asked about. On the other hand, the people I met struck me as false helpers: in the age of demons I'd have seen them as spirits of temptation. I thought it over; I imagined those times filled with supernatural beings. I wasn't afraid, I was pleased: I'd reached the point of seeing everything around me as something concerned with my journey.

"Finally I reached the forge. Through the leafless trees I saw a light in the distance. Taking that as a guide, I hurried my horse, and the light vanished. Under the influence of my superstitious fears, I was taken aback again, and I hesitated. Vanity came to my rescue: I was ashamed of my childish fears, I wanted to be a man, and I kept going. Suddenly the ground beneath me was gone, and my horse and I fell to the bottom of a lake that the storm was lashing furiously. My first thought was that I was doomed. I felt a terrible pain in my hand: I'd hurt myself. I didn't know how to get to the bank, nor in what direction to turn. I repented my foolhardiness: I thought I'd struggled too boldly against all the obstacles. Courage by night, courage in solitude, courage against your own thoughts, are not the strongest support.

"I was despairing, when the light came on again; that was my only hope. I swam toward it, feeling like a man condemned to an evil fate… But no sooner had I reached the middle of the lake, where the depth of the water and the distance from the banks made the wind whip up waves strong enough to drive me back, when the light vanished again. Now I was sure it was some hand guiding me step by step to my death. The thought of giving up the struggle, if I managed to save myself, seemed like an honorable atonement I owed to destiny for my stubbornness in resisting it. No sooner had I made that resolve than the light reappeared and I heard a voice. I renewed my efforts and reached the bank. I heard my horse whinnying, as if to summon me to go. I ran to him.

"You were there! You, at that hour! You, opening the door to the general's house for me—the house into which I was supposed to bring such misfortune. I saw it as the final effort of fate, throwing me at you. Your voice was gentle and full of feeling. By the light of your candle, before the wind blew it out, for a moment I'd seen your face, so pure, so inviting of love. I found you so beautiful that now I was afraid; I no longer dared defy the destiny that would strike me the day I lived under the same roof as you. I was overcome by my fears, which the storm, the night, the danger I'd been in, and my meeting you had intensified to the highest degree. I can't recall what I said to you. I was intoxicated by a kind of faith in your powers. Finally I went away; I spent the rest of the night under a tree.

"Sleep calmed me, and the night took away my fears with it, and I came back. But, as a residue of my childish caution, I saw the chance circumstance that put my lodgings away from your house as a means to escape from the sinister fate I'd been threatened with. Henriette, you're listening to me with astonishment and perhaps with scorn: you hadn't imagined that a man who's been praised for being brave could be the plaything of such terrors; that sometimes they come back to torment him; and that even tonight they seized me, and it took all the fever of my love to overcome my fears when I came into this room.

"And yet almost everything that was predicted has come to pass. I got here in a storm, with blood running from a wound. I heard a word that told me I might not be who I thought I was: a man called me a bastard. And now I love you, I love you in spite of all the slander I heard about you, and even with the memory of it still in my heart... Oh, you know, I'm a madman: sometimes I get on my knees before your picture, and I worship you as the mostly saintly and purest creature in the world... And other times I despise myself for loving you, for loving you in a way unlike all other women... And I'm jealous."

"Jealous!" cried Henriette. "Jealous!"

Charles had suddenly grown calm and sad again. "Oh, don't ask me why, because if you insist I'll tell you, and then perhaps there'll be no more forgiveness for me in your heart."

"Oh!" she said, looking with pity at this strong man, whose energy and enlightened mind and great learning she'd so often admired; at this man who was shaking like a child, and who'd been reduced to admitting to her all the follies of a confused soul. "Oh, you must be terribly miserable!"

"Miserable! Indeed, and yet I wouldn't exchange my life, my life torn by cruel doubts, for all the tranquility of my earlier days. Listen, Henriette, you've just learned what I suffer in the feverish hours in which, to flee my own thoughts, I run through the forest like a madman; in those hours in which, standing among the local men, I contend with them against the dangers of the boiling iron and the roaring flames, hoping to feel something that distracts me from you; but it's impossible. The time to see you again comes before I've managed to think of anything else, and the moment I'm in your presence again everything else fades away. I look at you, I see you, and I feel nothing but the blessing of seeing you and looking at you. When I'm away from you, away from the delight that absorbs me, I've often said to myself, 'She's loved another man, she's given herself to another man.' And I redden with anger, and I cry, 'Thank God she's not an angel! She's not safe from a fall.' Other times, you know, I make up a story: I make you so pure, so innocent, that I despair, and I say to myself, 'If I ask for her love, she'll believe I'm insulting her, that I think she can be seduced, because I think she's been seduced before.' And in my solitary nights, how many times have I dared think of you, because you're beautiful! How many times have my desires dreamt of your hand in mine, your heart pressed to mine! How many times have I dreamt I could give up my life for a single one of your kisses! All of that consumes me, transports me... Here I am! Here I am beside you! I come meaning to say to you... 'Are you innocent? Are you guilty? Will you be mine?... Do you want me to die?... Do you want us to die together?'... And then I get here, and I see you! I see you, Henriette! And your spell over me begins. I lose my anger, I lose my doubts, I lose my desires. Everything blows away in a puff of your breath, everything melts in the fire of your eyes. To see you becomes all I can do. Your presence intoxicates me and fills my soul."

He fell to his knees and went on, "Oh, let me see you!... That's all I ask!... I told you, don't answer me!... I'm not asking you anything!... I'm not accusing you! Don't justify yourself! Hate me! And you must hate me, I who came here to break your heart without mercy, who annoyed you with the tale of my torments and my doubts... But—I'm asking as a wretch who lives off his sorrows—let me see you!... I'll stop speaking to you, if you want!... If you want, I'll see you for only a minute a day! But allow me that! Oh, Henriette, Henriette, how little I loved you when I wanted to die! Now, for me, to be alive in the world in which you are, to live as an outcast, to live in torment, is still happiness. It means seeing you! It means feeling your presence! It means loving you!"

With those words, the wild excitement filling Charles was extinguished. His voice conveyed such saintly resignation, his tears flowed so sincerely and tenderly, that Henriette also felt her spirit being relieved of all the strange and violent emotions Charles's story had put her through. Her pride, which made her so uncaring of her father and so reserved toward d'Aspert, made her realize that the man who loved her this way, and to whom her life must surely seem guilty, must be suffering terribly. Because of the despair they provoked, she forgave suspicions that, from anyone else, would've offended her; and she rewarded his love with the holiest words she could've uttered at that moment: "Charles, I'm innocent."

As she spoke she wiped the poor man's eyes, which were bathed in tears.

"Oh. I knew it!" cried Charles, taking her in his arms—so happy that she could hear his heart beating and see his whole body trembling. "And you, Henriette? Do you love me?"

"Yes," she answered, so quickly and quietly that she seemed to be afraid she'd regret her words. Then, putting both hands on his eyes, she repeated, "Yes, I love you." She imagined that, if he couldn't see her own eyes, so troubled and so full of love, he wouldn't sense her body trembling and her voice shaking.

There's no love so saintly that it doesn't make your body burn all the way down to the bones when a hand touches your brow, when another's breath warms the air you breathe, when you feel another's chest pounding against yours. Charles lifted Henriette in his arms.

"Well! What do you want?" she asked, putting her hands together. "Oh, no!... No!..."

He opened his arms, and gazed at her like a submissive slave.

"Oh, no!" she repeated gently and consolingly. "You know that's impossible."

He lifted his desperate eyes to heaven.

She went on, "Listen, Charles, you can see, I'm not hiding it from you: you love me the way no woman deserves to be loved, unless she were capable of facing anything for such a love. But between us nothing remains but the bonds of the world and of honor. Yes, Charles, Charles, if the man I'd be harming had picked me up at random in society, like so many women men seek out just to put an end to a life of loneliness, yes, I'd be yours now. But you see, he chose me the same way you love me: with my misery and my shame. Oh, don't push me away! He didn't devote himself to me with the love I'm grateful to you for; he didn't offer my heart a heart whose sufferings and even whose doubts make me cherish its tenderness. But he offered me all that was great in him, all he had that was dignified and noble: his name."

"His name!" cried Charles. "Which didn't protect you, which didn't put an end to the ugly slander!..."

"Well, did he know about that? What could he have done? What could you yourself have done?"

"Me? Oh, me!" he replied with wild glee. "I'll wipe from the face of the earth anyone who speaks your name with scorn... I know how many of them there are... Where they are... Oh, those despicable wretches, who have only one life each to give me!"

"Fool! What a fool you are! Why should you care? Why should we care? Life is here! Happiness is here! Oh, let's not expect anything from other people."

As she spoke she smiled at him so gently that he felt everything that wasn't her voice and her will die away within him.

"At least we'll be innocent," she added, "and no matter what misfortune befalls us we'll bear it together, without lowering our eyes before each other." She'd therefore reached the point where innocence was her entire reason for not giving herself to him. She hadn't thought that when she'd come to this rendezvous.

He replied with the confidence of a happy man who believes he's achieved all the happiness he wants. "Oh, forgive me!"

"Fine, I forgive you."

How much love burned in that forgiveness! How well that woman understood the sacrifice he was making for her! Oh, what secrets must veil the nights of a woman in whom youth has remained sterile, and who hasn't slept dreamlessly!

They sat together in silence. The voices of passersby warned them they weren't alone in the world.

"My God!" she cried. "Three o'clock!... Go home! Get out of here!"

"When will I see you again, Henriette?"

Seeing her again already meant being alone together in the night: it no longer meant the parlor, with its furtively exchanged words and sidelong glances.

"Soon, soon..."

They parted. Only the next morning, when they saw Madame Bizot, did they remember that their encounter the night before had been intended to be entirely about her

.

XIX. REFLECTIONS

Much has been written on all kinds of subjects, much above all on women and love; and generalizations have been written about questions that are almost always a matter of individuals. Because love belongs to all social classes, it's been assumed that it must proceed the same way in all classes—that because it's a passion belonging to all eras, it must be the same in all eras. People strongly criticized Rousseau's "acrid kiss," saying no girl would speak so freely of her physical impressions. That might be true today, when we have prudishness in the midst of depravity, when worldly women no longer fall in love but reach agreements. Since everything they call love is artificial, planned, calculated for amusement, without risk, they don't get carried away in expressing it. So what they look for in a man is neither brains nor looks, it's rank.

At the time of that "acrid kiss," a man's and a woman's physical qualities had something to do with their desire to please and possess each other; they didn't pretend to scorn sensual pleasures; the body was important. In those days people tried to raise lusty children. Mirabeau laced his smoldering pages on love with medical lectures, and spoke of nothing but wild pleasures and unbearable abstinence. Diderot wrote very funny dirty stories; Crébillon did the same. Lesser novelists, like Rétif de la Bretonne and Marmontel, explained the effect of a shapely figure and an elegant leg. Colardeau found nothing better to give Héloise to say than the line, *Cover me with kisses! I'll dream of the rest.*

Just between us, that strikes me as the most disgusting expression of something that's well worth the trouble. *The rest*, separated from *Cover me with kisses!*, is the most shameless piece of filth ever printed. And yet *the rest* has been much admired. Anyway, aside from his choice of words, Colardeau shared his century's ideas. Whether all those writers just echoed the customs of their time, or whether they brought them into being, the fact remains that people loved each other very physically.

These days women of decent status, which is to say lawyers' and stockbrokers' wives and women with a position at court, would blush at even seeming to think about it. And yet the age of love affairs stupidly referred to as platonic is over, if it ever existed. I don't believe even masculine chastity was ever a virtue much admired. The story of Joseph has

231

always been ridiculous, and I don't know of anything more contemptible.[74] But even he was far above that Combabus, a practiced courtier who was in love with his master's wife: when he was given the task of guarding her, Combabus castrated himself to ward off the risks of his passion, leaving with the husband the guarantee of his fidelity, enclosed in a box.[75] Compared to that, Joseph, who left behind only his coat, was an outright libertine.

Of course our women—and I still mean women of status—would run out of ways to mock a simpleton like that. And yet if you told them a woman had surrendered herself just because she was a woman, they'd feel entitled to call her a whore. Given all that, it's hard to know why those women yield to a lover, unless it's a matter of calculation—and by calculation I mean what they want to tell us and perhaps what they believe.

According to them, to yield to a lover is to give him the ultimate proof of a love that for them lies only in the heart; a proof which, they claim, gives them no pleasure, and is actually distasteful to them, and which they'd gladly do without; but which, when it's accompanied by these words—"Oh, you don't believe I love you! Well then, if that's what you want, I'll lose my honor, but at least then you'll believe in my love!"—turns it into a sacrifice and preserves the full sanctity of their passion, whereas their lover is just vulgar and infatuated and thinks having possessed them counts for something. Everybody believes things like that when they're young, because out of a thousand women there's one for whom those feelings are sincere, and you have to be clever to detect the counterfeits.

People even believe it when they're madly in love, which is the same thing as being young. The admirable or idiotic thing about love is that it fills your heart with all the illusions you had when you were twenty. Consider the follies of youth and of old age: they share the same nature. If midlife is spared, it's not because it's stronger or cleverer, it's because it has other preoccupations. At twenty, ambition, desire to make your fortune, love for children, haven't yet arisen. At sixty they've already passed: ambition is satisfied or scorned, fortune is won, love for children, which would be a defense, has grown lukewarm because it's pointless; and the heart, with all that remains of its energy, grabs hold of a feeling that has

[74]In Genesis 39, Joseph resists being seduced by the wife of his master, Potiphar. He escapes from her bed, leaving his coat behind.
[75]This anecdote comes from Lucian. The woman was Stratonice, Assyrian Queen of the Seleucid Empire in the early 200s BCE.

the benefit of being rekindled by means of a pretty girl who needs to sell herself. In any case, when you're in love you fall for all those protestations of coldness and prudishness; and when you're young and a woman is willing to give herself to you, it's literally her honor you think you're taking from her, and that makes you very grateful for her sacrifice.

As for me, I think there's some other motive or force that drives their decision; and I'm convinced that any woman who's really committed to her duty will never grant a rendezvous to the man she loves. That's what happened to Henriette after she'd answered Charles's question: she soon found a thousand excuses to put off their next meeting. Henriette was a woman who was honest with herself. She loved Charles, and had spent a minute in his arms; she'd found out there's no willpower that can resist what stirs and disturbs and intoxicates you. The woman who says, I'll stay with my lover for hours on end, and I won't lose the self-control of refusing him, is a fool and a child. Either she's lost her mind or she's never yet been in love.

Meanwhile Charles requested that rendezvous with pleading eyes and furtive words. He seemed to doubt the love she'd avowed; and in spite of all, Henriette was alarmed by that doubt. But she didn't want to reassure Charles at the price demanded by almost all lovers. And since her resolve was genuine, even at the cost of losing the love she cherished and seeing it flee, she preferred that misfortune to the risk of being alone with Charles. Some people will look down on Henriette for having that fear about herself. They'll weigh on a stern scale the virtue that anticipates weakness, and that weakness will seem despicable to them because it arises from confused feelings. Perhaps they'll be right; perhaps this isn't the way to write a novel—to which I'd reply that this isn't a novel. But the opportunity to fall arises once in every love story: it's like a condition of existence. So the opportunity arose between Charles and Henriette. Here's how.

XX. HOW IT ALWAYS HAPPENS

D'Aspert's health was worsening noticeably enough to concern him. He wasn't afraid of dying. Of course it made him sad, but he wasn't afraid; he wasn't terrified, as some old men are, by the smallest thought of death that crossed his mind. He could hear of someone's passing without becoming anxious about himself, he could meet a funeral procession without growing pale, and see the curate without trembling. With that attitude, sensing that the gout was moving from his legs to his chest, he thought to put some order in his affairs. He wanted to draw up a will. In that will his property was divided equally between Henriette and Charles Dumont. But d'Aspert, who'd let time go by without solving the mystery of Charles's birth, didn't want to carry to his grave the doubt with which he'd lived. The truth is, he'd never explicitly given up on learning that secret, but he'd always put off the moment. The time had come when more delay would be unwise. He reached a decision: he'd just suffered through a crisis that had alarmed everybody, Charles and Henriette's care had saved him once again, but a new attack could occur. One evening he asked Henriette to stay alone with him after everyone else had withdrawn.

"Henriette," he said, "this morning I completed my will. Its terms are irrevocable. Whether or not Charles is my son, nothing in it will change. But I can't face the idea of leaving this world without knowing by what name I should bless him. I should've found it out long ago, but I didn't dare. Happy tranquility makes you selfish: you become afraid of upsetting your life. And perhaps I was right, perhaps it wouldn't have made us any happier, perhaps even now I'm wrong to try to throw light on this murky question. Who knows whether I'm about to inflict some terrible blow on Charles? But what can I do? I'm afraid to die with a lie on my conscience. I have to question Charles."

Henriette approved his intentions, and—through the tears she shed at what d'Aspert was telling her—she said she too thought it was his duty. Death lends a solemnity to all the actions of life. There's no oblivion so sure in the grave that we don't care to put our consciences in order before descending into it, even if it's just with respect to ourselves.

"Since you agree with me, please take charge of the task. I've told you enough for you to be able to question him skillfully. Anyway, all you have to do is to talk to him about his father, what happened in Rome, how he got there. My son was coming from Verona and had lived in England; he was accompanied by a servant. Those few circumstances will be enough to know if it's him."

"But why not do it yourself? It would be much easier for you to detect the truth you seek in hints that would be insignificant to me."

"No, I feel that I'd get upset, and ask him questions that are too direct and that might perhaps give him a hint of what it is I want to know. Because you understand, Henriette, if Charles isn't my son, he must remain unaware of even my slightest doubts. If, on the contrary, his answers show that he is, I'll tell him the whole secret of his birth: knowing his mother's name is bound to be useful to him. Be careful to bring it up as if by chance. Stay here alone with him after everyone has retired. And pick one of those moments when the conversation becomes more confiding and intimate because other subjects have been exhausted. I'm leaving the job up to you. Only a soul like yours could've made the last years of my life so happy. You've endured my solitude, my suffering, my pain, my infirmities; you'll add this blessing to so many others."

Henriette agreed. The sacredness of the task she'd just been given shielded her against Charles's love and her own. She realized she could be with the man she loved with impunity while thinking of the duty imposed on her. But so many things can conspire, without our knowing, to tear down the ramparts we think are unshakeable!

First of all, she didn't carry out her mission the day she received it, so moved had she been by the words of a man who foresaw his own death and spoke of it so simply, and by her vivid memory of his thanks for the happiness she'd given him. A few days went by. D'Aspert's health took a reassuring turn. Still, he asked Henriette whether she'd questioned Charles. She'd honestly tried to find an occasion, but it was difficult to get him to talk about anything besides his love. Finally, under pressure from her husband, she decided to give Charles a time for a rendezvous, rather than wait for him to ask her for one, and to tell him plainly that she had serious matters to discuss with him. Just in case, she counted on the subject of Charles's secret to forestall his love talk. She thought she'd foreseen everything. Partway through the evening she told him, in front of her husband, who was well enough to have come downstairs, "Charles, please don't leave tonight without having spoken to me. I have to talk to you."

A rendezvous given so publicly perhaps surprised Charles, but it didn't make him suspicious. D'Aspert gave her a nod of approval that everyone, even Charles, could see, and it was clear it must be about business. Charles, it has to be said, received her invitation unhappily: that wasn't what he wanted. Though he wanted to be alone with Henriette, it seemed to him that the thoughts of everyone who knew about their rendezvous would be present to witness it. He replied coldly, and his coldness wasn't an act. He wouldn't have believed that Henriette could have the boldness of so many women, who'll misbehave so openly that it seems impossible to suspect them of anything. So he waited, with an impatience more curious than stirred, for the moment when they'd be alone together. When it rang ten o'clock everyone withdrew.

There are a thousand trivial things that can change the nature of a scene, things we believe to be insignificant but that become all-powerful without our noticing. If anyone has the gift of knowing about those things, perhaps it's playwrights, who succeed or fail through tiny incidents the audience isn't aware of, though it's they who judge the results: an awkward word, an inopportune entrance, can kill the most touching scene. Whereas a hypocritical evasion by which a character ducks a difficult moment, or gets past it, often counts as if he'd beaten the challenge directly. That's because in the theater, as in life, it's almost never people's fundamental underlying thoughts that determine the success of an action: everything lies in the details, and it's those details that the writer must be sure about and must know how to set in the right place.

We've explained Henriette and Charles's situation. If everyone slowly withdrew and they were left together, the first moment of their rendezvous would've been awkward. Certainly they wouldn't have thrown themselves at each other, delighted to be alone: the influence of those who'd retired would've left them still behaving almost formally with each other. He would've asked her what she wanted; she, not knowing quite what to say, might perhaps have told him the honest truth—in which case something besides their love would've prevailed at that meeting, and the strangeness of what Charles would've found out would've distracted him from his passions.

It transpired differently, because of a precaution Henriette took, perhaps as a final safeguard: she left the parlor to help d'Aspert back to his room. The general kept her there a long time. Meanwhile Charles was alone, and the night advanced. All the noises in the house, which would've watched over them, so to speak, at the beginning of their rendezvous, fell silent one after another. Charles was completely alone, and the mystery of the upcoming interview was reestablished with the silence, and with the lateness of the hour ringing on the clock. And still Henriette didn't return. Charles's curiosity, which at first was interested only in what she could want, turned to impatience. Gradually he came to fear he wouldn't see her; he imagined the general was suspicious, and was detaining her; he suffered all the alarms of a secret, guilty tryst; he went through all of its turbulent emotions. Soon the rendezvous, which moments earlier had felt unsatisfactory to his needs, now seemed like a joy that would escape him: the moment he was afraid to lose it, it became more precious than anything he could imagine.

Meanwhile he listened: the whole house slept. All the sounds that can be heard for a long time in an isolated house in which five or six people are heading to bed—the doors opening and closing, the comings and goings, etc.—had ceased. There was total silence. Charles's fears had already turned toward genuine terror: a thousand unpleasant conjectures crossed his mind. Several times he was tempted to go up to Henriette's room. He'd opened the parlor door, and a dozen times he'd gone as far as the foot of the stairs. Then he came back, imagining he'd waited there a long time, though barely minute had gone by. His heart pounded. He reached the point of thinking of nothing but to give up hope, when he heard a door open quietly, and close quietly. A light footstep crossed the long corridor and came down the stairs. A dress brushed the steps. It sounded like someone afraid to make a noise.

Charles rushed out and saw Henriette. "Ah, it's you!" he said, taking her in his arms. "It's you, at last! My God, it's you!"

"Have you been waiting for me a long time?" she replied, surprised and moved by that outburst of joy at seeing her, by the feeling that was so different from the approach she'd prepared, but which she couldn't rebuff, because she hadn't considered it in her plans.

"Oh, I was afraid. I thought you wouldn't come."

His shaking, halting voice revealed the distress he'd felt, and she wanted to comfort him. "I promised you I would," she said, lowering her voice.

"It's been so long since you made that promise, so long! But here you are… Yes, here you are… Here you are!"

Meanwhile they'd returned to the parlor. Henriette had sat down in one of the large armchairs I described to you. Yes, that's where she was, slim and lithe, her white dress setting her off against the dark velvet background. And he'd placed himself on his knees before her, worshiping her with his eyes, and repeating as he kissed her white hands and her knees,

"Yes, it's you... It's you, here you are." As if a long or dreadful absence had separated them.

She smiled as she looked at him. How can you defend yourself against the happiness you give? Isn't that the most seductive of all triumphs? "Come now," she said. "Calm down, Charles. Have a seat here."

"Oh, no, no, let me look at you, let me see you. Do you know how long it's been since I've seen you or heard you?... Oh, you're so beautiful!"

"Please, Charles, not like that. Don't talk to me like that... Come on, be quiet." And with those words she put her hand over his eyes. What were those eyes saying to her?

"Henriette! Henriette! Henriette!" He spoke her name like an invocation, each time giving that name an inexpressible feeling of desire, love, prayer.

"Well... Charles... Yes, I love you... I love you... Come now, listen to me. Let's talk."

Talk! Oh, Father Olivet would certainly have wanted to know about that interview when he created his *Dictionary of Synonyms*,[76] in which he tried to distinguish the nuances of every word! For here were two people who were speaking and replying, and who weren't talking.

"No," said Charles, "no, not yet. I'll listen badly, I won't understand you. Let me look at you... Let me look at you for a long time... forever!"

He'd crossed his arms over her knees and pressed his chest against them. There before her, he looked up at her from below; whereas she, leaning back in her chair, her head resting on her hand, surrendered gently to the ardent contemplation that pierced her. There was a long silence, a silence during which, with their eyes locked, each on the other's, they felt their souls melting together under the beam of their gaze. Astonishing delight poured from each to the other, a flood of ineffable joy that would drown life if it didn't finally overflow. But when the heart is too full it refuses it, and then it spreads outside and eases the heart through words and sighs.

"Henriette!" he said, trembling all over.

"Charles!" she replied, letting her eyelids fall over her eyes and releasing a long sigh.

"Henriette!" he said again, in a tone that turned one word into more than a long speech, more than vows and transports of joy.

---

[76]Abbé Olivet, *Dictionnaire universel des synonymes de la langue française* (1788).

She passed her hand across her eyes and suddenly got up. "No!" she said, resting both hands on Charles brow; he'd stayed at her feet and put his arms around her. "No… I'm out of my mind… You're out of your mind… Go away! Go away! Tomorrow… I'll see you again." As she spoke, her teeth chattered and her knees buckled.

"Listen," he said, "you love me!"

She didn't answer; her whole being answered for her.

"You love me!… You belong to me!"

"Oh!" she cried, tearing herself away. "Be quiet…" She gave a long, troubled look around. Seeing nothing but the solitude of that vast parlor, lit by the feeble light of a candle, she went on, "Go away! Go away! We're dooming ourselves!"

"Oh! Do you really love me?" he asked, rising and taking her in his arms.

"Oh my God!" she said, turning away her head. "Leave me, I beg you, leave me." Since he was pressing her to his heart, she said, "Oh, you're hurting me!"

He pressed his lips against the mouth that trembled as it spoke.

She escaped as if red-hot iron had burned her, and cried in despair, "Oh! You're pitiless!"

He tried to approach her.

"Never!… Never!…" She said, pushing back with her delicate arms against her lover's arms of steel. "Oh! Listen to me!… Listen to me!… You love me… Don't you? Well then, don't dishonor me, don't drive me to my death!" And when he let her go, she murmured dully, "Yes… Go away, leave me… Yes, you love me."

She dropped into a chair and hid her head in her hands. She began to cry.

"Yes, I love you!" said Charles in a different tone. "Yes, I love you!… But you?"

"Oh, me!" she said, raising her tear-bathed eyes to heaven. "Oh, me! I don't love you, is that it?"

"What do I know?" he said in anger and despair.

"My God, he doesn't know!" she replied with a bitter sob.

"No," he said with ruthless energy. "No, I don't know… You've told me so… I used to believe it… I no longer believe it. No, you don't love me! No, no, no!" he repeated almost angrily.

"What do you need, to believe it?" she asked, giving him a wild look. "That I give myself to you? Is that what you want?… Well then, so be it!

239

It'll drive me mad! I'll go mad… It'll kill me!… Yes, you know, tomorrow either I'll have gone mad or I'll die… But if that's what you want… If that's what you want…" And then violent sobs kept her from speaking.

He fell back on his knees before her. "Henriette! You're crying! You're crying! Have mercy! Oh, have mercy! What do you want from me? My life… my honor… some crime? Speak, and I'll give you everything… If I had a world to sacrifice to you, I'd shatter it at your feet. Oh, don't turn away, Henriette! Because I love you… I love you… Oh, tell me you love me! Tell me you forgive me!"

Henriette, calmer now, held out her hand to him. "Yes, I love you!" she said. Then, taking his hands in hers, she added with a kind of intoxicating sadness, "And believe me, my own Charles… Believe me… If I refuse you, it's not because I'm afraid you'll deceive me, that you'll forget me! Oh, no! You love me better than that, don't you? But look… We'd be miserable… I swear, we'd be miserable."

"You would!" he said, continuing his reproaches, but so gently that he provoked pity. "You'd be miserable!… You love me, but not with the kind of love I have for you."

"Oh, don't talk that way" she replied, caressing his brow with her burning hand. "You think I don't need courage to resist you?… You think it's only you I have to struggle against?"

"Oh," he said, in a tone in which pleading love seemed less dangerous, "so you understood what I'm suffering?"

"Hear," she said, taking his hand, "feel my heart."

And she placed that hand against her pounding heart. Reckless woman, who trusted to the first respite in the struggle, thinking no new excitement would arise. Her heart beat quickly.

Charles, gently drawing Henriette into his arms, pressed his chest against hers and said very quietly, "Oh, let me feel it this way."

Then he sought her lips. For a moment she surrendered… Then, shaken to the depths, she stiffened her arm against his chest so as to get out of the grip that bound her to him. But she couldn't free herself from his kiss… Her strength was exhausted, and her arms dropped as if they were dead.

He took her away from the light in the parlor. She rested her head on his shoulder, like a broken, failing flower; and as they crossed the threshold of her boudoir her dying voice murmured these muffled, halting words: "Oh, this is death, Charles! This is death!"

But he didn't hear her! Or, if he'd heard her, would he have believed her words? And even if he'd believed them, what did it matter? Doesn't there come a moment in love in which nothing is an obstacle? Is death so terrible that it has ever stopped a passion?

Then, a moment later, they'd assumed the same position as at the beginning, in the parlor: he on his knees before her, she seated in a chair, her body upright, her eyes locked in his, her hands in his hands, which she couldn't feel. What was she thinking about?... Or was she even thinking?... Did she have any idea what had happened?... Was it fear? Was it remorse? Charles looked at her without daring to speak.

At that moment a noise rang out overhead: it was repeated blows with a cane against the floorboards. At the sound, Henriette stood up. Her face seemed to be lit by some terrible memory. She gave a muffled, torn cry. Lowering her haunted eyes to Charles's face, she said, "Do you hear that? It's your father."

She'd just seen her guilt, and seen it as horrifying as it could be. Remorse had turned a doubt into a certainty, and she felt the inconceivable, inevitable need of suffering: to push it to its extreme. Who knows whether her cry also contained the instinct of human pride, that leads strong souls astray and makes them scorn ordinary things? With those words Henriette elevated her sin beyond the commonplace: she made it into incest.

Meanwhile she stood still. The noise began again.

"It's the general!" said Charles.

"It's your father, I tell you. Your father, who's going to ask me... who you are..."

"Who I am?" he cried, thinking she was losing her mind.

"Yes," said Henriette, who really was losing her mind. "Yes, who you are. He's going to ask me if you're his son. What do you want me to tell him?"

"Henriette! Henriette!" he cried, trying to hold her back.

"Do you want me to tell him you're my lover?"

"Oh, not so loud, Henriette, not so loud... You'll doom me."

She looked at him with sublime scorn. "I'm doomed! And you're a coward!"

He went pale, not at the insult, but at her exaltation.

"I'm doomed!" she said, slapping her head in despair. "I'm doomed! I'm doomed, sir!"

"Oh, not so loud," he said, clasping his hands. "Not so loud..."

"And what if I want him to hear me? What if I want him to kill me?... I'm not afraid of dying."

The noise resumed, more impatient, more demanding.

"Oh, woe on us!" he cried. "Woe on us!"

"Well then," she said wildly, "kill me... Better you than him... I'd prefer that... You can tell I still love you."

The noise grew louder.

"Oh!," cried Henriette. "You see? He's going to come down, and he's going to kill me!"

"Oh!" cried Charles, beside himself. "I hope he doesn't come... My God! I hope he doesn't come..."

"You'd kill him!" she cried as she rose, overwhelmed by the terrible look on his face.

"I don't know. But I don't want you to die."

"Well then," she said, shaking with fear, and before her was laid out such a disastrous series of crimes that she trembled at it even more than at the wrong they'd already done... "Stay here, I'm going to him."

"In this state!" he said, stopping her. "In this state! And what will you tell him?"

"I'll tell him... How do I know what?"

The terrible noise, the fatal noise rang out again.

"What is it you want me to tell him?" she cried.

He stopped. He was seized by a sudden resolve. "Stay here... Stay here... I'll go upstairs." And he rushed out of the parlor.

Soon he was back. "Henriette," he said, "go back to your room. I told him you'd spoken to me about my birth, and I'd gotten carried away, and I'd answered you angrily and almost offended you. And from that there'd arisen a discussion so animated that we hadn't paid attention to how much noise we were making."

"Thank you for having lied to him for both of us. I couldn't have done it."

"Henriette, when will I see you again?"

"Never," she said as she fled.

Was that vow going to be kept more than any other had been? Perhaps yes; but no doubt you won't believe it. How many people are there who, after having read this chapter—how many women especially—will discard this book with scorn, saying Henriette is a shameless debauchee, whose infamous behavior an honest woman shouldn't even know about;

how many, who can't argue from their own wisdom, will be outraged by the reason for her weakness and find her degrading!

Oh my, oh my, don't condemn this woman so fast for being a woman. You, who claim your own fall was the result of your total devotion to your lover's affection, and who, on that basis, have gone on to enjoy all the pleasures of love with a clear conscience, as long as it lasts—I have less respect for you than I do for Henriette. Sh didn't say to herself, "Now that it's over, now that I'm guilty according to some noble, subtle reasoning, let me enjoy the coarse rewards of my sin. That won't make it any worse." Oh, no! She had sensual feelings, but she also had a heart, a mind, a conscience, higher than yours. When her willpower came back to her, it came back honest and pure. She didn't believe she had to keep on sinning because she'd once sinned: she was truly remorseful.

After that aside to the majority of women, I must fall to my knees and beg their forgiveness. Forgiveness from those women who are in love enough to sacrifice everything for their love: fortune, rank, the world's respect, family; those women have understood love to be the only thing of value on earth. Who can say whether a rascal's greeting or a prig's invitation are worthy of the objects of their attention? Forgiveness from those women for whom that feeling serves as a kind of vengeance. To be insulted, scorned, and tormented by a husband's rejection, and to give him back everything you can in the way of insults, scorn, and torments, is a form of justice only a despicable husband could consider wrong. Forgiveness from those women who, with less energy, have sought from love some consolation for the same suffering. If that's a crime, we should kill a woman the morning after her husband betrays her: that would be less barbaric than condemning her to weep forever without a hand to wipe away the tears.

Let the legislators who abolished the eternal vows of nuns say it wasn't because human nature isn't capable of living that way, deprived of all the emotions we respond to. Why are they harder on a woman who loses those feelings than on one who never had them? For married women there's at least a contract that was broken by the signer, whereas for the nuns there's only aversion for what they wanted at first. Jesus Christ isn't unfaithful to his spouses.

What I find despicable is women who take advantage of their husbands as if they were well-behaved, and who enjoy their lovers in complete honor—insolent prudes, without either forgiveness or pity for those who have neither their cleverness nor their hypocrisy!—and who arm themselves with a husband too shy to risk a scandal, with too much integrity to throw the reflection of their wives' baseness on a family, or too pitiful to reduce their wives to the state of solitude and dishonor they inflict on others. Have contempt for those women!

As for Henriette, here was what she did: the morning after that very night, a servant handed Charles the following letter:

XXI. A LETTER

—Charles,

You're my lover. That's the first word I had to write in the only letter you'll ever get from me. That word must be my punishment. It's right that a man should have within his power the proof of my guilt, that he can use it against me, doom me, condemn me to dishonor, without my having a single refuge to escape to from it, without my being able to tell him boldly to his face, "You lied." This is written by my hand, signed by my hand: you're my lover. Now, to that man who has my dishonor within his power, I must add: I don't want you to speak to me, I don't want you to write to me; I'll tell people besides you, "Charles is my lover."

To prove to you that I haven't lost my mind, here are my reasons: If ever a woman had a duty, it's I. If ever a woman shamefully ignored her duty, it's I. I loved you, I still love you, you can see I'm not indulging in wordplay. But that's not what I accuse myself of. I gave myself to you, and that was my sin, my crime, mine alone. The first time you said to me, "I love you," I felt my entire being rushing toward you, and I was filled with a happiness that made my heart pound and clouded my vision. I would've given my life to have been free and pure, and to say to you, "Here I am." It's because I had that desire that, when I was away from you, I felt I'd be doomed if I saw you again; I fled from you.

Happenstance threw me back under the spell of our love. I'm not using that happenstance as an excuse, for I accepted it joyfully. Now I think I understand better what I did. That happenstance seemed to be accompanied by circumstances that would protect me from any weakness, and beneath that shield I hoped to experience once again, without risk, the delight of seeing you, hearing you, sensing your eyes on mine. I wanted to enjoy the innocent delights of a guilty love. It's true, I hoped for it, I wanted it. Out of the chaos of my desires, I chose the one which, according to common prejudice, doesn't leave a stain. That was my crime, that's why it was only right that you made me your mistress.

Now you could tell me, "The crime is done, what is can't be erased. The word adultery is written across your brow. Let's at least enjoy the pleasures of our dishonor." All men say that, in terms clever enough to persuade women. God knows, if you'd come to me to say that, if you'd staked your life and your happiness on the condition that I must always be what I was one time, God knows whether I wouldn't have yielded to you. I told you I still love you. So now you're strong, aren't you? Now you're saying to yourself, "She's in the first transports of unreasoning remorse; I won't confront it head on, I'll wait. My despair will lend me eloquence, and she won't be able to see me suffer without pitying me." And that's true, sir, you're right, your entreaties would make me miserable, but to protect myself from them I wouldn't say to my husband, "Charles is my lover." No, sir, I won't do it. I lied when I said I'd do it. Under the pretext of defending the shred of honor I invented for myself by deciding not to see you anymore, I won't go tell that man—whose trust in me was so genuine, and who yesterday thanked me once again for his happiness—I won't go tell him, "You're a dishonored husband." I won't go to the bed where he lies slowly dying and cry about my parricidal despair.

And the truth is, isn't every minute he has left to live worth my stooping to the shame of deceiving him? Isn't that the righteous punishment that awaits me: to have to smile at him, to speak to him of gratitude and devotion, when within me there's nothing but ingratitude and betrayal? Will the vanity of not being a hardened sinner be strong enough to give me the courage to rouse that noble old man from his trust and cry out, "Adultery and abomination are in your house!" Do I have anything left that's worth a single tear of that worthy man's? No, no, a thousand times no. You see, Charles, we must deceive him; but you must no longer speak to me or see me.

You don't agree. My God, will you finally understand me? We have to be dead to one another. Oh, can't you see that I've been lying since I started this letter? That there's an infernal being seated across the table from me, pointing to the true word I should write? Can't you see that I'm circling around it, searching for reasons that don't convince you? Don't you remember thinking I was mad when I let out that cry that terrified you? Or have you misunderstood the true meaning of that word?... My God, I'm telling you I don't dare... I feel like that word, once written down, will explode like lightning in this house... I'm afraid! I'm afraid! And yet it's been thrown in my face, and you repeated it to me... But it wasn't true... And now it is... Oh, if I didn't mistrust that thought, I'd go mad.

It's nighttime. I'm alone in my room. I look around... I feel like invisible beings are pulling my hair and strangling me. One of them is going to speak to me, he's going to shout out... the truth... No, my God! No, it isn't true. Make it not be true... Charles, you were called a bastard... If you are one, guess who your father is... Oh, now you finally understand me. Heavenly mercy, protect me! And you, Charles, want me to see you again, to give myself to you again, to speak to you! Oh, it's awful... Never, you understand, never!... You're lucky, you can die... I have to live: I have a father and a child. Do you realize that my life is some abominable destiny?... That it's suspended between two incests?... Do you understand that I don't know whether both are true? Well! I'm lying to you with every line. Do you know why I want to live?... It's neither for my father nor for my child... It's so I can repent... If God exists, I'll have to have suffered terribly for him to forgive me... And if hell... came to me with its infinite tortures, its wild laughter, its flames...

—Sir,

It's broad daylight. I found this letter on my table. I remember that when I wrote the final word I thought I saw phantoms around me, and heard their moans. I fell to the floor, from which I've just arisen... I'm sending you this letter. If it doesn't horrify you, may it make you feel pity!

Farewell.

—Henriette

XXII. DESPAIR

Charles had received that letter after a night filled with terrible anguish. The last words Henriette had spoken, her delirium, had lingered in him like a warning of calamity. When he got the note she sent him, a new horror took hold of him. Reading the part of the letter that had been written in the night, he'd trembled at seeing Henriette's mind going astray, getting lost. He'd paid more attention to the confusion of her ideas than to what they were saying. But when he'd finished reading, and in the final lines he saw she'd reread the letter with a cool head, after a fainting spell or a delirium that had lasted several hours, and that nothing contradicted what it said, he grasped the real meaning of the letter, and he in turn trembled. The Duchess of Avarenne's remarks, the somnambulist's predictions, what Aubert had said, all came to mind, and the idea that he might be d'Aspert's son took hold of him.

Certainly, on closer examination, the crime of Charles Dumont was the most odious. It was, if I can put it like this, a moral crime, one for which he had to forget all the principles of honor, that this old man had adopted him, fed him and put him in a state that his woe of being an orphan might never have ended; that he had finally done for him what he didn't have to; and that he'd taken advantage of what he'd become through these good deeds to bring dishonor onto this house? Was this not the most shameful ingratitude, the unpardonable crime? Well, a man, and I mean an honest man according to our social laws, is made in such a way that he's more frightened of crimes of morality than of nature. Ingratitude is a vice no matter where one lives or when; incest is a crime in some societies and in modern times. It's in the interest of public decency that decides legislation and it's because he's the child of the law that the law is responsible for punishing him while ingratitude is independent and one can profit from it as one wants. And Charles, if this was only his betrayal of his benefactor, would've felt a little remorse; but probably got used to it and forgiven himself that he was doing like so many others and out of an excess of passion.

But when the suspicion that he might be the son of d'Aspert, a suspicion that canceled out the gratitude he owed him, since he'd only fulfilled the common obligations of a father, when this suspicion became more grounded in his mind, he couldn't be more frightened of his crime or hate himself enough. The big word 'incest', so solemnly pronounced in our education, so frighteningly inflated in our stories, our poems, in the theater and sermons, this word was dragging him down and stripping him of all defense. He understood, without explaining anything to himself, without even thinking about it, that he couldn't see or talk to Henriette anymore. He didn't try to argue against the word incest. The adopted son could've found many good reasons against his benefactor; the bastard couldn't imagine even one against his own father. It's up to us to explain this propensity of the human heart. What if we try and make it not a crime? Let's see.

Could we say that there is in every man a social sense through which recognizes the good and evil that is done in society to the full extent of this good or evil? Isn't this what makes him so piously respect the laws based on just ideas of order and public interest, that make adultery and incest such serious crimes, even though human nature could repudiate them? In fact, what does nature care about incest and adultery? Should we say that they're crimes for other reasons than social reasons? But does the union of relatives offend anything but written morals? This is so true that incest was once more widespread than it is today, and it still exists but we talk about curtailing it. What is adultery? Isn't because it's a theft that we make it a dishonor? Destroy the inheritance of names and goods; make it so that one gets neither a name or fortune from a father and the adulterer who harms nobody is no longer a crime, no longer shameful. What can we conclude from this? It's that the laws, or rather the social necessities, that make morality, or at least a good part of it, and consequently it's a hard task to recognize these necessities and to make laws to protect them. I'd like to know if the gentlemen of the Chamber of Deputies have ever thought of this. They can answer that they're not stupid enough for this; to which we'd reply that more or less makes no difference and that we need something else besides living under bad social laws to decide to correct them.

Charles, therefore, was in a state of awful bewilderment. As long as the crime seemed to him certain, indisputable, he could feel only an unreasonable need to flee, to hide away from everyone. Finally, calm restored his doubt and this doubt was a consolation; but how to make it stop? How to clarify his real state? Who should he ask? D'Aspert? He was the worst coward. Henriette? He didn't dare; and besides, the outcome might be atrocious. The whole day was spent making conflicting resolutions; but among all the projects that were churning in Charles' soul, that of seeing Henriette again didn't surface. The thought of his crime was too glaring, it weighed too heavily for him to be able to have such a desire.

He was unsure of only how he should carry out the duty imposed on him, that of avoiding all relations with Henriette.

But the most miserable circumstances of life are much more powerful than the noblest sentiments. How could he leave the forge? On what pretext could he just suddenly depart? The explanation he'd given to d'Aspert about his meeting with Henriette offered him a reasonable excuse, and, if he used it, wouldn't it be d'Aspert who'd be looking for clarification? And he, Charles, could he get angry at a father who'd ask him: Are you my son? That was what he was thinking when a servant came with this mundane phrase that pulled him down from the heights of his ideas to suffer the trivial demands of life:

"Monsieur, the meal is served, they're waiting for you to sit down at the table."

Not going on account of illness would've brought everyone to his room an hour later, thus saying to d'Aspert: The scene yesterday was more serious than you were told. Then it occurred to Charles that Henriette had surely used this excuse of being ill so she wouldn't have to come down; he couldn't imagine her coming to eat. So, he went down.

When he entered he saw Henriette; she was standing in front of the piano; she turned around. Unusually, she was dressed up, and her face, at least as Charles saw it at the moment, was radiantly fresh.

D'Aspert didn't give him time to be confused. He said, "Well now, you haven't been seen all day; you're not going to act like my wife and pout because some sharp words were spoken? Come on, give me your hand and a hug."

Charles didn't know whether he should stay or go. Henriette walked over to him, holding out her hand: he saw nothing else around him; a low hum stunned him. Bizot took his arm.

"Ah, you're holding a grudge!" he said, leading him towards Henriette.

"Come on," d'Aspert, "total reconciliation, give her a kiss."

Henriette leaned forward and brushed Charles' cheeks. Bizot shielded the two from the general.

"There, everything's fine," he said. "Now let's sit down."

Charles looked like a madman. Henriette passed by him and whispered:

"Look at me?"

By the same automatic movement that had made him obey everything they wanted from him, he looked into her eyes. Henriette had put on blush to mask her paleness. Only her eyes, quivering in the sockets, revealed that she was struggling to stay calm. Charles was ashamed not to try what a woman could do. He put off till later to fathom Henriette's plans and her behavior.

The meal passed like on dull days: brief conversations now and again; everyone was too preoccupied by their own thoughts to take notice of the attitudes of the others. Madame Bizot understood it all as a lover's quarrel; maybe Bizot as well. Lussay was afraid that the general's living will had exposed some unpleasant explanations about the birth of Henriette's child. As for d'Aspert, remembering Charles' anger on the day he'd been called a bastard, he imagined that he had such overblown ideas on the subject of honor and sensitivity that he was bothered by a few clumsy words from Henriette; that, in a fit of anger, he had said something to her about her son and that from this came an argument in which it was easy to hurt each other. The matter was so delicate for both of them that he didn't want to ask about it: forcing them to repeat the accusations against each other would've been almost as cruel as the argument itself.

The dinner ended like this; the evening went pretty much the same way, and Charles and Henriette told themselves that since they'd spent this day like this, they'd do the same tomorrow, until a decisive step was taken to change the situation. The next day went the same as the following day, and day after day, they spent a week like this, during which time they got used to playing their roles.

But it was all they could overcome; they managed to reassure their exterior without ridding themselves of their secret despair. Their situation seemed unbearable to them; they could get out of it only by entering into a crime, which they both hated, and it seemed impossible to them to remain there.

It was Henriette who was the first to try to escape the obsession of her mind. It's been a very long time since I've heard this phrase: Man doesn't forget, he replaces. The distinction, which only sounds subtle, is exactly right. You kill one passion with another, one thought with another, sometimes a little activity is enough for this victory; but neither the heart nor the mind can stay empty when you have heart and mind. As long as Henriette kept this memory alone of her fault, she had all the remorse of that first day; sometimes it got worked enough up to make her as crazy as when she'd sent her letter to Charles. She felt no relief except when some household duty or a meeting put other thoughts in place of those hounding her. She was afraid to be alone and was ashamed to try to distract herself; for, she could only seek this distraction from people who made her fell bad about everything. How could she spend the day with Madame Bizot, with this woman whom she couldn't help comparing herself to, below whom she had sunk, and to whom she was embarrassed to resemble? Should she chose her father? But he might question her; and besides, he was always out of the house as usual. Should she talk to her husband? But every word, every glance would be a sword thrust. There remained Bizot; she couldn't lower herself to Bizot; besides, she considered him inadequate.

Perhaps in a different situation she would've turned her mind to the arts, maybe to gambling. And since I've let this word loose, I'll take the liberty to voice my thoughts on a very remarkable work of our time, maligned by the small-minded critics of our newspapers. I'm talking about <u>La Passion Secrète</u> by Eugène Scribe[77]. Almost no one wanted to see the huge talent of truth and observation in this work. The finer points were treated as false, because they were troubling. We've been challenged, despite the floor of the Stock Exchange crammed with gamblers, in our belief that gambling is a feminine passion. And why so? Because it it was an unkind truth for women, unkind for men who can be forgotten in a report; because, in the end, the public wants, above all, to flatter itself, to be shown with heroic virtues or vices so charming that they're better than virtues. But if you prove that it's selfish, harsh, engrossed in loathsome interests, it gets angry and tells you: This isn't true. Since I'm talking about it, I'll answer the objection you might raise from <u>Bertrand et Raton</u>[78]. Didn't the public love Bertrand, and wasn't he faithlessly, lawlessly ambitious, who sacrificed all honorable sentiments to the success of his ploys? Of course, but, what a witty liar, what a charming traitor! How right he was to mock all the fools around him! In our time of political corruption, with our present political fortunes, the honesty of our Men of State, who doesn't want to be Bertrand, and who doesn't blush for not being him, when so many knaves are him at such little cost? Moreover, Bertrand succeeded, that's the important thing. Does our century ever criticize anyone who's a success? Isn't success itself a virtue and genius? Ask our ministers; because, finally, they must have something: they have success.

---

[77]A comedy produced in 1834.
[78]A comedy by Eugène Scribe premiered on November 14, 1833.

Henriette, tormented by the desire to rid herself of the perpetual presence of her crime, was looking for an activity. What she found wasn't her choice, and was, therefore, all powerful. It's hard to force an idea on ourselves; but when we're in search of a thought to carry us away, we often find and followed one that is certainly not handpicked and that might seem impossible to us.

A political discussion produced the desired result. Well, all over France, a few living fragments of the spirit of the empire were being set in motion, a few men to whom the humiliation of France and maybe their own humiliation made it unbearable to tolerate the yoke of the old Bourbons. There were things that affected even the disinterested. Grenoble, Lyon, the telegraphed orders of Monsieur Decazes were grounds for cursing; after more than one isolated wrong, this swift justice lit more than one fuse, fired up more than one death pledge. In Henriette's soul it let off a cry that was, at first, very personal:

"Oh, how happy men are to get mixed up in these generous efforts of France! And when they don't succeed, it results in despair, a death that has not even the futility of suicide. If they're abandoned by all their friends, split from all their intimate relations, deprived of all personal hope, they can hang onto the great hope of the fatherland. No one asks them why; their life is taken only at the moment when, working in the interest of all, it becomes the heritage of all. They hardly ask if there were dishonor in this life before this epoch, and the misfortune is considered a title."

These words, cast out haphazardly, were, at first, only a symptom of the impatience of a woman who was content with the narrow life that our laws and customs made for her, as long as the space where she had to move around wasn't crammed with bitterness and sorrow, but who revolted against the slavery of her actions when the circle in which she was enclosed was bristling with grief and anxiety. Then, and only then did she curse her condition and desire to take part in the dangers of men, the chances of combat and death. Sorrow begat ambition.

No matter what Henriette said, she had to remain where she was: she would've like to get actively involved in all these movements that were secretly stirring up France, she would've offered her life and fortune, but the defiance and scorn of men would've rejected her. She at least got from it what she could, and, if she couldn't participate in action, she'd devote her mind to it. Every day she waited impatiently for news from Paris: she ardently read the debates of the representatives, took the side of the malcontents, got worked up by the great speakers, hated their enemies. Soon, conversations were a political arena where she called out everyone around her, astonishing them with the nuance of her opinions, stunning them with her boldness.

D'Aspert himself, who at first had smiled at his wife's enthusiasm, then had been enchanted by it, got alarmed even as a man who didn't care about disturbing his domestic peace for something overheard by a servant and reported to a crown prosecutor. At this time that was all it took for the authority to take a man away from his family and throw him in prison. Truthfully, the end of a prison sentence didn't scare d'Aspert; as a final result, his wife's talk would've accused him of conspiracy, which would've resulted in the worst the government's fears could inflict: death; and d'Aspert wasn't scared of death, but to get there he'd have to go down a path that did scare him. He had gout and had no desire to sit in a musty prison; he'd gotten used to the good life and couldn't think, without shuddering, about bread and water in a dungeon.

Denying that these little fears play a big part in the terrors that the bravest men feel in getting mixed up in a conspiracy, is denying experience. Every man who walks into a battle has more chance of dying than one who's involved in a plot, and yet, there are few who shy away from combat; and there are even fewer who dare to conspire. If you try to call their ideas of honor and affection obstacles, they'll answer that the citizens' hatred and contempt for power are sometimes universal, without finding twenty individuals to plot the downfall of this power.

To think that the people who had put themselves in the line of fire during the revolution of 1830 would've shuddered at the idea of being subject to an arrest warrant! Of course, there were more victims of the Bourbon resistance in these three days than they would've dared to toss on the scaffold if they'd been victorious. Well, if, instead of grabbing a rifle to fight, it was necessary to pick up a pen to protest, they wouldn't have found a fraction of those who got themselves killed: and truly, they would've found very few of them. No matter what you say, death isn't the greatest danger for a man in society. Separation from his family, depriving him of his usual comfort, the abrupt interruption of his daily habits, the whole parade of life, which is essentially life itself, that's what they're scared of risking and losing.

Although this fear controlled the moderate responses d'Aspert used to calm down his wife, this fear must have been powerless against her, since everything he feared losing, she was unhappy to be enduring. And he did nothing but fan the enthusiasm of Henriette by his resistance and arguments; and they almost all ended in this phrase: "If only I was a man!"

Another was also suffering like her, another was in the same situation of despair, and this other was a man. Henriette's words couldn't strike him without consequences. He, too, had searched for an exit from the intolerable suffering of his heart. Without a doubt, she wasn't the same as on that first day. The thought of his crime still horrified him; the sovereign prohibition, that this crime gave him no hope of love or happiness, also contributed greatly to his woe.

Having seduced the wife of his father was a terrible guilt; but not being able to assert his love for Henriette was an even more terrible despair. Finally, whether he took the opportunity to divert himself by this chance offering, or, which is more likely, he considered Henriette's speeches as an indirect warning and he found a kind of consolation in acting, once again, on his own ideas, in joining with her, once again, through this obedience and accomplishment of his desires, Charles focused his thoughts on the political issues that interested Henriette. And that was because she would've done, if she could have, what he did do, since he could.

I said that at the time of Charles' arrival, there were, among the people in the region where he'd come to live, signs of discontent, sounds of secret organization. Often around him he heard those words that needed only one acceptable response to be followed by a secret; but Charles, preoccupied with love, had seldom paid attention; and when these words were clear enough that he couldn't ignore them, he kept silent. From the beginning of his arrival, he had been the object of many hopes; his position as a former officer, his courage, his determination, even the Aubert affair, had brought upon him the attention of men who were leaders of the major political association in France. The lack of acknowledgment he gave to the mutterings around him at first deterred the initial intentions they'd had for him; but soon the influence he gained over the workers, the number of them he had under his control, made him a valuable conquest.

It wasn't just one man they'd get with Charles, it was a boss who could tell five hundred determined men, "Here's what we have to do"; and they would listen to this order without asking why, without wondering about the purpose of their actions.

He was also a man able to carry out what he'd ordered. He had the courage and the talent necessary for the task, and those who had their eyes on him believed they'd seen enough to know that once he was on their side, he'd see through to the end whatever he undertook.

Nothing, therefore, was easier for Charles than to get involved quickly and join in the plots being organized around him. Moreover, it took little effort for him to be understood, or rather, when he decided to pay attention those around him, he got what he wanted: activity and danger.

XXIII. BACK TO MAGNETISM

The nice weather came back. It brought the Duchess d'Avarenne to her land of l'Étang. With her came all kinds of gossip. She had, they said, got a nomination to the Chamber of Peers for the son-in-law to whom she'd choose to pass on her name and title. Julie was with her mother, and they talked a lot about the brilliant gathering of suitors that was supposed to take place in the chateau. However, no favorite had been chosen, and they were surprised that she'd left Paris under such circumstances. Once the initial excitement of this arrival had worn off, they stopped talking about it. Except that they believed a son of a filthy rich banker connected to one of the ministers would probably be the one who'd pay millions for the position and titles due to the Duchess.

In the meantime, life at the forge had changed a lot from what it had once been. The presence of the Bizots had kept the dinner parties going, although they had stopped being intimate or amusing; the general, completely crippled, got brought down, preferring the danger of this tribulation to the boredom of his bedroom. But when the Bizots left, everything fell apart. Henriette made a point of never leaving her husband's bedroom; Charles came to spend a little time there and then went home early; he was frequently absent; the general's business affairs gave him an excuse. As for Lussay, the return of the nice weather allowed him to resume his outings, even after dinnertime, and they barely saw him anymore.

Everything looked calm on the outside, and yet there was a vague sense of dread that seemed to herald disaster. Nobody knew where it was or where it came from: but there was an event looming. Everyone was worried, each had enough reason to be, and yet nobody blamed the gloominess on these reasons. Could there be an instinct that warns men of the misfortunes they're bound to suffer? Truthfully, I'm tempted to believe so. Or else what I call instinct might just be the intuitive observation of countless circumstances that are unrelated to one another, that have nothing special that should cause fear, and still, taken together, they produce a nameless terror, an awful dread of the present situation.

Whatever the case, a little while after the scene I just described, Henriette was alone with her sick husband. D'Aspert was a wreck; Henriette was sad. She told herself, "My God, how is this all going to end? My courage to live as I do is gone. Not a heart to confide in; barely a few hours when I can cry freely. And what is Charles doing? What's become of him? Not a word of explanation between us. Is it possible? Alas, could it be otherwise? How can we talk? What can we say? I'd die of shame and terror. But he hasn't even tried; for, in the end, my remorse has led me astray; nothing is sure, and there's even reason to believe that Charles isn't the son of d'Aspert. Oh, how pitiful I feel! But if we found out it was true, we'd have to kill ourselves. He's right not to want to know anything. Besides, I ordered him. He obeyed me because he still loves me... yes, he loves me: and me! But I'm vile to think like this. My God! If this man, who is here on the bed, could open my heart like a book, and read all that's happening there, how frightened he'd be! The poor man! He never dreamt that there could be so much vileness on Earth. What a cry of despair he'd let loose if he found out he was surrounded by this vileness! Certainly, it would be a very cruel discovery. Who knows what lies in the hearts of those we count on the most? Who know if Charles even loves me?

"This idea! Always this idea! I'll love this man unto death! If anyone suspected... Bizot knew it; his wife, she was jealous, I hurt her; she must suspect: in her place, I'd be sure. And my father... I dare not think of it. He who plucked out so many secrets from the magnetic sleep, if ever he caught on to my secret! I've been watching him for awhile, he talks to himself, he seems to have reached a long-sought goal; but in his satisfaction there's something that tells me he's planning a calamity. Nobody is so delighted for a good to come; people don't smile like that except for something bad they're going to do... What if my father, seeing that I haven't understood my soul or its intentions for a long time, what if my father read it in my heart and wanted to make me pay for the suspicions that my sorrow raised against him? Didn't I hold the word incest over his head? What if he wants to drop it on mine? My father.. Yesterday he stared at me for a long time with those fiery eyes... He uttered something about vengeance... If my father..."

Lussay entered.

Henriette couldn't believe it was him; it was too extraordinary that he arrived at the exact moment when she was thinking of how afraid she was of his presence. Then, when she was sure that it was him, she figured it was her inescapable predestination and she considered it the moment of climax.

Lussay made a faint gesture and whispered, "I have to talk to you."

"It's you, Lussay," d'Aspert said, having overheard, "what secret do you have to tell Henriette? Can't you tell me too?"

Lussay hesitated before answering, "In fact, you'll have to find out sooner or later; moreover, you alone can decided what must be done."

D'Aspert raised himself up on the bed to listen more attentively because Lussay was sitting like a man who had a long confession to make. "What's it about?"

"About Charles Dumont," Lussay replied.

"Charles Dumont?" Henriette repeated, whose conscience was so tormented that this name was heard like an accusation.

"Well," d'Aspert said, "what did he do?"

"He's lost, or nearly so: he's got himself mixed up in a conspiracy that wants nothing less than to overthrow the government, and there are traitors in this conspiracy."

D'Aspert turned to Henriette with a look of surprise and fear. "Did you know this, Henriette? That Charles is doing such a crazy thing?"

Henriette had known all too well. It hadn't taken long to imagine how desperate he was when he bowed to the political enthusiasm she had shown in his presence. It was the only devotion allowed to him, and he hadn't let it go: she was sorry and couldn't help saying, "Poor Charles!"

This adjective didn't correspond to what D'Aspert was feeling; but he said nothing, and turning back to Lussay, asked, "But, really, who told you this? Because, now that I think about it, exposing a conspiracy is pretty complicated; first you need the informant from the conspiracy, and then an informant of the informant"

"Well, the two informants are only one man," Lussay said, "and this man is Pierre Aubert."

"Pierre Aubert!" d'Aspert and Henriette blurted out together.

"Listen to me," Lussay went on, "and you, general, don't interrupt me with your skeptical observations: don't forget that this concerns the head of Charles, the head of your son."

"My son?" d'Aspert cried out.

"Your son," Henriette sounded strangely distraught, "his son? Are you sure?"

"Sure? No. I can only have the assurance of what somebody else told me."

"So, explain yourself!" d'Aspert shouted.

"Well," Lussay explained, "do you remember the day Charles chased out Pierre Aubert? I ran into him in the forest, swearing and cursing

Charles, the general, and you, Henriette. He needed a victim. He saw me and accosted me with insults and threats; he was getting all worked up and I expected that he was going to start a fight. I was alone, without weapons, I couldn't get away from him. However, I wasn't afraid: past experiences and continual exercise gave me confidence in my own power; I waited for the moment for him to step forward, I put my hand on his forehead and threw all the force of my magnetic fluid at him, saying, "Stop and sleep!" At that very moment, he stopped and dropped like he'd been hit with a club. But that's not what's most surprising about the whole thing; I've used this power on many men, and this worker had often been witness to my experiments. The imagination could've aided my power over him; my calmness in the face of his insults might already have surprised him; finally, I got a bigger result, a result whose terrible experience you'll soon see, a result that will be the completion of the promised revenge...

"But I digress; I'll get back to Aubert. Understand that from that day on, this man became my slave. I got him to tell me about his argument with Charles, more as an experiment than out of curiosity. That's when I learned he'd called him a bastard and I wanted to know why. I had a lot of trouble getting it out of him and it was only after more than a month of magnetism that I figured he was under complete control. He told me that when he was in Paris, where he worked as a locksmith, he ended up at a lawyer's to fix the some broken doorbells, when he overheard the name Dumont several times. He admitted to me that he'd listened, and that, in the little he could hear, they'd often repeated that Charles wasn't the son of Dumont."

"What's the name of the lawyer where this happened?" d'Aspert asked.

"Aubert couldn't tell me, nor the name of the person he was speaking with."

"So, where do you get," the general said, "that Charles is my son?"

"By pulling together a bunch of circumstances; all the care you took for Charles, your anxieties when you thought he was dead, your joy on seeing him again, and then a lot of things that didn't come into focus till the revelation hit me and made me remember them, giving me suspicions."

"So, it's just a suspicion?" Henriette said. "Well, heaven be praised!"

"Why?" d'Aspert asked. "Before you seemed to want him to be my son, and now..."

"Now..." Henriette balked.

"Ah!" d'Aspert said. "There's something between you ever since you had an explanation about the matter. Since then he has abandoned the house, so to speak."

"It's also since then," Lussay cut in, "that he got involved with conspirators."

This interruption, by bringing the conversation back to its real subject, saved Henriette from the embarrassment of answering.

D'Aspert continued, "Is it from Pierre Aubert that you learned about Charles' dangerous situation?"

"None other," Lussay said. "It was by asking random questions about his everyday activities that he told he was part of a conspiracy; then that Charles was also mixed up in it, and finally that, with no other means to avenge himself, he had denounced him along with all his accomplices."

"When did he denounce them?"

"At least three weeks ago."

"So, it's a cock-and-bull story," d'Aspert commented. "Would they have waited so long to arrest Charles and his friends?"

"What if they wanted them to compromise themselves more than they already have; what if they're waiting for them to somehow initiate the action?"

"But this Aubert ought to be scared of you revealing the secret he confided in you?"

"Did you forget," Lussay replied impatiently, "that this man, on waking up, had no memory of what he told me during his sleep?"

D'Aspert had such an adamant prejudice against magnetism that he refused to believe Lussay's revelations; still, it was so intriguing that he didn't know how to react; he finally decided to argue with Lussay.

"Why," he asked, "didn't you tell us earlier?"

"Because I had sworn never to betray the secrets that I might obtain by my power: my mission here is a vocation that demands the same confidentiality and integrity as a priest hearing the confession of a sinner."

"That's absurd," d'Aspert said, "since you're telling us today."

"It's because only today I learned of Aubert's denouncement, even though it happened awhile ago; but don't think that I'd be doing this if the man hadn't given me the right to betray him since he himself betrayed his accomplices. You know my opinions: they're the opposite of the conspirators; but it's not my calling to use the sublime science against spies; my calling is higher and nobler."

"More of your foolish fantasies!" d'Aspert shot back. "Try, instead, to find some way to save Charles."

"So, you do believe me?" Lussay asked, whose joy at having misunderstood d'Aspert's disbelief was stronger than his concern about Charles' safety.

"I believe you! I believe you!" d'Aspert shouted angrily. "What do I know? And you, seriously, do you yourself believe what you're saying?"

"I've done my duty," Lussay responded, "now it's up to you decide."

"Damned maniac!" Lussay barked. "He's crazy!"

Perhaps, at this moment, the quarrel over magnetism was about to start up again and make them lose sight of the real subject they should've been discussing, but a loud noise was heard inside the house. Someone was banging on the front door and yelling, "Open up, in the name of the law!", as the servants were asking questions through the door. They had to open it: the police were there, surrounding the house. They demanded Charles Dumont and they searched thoroughly, but didn't find him. Finally, the officers came to the bedroom of d'Aspert where the general asked on what orders they had violated his home. The lieutenant in charge showed him an arrest warrant for Charles Dumont, accused of participating in a conspiracy to overthrow the king's government.

After Lussay's revelations, this warrant was no surprise except for the rapidity of its arrival; but what was surprising was who had issued it. It was signed by a Special Information Commissioner who was none other than Baron Premitz. Hearing this name, Lussay broke out in such wild laughter that he could reasonably be mistaken for a madman.

"At last!" he cried out. "Oh, a supernatural power has sent him to me. Where is he? I have to speak with him."

The lieutenant, imagining that he was hoping to get some favor for Charles, answered, "I left him yesterday in N..., but tonight he should be at the chateau in l'Étang, with the Duchess d'Avarenne. If you go there early tomorrow morning, you should find him there."

"Tomorrow," d'Aspert said, "will be too late. Get the horses ready and get me dressed. Henriette, we're leaving."

"Yes, yes," Lussay agreed, "right away, I have to see this man."

"And I have to see the duchess," d'Aspert added. Then he addressed the lieutenant, "Monsieur, may I ask you to do something for me? Would you delay following through on these orders until I've seen Madame d'Avarenne?"

"That's not possible," the lieutenant admitted. "In the first place, I'm not authorized, and besides, my men are crawling all over the area with orders to arrest Dumont, whose description they have; they're supposed to bring him here and we'll take him immediately to N…"

"Well," d'Aspert said, "since your orders are so precise, and I know better than anyone that you must follow orders, grant me the favor of taking Charles to l'Étang. I can guarantee your kindness will be excused by Baron Premitz."

"But," the lieutenant replied, "as much as I'd like to do what you ask, I've got orders not to let anyone leave this house until Dumont's been arrested; we can't let him be warned and give him the chance to escape."

"Monsieur," d'Aspert said, "I'm leaving with my wife and her father, only one servant will accompany us; give us two men as an escort and I assure you that we won't stray from the road to the chateau of l'Étang. It's barely three leagues; we'll arrive in ten hours at a steady pace."

"General," the lieutenant replied, "I'm doing more than I can and than I should; but I haven't always been a police officer. I was in the army in Russia, I knew Charles Dumont; I was under his command in 1809; so, I won't refuse you: what will happen will happen, they can fire me if they want."

"If they fire you," the general said, "you will have a place here that will be better than what you'll have lost."

During this conversation, the general had stood up. With Charles in danger and the decision he had made about it, he had found a new strength and energy that he hadn't thought he was capable of. Lussay had got ready, Henriette as well. It would've been very easy for her to stay at the forge, but she knew that the tragedy of this whole affair was coming to a climax; she couldn't imagine it being favorable, but she had no idea how to escape it. Her whole life seemed stamped by a fate that had never let her act freely, and consequently she just gave in, not worrying about anything but getting out of the present situation, in any way possible. At last, they left.

XXIV. A LOT OF INCIDENTS

In the meantime, a completely different scene was taking place at the chateau of l'Étang. A brilliant gathering had assembled; it was the day appointed for the signature of Julie's contract with the son of the banker, the very elegant, young diplomat, who was promising his wife the finest horses and the most magnificent house in Paris. There was a big dinner at the chateau; the departmental authorities, the nobles from the region and a few friends from Paris made a big enough crowd to give it the air of an aristocratic celebration. The duchess was once again feeling something of the former splendors of her house: she had no doubt that all the old privileges of the nobility would soon be given back, and, at this moment, she was so exhilarated by the idea that the word "vassal" sometimes escaped her lips when talking about the farmers, and almost always "bourgeois" when she wanted to belittle someone. Her future son-in-law, as bourgeois as he was, and from the most typical bourgeoisie, unable to trace back to his grandfather without admitting that he was a clerk for a tax collector, found everything perfect because he was already wholly dedicated to the dukedom coming to him.

The entire salon was lit by candles, gloriously decorated; the notary of the region, to whom they had brought a contract drawn up by a famous lawyer in Paris, and who had got himself a brand new, black suit made, counting on the fat fees he was hoping to get, this notary was keeping a close eye on the duchess, like a fireworks expert waiting for the sign to start the show. The duchess made the imperceptible sign; servants brought in a table with candlesticks: it was all very dramatic. It was old drama. Nevertheless, along with the servants who were setting up the decor, another came in and handed the duchess a card; she glanced at it and looked troubled. She gave it back and ordered the notary to begin. While they were listening to the reading of the first articles, a servant, with terror written all over his face either from the order he'd been given or from the nerve he'd had to carry it out, slipped behind the duchess and handed her a note. Madame d'Avarenne turned pale, and leaned over to the servant, who nodded to the question she asked him. Then, with impotent rage, she stood up and waved to the notary to continue. The future son-in-law, seeing that she was leaving, went to her and spoke with that financial acumen he'd inherited from his father:

"Can I be of service? I've got 200,000 francs in my wallet."

The duchess glared at him with such astonishment and contempt that he saw he'd made a big mistake. The poor kid was so dazzled by what was happening around him that he thought he was in some kind of vaudeville melodrama in which there was always someone coming to take the manor from the noble while he's marrying off his daughter, and the son-in-law pulls out his wallet and finds the exact sum needed to save the family honor and home. The duchess, outraged by the stupidity of her son-in-law, even though she greatly appreciated his fortune worth twelve million, replied like a grande dame and in the insolently rude voice she reserved for petty people:

"Do you take us for beggars?" And she walked out.

Outside the salon, she asked the servant who had brought her the two messages, "Where is he?"

"In the blue room."

The duchess went there. A man dressed for traveling was sitting there. On seeing the duchess, he stood up and said, "There you are, finally!"

This man was Baron Premitz.

"Well," the duchess responded, "what do you want?"

The baron went to close the door and motioned her to sit down.

"You tried to get away from me," he said to her, "you betrayed our agreement: I've come to remind you of it."

"Our agreement?" the duchess retorted. "I don't understand; that I promised you what I did? Aren't you exactly what you were hoping to be? Commissioner, State Councilor?"

"I was hoping for more," Premitz said, "and you know it."

"Monsieur, there is a social position whose influence can go only so far. I was able to ask a minister to make you what you are; I couldn't ask him to quit and make you minister."

"But," Premitz said, "did you get nothing else but what you gave me? What about this nomination to the Chamber of Peers and passing on your title…"

The duchess cut him off and snapped, "What are you talking about?"

"Oh, don't play at being angry or surprised. You know very well what I'm saying, even if I don't have time to explain it; and the only proof I need is that you didn't tell me about the favors you got; that you ran away from Paris to carry out your devious designs here, hoping that, being confined to my prefecture, I wouldn't find out about them. But here I am, madame, and you'll have to explain yourself. The marriage of your daughter with this young man cannot take place."

"Why?" the duchess asked.

"Because I don't want it to."

"Monsieur," she replied furiously, "don't forget that I can run you out of here."

"Madame, don't be ridiculous, please. You know very well that you won't do that; you know that tomorrow my response to any bad behavior on your part would be a letter addressed to the man responsible for all the credit and favor you hold; you know that this letter would take everything away from you in an instant. Look, madame, here's a note from you that I got you to write when you believed I was an accessory to your intrigues. It looks clear enough to me. And here's another in which the whole mystery of your supposed so is brought to light. Come now, madame, tit for tat."

The duchess was overcome by the audacity of this villainous Premitz, "But calling off the wedding will create a scandal that I couldn't face."

"A scandal for a scandal, madame, I'll make you suffer one that would make a canceled wedding quite trivial."

"But monsieur, Julie loves him!"

"Ha ha," Premitz snickered and shrugged his shoulders. "Let's talk sense and not say such things. You think I'm an idiot?"

The duchess, already stunned by the arrival of Premitz, who had given her time to gather her thoughts, needed to pull herself together. After a moment of silence, she told him, "Well, monsieur, let's suppose that I give in to your demands, do you think that this favor would be given to me whenever I wanted? Don't you think there'd be scrutiny the minute I got it granted? Do you believe that I can hand out favors as I please to the first comer?"

"The first comer!" Premitz exclaimed pompously. "Are you referring to me?"

"Who and what are you that I should make you a duke and a peer?"

"I am one of those who become one by their own strength, by the services they render and the merit they show; but I'm also one of those who are happy to shorten the path when they can. Anyway, since it's futile for us to waste time on empty discussions, understand that when I learned about your projects, I rushed to Paris and, not finding you there, I took time off to come to l'Étang. This decision got some people thinking it was for a mission that required an active, determined man who scoffed at danger and mercy. The success of this mission will give me the right to whatever reward I deem worthy. Maybe this would be enough, but it's not certain, so I need to act quickly. And if you must know everything, know that this place you'll give me won't be the peak of my career: this will be but one step to climb as high as possible under this monarchy.

"The time has come for me to lay down all my cards. I know you have a secret that could ruin you; well, there's one that can ruin me too; but since we'd fall together, you'll think twice before betraying me. They publicly chased out of France a group that secretly remained and that wants to rise up again. It's already living here safely thanks to men whom it won over on many levels of the State; but that's not enough for it: minor police officials and petty administrators, it's still running into resistance among the higher nobility whose devotion to royalty allows them to fight without needing to use the common name of liberals or revolutionaries. A man placed in the High Chamber, a man in the process of being everything they could want, would be so valuable that this group would throw all their support behind him; they're looking for one man and they'd spend millions on him; but there are difficulties, and these difficulties would vanish into thin air if this man were one of the most influential and devoted of the group, if this man were me…"

"You!" the duchess cried out. "Who are you?"

"Madame, I was raised by Cardinal D…, even though I'm French; this might explain to you my life in Paris without any apparent means of support. I said I'd tell you my story; it's a strange one; but we don't have time right now; we have to act, you have to stop the signing of that contract."

These revelations of Premitz came so fast that they stunned the duchess. Without delving into the truth of the baron's assertions, without determining whether the future he seemed to be promising was possible, she gave in to the fear he inspired in her.

"Well," she said, "we'll see, we'll talk about that later."

"So be it," Premitz said. "Let's not go crazy: I don't want you to see what you're about to do as a huge sacrifice; but that contract cannot be signed: it'd be a hard commitment to break. There's more; your son-in-law has to walk away from the wedding, and I'll take care of making sure he does."

"You're talking about an insult," the duchess said.

"No, madame, he will walk away feeling unworthy. You only have to play the role of a woman who was mistaken about her choice. Allow me to write a note to him."

Premitz wrote and gave her the following message:

Monsieur,

On your last mission in Rome, you made secret promises concerning the court to support, with all your power, the reestablishment in France of the Jesuit Order. The minister views this conduct as merely reckless enthusiasm; but it has ordered me to warn you that, although he does not want to make this a cause for dismissal, it will, nevertheless, be an insurmountable obstacle for your entering the Chamber of Peers. Your marriage to Mademoiselle d'Avarenne will not lift this obstacle, and Madame d'Avarenne will be informed. It is up to you, monsieur, to make sure the cancellation of the wedding impacts nobody but you. We will be grateful to you for everything you do to take all responsibility and spare the duchess any false allegations. The disregard of your past conduct is at stake.

"And it's you," the duchess said, "who are making him guilty of crimes that are yours."

"It'll fall from wherever I drop it, that's what makes the difference between fools and great minds."

The note was sent, and the duchess announced that a grave illness was forcing her to delay the signing of the contract until the next day. The son-in-law figured it'd be best to go to his room, and Julie went to her mother's room, where she had gone with Premitz. But her mother refused to see her.

They were only for only a few minutes when the duchess was informed that three people had just arrived at the chateau, and that one of them was the Count d'Aspert, demanding to see her privately at once. The duchess was astonished: the two of them had no relations; the old friendship between Julie and Henriette had never struck up again in the countryside.

But Premitz hastened to say, "I think I know the reason the general came here; let him in, we'll figure out what to do depending on what he says."

The duchess gave orders to show him in.

While a servant went to get the general, Premitz told the duchess the real reason he himself had come, and about the arrest warrant for Dumont. Then, D'Aspert came into the room where, thirty years ago, our story had started. He couldn't help pausing just inside the doorway and looking around. The duchess guessed his thoughts and was herself a little dazed by this unique encounter.

D'Aspert advanced and, after seeing Premitz, said to Madame d'Avarenne, "It's only you I'd like to speak to."

"Whatever you have to say to me, you can say it in front of monsieur; he knows all my secrets," the duchess responded.

"And does he also know OUR secrets?"

"All," she answered curtly.

"Yes, monsieur," Premitz broke in, "the duchess thought she should tell everything to the man she will soon be naming her son-in-law."

"Her son-in-law!" d'Aspert blurted out in astonishment.

"The name doesn't matter," Madame d'Avarenne said, disturbed by the insulting tactics of Premitz, who was assuming his hopes were fore-gone conclusions, "monsieur knows everything."

"And this son-in-law," the general looked at Premitz, "is he bringing you, as the first wedding present, the head of your son?"

"The head of my son!" the duchess cried out in dismay. Then, shak-ily, she said, "You mean this Charles Dumont..."

"Is the child I took away from you in Rome."

"Ah!" Madame d'Avarenne cried out again. "You wanted him; you needed the child, and look where you led him, to the gallows!"

"You have the power to save him."

"Me? How?"

"Monsieur," the general said, pointing to Premitz, "is the man who can close his eyes to his escape and, if you want it, he can do it."

"And I really can," Premitz said, "if this young man is the son of the duchess. Don't forget, madame, that Monsieur Dumont was questioned by you and said nothing that might lead you to believe what you are believing about him."

"Of course," she said, "but the questions that I asked him were vague, not precise enough to awaken dim memories. At the time, needing to keep my interest in his answers concealed, I didn't question him frankly."

"Well," Premitz said, "that's what's needed now, which we can do tomorrow."

"Tomorrow," d'Aspert asserted, "Charles will be stuck in the city jail, and his fate will be beyond your power; other judges will take over his case and not allow him to escape. If Charles is arrested tonight, he'll be brought here. And here you can order him to be locked up in a room chosen so that he can slip out. I know all the hallways and cellars of this chateau, and I can, without compromising you, guide him off the property."

With the words, "I know all the hallways of this chateau", Premitz couldn't help smiling at the duchess, and he smirked at d'Aspert, "You have a good memory."

"Monsieur," the duchess barked, "see if the young man has arrived."

Premitz rang. Charles had just been brought by the police. In the salon where they led him, he had found Henriette, whose father had left to get information and who was waiting for her husband. When they saw each other in this state, she, in a corner, devastated, pale, dying, he, hands bound like a criminal, they gazed at each other like two accomplices awaiting their punishment.

Charles walked up to her and she whispered, "So, you couldn't get away?"

"I didn't want to. At last, it'll all be over soon."

"Ah!" Henriette hid her face in her hands, "I'm the one who killed you."

"Is it remorse or pity that makes you say such things?" Charles said. "Are you sorry that I'm dying?"

"I don't know," Henriette sighed. "Death atones for so many things. I wish I were in your place."

"Henriette," Charles said, "you life is needed for someone's happiness, keep it: the happiness we can give is an obligation to live; mine is hopeless, since I have to live without you. So, don't be sorry about my death... because I still love you."

"Oh, you're going to relinquish your remorse, I'll have to keep mine."

Charles had to go see Baron Premitz. He followed the servant who had come to fetch him, and appeared before the duchess, the general and Premitz.

"Charles," the general spoke with an unsteady voice, "you have to answer honestly the questions that the duchess is going to ask you; she has the right to make you do so. It'll mean your safety. Think hard abut your childhood... remember the things that struck you the most, and don't hesitate to mention the vaguest memories; they might provide a clue."

"Where did you spend your first years of childhood?"

"As far as I can remember, it was in France."

"Do you remember the name of the city you lived in?" the duchess asked.

"The name... I can't remember... but it was a French name."

"Were you ever in England?"

"I remember having been in England... I crossed the sea to get there... the ship, the sea, they're still engraved in my memory."

"You remember the trip," the duchess said. "So, as a child, you moved from France to England?"

"I think so. I feel like I spent a very long time at sea."

"That's strange," the duchess uttered.

"I can explain that," Premitz jumped in, "and the general can verify that the facts I have are accurate. Captain Dumont served in America; he was taken prisoner and brought to England; he came to France later, only after the Peace of Leoben[79]. It's the trip from America to England that he remembers."

"That's true," the general agreed.

"Were you with your father?" the duchess asked.

"No," Charles replied. "I only saw my father again in Italy..."

"Who brought you?"

"A servant brought me to England."

"Was this servant an old man with a slight limp?"

"I don't know."

"An old man with a limp..." Premitz wondered aloud.

"Did he used to call you Count?"

"No."

"Count!" Premitz repeated, as if racking his brain for clues.

"This servant, was he called Louis?"

"Louis Feret!" Premitz blurted out.

"No," Charles said, "it wasn't Louis..."

The duchess looked at Premitz, "How do you know this name?"

"Oh," the baron looked unusually troubled, "do continue; I'll tell you alter."

The duchess resumed, "Do you remember a man who was very affectionate and was called monseigneur?"

"No, madame, no."

"Monseigneur," Premitz echoed again in a whisper. "Oh, that's it—monseigneur."

"Let me, please," the general broke in. "There's a more recent memory that can clear everything up. Do you remember arriving in Rome

[79]Signed on April 18, 1797, between the Holy Roman Empire and the First French Republic to end the War of First Coalition.

with a servant you got separated from; and then taken to a soldier who said that you were Charles Dumont?"

"No," Charles said, "I've always had this name."

"Charles Dumont," Premitz repeated, "Charles Dumont... so, that's the name... that you said to that child. And you left him in your palace, which was pillaged the next day."

"How do you know that?" d'Aspert asked.

"Oh, I'll tell you," Premitz promised as he turned pale. "I will tell you. Go on."

"Lastly," d'Aspert asked, "do you remember a sergeant named Bazile coming to get you?"

"Yes," Charles said, "a sergeant found me at the door to your palace... I see myself sitting down, crying and calling for you; because my father... or the man who called himself that, had told me that you would accept me like a son."

"Why do you have doubts," d'Aspert asked, "that he was your father?"

"Because they tried to make me doubt it. While I was in England, they told me: 'Your father is a prisoner and you can't see him.' Then he left without taking me; then he wrote that they'd bring me to him, and I only got there a few days after he'd died... I barely knew him, and, if I must be frank, once I'd been led to believe that he wasn't my father... his abandonment and your cares made me believe that I owed more to you than my fortune."

"And who planted this doubt?" d'Aspert asked.

Charles turned pale and cold; the horrible night when Henriette cast this doubt loomed up before him.

"We're getting off the subject," Premitz said. "Monsieur here is very much who he appears to be. He is really Charles Dumont. You can't doubt it, madame..."

"Why not?" the duchess asked.

"Because," Premitz pulled her into a corner of the room and whispered, stammered, "because he doesn't remember that it was his mother he was going to see in Rome, and not his father; because he didn't keep the portrait that his mother gave him; because he doesn't know the name Louis Feret who went with him; because he doesn't remember the woman, who was as pretty as an angel, who gave him, when she hung the portrait around his neck, this strange thing to say: 'Charles, you tell the gentleman you're being brought to: Love me for the love of this lady'..."

"Good God!" the duchess exclaimed.

"Madame," he spoke more loudly, "this young man is not your son. Take him away!"

"Where?" The general cried out.

Premitz sneered, "To the room where you can get him to escape."

"Monsieur," the general continued, "this isn't over. Madame," he turned to the duchess, "if Charles Dumont isn't the one you're looking for, he's still just as dear to me... Save him at any cost: I have the right to demand this."

"The right!" Premitz retorted. "Because you left the other to the whims of poverty and death?"

"The right, monsieur, comes from my faithfulness in keeping a secret that today is making your fortune as the future son-in-law of the duchess."

"Oh," Premitz said, filled with an inexpressible and somber joy, "... her son-in-law... No, no... better than that."

"What then?" d'Aspert asked.

"Nothing... nothing," Premitz uttered, "take this young man away."

D'Aspert shouted, "You can do that, but it won't be without consequences... I'll talk, I swear, and this whole tower of grandeur will come tumbling down when I do."

"You'd do that?" Premitz growled with fierce hatred written all over his face.

"Yes I would, to save him I'd confess everything, and I'd tell it to someone who will throw you back into the mud you're trying to crawl out of."

Premitz suddenly changed the expression on his face and his voice sounded gentle, "If that's the way it is... I'll put a stop to your indiscretion... I'll do something I don't want to do."

He rang, wrote a note and gave it to a servant. A moment later, the police lieutenant entered, followed by all his officers.

"Arrest these two men!" Premitz ordered, "and keep them under close watch, separately; let them communicate with no one, no writing or talking to anybody at all."

The order was so surprising to the general that he was left speechless. Charles wanted to resist.

"If you you want to save yourselves, stay calm," Premitz said.

They took the two men away.

"And what are your plans?" the duchess glared at Premitz with heartless dread.

As he left he declared, "I don't know... I'll talk to them tomorrow... tomorrow... Ah, now there's a future."

On the way to the room, Charles passed by the room where Henriette was waiting.

"Where's my husband?"

"Arrested," a policeman responded.

Charles didn't answer because they had gagged him.

XXV. DENOUEMENT

Premitz had gone back to his room. He was sitting at a table and pondering; one project kept coming back to mind, to accomplish Madame d'Avarenne's first plan: the one that had first struck him with sudden joy. But Premitz was too cautious to not mull it over for a long time. It was such a magnificent project! What a future! His imagination got lost in his rising fortune; but to succeed, how to get it? Thanks to Dumont it was easy. But was it a free from doubt? Would d'Aspert keep quiet? Oh, if only d'Aspert were dead! If only he would die! Premitz thought about it, for a long time.

However, something rose up and stopped him. There was, along with the name d'Aspert, such a sacred title, even for an ambitious man. If anyone could've seen Premitz at this moment, his face radiating such joy, looking so serious and determined, standing up to do the deed, then freezing as if an invisible hand had grabbed him, then dropping back down into his chair as if overpowered by a greater force, he would've recognized the infernal debate before a crime is committed. The future wasn't smiling anymore, because it had to get through a parricide to be fulfilled; and he remembered the past. Premitz looked so scared that he must have seen a hideous crime in this past. He stopped himself at this point, because he had turned pale and was trembling, when the door to his room opened.

"It's me," Lussay announced.

"You!" Premitz shouted, unexpectedly caught in the middle of this thoughts, "You, the father of Henriette... What do you want?"

Why was Premitz thinking of Henriette?

"I want to talk to you about my daughter."

"Your daughter... to me? Why?"

"Oh, because you have to know about a discovery I've made."

"I don't want to... I don't want to know..."

"Sit down and listen," Lussay commanded while raising an imposing hand.

"Monsieur," Premitz said, "I don't have time to listen to you."

"Sit down," Lussay repeated, looking like a wild beast about to pounce on its prey.

Premitz looked away and sat down.

"Look at me!" Lussay ordered.

Premitz was fidgeting like a man trying to escape binding chains.

"Look at me!" Lussay repeated.

Premitz looked at him.

"You don't know," the old man said, "that I discovered a great secret of magnetism."

"Ridiculous!" Premitz stammered.

"You're lying… and you're scared," Lussay said.

"Monsieur… let's get this nonsense over with… I don't believe you."

"You're lying again… You must believe… You who had the power to impose a sleep as deep as death."

"Monsieur… monsieur," Premitz was floundering under remorse or else under the power of Lussay, "I'm not here for you to use as an experiment."

"On the contrary, I'm going to show you something extraordinary. It's that the experienced practitioner, whose power over everyone seems irresistible, is but a child's toy in the hands of someone who has found him out. You said to a crazed woman, 'Remember!', and she remembered; you said to a young woman, 'Sleep!', and she fell asleep."

"Who cares!" Premitz leapt up. "Who cares what I did!"

"Well, I do," Lussay said, putting his hand on the baron's forehead. "Sleep and remember!"

Premitz dropped into his chair, motionless, staring straight ahead, wide-eyed: the mesmerist had won. Lussay sat in front of him and gazed at him for a long time. He was laughing quietly: it was the laugh of a cannibal before his victim! He was filled with pleasure as he devoured him with his eyes. Finally, after half an hour of this gazing, he told him:

"Call for General d'Aspert and Charles."

"They've been arrested," Premitz said, looking like he was awake, except for the eerie stare he kept.

"Write a note to let them go free and be brought here."

Premitz wrote, but without even looking at the paper. Lussay called a servant, gave him the order for the lieutenant and told him to inform Henriette and the duchess. Then he sat back down in front of Premitz, holding him chained, so to speak, with his eyes.

Everyone was startled by the condition of Premitz and the wild look on Lussay's face. The former didn't see them come in. The latter pointed to the chairs. They looked at each other anxiously. The duchess addressed Premitz.

"He's as deaf as a judge," Lussay said.

Then he motioned to Henriette to come over; he took her hand and, putting it in the hand Premitz, he spread his arms from one to the other, as if make the fateful enchantment pass from Premitz to Henriette. At this contact, both of them shuddered, and Henriette, struck with terror, fell to her knees.

"Do you know this woman?" Lussay asked.

"I know her…"

"Did she suffer the infamy of a great crime?"

"Yes," Premitz said.

"Tell us about this crime."

Premitz shifted in his armchair, moaning faintly. He didn't answer.

"Tell us the crime!" Lussay boomed.

"The crime," Premitz stuttered as his whole body shook, "is incest."

At this word, everyone was stunned. Charles and Henriette felt like the hour of truth had come. They had left the chains and gag on Charles, otherwise he would've cried out for mercy or smashed in the head of Premitz. D'Aspert listened, not understanding why he was so terrified; the duchess looked at everyone trying to guess who the word was meant for, this word that had already struck her, the one who'd been forced to promise her daughter to Premitz. As for Lussay, he didn't budge.

"Incest," he thought, "that's not it." Then he spoke aloud in rage, "Answer! Tell us the crime!"

"Incest," Premitz repeated.

"Who did it?"

"The son."

"Mercy! Mercy!" Henriette collapsed to the ground. "Father, father, enough already!"

Charles snapped his gag with his teeth and broke his chains; he wanted to lunge at Premitz, but Lussay held him back.

"But isn't the crime yours," he shouted, "for abusing your infernal power against her?"

"It is," Premitz admitted.

"So," Lussay went on, "who are you to accuse yourself of incest?"

"I'm the son of Jean d'Aspert and Madame d'Avarenne."

"Well, I'll be," Lussay said.

And with a swipe of his sword he knocked Premitz to floor next to Henriette.

Three years later, in a small town in America, they celebrated the wedding of Charles Dumont and the widow of Lieutenant General Cound d'Aspert. Lussay died in this town one year before the marriage.

Note from the Publisher

This translation of *Le Magnétiseur* was initiated by the wonderful Stuart Gelzer, who sadly passed away much too soon on April 23, 2025, at age 65, from cancer complicated with liver failure.

He was only about 40 pages from the end. To be accurate, Stuart stopped on Page 248 at the end of paragraph 1 of Chapter XXII. We were lucky to have Michael Shreve complete the job, according to Stuart's instructions.

Throughout his life, Stuart gave encouragement to all ages as a writer, translator, photographer, explorer, a film editor, a teacher of film editing, a screen writer, a drama and theater director, and as a scholar, an historian, an avid student and performer of Georgian folk music, as a fast friend, brother and uncle.

If you are moved to give in his memory, Stuart had designated the Ted and Margaret Jorgensen Cancer Center, 2400 Unser Blvd SE, Rio Rancho, New Mexico 87124, as his choice for a gift in his memory.

J.-M. L.

www.ingramcontent.com/pod-product-compliance
Lightning Source LLC
Chambersburg PA
CBHW030356020726
47493CB00003B/846